CEO

Patricia E. Gitt

This is a work of fiction. Names, characters, places and incidents either are the product of the author's imagination or are used fictitiously, and any resemblances to any actual persons, living or dead, events, or locales is entirely coincidental.

Second Edition   ISBN: 978-1-7341584-0-3
First Edition   ISBN: 1-40102750-4

This book was printed in the United States of America.

Also by Patricia E. Gitt

FYI An Unintended Consequence

TBD – to be determined –
        A game changer

ASAP -as soon as possible-
        A settling of scores

Book Interior Design by Soumi Goswami |
soumi.goswami.pub@gmail.com

Published by
Athena Book Publishing
New York, New York
Athenabookpublishing.com

To my parents, Cornelia and Michael Gitt, for their love and wholehearted support.

This book as been brought to life through the skillful guidance of Lou Willet Stanek, teacher and muse.

Along the journey, I had the invaluable friendship of fellow writers Maria Smith and Gillian Coulter. They kept the story alive and its author on track.

The final manuscript was improved by the constructive comments of the following friends: David Andelman, Marty Appel, Bernard Block, Deborah Diamond Fisch, Sheila Kayne and Andrea Martone.

To all of my friends, thank you.

PROLOGUE

Excerpt from *The Wall Street Journal*

Chief Executive of United Chemicals Dies

New York, July 4, 1998 - Jack Foster, Chief Executive of United Chemicals, died suddenly yesterday of a massive coronary, at his home in Connecticut.

During Foster's thirty-year stewardship, UCC became a world wide industrial leader in petroleum and mineral products. Foster's attention to the bottom line was reflected in UCC stock, rising in value during his tenure, from $18 to yesterday's closing price of $45.

Foster's wife, Susan, died in 1989. The couple had no children.

CHAPTER I

September 1998

"How in hell did a woman become CEO of UCC?" Pamela Green muttered to herself while negotiating past the long bar at Mickey's, her favorite hideaway. The bright, young reporter for *Economic World* magazine always spoke to herself when sorting through a problem.

"What's that?"

Looking toward the back of the restaurant, she saw Skip emerging from the kitchen. Her long-time buddy must have been helping Mickey, the owner, prepare tonight's entrees, she thought. As the compact, athletic man ambled toward her, she saw a welcoming grin soften his lean face. Throwing a dishtowel over his shoulder, he enfolded her hands in his callused paws.

"Nothing. I'm having a one-sided discussion."

She saw him nod in acknowledgment. They had been friends for ten years. Skip, a corporate dropout, was always there to listen to one of her acerbic views of his former world. Then he'd tell her she was just parroting her profession's liberal bias against big business, pat her on the shoulder, and, in his annoying way tell her that she knew better.

"Thank God your crowd doesn't begin until 4. I need quiet, and a strong cup of Java." Swinging her tote bag off her shoulder, she continued striding toward her usual booth, where a large mug of coffee sat waiting.

"How did you know I'd be by today," she said, seeing the coffee was freshly poured and steaming. It was as if Skip knew things about her before she did, and the accuracy of his observations was unsettling.

"I saw you a block away. I knew something was bugging you when you walked into the corner mailbox."

The concern on his handsome Irish face told her she was more upset by her upcoming appointment than she had realized.

"Yeah. I get that way when I'm trying to reconcile a shot at some major bucks with my journalist's ethics."

"Oh? And which one of your rigid principles are you about to break?"

"Never mix money and business. It could screw up my reporter's rep."

Settling into the booth, she was glad Skip was slipping into the facing seat. It wasn't often he could stop what he was doing to join her. He took his responsibilities as the owner's son seriously. Beginning his non-stop day at 9 AM and not letting up till closing at 2 the next morning.

"What's really eating you?"

"I have an interview in forty-five minutes with the VP of Public Affairs at United Chemicals Corporation.

I'm doing a book on their new CEO. Would you believe it's a woman?" Panicked, her flushed faced looked up at him. "Skip, this is top secret. You have to swear not to tell a soul."

"Cross my heart."

Watching him do just that with a silly grin, she knew he wouldn't share this nugget of information with anyone. Skip was the only man she'd trust with her life. Or, with her job, which was her life, digging up and keeping secrets till they're ready to be revealed.

"Isn't that good? UCC is one of the global giants. It could be your major break out of the minor leagues. Haven't you always wanted a crack at one of the *Fortune* 500?"

"Yes and no. I need access. I'm afraid of the cost. They may want to tie me up in paper. Own me."

"Nobody can own you, Pal. Not you."

As if her clouded vision had suddenly cleared, she said "That's true. And, I'll earn my fuck you money."

"What?"

The surprise on Skip's face had her smiling. "My fuck you money. The amount I can bank and tell anyone I dislike, to go to hell. My freedom to tell John Holmes which assignments I want, and how I want to write them."

"Sounds like you're dating another loser? You always get your Irish up when they misbehave."

This wasn't the time to update Skip on her social life. Instead, she'd hide behind her screen of jaunty independence. "I can't get my Irish up. I'm Hungarian.

Why not act like a waiter and get my burger? I'll call you when I need my head shrunk."

Of course she couldn't fool Skip. He knew the rest of her life was a mess and he never approved of the men she dated. *Too bad I can't date a hunk like Skip. He wore those faded jeans like the men in one of her fantasies.* "No way," she mumbled. "With my luck, I'd go out with him once and lose my best friend."

Pamela usually stopped by Mickey's for a 3 PM meal between the bar's busy lunch and after-work crowds. By now, the midtown hangout for young reporters and writers was a second home. The quiet interlude in the bar's busy day provided her with a haven to puzzle out a new assignment, line up questions for an interview, or scope out an idea to present to her boss, John Holmes, the editor of *Economic World*, corporate America's leading business magazine.

Sipping her coffee and refastening the ribbon-covered elastic around her stick-straight ponytail, Pamela was lost in thought. *How would she do at the interview? Would they agree to help her write the factual story of the first female to lead a Fortune 100 industrial corporation?*

"Here. Your burger," Skip said placing the plate in front of her. "Why are you upset? You'll write your book and that'll be that."

"It's a toss up. If they like me, I'll get to write an authorized bio. And, if I don't get their OK, I'll lose the chance of finding out who this stranger is and how she became the first female CEO of an industrial megapower.

Not to mention the loss of my book deal. It's predicated on having her participation and approval."

"You know I used to work for UCC. They're OK."

At first she was surprised that this private man offered any personal tidbit. Then she remembered Mickey telling her with all the pride of a father for his only son, that Skip had been on the fast track as assistant comptroller at a major corporation. Looking at his bar uniform of black cotton T-shirt and jeans, she had trouble picturing him in corporate pin stripes.

"Yeah. Something in upper management, wasn't it? Didn't you like Big Brother?"

"I left Ms. Independent, because Dad got the big C and needed me here. Even after surgery and chemo, he needed me to look after things."

"Don't get huffy. But that was ten years ago."

"Well I got used to being here. And Dad still depends on me."

She felt sorry for baiting him. Skip really did like running Mickey's. He didn't have the New York ego that required identification by what you did for a living. He was secure in who he was.

"Anyway, if I left who would help you solve your problems and get you out of one disastrous relationship after another?"

"Right. Maybe my bad luck with men is due to your bad advice." Seeing him grimace, she quickly said, "Sorry. It's just that this interview has me on edge. My fingers are itching to get to the bottom of this corporate mystery. If she's for real, she's shattered that damned glass ceiling. What a story!"

As Skip walked away, Pamela began to nibble around the edges of her burger, her mind a whirl. What's it like to head up a corporation? Have everyone at your beck and call, instead of her crummy life of running after the next news-breaking story? Did a female CEO get a seven-figure salary like a man? Was she hired because she was different from other women, or would she change the job because she was a woman? And what did this person look like? A prickly matron or *Cosmo* cover girl?

Stopped cold at the thought that she'd have to be ugly to be good enough for the job, Pamela took stock of her own appearance. I'm certainly no cover girl. More like a girl down the block. The ones boys fixed their cars with, not for. "Shit. I'm smart, good at my job. By my scale for success, I should be aiming my sights for the Pulitzer." You're getting squirrely, she thought, looking up as Skip refilled her mug for the third time. "Thanks. Hey. You're a good judge of character. Maybe you could give me some tips?"

"Like what?" he said and slid back into the booth.

"Like what would you look for in a woman?"

With a white-toothed grin, Skip looked like she'd given him the best of compliments.

"The obvious first. Size her up as a possible conquest."

"You? In all the years I've know you, I've never seen you act like a macho cad. You don't come on to every pair of legs draped over a bar stool."

His grin had turned into a full-blown belly laugh. "You flatter me, but I'm only human."

The look he gave her was about to melt her lipstick. As quickly as Skip had turned on the sizzle, he returned to normal. Thank God, she thought, breathing a little easier; he seemed unaware of his effect on her.

"Once I've determined working girl or free spirit, married or single, I want to know if she's real or phony. Is she someone trying too hard? Augmented body parts, too much makeup, faking who she is and where she comes from? Or, is she one of those rare birds who is a unique combination of looks and brains, like you."

Ignoring his compliment because she didn't believe she was anything special, Pamela returned to business. "Skip, what if she's a fraud?"

"What do you want? To sell a book, or do your usual digging beneath the facade?"

"One of my problems with today's meeting is to get them to want this book written. I don't want to be used to write a cover-up."

"Keep looking for mismatches. Skillful makeup and chewed nails. Sophisticated clothes and nasty mouth. Does she have a temper? Is she as cool at the end of a long day as she was at the beginning? Who are her associates? Are they all cut from the same cookie cutter or, is she democratic in the selection of her staff?"

"I guess I'll know if she's smart. But not if she's a fake."

"Go beyond the job. What are her hobbies? Favorite book? And how recent were her selections? If someone tells me that their all time favorite book is *Gone With The Wind* or *The Catcher in the Rye*, I know they haven't read anything since high school."

"Is that all?"

"No. You're a feminist. See if she's a Sister. Does she like men? For all your sass, you really like men, or I wouldn't have talked to you that first day you walked in here."

"How do you tell when a woman likes men? Don't give me that look. I'm not talking about a bimbo!"

"A woman who likes men is comfortable talking about real things. The day-to-day politics of life."

"You mean the Yankees."

"I mean the problems of taxes, corruption, cops on the street. Life! Not artsy stuff, or the latest fad diet."

"Thanks Skip. I may put you on retainer."

"Any time, Hot Shot!"

Noticing the regulator clock over the bar mark 3:45, Pamela jolted into action. Barely pausing as she handed Skip a ten for the cash register, she called, "Take any extra off my tab."

Just as she reached the door, Skip called out, "Joe's just finishing up and his cab's out front. He said he can get you over to Park and 50th in less than five minutes."

Nodding to Joe as he led her out to his cab, Pamela whispered a personal prayer, "Don't let my loathing for corporate fools prevent me from doing this book."

*   *   *

Joe was good to his boast, having sped her the six traffic jammed blocks in record time. Handing him a healthy two-dollar tip for the less than five-minute trip, Pamela gave him a parting thumbs up.

Approaching the building's glittering tall windowed entrance, she saw her image reflected back. "Yuck," she muttered, noticing her hair had once again escaped its elastic band. Quickly refastening the elastic, she dashed toward the bank of elevators designated for the 50th floor.

"Keep quiet and let this guy, Cray, do the talking," she cautioned herself, as the elevator opened on the executive floor of United Chemicals Corporation. Catching her breath, Pamela stopped to stare out the expanse of windows with their view of the city laid out fifty floors below. The absolute quiet of her surroundings screamed power. Twisting the strap on her tote bag, she walked the empty corridor toward a male receptionist, sitting behind a semi-circular polished wood desk, centered in front of the wall of windows. The welcoming floral arrangement cost more than a week's pay, she thought.

Looking at the older man, with neatly trimmed mustache and clipped thinning dark hair, she saw that he was clearly in control of his responsibilities as corporate barrier.

"I'm Pamela Green of *Economic World*. I have an appointment with Charles Cray." As the man's rich voice conveyed this information into a telephone, Pamela looked at her watch. Well at least I'm on time, she thought, walking toward the windows and the view that held her enthralled.

Five minutes later she was ushered into a soft, gray environment to meet Charles Cray, a man over six feet and slim, with a barely controlled head of red-gold hair, a color she had only seen on women. But it was his eyes that threw her off stride. They had a gentle, welcoming expression, not the cool secrecy of a manipulator.

"Ms. Green, I'm sorry to have kept you waiting. I was arranging a security pass for you. I am afraid passes and security checks are a necessity these days."

Still somewhat off balance, now because of Cray's charming manner, Pamela allowed him to guide her to a seating area in the spacious office suite. Sinking her taut, five foot frame into a gray herringbone sofa long enough to seat four with comfort, she watched as the elegant figure casually moved a leather club chair to a more intimate distance.

"May I call you Pamela?"

His voice was as inviting as his greeting she thought. Not trusting her tongue, she nodded her approval and was further surprised as Cray launched into a remarkably informed chat about her previous work.

"Your well researched treatment of the Midlands Savings & Loan collapse provided even me with some new insights."

Delighted that he was well versed in no less than two of her all time favorite assignments, Pamela finally reverted to her normally animated self.

"Mr. Cray, I imagine in your position you have a varied diet of required reading. I'm flattered that you remembered any article of mine." What else has he read about me, was what she wanted to know?

"Call me Charles, please. As a matter of fact, I'm a faithful follower of *Economic World*. Your editor, John Holmes, has an unusually accurate nose for breaking issues. If UCC hasn't been mentioned, I figure we must be doing very well indeed. You see I spend just as much time trying to keep our activities away from the media as our Director of Advertising spends in buying space.

This guy is so smooth he'd have me voting Republican if I'm not careful, she thought.

"Which brings me to you."

Finally! Down to brass tacks, her mind was poised for the curve ball.

"Pamela, I have reviewed your request to have access to Melissa Horn, our new CEO. You wish to write an authorized biography. Before we get to the details, there are a few things I need to know. Cooperating with your project is somewhat a delicate matter. I must be sure that you understand why Ms. Horn was selected for her position. It's important that you are sympathetic to our goals."

Here we go, she thought as she tucked her skirt closer to her legs. "Charles, to be frank, I'm not used to playing on a corporate team. Why do you need my approval of UCC's actions? Knowing my past work you must realize I shoot straight."

"Exactly. You don't seem to let your personal bias interfere with the truth. Very admirable, I may add."

A plain talking guy? I'd better level with him about my status at the magazine.

"John Holmes understood that this would be an independent project of mine. I would be under no obligation to provide him with information. But he asked me to tell you he would expect to have the first right of refusal for publishing excerpts from my book, and an exclusive interview with Ms. Horn for *Economic World.*" Leaning toward Charles, she added, "And I want the byline."

"That's fair enough. Agreed. And now that we've defined our turf, just what do you think of a woman as a chief executive officer of an industrial corporation?"

Sitting a little straighter, Pamela reminded herself to curb her cynicism. "I'm curious to know how someone, especially a woman I've never heard of, got a shot at such a plum. My feminist hope is she's smart, capable, and will be honest. When I work on a personality piece, I try to get inside the person. Learn about their on-the-job history, while studying their style of leadership."

Shit. Was that crossing of his legs a sign of disapproval? Have I gone too far?

"Believe me, I want to like Ms. Horn. I'm not looking for dirt." Unless there's dirt to be found, she thought. "It's just that she is the first. It's really the news story of the decade."

Watching for some clue, she saw Charles was thinking about what she had just said. He sat there with that easy manner of his, yet his face was a study in concentration.

"You might tell me why you'd allow a journalist to have access and write an authorized biography, in the first place."

Now she had his attention. As though he had just made up his mind about her. "Yes. Our needs and your loyalty. Let me see if I can level the playing field a bit and address some of your concerns. Ms. Horn, as you have just noted, did not rise through the hallowed halls of UCC. She has been hired by the Board of Directors because her plan for the corporation was the one they felt had a chance of bringing us into the 21st century."

She was about to interrupt when he held up his palm to stop her.

"You have also just voiced one of our major concerns. That Ms. Horn's position will make her the target of the media and inhibit her from being able to do the job she was hired for. In screening your work, I liked the fact that you tried to understand the person behind the job. In Ms. Horn's case, I think this will be difficult, but critical. She is by nature a very private person."

"You want the unvarnished truth?"

"Truth, but limited to her business credentials. We'll leave the exposés to the yellow journalists, shall we?"

The truth from a corporate spin doctor? This sounds fishy. "I will want to meet Ms. Horn!"

"You will be working quite closely with her. One of the reasons I wanted to meet you is to see if you were as forthright as your articles. You see Ms. Horn expects everyone around her to be frank. She won't have much time to give you. But I think you'll get to see the person behind the job."

"Charles, is this arrangement going to be on the level?"

She had to know if she was being suckered. This was the strangest interview she'd ever had. One minute she's told that they would help her write a truthful book. The next she's told the information would be limited. Hell, she thought. Corporations are always limiting a reporter's access to information.

"Pamela, I know corporate America is not well thought of by the press. But, aren't you tempted to find out if we are the honorable citizens we say we are?"

Why couldn't she answer him?

"If you learn anything from M.L., it'll probably be that corporations are headed by people who are serious about their responsibilities to the thousands of people who depend on them for their livelihood."

"In today's downsizing environment?"

"That is a cross we always have to carry. To be profitable and answer to our shareholders sometimes requires layoffs. We try not to over staff. Our goals are to provide our employees with job satisfaction, our shareholders with a sound investment return, and our customers with quality products and services."

She was surprised by the strength of his convictions, thinking he's probably the only one in the USA who still feels this way. But he wasn't CEO, he was VP of Public Affairs. It was his job to win the approval of the media and the public. Hers anyway. It was just too textbook. Where was their hidden agenda?

"You've made me even more curious. If this book is to be accurate I'll have to present Ms. Horn's qualifications as I see them. Can she do the job?"

"Pamela. For reasons I won't go into right now, she has to!"

CHAPTER II

"Yes, Charles. Then this Pamela Green's our best shot at damage control? I'll review the videotape you sent over. Good work."

Melissa Lynn Horn watched as E.F. Haynes hung up the library phone. His broad body relaxed in a casual stance making all 5 foot 11 inches of him looks shorter.

"You know Charles Cray is in love with you."

E.F.'s Texas drawl, tempered by forty years of living amid the steel canyons of Manhattan, cut into her thoughts. Why would he say something like that now? she wondered.

"We have an understanding. That's all."

"An understanding? Don't lead him on Melissa. He's too fine a man."

"Honestly E.F. We've been friends for so long, I guess I keep hoping he'll give it up. What's gotten into you? We have work to do."

"Listen up gal. You'd be hard pressed to find a better husband. He's brilliant. He's kind, and he has a sense of humor. You're alone too much. It's not healthy."

"You're a fine one to talk," she laughed. "You're the one in his prime. Rich, distinguished, on the Manhattan women's social roster of most wanted. So, when was the last time you went out on a date?"

The sheepish look on his face was her reward. E.F. could never push her into doing something he wouldn't do himself. And dating wasn't part of either of their lives. He hadn't romanced anyone since his wife Carol died twenty years before.

Walking over to her dearest friend, she gave his shoulder a gentle squeeze. "E.F. I may be alone, but I'm not lonely." She didn't want him to worry about her. "Ever since I moved upstairs, I've felt more at home than in the house I grew up in. Who else would take some strange female under their wing like a protective father?"

"Honey, life without you would be empty. But, I can't give you advice and not take the same medicine. Maybe you and I should become lovers?"

"Not this stone maid for you," she shot back. "Pruned of all distractions for the flowering of my ambitions. You need a passionate affair of the heart."

"Maybe you're right. We lean on each other too much as it is."

She felt his arm around her waist, as E.F. steered her toward the sofa. She could see that his sentimental moment had passed. They didn't delve into one another's demons, never had. Theirs was a unique business relationship, living and working together like close family. But her thoughts returned to E.F.'s concerns for her personal happiness. It was sad that she couldn't accept Charles' attentions. He was the fabled prince in every way. I better chalk it up to a piece missing in me, she thought, not for the first time in recent months.

Melissa had seen all her mother's vitality drained by a lout of a husband. Her father used religion as a straight jacket, binding both women to him with fear of the Lord. These many years later, she realized it wasn't the Lord they feared at all. E.F. had released her from that barren existence and opened her up to feel and crave life, and with his training and encouragement she had thrown herself into her career. Now he was trusting her to lead UCC out of stagnation. Naming her CEO was the latest example of his faith in her abilities.

Dear E.F., she thought. His own hectic life was one of limitless horizons. He was even more driven than she was. Or, was she mistaking his encouragement and support of her career, with her own drive to excel? It was one of many questions that she kept putting aside, not wanting to put a chink in her confidence.

"Honey, our problem of the moment, is this videotape. Charles thinks your best bet at damage control is to assist this Ms. Green in writing her book. Want to look at the interview?"

"Yup. Sooner the better." It was getting uncomfortably close to the time when she'd be out on her own. This reporter was to be her protection. As if any reporter could be trusted, she thought.

The two were seated side by side on the library sofa as the videotape began to play. Reaching for her glass of wine, Melissa thought of all that was riding on her plans as the new CEO of United Chemicals Corporation. And *Charles thinks this reporter will be the key to my launch. What did he see in her?* She couldn't voice her real thoughts. This was a course of action she'd recommended. Hire a reporter to shadow her for one week. Use this journalist to validate her position, explaining how she had earned the credentials to be CEO.

"My new best friend." Her sarcasm didn't escape E.F.; he patted her hand. He knew only too well her distaste for publicity.

"Well, well. A feminist in the flesh! Trim, pared down wardrobe, dressed for action. I'll bet she shops at the GAP," Melissa said, secretly relieved to find the young woman was bright and hadn't talked Charles to death about how good she was.

"Charles might be right," E.F. said in response. "You have to like her style. She's all business."

"She has a brashness I like too. I'll bet she won't miss much. But, I suspect she's no friend of corporate America."

"As a matter of fact, the file of articles Charles sent over has some surprises. It seems our Ms. Green, while wanting to champion a social agenda, is smart enough to report the truth when she sees it. She's the one who actually took the side of that Bank Director in the S&L exposé. Here read it for yourself."

Taking another sip of wine, Melissa stretched her arms overhead to release tension. "I'll read it after dinner. That's not my main worry. After years of working quietly behind the scenes, I doubt that this reporter will believe in my having earned the right to be CEO. And if she doesn't, we're sunk."

Getting up, Melissa began to pace the room, unaware of the picture she made as her silk jumpsuit flowed over her slim body with each graceful step. Stopping in front of E.F., she kneeled down and placed both hands in his. "Until now you've allowed me to work behind the scenes. Any time a journalist even got close you had Charles sidetrack him. So what's to keep our Ms. Green in line? You two did too damned fine a job of keeping me a secret!"

"That's why we're going to insist on a contract! It isn't as if you haven't passed your trials by fire."

"How are you going to censor that firebrand?" Agitated by the thought of a reporter critiquing her capabilities, she jumped back to her feet.

"We approach the project in stages. First, have Ms. Green write an outline. We can edit that, if necessary. If, as Charles expects, Ms. Green becomes our ally, then we can encourage her to emphasize certain elements in your training. I expect we'll have to give her Editor an exclusive interview as well. We'll simply recommend these elements be included in the *Economic World* article. By that time we'll be set. All plans in place."

"What makes Charles think she'll become a willing participant in our plans?"

"Because she's a feminist. She has to root for you to succeed. You are the first woman to run a global industrial corporation."

She knew that. This was the thrill of her life. She'd reached the pinnacle of her career. "And, what if she doesn't become an ally?"

"Then we rethink stage two."

Looking at the canny horse trader, she saw that he was relaxed. His favorite polished boots peeking out from under the crossed leg of his gray flannel slacks. E.F. wouldn't worry about something he'd already researched and accepted.

"You know what I'm worried about? Not the job. I've spent years training for that. How do I keep her out of my private life? I cringe to think of a reporter learning that we live together." Her palms felt cold and wet. "I know we're completely respectable with my separate apartment. But you've got to admit it looks a lot more intriguing than it is."

"Melissa, for the time being she's on our leash. And, by the time her contract has expired you will have proved yourself to more than this little gal. Charles will keep a close eye on her. Listen to him. He's saved my bacon more than once."

"So Charles is going to have this hot shot treated as my new best friend? How can she not see our relationship?"

Having E.F. laugh at her wasn't helping her nerves.

"With your schedule, a personal life won't even crop up. Even if it does, she'll see that being CEO isn't a 9-to-5 job. I'm sure you'll handle her."

But Melissa was secretive about her personal life, past and present. It was an old habit that kept her safe from cruelty of others. Once her grade school classmates had laughed at her early curfews, her not being allowed to wear lipstick, her dowdy clothes. No one laughed now, she thought with pride. Now, people saw a fashionably dressed lady. She vowed long ago, that this cool exterior would be the only M.L. Horn outsiders would ever see. Secrets had become her way of life. A public facade was her protective shell. And just as E.F. had said, there was no social life planned for anyone to comment on. She was betting on carefully orchestrating the week, at least that was the plan. But now it's about to become real.

She had loved working for E.F. from the very first day. That was fifteen years ago when she'd just graduated law school. She'd been hired to be his assistant at E.F. Haynes Associates. It was a management firm, geared to E.F.'s wide-ranging business interests. In those early days, they worked side by side, real mentor and protege. It was fun and even brought Melissa the surrogate family she longed for. Then came the trials by fire, six-month assignments at one down and dirty business after another. First mining, then metal fabrication and automotive parts, she'd been trained, tutored, and tested in each, working her way from the bottom up. Now, as one of the Directors of UCC, he'd had her nominated and named CEO. In a few days, she would officially join her corporate peers, assuming the mantle she'd worked toward all her adult life.

"Melissa, if I've learned anything in my dotage, sticking as close to the truth as possible, is the best policy. It does help, of course, to be able to charm your critics. But, in that my dear, you are extremely adept."

"You're not old." Her smile filled with her love for him.

"Maybe not, but looking at your youthful face, I feel it."

His trust and faith helped calm her nerves.

"We have nothing to fear that can't be controlled," E.F. said. "Let's go in to dinner and leave the gossip to those who will. We have done nothing wrong and have nothing to apologize for!"

As E.F. led her into the warm Chippendale appointed dining room, Melissa reflected on their relationship. Would this reporter want to see where she lived? Peek into their home? And if she did, would she see a townhouse with two separate apartment entrances, or the underlying relationship of a man and woman living together?

Looking across the highly polished cherry wood table where they shared most meals, Melissa warmed at the site of her friend and soul mate. Graying temples enhanced his youngish sixty-five year old face, etched by life. As a roughneck in the oil fields, the young E.F. had earned and lost at least one fortune that she knew about. Now a millionaire many times over, E.F.'s wealth, as he often reminded her, was a by-product of his fascination with corporate finance. His thick square fingers were now free of crude oil, and his strong body softened by 65 years of life. But he fit so comfortably into his conservative British cut blazer and slacks, she had trouble thinking of him as the poor orphan he'd been. Somehow she couldn't place E.F. in a pair of torn jeans with a dirty face. Or, as a scrappy youngster, fighting for his life.

"You know E.F. I am a little skittish."

"About what? Your new position? I know you can handle that. It's no different from your assignment at Cole Automotive. And your game plan's been upgraded by the best research available."

"It's not the plan, that worries me. It's coming out from behind you. Being the focus of everyone's attention. I can get the job done. I would just rather work behind the scenes like I always have."

"Melissa, I'm looking at a mature leader who happens to be a damned attractive gal. We've talked about this before. This is what we've been working toward. And you've always told me that being female has been your ace in the hole. The stakes are higher, but the tactics are the same. Now use your visibility. Make your grab for control. Why, they're mere boys, compared to you."

"Right!" she answered, sitting straighter in her chair. E.F. always stiffened her spine. She wouldn't back down now.

Acknowledging her readiness to do battle for UCC, Melissa raised her glass of Saint Emilion in salute. "To Success. To breaking tradition or balls. What ever works," her mischievous smile filled with delight at E.F.'s lusty laugh.

"That's the ticket. The crafty leader I know and love. Remember it's a game. Line up your players, set your strategy and knock'em dead."

"And what will you be doing while I'm playing with the big boys? Implementing stringent budget cuts and a major staff reorganization?"

"Keeping score, of course. Watching your backfield. Stepping on all those cockroaches you're bound to scare out into the open."

CHAPTER III

The library desk sat in a pool of light, off to one side of the darkened room. The heavy damask draperies were pulled closed to hide New York's Upper East Side skyline, eliminating any clues to the time of day. William Smythe Foley, Counsel for United Chemicals Corporation, was a nocturnal creature who thrived in the shadows. Bright light made him nervous. Now, after a full day at his office, he was home, immersed in his private world. A world recently devoted to ruining UCC's new CEO, M.L. Horn.

That weakling chemist was worth every penny of the $5,000 I paid for him, Foley thought as he read a confidential, patent application report, laid out on his desk's leather framed blotter.

"Well, well, they got their patent for the manufacture of synthetic hyaluronic acid, now they can replicate the costly natural stuff for pennies. From cocks-combs to cosmetics. If there was ever a way to print money, the cosmetics industry is it," he said as he completed reading the summary.

Picking up the telephone, he punched in the number of Quinn's Bar. Leaning back in his high back desk chair, the small man dressed in Lord of the Manor splendor cut a cunning figure. With ruby velvet smoking jacket, black slacks, and white silk ascot, Foley looked like one of the portraits he had long admired in Boston's Museum of Fine Arts. As if he could hurry the ringing phone, his slippered child-size foot began tapping out a silent beat.

"Scully? This was what I wanted. I'll have your money delivered to Quinn's later tonight. Don't forget, not a word to Quinn!" Hanging up, Foley thought that Scully hadn't needed to answer. He hardly spoke anyway. The perfect errand boy.

Once again hunched over the report, Foley began to list possible markets for this remarkable new creation of science. It was really science copying Mother Nature at her best.

"Medicine, cosmetics, pharmaceuticals, even horse racing. Hell, I can't lose."

Next, he called Bruce Dearling at Neuwirth Investments. Dearling was integral to his plan.

"I need more BioTech's stock, but stop short of the 5% rule. I don't want anyone tracing my trades. Also, think of how I can significantly increase my position in UCC. Research the numbers," he barked into the mouthpiece, never acknowledging the man by name. "Don't limit yourself to outright buys, include options and buying on margin. Get back to me by Tuesday."

Hanging up, Foley promptly dismissed Dearling from his thoughts. Reaching for his first scotch of the evening, he sipped its smoky richness, looking around the book-lined study of his large, pre-war apartment. The room was a replica of one he used to pass as a boy in Boston. He remembered scurrying home long after dark and passing the Back Bay mansion, its windows so clear that the main floor library reached out to him. It always glowed, warm and inviting, in candle and firelight. Sometimes he'd stop, close his eyes and imagine his chilled bones being warmed by the glowing fire. And as he hurried home he'd dream of having a book filled room like it one day, and money enough to have a fire, even on the 4th of July if he wanted it.

"Now I do," he swore, relishing the thought. The proof was all around him in the cost of his apartment and furnishings. The fruits of more than two decades as a private attorney representing major corporate clients. Then he remembered joining UCC as corporate counsel, giving up his independence, because it promised him a future of power. As their CEO he'd control not only his personal wealth but also the corporation's billions.

Foley's mind began to savor another kind of power that would soon replace the position he'd lost, the power of owning something everybody wanted. His small mouth curled in a cruel smile, as he thought of the honors and favors that would be asked of him by the rich and famous, all because he controlled the new magic elixir, the secret to prolonging a youthful body.

There was no stopping him. His plan was in place. To become a member of society's A List. "To my New

World," raising his glass in a private toast. "Where money and power are the only pedigrees that count."

The shrill sound of the unexpected telephone call snapped him back to the task at hand.

"Yeah?"

"Mr. Foley, it's me, Bruce Dearling. You hung up before I mentioned that I need your signature on the stock transfers for tomorrow's trade."

"Yeah. Come on up. I'll be expecting you. And Dearling, bring along your projections. We need to go over your upcoming buy and sell strategies."

Carefully unlocking his bottom desk drawer, Foley withdrew his file on Bruce Dearling. He had literally bought the man skin, bones, and soul.

Thinking back twenty-five years to his first job out of Georgetown University Law School, Foley remembered first spotting Dearling in the library of Longworth, Glen and White, a Washington D.C. law firm. Foley had relished that job, and his position as one of the bright young attorneys hired that year. Dearling had been a lowly file clerk, studying for his stockbroker's license. His job had been obtained as a favor to his well-connected father. They made an odd pair, the scholarship lawyer and the silver spoon clerk, but from the beginning Foley knew this was a man he could use.

Sipping his drink, Foley remembered that first hectic week. He had been in all his glory. Even though he had been sent to the firm's law library to research precedents, the assignment had been for a major client. A corporation accused of stock manipulation. As he remembered it Dearling had approached him. "Mr. Foley." Looking up from a pad filled with tightly scrawled notes, Foley had stared into the bespectacled watery blue eyes of a lanky blond man his age.

"Yes?" Imagine being called Mr. Foley, he had thought. He had always liked the respect with which Dearling addressed him.

"I'm Bruce Dearling. I'm a file clerk here and was told to gather this information for you."

Foley wouldn't have given Dearling another thought except he then offered, "The crux of your dilemma can be resolved by using the strategy found on page three of this file. I marked it for you."

Nodding at the strange man, he had taken the file and opened it to find a note with an arrow pointing to a paragraph midway down the page. It had been a summary of a prior legal action taken in a similar situation to the one he was researching. When he had looked up, Foley saw Dearling had left as quietly as he had arrived.

He was such a timid guy, Foley remembered. Dressed in Brooks Brothers navy and chino. "If I'd dressed that way, I'd never have been hired," he grumbled. It was a painful memory, learning that he had only been the hired help, Dearling was part of the WASP family. Yet they had become office friends. "Yeah, both intent on becoming rich," he muttered. "Even then, Dearling really knew how the financial market worked. Still does." Foley's respect was voiced reluctantly, even for his own ears. After all Dearling was Foley's hired help now.

Closing the file, Foley thought it had worked out just as he planned all those years ago. He had marked Dearling then as a means to accumulating his wealth. Dearling needed his cunning. He'd wanted to prove to his overly rich family, he could make his own fortune. Foley remembered savoring the moment when Dearling finally admitted that he didn't have the guts to fly close to the edge. That the best he could hope for was a six-figure salary as a broker at some large firm.

With a smugness for his own planning, Foley recalled how he'd watched and waited for the right moment, and had been there to offer Dearling a position as the head of Neuwirth Investments, a front for Foley's driving ambition and greed.

Now, eighteen years later, Dearling was a willing participant in his plans, earning a percentage on all Foley's trades . . . just as if he had still been with a large brokerage house. And, as demanding as Foley was, Dearling accepted his place, which to the world was head of Neuwirth, along with his share of the growing wealth of the firm. It didn't matter that Neuwirth was owned by WSF Inc., of the Cayman Islands. Or, that Foley owned WSF lock stock and barrel. His role was to keep Foley's activities hidden.

"OK, Dearling. You're on track," Foley said placing the file back in the desk drawer. He liked to keep track of Dearling's growing income, always fearing that if Dearling finally amassed his fortune, he would terminate their partnership. Not likely! There would never enough money for either of us, he decided.

Picking up a memo, from a pile of work that he had brought home from United Chemicals, Foley growled, "That Bitch. Just because she's CEO doesn't mean she can tell me how to represent the corporation. She's got balls, I'll say that. But she's not going to tell me how to do my job. Damn the Board of Directors! How could they make a woman CEO? She'll ruin us. Bending his head closer to his notepad, he thought, let me see if I can bypass her on this one. She's so busy playing Bossman, she'll never know what happened." Chuckling to himself, he began creating another problem for Bitch Horn to handle.

The building phone buzzed, reminding him of Dearling's arrival. Picking up the house phone he barked, "If it's Mr. Dearling, send him on up." Getting the doorman's confirmation, Foley cleared his desk muttering, "The plan's almost set. Now, to rework the numbers. I can't be this close and come up short of funds. Dearling will have to find a way."

CHAPTER IV

Rubbing the bridge of his aquiline nose, Dr. Lawrence Henderson, founder and President of BioTech was feeling his 62 years. "How can I be so tired?" he complained to the walls of his clinic-like office. Buzzing his secretary on the intercom, he wearily asked, "Emily. Do you have any apple juice out there? I need a pick-me-up."

Removing his wire rimmed glasses, he began to clean the lenses of imagined streaks. This merger with UCC had better come through soon, he thought. I need those funds for two more clinical trials. Without test results they'd never get FDA approval in time to market hyaluronic acid injections this year.

"Why does the FDA make testing so difficult?" he remarked to a surprised Emily who was standing in front of his desk holding a glass.

"Dr. Henderson. Your apple juice?"

After 40 years at his side, she should be used to his outbursts about the FDA, he thought.

"Yes. Thank you Emily. Do you have a minute?" he asked as he sipped the cold juice and straightened his tall spare frame, to release the tension from long hours at his desk.

"Of course, Dr. Henderson."

"How soon after the merger papers are signed can we obtain our funds?"

"According to Ms. Horn, the budgets have already been established. You'll have access within 24-hours of signing. She said that was the soonest the bank would allow."

"Dear Melissa. That should be fine. Are we set up to begin the first trial at Orthopedic Hospital? Do they know we'll need a population of 100 knees?"

"It's all in your proposal Dr. Henderson. According to Dr. Gangis, the arthritis clinic will have more than enough patients to satisfy our requirements."

"I wish that this additional test wasn't necessary. Those patients scheduled for the placebo will have their hopes raised and won't be helped at all."

"But Dr. Henderson, when the FDA approves X-43, you will be able to offer those patients their first treatment's free of charge."

"Yes Emily. It isn't as if we've targeted patients with advanced stages of deterioration. There'll be plenty of time to relieve their pain after the trial is completed. Anything left for today?"

"You're meeting with Dr. Emery in ten minutes."

Taking another sip of the cold juice, Dr. Henderson nodded. "OK Emily. Let me know when he arrives."

Watching his secretary leave, Henderson steeled himself for a truly unpleasant task. He wished all his employees were as honorable and diligent as Emily was. Unfortunately, even with his ability to pick the good employees from the flotsam and jetsam of job candidates, he occasionally made a mistake. Was George Emery one of those mistakes?

Henderson thought about the reason that he had hired Emery in the first place. It had been the young man's dedication to research. Very few people had a love for the time-consuming, all-absorbing rigidity that the field required. Or the discipline it entailed to prove a theory absolutely.

"What had gone wrong? Emery had so much promise," he worried aloud, as his intercom buzzed.

"Dr. Emery is here, Dr. Henderson." Emily's voice emanating from the speaker on his desk.

"Please show him in, Emily."

Standing to greet his young employee, Lawrence Henderson noted a peculiar pallor to the young chemist's normally sallow skin that was stretched over his bony face. He was always brooding about something, Henderson thought. But, today he also saw that Emery's nails were bitten to a ragged mess.

"I'm pleased you could break away from the Lab to join me, Dr. Emery." He saw that his junior chemist was unnaturally fidgety as he acknowledged the greeting.

"We haven't met outside the lab in the . . . how long have you been with us George?" The question was designed to force a response and hopefully elicit some clue to the young man's state of mind.

"Six years Dr. Henderson," Emery answered as he sat in front of his desk, crossing his legs into a tightly held knot.

"I was wondering how you like working for us?" Henderson began. Trying to get his visitor into some form of a conversation.

"Fine. Sir."

"Are you involved with Henry's hyaluronic acid project?"

"Not directly Sir. I helped collect data for the patent application, but the real work was done by Dr. Markem's team."

"I see." Looking directly at Emery, Henderson saw him re-cross his legs. But it was George's eyes that were disturbing him now. They were too bright. Maybe the boy was ill, he thought. That would explain his skin color and his slightly crazed appearance.

"George. I wonder if you might help me out with a problem."

"If I can Sir."

"It seems that copy #5 of the Hyaluronic Patent Application Report is missing. The copy assigned to your office. Do you know what happened to it?" "Were the reports numbered, Sir?"

The sudden burst of dew on Emery's upper lip confirmed Henderson's suspicions that all was not right with George Emery. Had he something to do with the stolen report?

"Yes George. It was critical to keep that information under lock and key. Do you have any idea where it is?"

Even though there was a sudden edge in Henderson's voice, Emery didn't reply.

"I'm deeply concerned because the report outlines our plans to market hyaluronic acid. You know, for use in treating arthritis, as a delivery system for medication, and of course the numerous cosmetic applications. I wouldn't want our competitors to get hold of that information just now. We need time to perfect our basic formulations before we can go into full production. Any leaks at this stage could ruin us." And squash our merger with UCC, Henderson thought.

Watching closely, Henderson noticed that Emery's bony chest had stilled, as if he had stopped all bodily movement. What the Hell's going on, he wondered. Emery had changed from a normally intense man into a stranger.

"You aren't looking very well, George. Have you been ill?"

"Actually, I have, Sir."

Henderson was watching, as George's fevered eyes began looking for a way out. "Well, why didn't you say so sooner?" he replied, with an amiability he didn't feel.

"It's not something I like to talk about Sir."

"Well I can't have any employee of mine ill." Pushing the button on his intercom Lawrence Henderson asked his secretary to get Sam Levy on the phone. A friend for more than forty years, Sam was also BioTech's company doctor.

"Dr. Henderson. Really that's all right. It's just a bronchial thing. I'm susceptible. I'll see my doctor tomorrow. Really it's okay."

"Not at all." Picking up his phone at Emily Roberts buzz, Henderson began a one sided conversation with a missing Dr. Levy. "Hi Sam. Yes, everyone's fine. I'm in a meeting with one of my bright young geniuses, George Emery. Oh? He hasn't had a company physical in two years? I see. Yes. I'll have him stop by within the hour. Thank you Sam. Bye." Hanging up the unconnected telephone, Lawrence played out the script he and Levy had prepared to corral Emery into a legitimate company built corner. Henderson had watched George Emery change over the past year and suspected he was hiding an illness. He couldn't afford to have any of the company's research projects contaminated. So, he and Sam had plotted to get George in for a complete medical check-up.

"George, you must be extremely tired working the hours you do. And not feeling well can certainly add to your fatigue. I want you to run right over to Sam's office. He'll check you out and we'll continue this chat Monday."

As kind as he wanted his words to sound, Henderson watched a shaky George Emery stand to leave. As he reached the door, Emery started to say something, but all he heard was a whispered, "Thank you Dr. Henderson. I'm sure I'll be fine."

"No, don't thank me. Just get well. See you Monday."

No sooner had Emery left then Henderson dialed Sam Levy.

"Hi Sam. He's on his way. Yes, I'm sure he's ill. His eyes, they're too bright. His skin is stretched so thin, you'd think he was starving. Get those test results for me. And while you have him, get as complete a medical history as possible. We may need it for leverage. It might be a mental breakdown. Could even be drugs. But that wouldn't be George. We have to know what's wrong with him. Maybe then we'll have an idea what the Hell he's been up to. Thanks."

CHAPTER V

Pamela never entered John Holmes office without a brief fluttering in her stomach. After eight years, he could still throw her at least one curve, often upsetting a preconceived approach to an assignment. As the no nonsense Editor-in-Chief of *Economic World*, he was something of an extrasensory leader. His staff often wondered if their assignments were merely will-o'-the-wisps. Pamela knew that Holmes hadn't an ounce of whimsy in him and his off beat assignments would often prove to crystallize a current theory he was pursuing for the magazine.

Glancing around his Spartan glass enclosed office she observed the usual beehive with editors, reporters and secretaries, running in and out. She was left to find her own way to the one chair free of piled folders.

As she settled, John Holmes acknowledged her, eyes reflecting a mind traveling faster than the speed of one of his news gathering computers. Bow-tied collar loose on his scrawny neck, Holmes had the body of a zealot.

It was as if his over active mind had burned away any extra flesh.

"That's all for now Linda. Hold all calls," he directed to the departing group. "Well? How did it go?" Holmes demanded as he stood to close the office door. Settling back in his chair with thumbs hooked on his narrow belt, he sat waiting for her to answer.

"I don't know. Charles Cray was polite, but I got this crazy feeling that it was a look see, as the models would say. He was charming, but a little distracted. As if the decision to allow me to write an authorized biography had already been made before we met. What he said though, was that he'd make his recommendation to Ms. Horn and would be in touch."

"You don't give yourself enough credit. As a matter of fact, you did very well. He said yes. Your official biography of one of UCC's best-kept secrets, Melissa Lynn Horn, CEO should cost me dearly, he grumbled. With your newly acquired independent profits from that book, I'll have to give you a raise, just to keep you on staff."

Jumping up from her chair, Pamela had all she could do to keep from running around her boss's desk, to hug him, something he would have hated. It was hard not to react to the news. She knew he was pleased for himself first, then for her.

Pamela had learned all of her reporter's skills from John Holmes, developing into a journalist she knew he respected. Her once overwritten pieces were now brisk, spare, as was her personal style. He trained her well, she realized. No matter how hard he'd pushed, she'd always come through. She's never taken the snide point of view, regardless of the level of sleaze she'd uncovered. John often told her he liked the skeptic in her. Her desire to prove to herself that the subject of her research was real. And that meant digging for those hidden bits of dirt. Analyzing every speck she uncovered to learn a complete truth she could accept. What was it she was always telling him? "I don't have to take them home to meet my mother, I just have to believe they had a mother."

"You might be interested in a note I just received from our Mr. Cray," his sharp voice cut into her thoughts.

Seeing the Tiffany note-sized paper he dangled in front of her, Pamela leaned over his desk to grab it from his hand. Reading aloud,

Dear Mr. Holmes:

After careful consideration of Pamela Green's request to have our cooperation in the preparation of an authorized biography of UCC's new CEO, Melissa Lynn Horn, we have decided to give her our consent. Along with our consent, we will provide access to Ms. Horn for one week.

If it is agreeable, I would like for you and Pamela Green to join me for luncheon, 12:15 next Tuesday, at the Four Seasons.

It is my hope that both of your schedules will permit you to accept, and to forgive this short notice.

Sincerely,
Charles T. Cray
Executive Vice President
Public Affairs

"Why does he want to invite both of us to lunch? And, why didn't he write directly to me? It is my book!"

Sitting further back in his swiveling desk chair, John Holmes seemed to be temporarily lost in another world, and did not immediately answer. Pamela sat somewhat impatiently, waiting for him to share his thoughts.

"He's one cagey fellow! I think he wants to be sure that I won't interfere with your manuscript. Since nothing has been signed, he is still free to select another writer, one he feels confident he can control. It looks like he wants an authorized book written."

Pamela sat quietly, waiting for John to continue. She knew he was reviewing her situation looking for problems.

"I remember meeting him at a press conference in the early '70's. He worked for one of the large public relations firms and his client was the leading manufacturer of aerosol containers. It was to be the first discussion with the press on the growing concerns over the impact of fluorocarbon sprays on the ozone layer."

Coming out of his thoughts to look at her, she saw that he looked unusually relaxed.

"Of course we know now that fluorocarbon sprays were poking holes in our atmosphere. And they were removed from the marketplace. But the level of scientific expertise presented at the conference introduced me to some new information."

Sitting straighter in her chair, she watched and waited again for him to continue. She knew that public relations agencies were known to if not color the truth, at least provide only the positive side of a story. What he told her about Charles Cray could be very useful in her upcoming dealings with the man.

"While I didn't buy Cray's client's argument, I was able to launch my own research using some of their experts. Anyway, I came away from that press conference with a greater respect for the art of public relations. Cray had established a platform of experts for the media to question. He positioned his client's point of view, but in doing so actually gave anyone bright enough to read between the lines, information on an issue that at that time hadn't been a clear cut one. If that panel hadn't been as august as it was, then my view of Cray would have been lumped with all the other flacks. But he had an integrity that I admired."

Pamela knew her boss rarely had a kind word for the spin-doctors, his pet term for PR types. She was surprised he found one he liked. "Will I ever understand you, Boss? Just when I think I've got you cold, you pull another rabbit out of your hat."

Looking very smug indeed, Holmes said, "I'm curious as to just what Mr. Cray has up his sleeve this time. We may or may not get an inkling at lunch, but the meeting should prove enlightening."

Why was he looking at her like that? His scowl was making her uncomfortable. As if she'd done something wrong.

"Get your hair done and buy yourself a power suit. On me."

"John, I didn't know you cared. What's up?"

"You don't have that sophisticated-journalist look. Like those gals on TV. I want you shown off to good advantage for our lunch at the Four Seasons. How much is a woman's suit these days?"

"If you are talking about an executive woman, and not a reporter's outfit, about $1,000.00 should take care of it."

She had to smile at the shock registered on her boss' face.

"Here is an authorization to draw an $800.00 advance. Use it on your new look."

"I see that my book is important to you as well," she joked, as she grabbed the chit before he could change his mind. Saluting her boss, she pivoted and marched out of his office. She could hear him yelling as she walked down the hall. "Linda, I want the "Dun and Bradstreet" on United Chemicals, the "Who's Who" listing on Melissa Horn, if it exists, as well as their write-up on Charles Cray and every UCC board member. Also check our research department for any personal information on these people."

If there were anything funny going on, John would keep her informed. He wanted to get to the truth as much as she did. Feeling better knowing that she would get John's permission to take a leave of absence to write her book, Pamela wondered why her Boss, who was known to squeeze a rock for water, thought a new look was important. She'd never thought much about her wardrobe. It had to be durable and travel. Other than that, basic black and brown seemed to go anywhere.

CHAPTER VI

In a downtown brokerage office the telephone had just rung with a buy order for 10,000 shares of BioTech at $22. Looking at his computer terminal, Tim Lynch noted that at last weeks drop in the market, this same caller had purchased another 10,000 shares at $19. He had never met the caller who was trading the account of Neuwirth Investments. All he knew was that his client was a private investment club with a recent small but sparkling track record for picking stocks in companies that were about to make news.

Wondering aloud, "Should I purchase 100 shares for my personal account?" Tim tried to remember if he had read anything that would recommend new interest in BioTech.

Tim was too junior to be privy to any gossip shared by the firm's partners over lunch. A neophyte at Morrison, Sherman and Temple, Tim had been a retail broker for only two years. But he was of the breed. From the well-starched collar of his custom made shirt to the buttons of his bright red braces, Tim was molding himself for a Wall

Street success. He lived for the daily rush he got trading other people's accounts.

Lost in thought, his short dark hair, cut close to the side of his head, Tim squared his shoulders as he searched his computer for information.

Finding the latest corporate analysis, Tim remarked aloud, "Oh yeah. I remember now. BioTech's been going through a tough time." Continuing to look for a clue as to why his client wanted more of their stock, Tim read their most recent two quarterly reports. Both stated an increase in the loss was due to ongoing promising research.

You haven't had an increase in new revenue sources in five years, he thought. What's going on here? It says that BioTech is expanding its product pipeline. Maybe these guys at Neuwirth know something's about to break? If I stay lean I can gamble $2,200, he decided. "I think I'll follow their lead." quietly murmuring his plans

Entering the Neuwirth order, Tim then made a note on his calendar that he was purchasing 100 shares for his own account on a hunch. Keeping a meticulous diary of his trades would hopefully prove his honesty if it were ever questioned. He knew that the firm was paranoid about their brokers' access to market information. They didn't want any employee jeopardizing the firm's pristine reputation. After the scandalous 80's, Morrison, Sherman & Temple had tightened up the firm's practices. Tim's training had been filled with these new rules. But the firm still allowed their employees to maintain personal accounts. And Tim was just as earnest in developing his fortune as he was in aggressively trading his clients' portfolios.

"One day," he promised himself softly. "I'll have a personal account important enough to open doors to the men that shape the market. And, just maybe, playing in the big leagues I'll get to meet Michael Milken." His dreams voiced in the softest of whispers.

Milken was the reason Tim had become a broker. He idolized the man who created the high-yield market. And even after his hero was sent to prison, Tim kept track of Milken financed companies, watching them grow.

Tim would get together with his equally driven friends for after-market drinks. They often remarked about the brilliance of a guy who enabled small companies to finance their growth just like the *Fortune* 500.

Over drinks they'd play Milken Trivia. Fashioned after baseball trivia, it became a mark of membership in their clique. In rapid-fire succession, they'd toss questions back and forth. "How much did Turner's initial issue raise to expand CNN?" "What was the date MCI got their financing to challenge AT&T?" "What was the size of the offering that enabled HBO to strengthen their franchise?" And each evening they'd wrap with a group cheer. Building a pyramid of hands, they'd chant, "High-Yield-High-Times." This was Wall Street's newest group of young men on the move.

For Tim, defending Michael Milken was akin to a religious crusade. He often reminded the naysayer's that two hot industries, cellular telephones and cable television, owed their very existence to junk bonds. And when questioned about the loss of jobs due to corporate takeovers, he'd pull a wrinkled *Wall Street Journal* clip from his vest pocket, and read to the ignorant skeptics.

> "The high-risk securities market created by Milken added some 12 million jobs to the economy at the same time the *Fortune* 500 firms were decreasing employment by some 4%."

As he fingered his Mont Blanc pen, Tim whispered, "Neuwirth Investments needs watching. I think they know more than they're supposed to. This account could launch me into the major leagues."

CHAPTER VII

Standing in front of the tabletop bar that was always set-up and ready in the library, E.F. turned and smiled at Melissa. She watched as he took in her appearance and winked.

She had been relaxing on the sofa, part of her usual Sunday afternoon at home with E.F. Today, she felt like cheering herself up and had dressed in a green silk jumpsuit she knew he particularly liked. He'd often told her the color sparked the red highlights in her auburn hair, reminding him of fireflies on a summer evening.

They had spent the morning at separate chores, meeting at 4 for their ritual drink and chat before Sunday dinner. Today she needed something to clear away the clouds of doom. A dose of harmless flirting with E.F. was just the thing, she thought. The two very private people enjoyed a special closeness that had grown so naturally over the years of similar afternoons spent together.

"After a hard week, it's time for a drink. How about a scotch, Honey?"

"So we're into a serious bout of relaxation are we E.F.?"

"Yup! One more week and you're on your own young lady."

"At last," she sighed with exaggerated glee. "Now I can prove just how capable the gentle sex can be."

"Honey, I hope we can always find time to be together like this."

E.F.'s sudden switch in mood was as sharp as the sharp ring of ice dropping into the crystal glasses. "We will E.F.," she promised, trying to keep his mood light. His somber tone, she noticed, matched an unusual downward cast on his life-worn face. "After all we'll still be living here. If the outside world dares to intrude, we'll pull up the drawbridge and keep it out."

Handing her a drink, E.F. went to stir up the fire. She saw that he was lost in some private thought. At the sudden ringing of the library telephone, E.F. moved quickly away from the glowing fire. Rushing to stop the phone's jarring sound seemed to be his only goal. She knew he never received calls on Sunday. The break in their peace was not welcomed.

"E.F." he said growling into the receiver. "Oh it's you Larry."

She saw him smile, releasing him from his sour mood of a moment ago. "So that's it! Yes. I'll check into our end, first thing in the morning. Something is definitely out of whack. She's fine. Yes, we'll see you for dinner next week.

I'll get back to you on this just as soon as I learn anything. Night, Larry."

Alerted by E.F.'s thoughtful frown Melissa asked, "Does Larry have a problem at BioTech?"

"Yes. It seems that he's missing a copy of his Patent Application Report on hyaluronic acid. He suspects foul play. That one of his scientists was manipulated into stealing it."

"Did he say why an employee was suspected?"

"Yes. It seems this poor bastard got AIDS and needed the money for outside treatment. He thought he'd be fired if he was found infected."

"But Larry wouldn't fire anyone who got sick."

"You and I know that. But this fellow was desperate. He was contagious and thought that because of the sensitivity of his work in the lab, Larry would have to fire him."

"Does Larry know who bought the report?"

"Nope. He hopes it's not a competitor. But the funny thing is that because the patent was approved, the report won't really help a competitor. They can buy natural hyaluronic acid. It's expensive, but available in the combs of roosters. But without BioTech's process to produce it synthetically, it's just too costly for any company to compete with them. So the question is who else would profit? Someone who is trading BioTech stock? Or, someone who knows we plan to buy BioTech?"

"That can only mean one of my staff," Melissa snapped. So much for a relaxing Sunday at home, she thought.

"Damn, if you haven't got something there. I'll check them out first thing tomorrow."

"E.F., why not have your broker check the movement in both UCC and BioTech stock? If there's any parallel activity in both, maybe we can flush out our rat?" Reflecting on E.F.'s connections, Melissa hoped they would be able to identify a sizable individual transaction, or newly active account trading both stocks. In situations like this, it helped to have friends.

"While we're discussing troubled waters, have you given any thoughts to your week with Ms. Green?"

"Yes. I'm thinking it could be an opportunity to test my power outside the Boardroom."

"What's cooking on that pretty brain?"

"Let's assume our feminist is accustomed to living in the rough and tumble world of men. And let's suppose her attitudes toward corporations have been colored by exposé's on the less than admirable among us. It might enable me to use her own career struggles, as a mirror for our current strategy. You know, iron hand in velvet glove sort of thing."

"Melissa, let me remind you of our hidden agenda. We don't want our plans to wind up on the cover of *Economic World*! We want to shape her book."

"We'll have her under contract, won't we E.F.?"

"Yes."

"And Charles told you she was a straight shooter, at least as far as he could determine?"

"Yup."

"Well then, how about a little dose of honesty? Confront her with the magnitude of our problems and let her evaluate our plans? I'm certain that if we aren't too controlling, she will agree with a minor tweak or two on her information. Charles said that without our cooperation, she doesn't have a book deal."

"Evaluate our plans to whom?" the alarm evident by the resurfacing of his Texas drawl.

"Me? No. How about Charles? He's very good at eliciting confidences."

"And just when will you find the time to plot out your little game of Truth or Consequences?"

"Well since I'm about to lose my independence, I thought I'd sneak away for a last weekend as a private citizen. I need to iron out some knots in my psyche with a dose of sun and sand."

"Want me to join you Honey?"

She purposely kept her voice light. "Not this time E.F. I need some solitary R & R. I'm afraid I'd only have fun if you joined me."

"You know I can't help worrying about you. Larry's new situation will work itself out. But you must be prepared for a very demanding week. Our Ms. Green is no fool. She's going to be looking for trouble. So while you're tanning that pretty body, remember you've earned the right to be CEO."

So that's what has been bothering him. The dear man. Here he spends fifteen years training me to take his place and now he's afraid to let his chick fly. "I'll be all right, E.F. But I do need some time to myself. Thanks for understanding." Her smile and gentle squeezing of his hand had brought a smile to his lips.

"OK. But call me if I can help."

She was glad he was accepting her need for privacy. It was one of the many things they had in common, she realized. And while I'm away, I'll bet he's going to do a little digging of his own. It wouldn't be the first time a CEO was bushwhacked by a colleague. That and a market check should help rout any snakes from the woodpile, she hoped. E.F. was resourceful, not to mention well connected, she thought. With his contacts, he should be able to locate Larry's thief and uncover any of our enemies.

CHAPTER VIII

Lying on the turquoise striped pad of the wide beach chaise, Melissa enjoyed breathing the still cool, early morning air. As the sun began to warm her skin, she concentrated all her energies on a Yoga exercise called the Corpse. Silently she commanded her body to follow her directions. It was a slow process of first tensing an isolated part of the body, and then relaxing it as she exhaled.

Having unkinked every part of her body, she lay suspended in a limbo of calm, listening to the soft pulsing surf. It was hypnotic. No honking horns, screaming fire engines, or wailing sirens. Just the blessed surf and sun and softly blowing breeze. Luxuriating in a way that she could never duplicate in the more populated resorts, Melissa said a prayer of thanks for this secluded sanctuary.

She had fled to the isolated island of Largo Verde in the British Virgin Islands, to recharge her batteries for what she was sure would be the fight of her career. Her public unveiling as CEO of a major global corporation. It was a position she had worked towards all her adult life.

Allowing her mind to drift, she found herself in a far distant time listening to her mother's warning about wasting hard-earned money.

"You shouldn't go spending your money frivolously, Dear. You'll need every cent you earn for college." By frivolous her mother had meant her purchase of a book on the great museums of the world. I'd saved for two months to buy that book, she remembered. It was my book of dreams. A peek at life beyond Pittsburgh.

What would Mama think of me now? Here I am, lying at the edge of the deep aquamarine sea so clear I can float face down and watch the fish feeding. "Mama would count out the wasteful expense of taxis, airfare, and by the time she heard the cost of my accommodations she'd accuse me of having done the Devil's work to be able to spend money so freely," she muttered.

Funny, people say you never miss what you don't know. I always knew I was missing something. Sighing to herself, she thought of E.F. You don't know how many doors you've opened for me. She wasn't thinking of her career now, but of finally having warmth and happiness in her life. Late evenings spent sharing books, theater, and film classics with E.F. He even enjoys coaching me in chess and bridge, she thought.

Why was she surprised? It's easy to play if you have someone to play with. But why is it so easy with E.F., and so difficult with anyone else? Taking a deep breath to release a knot that had formed in her stomach, she wondered if she'd ever outgrow that feeling of aloneness that was by now so much a part of her.

"Excuse me. Do you mind if I join you?"

Shading her eyes as she looked up at the source of the question, Melissa saw a well-built, slender man about her age watching her. His question had been politely asked. Something in his voice told her he would leave without another word, if she said no.

He was wearing a striped towel in the Largo Verde colors of turquoise and white, casually draped over his shoulders. But it was his face that stirred her sympathy. Its sharp angles and planes shadowed a haggard tightness around the eyes and mouth. While annoyed to find anyone close enough for conversation, somehow this blond stranger didn't seem to threaten her quietude. Reluctantly, nodding her assent, she closed her eyes and resumed her lazy reflections and her own company.

Melissa was only slightly aware of the young man spreading his large sheet sized towel on the clean unmarked sand beside her, and then move his body to shape the underlying sand to his comfort.

* * *

"Miss. I've brought you a cool glass of pineapple juice."

Melissa's dozing was interrupted by her houseman, George. Looking up at George's smiling face, she noticed the sun had moved higher in the sky and estimated it to now be around 11. She had been lying here since 8 in the morning of her first day in retreat. Leave it to George to let her know when it was time for a break. He and his wife Mary came with the cottage. She noticed that George, having seen her with company, had brought enough juice for two.

Sitting up and adjusting her chaise, she took the offered glass. Glancing over at her silent visitor, she noticed that as she had expected, they were the only two on this part of the beach. How long had he been lying there? Probably two hours, she calculated. Unusual, she thought. He hadn't moved close enough to be on top of her. Just close enough for conversation. Wanting to thank him for not bothering her, she decided to offer him the extra glass of juice.

"Excuse me."

Waiting for him to answer, she watched as he opened his warm blue-green eyes and without a word, offered her his full attention.

"Would you care for a glass of pineapple juice? George has brought more than enough." She tried not to stare, but he was very handsome. His almost hairless bronzed chest and shoulders were no strangers to the sun and he had a light dusting of yellow down covering his well-shaped arms and legs. His quiet manner made her wonder who he was and why he was there. Watching as he accepted her offer, of the glass of juice, she saw that he was easy with his body, like an athlete of a sport requiring flowing movement, maybe tennis or swimming.

"Thank you for sharing your beach with me. It felt lonely outside my cottage."

His voice, while deep, had a gentle clarity that was easy on her ears. "You've been a good neighbor, respecting my privacy. Thank you."

"My name is Hugh," offering Melissa a lean strong hand. She was surprised to see that his nails had that cared for look. Possibly, by a manicurist.

"Mine's Melissa."

"Melissa. That's a pretty name, but so formal. You look more like a *Lissa*, to me. I was watching you from around that bend and wondered what your secret was?"

"Secret?"

"For being so relaxed. Lissa fits the woman I saw earlier."

"Lissa it is, then," smiling at the easy way in which she could talk to this stranger. Another name to add to my list of M.L. and Melissa, she thought.

"I'm afraid I watched you for some time. I'd never seen anyone so at peace. I wouldn't have bothered you but I'd hoped that your secret for relaxing would rub off on me."

"Has it?"

"Yes. I haven't been this calm in almost two years. I'd forgotten what it felt like."

"Mm. I know what you mean. I need to unkink every so often and when I do, I usually come here. It's this place."

"Why is it so quiet? Where is everybody? And I only saw one restaurant. Don't people eat?"

"I take it that this is your first time on Largo Verde?"

"Yes. It was recommended by a doctor, friend of mine. He shanghaied me. Packed me up and shipped me out. I don't even know where I am. But Mark was convinced that if I didn't get away I'd have a breakdown."

So that explains the dark shadows under his eyes, she thought. Exhaustion? Maybe, job stress?

"How trusting to allow someone to pack you up and ship you someplace new."

"I was too tired to care. What is this place anyway?" Hugh asked, perking up with interest.

"This is Largo Verde, a man-created heaven. The South American industrialist, who built it, knew some would pay dearly to get away from the world. Usually it's people with active business or social lives. Or, those in the public eye. The Club is available for diversion, but most visitors enjoy being pampered by the staff in the privacy of their own cottage."

Finishing her drink, Melissa stretched out again and closing her eyes politely discouraged any further conversation. But she didn't stop thinking about Hugh. Who was he? No man can be that handsome without his ego showing. Listening once again to the soothing sound of the lapping water, she began to accept his quiet company.

Melissa wondered if he was alone? He wasn't wearing a wedding ring. In fact the only jewelry he wore was an expensive sports watch. She had just begun to doze when she felt someone gently shake her arm.

"Don't be alarmed." It was Hugh's low-pitched soft voice. "You should probably call it a day. You're beginning to fry."

Melissa saw only concern on his handsome face. Glancing over to his hand, she saw the white imprint his fingers had left on her skin. "Thank you Hugh. It looks as though you saved me just in time. I owe you."

"Not necessary. You're already paid in full." His smile eased the tension around his mouth.

"Well I'm going to take one last swim. Care to join me?" She was very aware of being drawn to this unusual man.

"I'd like that."

As Hugh followed her to the water's edge, she was impressed again by the graceful way his muscular body moved in his very brief Lycra suit. He could model swimwear, she thought. Entering the water at his side, she began to swim, matching each stroke of her arms to his. He swims easily, an athlete definitely, she thought.

They swam for ten minutes before Melissa turned and headed for shore. Emerging from the sea Hugh commented, "You swim like you were born in the water."

"Not exactly, but I was on my high school swim team. You swim well yourself."

"Me too." he chuckled. "School swim team. Although, almost everyone in California swims."

"Oh you're from the West Coast?" Thinking now that if she replaced his tired expression with an easy grin, she could mistake him for a sun-baked surfer or tennis club player.

"Yes, and you?"

"Oh, the East," not sure why she didn't want him to know where she was from. As if knowing would change things. Anyway, Lissa didn't really exist.

Standing awkwardly, and not knowing what to say next, Melissa realized that if she went in now, she'd never see him again. She wanted to get to know him. She was drawn to this stranger by his warmth. He was the most non-threatening man she'd ever met. It made her feel bold by comparison. "Would you accept an invitation to dinner?"

A little boy's grin lit up Hugh's face. "Lissa, I think that would be a wonderful idea."

Her invitation had been hesitant, so she quickly added, "Why not stop by at 6 and we can have cocktails on the beach. You'll be just in time to see the magnificent colors of the setting sun."

Watching as Hugh bent to pick up his towel, she heard him say, "She's shy!"

Shy? That's a new thought. Well I guess I am at that. Then her normal caution intruded on her thoughts. What the hell are you doing? He's a stranger. Not willing to give in and revert to her solitary plans, she wondered, maybe I can pretend with him and turned to walk toward her cottage.

*   *   *

As she began to apply a dusting of blusher to even out her sun-reddened face, Melissa chided her image in the bathroom mirror, "It's *only* an invitation to dinner. He's a gentleman. We'll just share a meal and talk," realizing how out of character and unconvincing she sounded even to herself. "Any way, George can always escort him out if there's a problem." Defenses in place, she turned her attention to dressing.

Melissa found herself submerged in an unaccustomed attack of nerves. "Oh stop it!" she ordered. Standing in front of the bedroom mirror she saw her reflection of tropical colors draped into a one-shoulder, ankle-skimming sheath, staring back. "It doesn't have to go anywhere. But if he's as sensitive as he appears maybe I should go for it?"

You don't know anything about him, her conscience screamed.

"No I don't. I don't care if he's a stockbroker or stockman from the Outback."

Staring at her reflection she saw a stranger, a woman with a flushed face and eyes that sparkled with life. "Men enjoy one night stands. Why not me? I'll think of this as a holiday from myself. And, just maybe, this time, it'll be okay."

Unaware that she had crossed her fingers for luck, Melissa went out to give last minute instructions to Mary and George. It was almost six. She decided to wait for Hugh on the beach.

As Hugh rounded the turn of the beach, made sharper with the incoming tide, he saw Lissa standing barefoot at the edge of the surf. Stopping to watch her looking out toward the sun, poised for its drop over the horizon, he wished he could be sure of his ability to act naturally. "There's nothing wrong with my acting. It's my reacting that's not up to the task. Oh shut up. Can't I just enjoy having dinner and some pleasant conversation with this pretty woman? Or am I to be dogged by my problems all night," he said in disgust.

Not wanting to approach her and interrupt her mood, his thoughts returned to his problems. Damn! I had to leave LA to be cut down to size. This gorgeous creature has no idea of who I am. Where has she been not to have seen my face on some magazine cover? Shaking his head, Hugh was surprised to realize he'd finally accepted his overwhelming celebrity.

"Maybe Mark is right. I just forgot who the private Hugh Baron is. Could this wonderful, unassuming woman help me find myself? Will being myself finally be enough?" Not wanting to be late he picked up his pace as he walked toward her.

He watched, as Lissa looked up at his approach and smiled the first full smile he'd seen her wear. Catching his breath he waved and reaching her side handed her the bottle he'd been carrying. "Something from Mark. He said brandy and moonlight were part of my prescription."

"Napoleon. Your doctor has good taste. We'll have to follow his orders. But for now, would you like a Mai Tai?"

Hugh accepted the glass and turned to follow her gaze just in time to see the last rays of the sun spreading out over the darkening sea.

"Is it the air or the water that creates those hues?" he asked.

"They say it's the way the impurities in the atmosphere break up the light. I always stand here and try to touch them."

What an innocent thing to say, he thought, watching Lissa for any clues to who she really was.

*   *   *

She lay expectantly as Hugh's tongue flirted with her ear. After two short days, Melissa's skin had begun to anticipate his next move. A prickling of tiny nerve endings preceded his gentle touch, awakening her body to more than a longed for passion.

How odd, she thought. Here I am pillowed in Hugh's arms. A man I don't know, and he's introducing me to my own body.

Hugh had begun to kiss her mouth in his very sexy and tender way. She couldn't get enough of those kisses. As her mind shut down, erased of all thought, her nerves began to spark like hot wires. Feeling a trembling start deep within her, she closed her eyes to feel her skin, and taste her mouth as it kissed Hugh's salty skin. Digging her fingers into the smooth muscles of Hugh's back, she wrapped her legs around his waist, and began to move with him. Closing her eyes, she felt her emotions unleash, her body no longer in her control, alive as if awakened from a long sleep.

Their release hadn't stopped her trembling, her mind still possessed by their passion. A feeling more intense than her orgasm. A need so deep she thought, my God, I'm crazed.

The lapping surf had once again lulled Hugh into a semi-sleep. Watching his eyes move beneath his closed lids, Melissa felt a rush of tenderness. My life starts tomorrow, she worried silently. What am I going to do? I can't just say good-bye. But what would he think of the real me? Imagining him at a UCC cocktail reception, she smiled as she pictured them as a couple. His body was made for a tux, she thought, and could almost feel them together, dancing.

"Lissa, where are you?" Hugh's sleepy voice nudged her back to the present and her fears.

"Right here darling." Snuggling deeper into his arms for warmth.

Turning her toward him, she felt him lift her chin and watched him study her face. "Not all of you."

Looking away, she realized that she couldn't share all her thoughts, so with a soul deep sadness, answered. "If you must know, I was thinking of tomorrow, and saying good-bye." The very thought was breaking her heart.

Hugging her to him, Hugh nibbled her ear. "Good-bye seems so final. Aren't we going to see one another when we get back to the real world?"

Can we? Will we, she wondered. "Hugh where did you come from? Why were you so exhausted?" She had to know more about him.

"The real me didn't fly to this Garden of Eden. You saved my life. If we hadn't happened, I'd probably be the mental case Mark threatened I'd become."

"But why?" Seeing him turn away, she lay back in his arms, waiting for him to continue. But he remained silent. *So he has secrets too. A broken romance? A hard-nosed boss? He's too decent to be in any real trouble.*

"Hugh, part of the magic of this place is to be removed from our lives. There are no career pressures," *or last names* she thought. "We're free to be ourselves. Darling what did you mean by not being real? You are the most real person I've ever met."

Gently he took her face in his hands, "Thanks to you. You couldn't have known. I've been impotent for almost a year?"

"You?" Sitting up, she smiled at the insanity of his statement. "Me maybe, but certainly not you."

"*You?*"

She had to make him know how special their time together had been. "With you I'm alive. I always thought I'd had a piece missing."

"Lissa darling. Just being you is sexy. You don't suffocate me. You absorb love. You must know what you do to me?"

Feeling tears building, she turned her head to hide them from Hugh. "Lissa. You don't have to tell me why you're crying but let me tell you a little something about myself."

She wanted to stop him. If he shared his secrets, she'd have to share hers. But Hugh just held her, gentling her in his arms.

"Hush. Just listen. It might help explain. I live in a world of images. Everyone preens and postures their way through a kind of life. Sometimes these images take over. In my case, I lost the real me. The boy, who worked summers on a farm in Illinois. I even forgot the values my parents drummed into my thick head. But living as an image freezes your soul. And the man you first met had become almost soul dead. So don't you see? Loving you has breathed life into me? You're real. You're bright. You share your feelings so openly. There isn't a calculating bone in your body."

Pulling away Melissa sat up, threw her legs over the side of the bed, and burying her face in her hands, let out a strangled moan.

"What's wrong Lissa?"

Wrapping herself in a corner of the bed sheet, not having the courage to face him, she realized he hadn't told her who he was.

"I'm here to get ready for the career opportunity of a lifetime. But instead of resting and planning, I met you." Looking into Hugh's troubled eyes, she decided not to tell him everything.

"I have always thought I was frigid." Ignoring his look of surprise, she looked away. "My family was very strict and straight laced. And in college, my first boyfriend hadn't noticed my less than enthusiastic responses to his lovemaking. I didn't know anything was wrong. I thought I was just incapable of the kind of feelings my girl friends talked about." Touching his cheek, she caressed his face with her eyes. "Those feelings you awakened in me. I've never felt this way. Oh Hugh, I'd love to go on seeing you. But it's not possible. You're out West, and my life's so complicated."

As he pulled her back into his arms and began to rock her like she was a wounded child, she thought, and you think I'm so open and honest. Her soft tears were becoming a quiet deluge.

"Hush darling. Here," reaching into a pocket of his discarded jeans, he pulled out a business card. "It's my private number. You can leave a message for me if I'm not there. Someone will see that I get it."

Her tears had stopped, but her sinuses were raw from blowing her nose. Reaching for another tissue to wipe her eyes, she studied the small ivory colored card engraved with only a phone number with an LA area code, and wondered if she'd ever call Hugh. Leaning back into his arms she began to hiccup. Trying to hold her breath to still her maddening condition, she thought, maybe, when I've finished UCC's first round of executive initiatives I could sneak away then. Find some way to meet. If not in New York, we could come back to this wonderful place. Thoughts of not having to lose Hugh had cured her hiccups.

Now lying quietly in his arms, she heard him whisper, "Lissa, my darling. Don't worry about tomorrow. God couldn't be that cruel. We'll go back to our lives and when we can, we'll find time to be together. I promise."

CHAPTER IX

E.F. and Larry Henderson sat huddled in front of the library fire. Cigars and brandy sat cooling on the highly polished table at their knees. Their voices, one in a drawling Western vernacular and the other with a clipped Eastern educated rhythm, rose and fell as they battled through their problem.

"I don't know how serious this theft is, E.F. But if our plans are leaked to the wrong people BioTech's stock will shoot up."

E.F. wanted to slug someone. His custom-made shirt was almost splitting its seams as it stretched over his hunched shoulders. "If that happens Larry, UCC can't buy BioTech."

"I won't sell to anyone else. Damn it."

"Friendship aside, UCC needs BioTech. Melissa's plans will revitalize the corporation. She figures that mining and petroleum products are our past. They can't give us the kick in the ass we need to pull out of this slump. BioTech can."

Larry and E.F. had planned to merge their companies. As E.F. often said, "We're too old for this day-in and day-out shit." Melissa was their hand picked successor. Their promise that the integrity of the two companies would continue long after they were gone.

"Only UCC can guarantee that my research will be used to help people. I don't want my life's work to be at the mercy of some moral bankrupt, only interested in profits."

Looking at his old friend, E.F. was amused to see that he was disheveled. For Larry, that meant tie undone and French cuffs rolled to his elbows. Hell, even when they played poker with the boys, Larry was as neat as one of his laboratories. They were cut from different bolts of cloth. His was horsehair, and Larry silk, spun fine by his wealthy family. Yet they were closer than brothers, especially since the death of both of their wives.

"Tell me again about the missing patent application report. Maybe it'll trigger something."

"Emery, the poor schmuck, doesn't know who purchased it. He told me he'd been contacted by mail with an offer to meet someone with a business proposition."

"Your people are loyal. You have a knack for picking them that way. Why would this one betray you?"

"He was desperate to protect his wife and daughter. He thought I'd fire him when we learned he had AIDS. So he called the number printed in the letter. He didn't think he could actually hurt us. After all we did get our patent."

"Would you have fired him?"

"Of course not. He's an asset, or at least he was. I could use him to help gather data for those endless FDA reports."

"So then what did this kid do?"

"Emery said it was an impersonal arrangement. He turned over a copy of the report to a messenger, who handed him $5,000 in cash. No questions. No paper trail."

"But Larry, he's a scientist for Christ's sake. He'd have to have asked questions."

"Yes. But none were answered. Just that the report was for private eyes and no one would be the wiser."

Lawrence Henderson and E.F. went back some 30 years. Sharing a lifetime of dreams and their growing business successes. And E.F. had to have UCC buy BioTech at its current low market value. But the stock price was sure to triple when the value of Larry's success in producing synthetic hyaluronic acid was made public. Too costly as natural substance, the miraculous substance at more affordable prices would revolutionize many medical and cosmetic treatments.

"You know I must continue my research. BioTech's sale to UCC will guarantee me access to lab and staff. And you'll be relieving me of all those administrative chores. Can't you move up the merger?"

"Just where are you in your schedule?"

"If I can complete two clinical trials at Orthopedic and Joint Diseases in two months we can go into full production of our first formulation. Hopefully, we'll be on the market by spring."

"I get confused with all your formulations. Just which one are you testing now?"

"The one we've been using on race horses for the past five years. By injecting their knees with X-43, we've increased their ability to absorb the pounding they take during a race. I'm so sure of our new formula for humans that these clinical trials are only being done to appease the FDA. Damn it to Hell E.F., hyaluronic acid has been safely used in eye surgery for more than a decade. All we've done is develop a way to manufacture it in a laboratory at a viscosity suitable for human joints. With an injection twice a year, arthritic crippling of knees, elbows, even fingers can be delayed for years. Imagine E.F., we'd have delayed your hip replacement by at least ten years."

"I'm sold. But who's our thief? What can he do with your report? He still can't manufacture your process? It's protected."

"For the life of me I don't know. But I'll be more comfortable if we can finalize this merger before the clinical trials are completed. I'm not sure I'll be able to keep our success a secret after that.'

"When Melissa gets back, I'll tell her to get cracking on the closing."

Looking relieved, Larry changed the subject. "Where is our gal? I miss her."

"She took off on one of her retreats. Next week's going to be sheer hell for her."

"What's been going on? I seem to have missed a step or two."

"We're having a reporter follow her for a week. This gal's going to write her authorized biography."

Larry began looking around the library. "Aren't you worried that a reporter will discover Melissa's apartment on the top floor? Think you're living in sin?"

"Nope. Not if she's careful. The entrance has been carved up to look like two separate residences. And the elevator's marked for only two floors. The other buttons are hidden behind the Lalique mirror. So even if this reporter sees Melissa to her door, she shouldn't leave any the wiser."

"I guess appearances are correct enough. Too bad you two aren't blood relatives. You've already been family longer than most marriages these days."

"I'd love to shout to the world that Melissa's family. But she's afraid of the snickering and backbiting it would cause. This way we just work together. No public appearances to raise questions. Maybe once her abilities have been proved to all those skeptics, she'll be validated as UCC's rightful CEO. Then, hopefully, it won't matter so much."

"Well, she's certainly ready. I know you're going to be real proud of her. Of course, I'm prejudiced. She was up against some real local players when she did the deal on that West Virginia factory for me. You know, without skipping a beat she had those red necks eating out of her hands. She was something to watch."

"I was talking to her last Sunday, and Damn if she didn't just grow up in front of my eyes. E.F., where did our little gal go?"

Shaking his head as he finally realized that his little gal was a stunning, sophisticated woman, E.F. gave his old friend a woebegone smile. "Where have I been to have missed the changes Larry? First into a no nonsense assistant, now as a capable leader." Next week our Melissa is going to belong to the world. I'm sure going to miss her!"

CHAPTER X

Turning a slow 360 degrees in front of her full-length mirror Melissa studied her reflection. "Just bland enough," she said with approval. The beige and black knit suit carefully downplayed her curves. A Chanel scarf and shoes, a Bottega Veneta bag, and delicately sculpted 18k gold earrings spelled sophistication. And her ear-length hair, combed off the face, fell in controlled waves.

"No one from the old days in Pittsburgh would recognize me now. A perfect look for the part. Goodbye Melissa. Hello M.L. Horn."

Passing the desk in her bedroom suite, she glanced again at the folder on Pamela Green. Charles had sent it over on Friday and she had already spent two hours this morning, trying to read between the lines. Picking up the folder and opening it once again, Melissa looked at an 8x10 black and white photo. "Well, Ms. Green. If I'm any judge, you and I could share a few war stories. I wonder if we'll get the chance?"

Studying the portrait she saw a natural looking, square face. Make-up was minimal, and good bones seemed to love the photographer's lights. "So you're not a plain Jane. Just built for action." How am I going to deal with you? she wondered. You're no doubt out to dissect me. Remembering the reporter's pithy articles, she sighed, "You're a bright and gutsy pro. I'd better stay several steps ahead of you."

Shaking her head, Melissa muttered, "Don't screw up!" She reminded herself that E.F. and Larry were depending on her to complete the merger that would secure UCC's future and free Larry to continue his research. She felt the enormity of her responsibilities with her every breath. Shit, one sneeze and I'll bring UCC, E.F. and Larry down with me. Shuddering at the thought, she muttered, "And in my spare time I have to train a new executive team, cut budgets, reallocate staff, and solve a few internal political problems as I go along." As if sarcasm could lighten the load.

Throwing a Cashmere cape around her shoulders, Melissa placed the folder and note pad in her briefcase. Without a backward glance, she headed for the elevator and basement garage where Ben was waiting to drive her the short distance to her office.

Settling into the back seat of the limousine, Melissa's thoughts returned to Pamela, with one recurring theme: I have to gain her trust, so maybe I'll be able to control her opinions. I wonder what she wants more than anything in life? A husband? Children? Probably a cover story in *Economic World*! I would. According to Charles she was in the top ten of her graduating class. That says a lot coming from Columbia School of Journalism. Could we be more alike than our jobs? Well Ms. Green, when I know that, I'll know how far to trust you.

At ten-to-eight, the car pulled up at the private entrance of UCC's Park Avenue office building. For two weeks Melissa had been using this entrance, unobserved by curious company employees.

While the elevator ascended to the 50th floor, a kind of metamorphosis took place, as Melissa pulled herself together into an almost military smartness. Backbone straight, face set, eyes straight ahead. Melissa knew that during office hours she could depend upon the disciplined posture and formal behavior to signal she was all business. Especially, to her executive staff.

Her staccato steps, muffled by the deep velvet carpeting, rapidly took her toward her corner office. The secretaries normally located along the main corridor of executive row, had not yet arrived. The day was still quiet. A time unofficially reserved for the early arriving corporate elite.

"Good morning M.L.," her secretary, Mrs. Hammond, cheerfully called, as she entered the outer area of her office suite. "I have your schedule, telephone messages, and agenda for your afternoon meeting." She had inherited Mary Hammond from her predecessor, Jack Foster. By now Mary was accustomed to her early arrivals.

M.L. had known Foster through E.F. And, since she began working with Mrs. Hammond, she'd learned even more about him. During his career with UCC, Jack

Foster had led the corporation to worldwide leadership in developing new uses for coal and petroleum byproducts. It had been Foster's curious mind that led UCC's research and development teams to create materials for packaging, plastics, and fibers. Some of the generic wonders of today's synthetic world, she thought. E.F. had been on UCC's Board for so long, Foster was almost part of his family. E.F.'s association with UCC, going back to the days of Tom Larsen, the corporation's founder.

Reviewing her day's agenda, M.L. was pulled from her thoughts by the prompt arrival of Charles Cray, at 8:20. He strolled in her office unannounced, reminding her of the ease with which they had always worked together.

"Good Morning M.L. I trust the material on Pamela Green was satisfactory. I think she'll work out just fine," Charles said, pulling up a side chair and unfolding his lean frame into it.

"We're a pretty calculating bunch," she reminded him.

"Nothing in this world happens by accident. It will be your job to make Ms. Green understand that. With all that's at stake, it's crucial she believe in our goals."

"Charles, I'd like you to take Pamela on a Cook's tour this morning."

"The complete circuit?"

"Why not? Dazzle her! She can't get into any real trouble. And I want her briefed on UCC's facilities and markets."

"OK. And this afternoon?"

"I'll take her to a meeting with Ed, Paul, Jason, Frank and Will. I'd like you to join us. We may need your honey-tongued twist on an issue or two."

"Ms. Green is here M.L.," Mrs. Hammond announced in the intercom connected to her phone.

"Show her in please, Mary" she replied, rising from behind her desk and moving over to join Charles.

Entering Melissa Horn's office Pamela looked out on Park Avenue and saw the Chrysler Building's Art Deco tower, through a two-wall floor-to-ceiling windowed expanse. Only a secure non-phobic could perch on the edge of the sky, she thought. Now I know why the corner office is the power perk.

As Pamela slowly approached the vitally attractive pair waiting to greet her, her first reaction was Wow! Standing side by side they had the ease of old friends. They even looked alike, she thought. Trim, slim and polished. She had loved the way Charles Cray dressed and looked. But no matter how she had pictured Melissa Lynn Horn, CEO, she had never dreamed of a fashion perfect woman with a body she'd have died for.

"Good Morning Ms. Horn."

"Call me 'M.L.' everyone here does. Welcome to UCC."

Clasping the well-manicured hand, Pamela gave a slight tug to the hem of her new jacket with the other. "I'm delighted to meet you at last Ms. Horn . . . I mean M. L. You're something of a mystery woman."

"Well that won't be a problem for you Pamela. For the next week, you'll be closer to me than my shadow. I hope you won't be disappointed."

Looking around the cream and powder blue suite, Pamela thought how she'd love working in this room. Normally, she was put off by sophisticated corporate types. But these two weren't aloof or forbidding. How strange? Usually the press is kept at arm's length, she thought. And I'm being welcomed as a valued employee. I'd better watch my step. And with that Pamela began to tune her senses for those unspoken clues. Looking for the real agenda behind their charm.

"Charles was just reviewing your week's schedule. Why don't we go over it together?" M.L. said as she led Pamela to a small conversation area across the room from a well-ordered desk. "Tell me, just what research have you done on us so far?"

"I've read all recently printed information on your Board of Directors. Skimmed an American Management Association text on the role of a CEO. And a recent *Wall Street Journal* profile on UCC. I must confess that my reading raised more questions than it answered."

"That was probably the best way to prep for your assignment." M. L.'s comments were more for Charles than Pamela. "You will really have to understand where UCC is today, before you can begin to appreciate my unique position."

"Pamela, M.L. is about to make history. With your help, we can inform the business community of her right to be UCC's leader," Charles remarked.

"I hope you're prepared for some very long days Pamela. Charles will be taking you on a tour of the Company this morning, followed by lunch in the executive dining room. I thought lunch might be a good time to review your approach to your subject. This afternoon I'll take you to an executive briefing where you will meet my staff."

"M.L. in checking with the SEC I learned that your appointment was made official two weeks ago. When did you actually take up your responsibilities?"

Pamela's direct question didn't seem to phase the attractive corporate leader. "I've been on the job for the past month. And for the last two weeks I've been working here with my staff. They're helping me put together the strategy and time frame for accomplishing some very important goals."

"Actually, M.L.'s spent the past two weeks in intensive preparation. Directing her staff and setting forth an operating plan."

"Really Charles. Don't let Pamela think I do it all." With a smile at Pamela, M.L. explained, "I am really the leader of a team of specialists. It is my job to learn, as well as lead. In that way we will be able to achieve the goals set forth by our Board of Directors."

Pamela couldn't keep her surprise from showing on her face. M.L. was being uncharacteristically generous in saying that she worked as a team leader, not a driven solo act. Was this simply a woman's approach to leadership or, was this CEO really different from the stereotype?

M.L., interrupting her thoughts, continued. "Pamela, I think we'd better explain our corporate structure. Then maybe you'll realize we all report to someone. In my case it is the UCC Board."

Nodding her understanding of the pecking order at UCC, Pamela asked, "Will we have any personal one-on-one time M.L.?" she liked Melissa's business moniker. It made her seem like one of the guys.

"Most definitely. Why don't you keep a list of your questions. We can go over them when we're alone."

"I'd appreciate that." Pamela promised.

"Charles do you have her schedule?"

As Charles handed her a soft leather covered folio, Pamela wondered how detailed the schedule would be. Opening the cover, she found a date-book and notepad with gold pen. The date book had been neatly filled in from morning to evening. It included the names, addresses, and business or social occasions that would make up each day's appointments.

This is a surprise, Pamela thought. Names and addresses? Easy access to everyone I meet? What am I missing here?

"As you can see Pamela, we have a lot planned. Even the after six events are business. Don't worry about transportation. As my shadow, you'll ride with me."

Before she had time to study the week's appointments, Charles had risen and was inviting her to join him for the company tour.

"Thank you for the nice welcome, M.L. I'm looking forward to being your shadow," Pamela said meaning every word. Following Charles, she wondered if she could ask him anything. Or would she have to play games to get the real low down. So far this seemed too easy. Authorized or not, she didn't want to rely on these people. She needed the truth, not what they presented as the truth.

*   *   *

"Have you caught your breath?" Charles asked as he pulled out Pamela's chair from the corner table. They were off to one side of the company's executive dining room, separated from the other lunch time clusters of people.

As he straightened the knot of his custom-made tie, Pamela tried not to let Charles see that she had been watching him over the top of her menu.

"Something wrong?"

"Oh no. I was just trying to catch the real you."

Breaking into a contagious grin, he winked. "This is it! Disappointed?" He stood still for her inspection, before sitting in a chair across from hers.

Pamela could see he was one with his image. Smooth. With a flirtatious sense of humor she liked. Damn if he isn't appealing, she thought.

Picking up his menu Charles commented on the day's selections, "Everything is pretty good. I prefer their salad. But the grilled fish is always fresh."

"Salad? Are you watching your weight?" she quipped as she reached for an impossibly thin breadstick.

"Always. And you?"

"Me too, but it's hard. I like all the wrong foods." She held up the breadstick as proof, catching Charles in the process of giving her a thorough once-over.

As the waiter took their order Pamela quietly reviewed her morning tour. Charles had answered all her questions without skipping a beat. Of course she only had a glimpse of each department. But her overall impression was that of a well-staffed organization. She hadn't seen a sloppy desk or chattering group of secretaries anywhere among the ten floors they'd visited.

"A penny?" Charles asked, bringing Pamela's attention back to the present.

Thoughtfully swallowing a bite of breadstick she replied, "Thinking about your tour."

"And?"

"Very impressive. Especially the seriousness of your employees." How had he managed that, she wondered. Sending out advanced warnings by electronic mail? 'Reporter on the floor. Stay alert?'

Nodding his head, she saw a lock of red-gold hair fall on his forehead. Of course, Mr. Perfect quickly put it back in place. God he's fabulous. A flirt, certainly. But she'd love to get to know him after hours.

Pamela began waving her breadstick like a pointer, "But that heart to heart with your R&D director was quite revealing."

"Why?"

She saw she'd caught him by surprise. "Am I right in assuming that within two years UCC's going to be in trouble? Isn't that when your patents begin to run out?"

"While you order, I'll introduce you to some of our other challenges."

He hadn't quite answered her question.

"In addition to developing new products, we are planning to move into a new field."

"Why are you expanding into a new field? I'd think you'd use your resources to support existing product lines?"

"Hmm, actually we are doing both. We mature a new product in five years. After that it becomes part of our stable of items and governed by market demand. This strategy has required R&D to keep new products in the pipeline. To be ready to take up any slack."

"I'm guessing that your petroleum and mineral products are the basis of all UCC's established brands?"

"For now. But our world is changing. M.L. believes our future lies in a new direction. And being a strong R&D company, we want to develop new products to meet those needs."

Charles' enthusiasm for his subject was obviously real. But he wasn't being specific, she noticed.

"And this is top secret?" she asked.

"I'm afraid so. For now, my hands are tied."

"That can't be the reason for this hushed up approach to launching M.L.?" Pamela stopped, noticing the twinkle in Charles eyes.

"I am really going to enjoy our association Pamela. You won't let me gloss over anything. But, you're right. M.L.'s position is unique. First of all she is an unknown executive and handicapped because she is a young and attractive woman."

"Charles, do you believe a woman can be a CEO?" There, I've said it. Now what's he going to do about it? He's a company man, she thought.

"I know M.L. can. But if you want my gut reaction as a man, then I have to say she's in for a fight. I was hoping you'd help her win it."

"Excuse me?"

"Come on Pamela. You work with the toughest of male chauvinists. Street beat reporters. Are you telling me you aren't as good?"

"Of course not!" Boy! He really knows how to push my buttons. "But I'm a journalist. I don't lead men. I work alone," she snapped, her anger beginning to flare.

"Well this female could lead anyone. Male or female. She has that gift."

"Gift? Isn't it a matter of power?"

"Yes and no. It's a gift if you can lead people by making them take you where you want to go. You'll get a sample this afternoon."

"Powerful men I've met look like they could move mountains. Power is a male thing."

"I'm surprised at you. What's more powerful than a mother's influence and control of her children? Power is about control, not brute strength."

"This is going to be a very interesting. You want me to follow M.L. Assess her leadership. Review her professional credentials. Then do a white-wash in print?"

"Too fast young lady. Where did whitewash come in? You're underestimating your research."

Nodding her acceptance of his assumption that she'd accept their story, Pamela, resumed eating her salad. Just as she was about to pick up her glass of water when she felt Charles watching her.

"Can't we be friends? I don't like making enemies of pretty women."

Seeing the impish dimple at the corner of his mouth restored Pamela's humor. Friends. I'd like that she thought.

"Anyway, I'm sure you're going to be more interested in M.L.'s corporate problems."

Was Charles teasing her? Hinting that she was really going to see some of UCC's behind the scenes secrets?

"Yes. But won't some of those problems be because she's female?" The words were out before she could stop them.

"Are you playing devil's advocate? Or are you trying to get a rise out of me?" he shot back.

Looking at the beginning of a wrinkle on his handsome face, Pamela had to smile. "A little of both. Call it testing the water?"

Somewhat mollified, Charles continued, "M.L. will have to address our future. Plan steady growth in a new era. When you lead a corporation this size you learn early on that its very size can be its biggest problem. It's expensive to run one plant. How about 10 located around the world? So you see, being female has nothing to do with the business ahead."

"I've never thought of a plant as a problem. Unless it's no longer producing something the public wants." Shaking her head as she reviewed what she had just said, Pamela's thoughts spilled aloud, "So that's where your new direction comes in? Now I'm beginning to understand. UCC's poised for some major campaign."

"A+. I told you you're smart."

"And you said there was something else she had to do?"

"This is the tricky one. If any of our plans falter, the prejudice against women as leaders, will be fodder for newspapers round the world. Just the excuse for our enemies to attack."

"How?"

"If you were a competitor and thought a female was ruining the company, wouldn't you go for their jugular? What bank would continue to favor us? What broker would recommend our stock?"

"I see. Charles will you always answer my questions?"

"I'll be delighted to. And don't short change M.L. You can ask her anything."

She prayed she could. Leaning back in her chair, lunch forgotten, she quipped, "I'll just have to keep my eyes and ears open."

"And that sharp mind."

She acknowledged Charles' flattery with a crisp military salute.

CHAPTER XI

"Tim Lynch?" the caller asked.

"Yes?" Tim recognized the man as Bruce Dearling, President of Neuwirth Investments. He was a relatively new customer, trading in small blocks of obscure stocks.

"I'm interested in opening a new account."

"Yes Sir."

"What's the current Am Ex price for BioTech?"

Tim scanned the American Exchange ticker frantically. As if speed, would lock up a new account. Finding the information he eagerly announced, "BioTech's at 2 and 3/4's Mr. Dearling."

"I see. Open a new account in the name of Smythe for me, with 10,000 shares. You can send all paperwork to my attention."

That's weird, another new account, Tim thought, as he automatically took notes. "But . . . ." wanting to ask about payment, but was interrupted.

"I'll messenger a cashier's check for $30,000 before today's market close. Are we in business?"

"Er, yes Mr. Dearling. And the extra funds?"

"Be creative. I'll need them in one week."

"Yes Sir!" An enthused Tim was already seeking a profitable home for the extra $2,500. Commissions were always charged over and above the amount of the trade. He'd make money on at least 3 trades within one week. I've got to get him into something hot. Maybe I'll even be able to churn his account for short-term action.

Trying not to sound too eager, Tim asked, "Is there anything else I can do for you?"

"Not for now. I'll be in touch."

The abruptly cut phone connection buzzed in Tim's ear. "What's he up to," Tim said to himself, thinking that Neuwirth now had three accounts heavily invested in BioTech. When they opened the second account, Tim had checked with the firm's research department looking for any flags placed on the stock. I'd better check them again. Something's not kosher, he thought. Dialing their extension, he wasn't surprised in hearing Roger's harried voice. "Roger, do you know a firm, BioTech? The one I called about several months ago. It's traded on the American."

"Nothing comes to mind."

"Well look it up. Then send me anything you find. ASAP."

Slumping back into his chair, Tim slowly swiveled from side to side as he thought of this interest in BioTech. "What's going down?" he whispered. "Out of the blue this small investment firm express a healthy interest in an obscure company. The market's into telecommunications. Cable, fiber optics, telecom infrastructure. What's BioTech into? Research already tracks the important bio-medical firms. Is it even medical? What am I missing? Could they be in genomics?"

A born worrier, Tim's fingers tapped his desk before they were calm enough for his keyboard, then resumed their tapping while he waited for the computer to pull up the firm's latest rating of medical firms. Needing something else, Tim reached for an unopened pack of cigarettes, even though there was a no smoking rule in his area of the office.

"What the Hell," he grumbled as he placed an unlit cigarette in his mouth. Could this client reverse my luck?

Tim needed a break. Janine was pressuring him to get married. If he didn't pay attention, she'd find someone else. His brother Bryan didn't think that'd be a bad idea. He said Janine was only interested in him for his money. That's a laugh. One day he had money. The next he could lose a bundle. What did Bryan or Janine know? But Bryan insisted that Janine didn't want Tim, just a way to escape life in Queens.

Maybe Bryan was right. Janine wasn't for him. "I don't have time for this shit! Concentrate! No one's going to hand me a break," he said as he began reading the data that appeared on his computer screen.

*   *   *

William Smythe Foley hung up his phone, Cheshire grin in place, enjoying the trap he'd set for Tim Lynch. From Dearling's report, this Lynch sounds young and hungry, he thought. And Foley planned to take advantage of his appetite. First he have Dearling give the kid a trickle of trades. Then he'd get a pipeline to Tim's inside information. It never occurred to him that Lynch couldn't tap the pipeline. He'd have Dearling show him how.

William Smythe Foley could always spot greed. First Dearling, Tim was next.

"Never work in a straight line," he muttered. "That's for chumps!"

Absently straightening all objects to square with the borders of his leather desk pad, Foley's laugh would have chilled anyone who'd heard it. Nodding to himself, he thought, "Greed is a goal of the weak. Power is using the weakness of others. Money is merely the way to keep score."

CHAPTER XII

"There you are, Pamela. How was your tour?"

M.L.'s warm welcome had been called from a small table in the back corner of her sky-filled office.

"Fine," she answered, as she walked slowly toward M.L. Damn! I'm beginning to like her and that's dangerous, Pamela thought, as she watched M.L. resume leafing through a file folder. What a control freak. Every paper in that folder is lined up, Pamela thought as she envisioned her own files, as untidy as her wastebasket after a night of writing.

"Join me," M.L. invited, indicating a chair across from her. "I'd like to brief you before we go into our meeting. Here," she slid over the folder she'd been reading. "You might like to scan this."

Pulling her chair closer to the table, Pamela placed her tote bag on the floor to her right, and opened the folder. She saw that the first page was a statement of purpose for the Executive Staff. The following pages contained the job descriptions for each of M.L.'s officers.

She noted that M.L.'s wasn't there and tucked that bit away for later.

"May I keep this? I'd like to make some notes."

"I'll have Mary make you a copy. We have a few minutes. Why not give it a once-over now?"

Pamela tried to ignore M.L., who seemed to be watching for her reaction. Afraid she'd never see the information again, she began to skim the pages using her finger to trace each closely typed line. Was M.L. trying to keep her off balance by piling her high with data? She hadn't handed her any corporate secrets, just a summary of overall plans. Something that with a little time and effort, Pamela thought she would have uncovered anyway.

"By the way," M.L. interrupted, "I've asked Mary to give you a copy of the minutes from this afternoon's meeting. She'll also provide you with a list of our phone extensions."

Pamela was hard pressed to keep her surprise from showing. She'd make a mental note to keep her eyes open for the stuff they weren't giving her.

"That's great. By the way, those notes you had included in my date book show a full plate. You seem to be on the go from sunrise to midnight."

"Actually, we'll be on the go." M.L. chuckled. "I thought reporters were accustomed to long days?"

"I'll keep up. I'm your shadow, remember? But there doesn't seem to be any downtime. Is your life all business?"

"My life has to be ruled by UCC's agenda. You don't think I got here to rest?" Pamela saw that M.L. was wearing a mischievous grin.

"You know how it is. We women have to work harder to stay even. I'll be looking forward to seeing how I do through your eyes."

She certainly had her attention. Maybe M.L. was a feminist. The old chestnut of working harder had always been true for her.

"This afternoon we'll be reviewing our plans to launch me."

"Are all CEO's launched?"

"No. But you'll see why launch me they must."

Before Pamela could ask another question, M.L. quickly added, "It's OK. I insisted on it!"

"You're not a ship for Christ's sake."

"Oh, but I am. A ship of war."

"Pardon me?"

"We are at war." Holding up her hand to quell questions. "Wait. You'll hear all about it in a few minutes." Pointing to the folder, she asked, "Finished?"

"Not yet. Can I have a couple more minutes?" Why is she rushing me? Now she's looking at her watch.

"Sure," settling back in her chair, M.L. left Pamela to finish her reading.

Meanwhile, the adjoining conference room was beginning to come to life.

"Hi Charles." A tall good-looking black man called, taking his time as he strolled into the wood paneled room.

A young Sidney Poitier if ever I saw one, Charles thought. He liked Frank Jackson's forthright approach to life. If I had been born in the wrong neighborhood, instead of on Sutton Place, could I have done as well, he wondered?

"Charles," the soft-spoken voice of another well-built man was next to greet him at the door to the conference room. It was Edward Cole, Executive VP of Human Resources. A college football star that hadn't wanted to go Pro, Ed was liked by everyone. He had no visible ego. No need to prove he was stronger or brighter. Yes, Ed would strengthen any team he played on, Charles thought.

"Ed. Over here," Frank called from across the room. "Do you have those notes I asked for?"

"Sure thing." Ed slowly moved around the large conference table to join his buddy.

Charles observed they're comradery, knowing that Ed and Frank went back a ways. The two were a management success story. Frank the operations man-on-the-line. Ed, the in-house personnel guru. Together they settled several violent miners' strikes and one near mill shutdown by two steelworkers unions. Charles had only met them six months before, but had instantly liked them. Both were down to earth, hard working men. Unlike most he'd met outside his social set, they had an old-fashion sense of honor.

"Ah, there you are Jason," Charles' warmth real, as he greeted M.L.'s Executive VP Finance. "All set?"

"Yyyes. I hhate presentations. I'm a background guy."

Smiling Charles understood Jason's embarrassment about his speech impediment. But Charles also knew that when Jason was involved in his subject the stutter disappeared.

"Why not sit by me? I'm over there. At the foot of the table."

"Thanks."

Charles would help Jason out if his tongue failed him. He'd done it before.

Charles stayed at the door, waiting for the last player on M.L.'s executive team. Like himself all present had been hired by E.F. to back her up. Funny he thought, rubbing his pocket watch chain, except for Foley and me, they're all from the corporate minor leagues. M.L.'s handing them a shot at the gold ring.

Turning quickly at a grumbled Hello, Charles nodded to William Foley as he entered the room. Well he's certainly waited until the last minute, Charles thought as he closed the door to the hall. Picking up the phone, he buzzed M.L.

"We're all here." Placing the phone back on the credenza, Charles turned his attention to the men in the room. Ed and Frank had their backs to the others and were in the middle of some sports story. He spotted Ed clasping and unclasping his gigantic hands behind his back. Frank's energy was thrown into his story telling with his arms, elbows and hands illustrating every word. Jason sat quietly reviewing his notes. Foley stayed to himself, comfortable in his own company.

Promptly on the dot of 2 PM, the door to M.L.'s office opened. Charles moved over to greet M.L. and Pamela, quietly saying, "And so we begin." Looking at Pamela, "Ready?"

Looking up into his serious face, Pamela acknowledged his greeting, "All set." Taking a deep breath, she followed M.L., with her eyes trying to see everyone and everything at once.

As they moved through the connecting doors, Pamela looked the room over. Handsome in its simplicity, it was really a setting for the charcoal gray and navy blue suited men waiting for them. At first glance the men all looked alike. Precise in their posture and wardrobe. On close inspection, she realized that each man exhibited little touches of personal vanity. One coordinated his tie and shirt. Another had a tie and matching pocket-handkerchief. And one little dumpling of a man, wore bright gold cuff links the size of hockey pucks.

Pamela felt a slight pressure on her elbow as M.L. began guiding her around the perimeter of the room. Moving as directed she was amused to observe the surprising warmth with which M.L. handled her introduction. One by one, each man in the room greeted her. Using her reporter's trick of memory, Pamela noted something unique about each. An antique pocket watch, small mole, hairstyle. All the time she was aware of the formality of protocol. It was M.L. who directed each chat. She was so skilled, Pamela felt she was at a social gathering, not amid lions in the corporate den. She has charm, Pamela thought. But does she have balls?

Finding herself back at the head of the table in front of the closed doors to M.L.'s office, Pamela watched the men settle in their chairs well spaced around the long table. M.L. nudged her toward the chair on her left, and Pamela saw Mary take the seat to M.L.'s right. Is it female against male, she wondered? The table was neatly segregated. Oh shit. Now I get it. M.L.'s isolated herself from her staff as neatly as if she had put them at a different table. What had she read in that management text? Power was position as well as control. M.L. was definitely in the power seat. Everyone else sat below her. Very interesting, she thought.

Pamela's attention was diverted back to M.L. There was something that reminded her of her father sitting at his Army Post desk. Always erect, as if a steel bar had been welded to his spine. That's it, she thought, she has the same Military bearing. Catching M.L.'s eye, Pamela thought, here we go, and opened the note pad hidden on her lap.

"Gentlemen, Pamela will be part of our war council this afternoon. As you know she is writing a biography on me. I have invited her to learn something about us. Help her better understand her subject."

War council? What the fuck, Pamela thought. They're actually going to share their plans with me?

"Charles. Why don't you begin."

Pamela saw Charles was doodling on the edge of his leather bound note pad. His gold pen occasionally reflected a sparkle of light from the chandelier centered above the highly polished table. "You have all reviewed this week's schedule. Pamela noted the unwavering firmness of his voice, his red-gold head set perfectly straight, his eyes seeking out the others at the table. There was no hint of the humor she had come to enjoy in him.

"M.L. will begin her official introduction tonight at the UCC cocktail party. The guest list is short. Some customers, but primarily bankers and our Board of Directors." Looking each man in turn, he directed, "She is not to be left alone. One of us is to be at her side at all times. Directing his gaze at Pamela, he continued. "You will probably want to stay nearby. But I'd prefer you not participate in any of M.L.'s conversations. We're stage managing her introductions." Returning his attention to the others, he continued, "We will be presenting M.L. with all the pomp and ceremony of a new CEO. Hopefully we can flatter our guests by having M.L. accessible, but still limit her exposure."

Unable to keep still, Pamela turned to M.L. and whispered, "That's so contrived."

M.L.'s lips barely moved, "Not really. I mean to have personal contact with everyone important to UCC, friend or foe. But tonight will not be the time to get involved with each one's problems. They're just covering my flank."

As Charles continued to review the week's schedule Pamela looked the others over. They certainly seemed a serious bunch, all eyes trained on Charles. Looking over to M.L. she saw her enjoying her position at the head of the table. Her Chanel suit was as unwrinkled as her brow, as if she had been starched and pressed into her clothes. The flawlessness reminded Pamela of a suit of armor. Remembering that M.L. had been working with these men for a couple of weeks, Pamela saw that they seemed to accept her leadership. But what had M.L. done to gain such support? she wondered.

"Jason," Charles called, bringing Pamela's attention back to the meeting. "This is probably a good time to present our current fiscal position."

This should be interesting, Pamela thought, as she began to study the small slim man. About 40, he had the wiry frame and look of a terrier ready to spring. Shuffling his notes, Pamela heard Jason's slight stutter.

"Er, as of this mmmoment, Jack Foster has left UCC in a fiscally sound position," his stutter diminished as he picked up speed.

"Our sales are a healthy $4.8 billion, an increase of 5% over last year. However," pausing to take a sip of water from the glass in front of him, "wwwe're at a turning point. If we don't get a dramatic infusion of new revenue sources, by this time next year we will have to begin to consolidate our liabilities through a major re-engineering effort . . ."

Pamela followed everything Jason had said and knew that re-engineering meant large-scale layoffs, possibly plant closings. Definitely trouble. So that's the war, she thought. UCC's life or death.

"If we are forced to downsize, our stock price will fall just at a time when we may wish to initiate a new offering to raise capital."

Pamela remembered Charles warning that anything bad would be blamed on M.L. And, UCC's stupidity in naming a woman CEO. Damn it anyway! Pamela's thoughts were already taking sides. I'm in this now. If I want her to succeed, I'd better pay attention to the fine print.

". . . So to prevent creating a self-fulfilling prophecy of a corporation on the skids, we'd better find these new revenue sources soon."

Jason paused to see if his summary had hit its mark. Looking toward M.L. he was pleased to see her nod of approval. He liked M.L. and had pledged her his loyalty. While he couldn't speak for the others, Jason remembered how she had reached him. She had taken the time to understand him. During a series of private meetings, she had role played the benevolent professor to his brilliant student, and asked him to reach out for new approach to UCC's traditional financial management practices. M.L. had inspired his oldest dreams. She had asked what he would do if the $5 billion corporation was his personal company? How would he make it a $8 billion firm? He could be the sole owner and director of the funds. He had only two limitations, his actions had to be legal and he couldn't print money.

Looking around the table Pamela saw M.L. nod in the direction of a blond, bulky athletic looking man who had been previously introduced as Edward Cole, V.P. Human Resources. Remembering her brief chat with this physical specimen, she was reminded of his wholesome personality. If leaders hired in their own image, Pamela thought, then just maybe this group could be the exception to the lean mean corporate club.

In a mild, Midwesterner's, unaccented voice, Cole began to summarize the important changes in the corporation's style of management.

"Experience shows that if you can make each of our 14,000 employees feel necessary, you have a more productive work force. Remembering our need to develop new products, you'll understand why M.L.'s tour of each plant is crucial. Not only will she be meeting with the plant managers, she will be unveiling a revolutionary incentive program to our employees. A program in which employees can earn shares of UCC stock based upon their contributions to the corporation's realignment. Rewards will be based upon development of new products or market opportunities, and of course, overall job performance."

While Ed continued to describe plans for their employee newsletter, and improved benefits package, Pamela saw how an area she called the hiring and firing department, would play its part.

"Ms. Green. Don't let Ed's nice ways fool you," the street-wise voice jarred her to attention. It was Frank Jackson, Executive VP Operations. Looking directly at this tough, scowling face, Pamela realized he had read her thoughts. The face belied his custom tailored appearance. The New York accent hinting of Brooklyn origins was worthy of a seasoned union shop steward. He may be black, she thought, but he's no token player.

"In operations, we need Ed's people committed to our schedules and production goals."

This Jackson was certainly a steamroller. But he had her attention.

Now leaning forward in his chair, his right hand clenched, Jackson continued, "Ms. Green, do you realize that we can be hamstrung by any one of four unions? When M.L. visits our plants she will also be leaving behind a manual establishing leaner employment levels, increased manufacturing goals, and a tightened budget. In two weeks we could be up shit creek without Ed's skills and M.L.'s razzle dazzle."

So much for tact, Pamela thought.

"Don't be put off by his tough delivery," M.L. said, turning toward Pamela at the same time that her slightly raised hand was reminding Frank to tone down. Turning her attention back to Jackson, M.L. said "Frank, since you've taken the ball, why not fill in the rest of the game plan."

As Frank continued in a more restrained manner, Pamela was reminded of her blue-collar cousins. She'd always enjoyed their rambunctious ways and was looking forward to matching wits with Frank at a later date. He's one mystery package I'd like to open, she thought.

M.L. was now introducing her Counsel, William Foley. "Will, please give Pamela a brief look at the global picture?"

"Sure thing."

Pamela hadn't paid too much attention to Foley since M.L.'s earlier introduction. Now listening to his heavy Boston accent, she noticed he sat shorter than his colleagues, and seemed older. A tailored dandy, with manicured nails, and well-barbered gray head of thinning hair, he reminded her of every corporate lawyer she had ever met. Is their arrogance something that they acquire when they pass the Bar, she wondered.

Sitting back, she watched as Foley directed his comments to the men. Pamela was reminded of something Skip had told her, that men uncomfortable around women, looked everywhere but at them.

"Our host countries, the Philippines and South Korea, to name two, are increasingly reluctant to grant us long term protection of our proprietary processes. But I'm working on a new wrinkle to leverage us into favorable position for our upcoming round of contract negotiations."

Pamela was somewhat surprised when M.L. politely cut Foley's presentation short. "William's also been negotiating the friendly purchase of a company, Pamela. He's too modest to tell you the importance of this acquisition to our future."

While her words were complimentary, Pamela wondered if M.L. was afraid Foley would divulge some sensitive information. He was, after all, the legal eagle.

Turning toward Pamela, M.L. cautioned, "Of course, the specifics must be kept from you for the time being."

Not sure if M.L. had been over heard, Pamela reddened from embarrassment, M.L.'s tone was clear. Don't trade away our secrets. She knew she couldn't relax her guard. Any wrong move would follow her all her working life.

Returning her attention to Foley, Pamela saw him graciously acknowledge his boss's compliment. "I'm just an old war horse, M.L., but I can still run at the bell."

Very smooth, Pamela thought.

It had been a long afternoon. But Pamela hadn't noticed the time go by. She had the feeling that she could work with most of the men. One or two might even talk to her honestly. The question that jumped to the top of her growing list was how they felt about working for a woman? Throughout the meeting she sensed an undercurrent. Was it nerves? Maybe fear? Did people who rose this high worry about being fired?

She had no doubt that M.L. was their boss. It wasn't that she bullied or shouted. It was simply that this group deferred to her. And it had nothing to do with her sex. Every time she opened her mouth it was to add something to their presentations. Or, to compliment them on their reports. Yet M.L.'s voice on occasion held an edge. Pamela would long remember how sharp that edge was when it was directed at her.

"Charles, Jason, Ed, Frank, William," M.L.'s attention was directed to each man in turn. "Your energy and original thinking have developed a campaign as unique as having a woman CEO. The tried approaches no longer work and the Board has empowered me, and through me you, to regain UCC's preeminent position among our peers. Gentlemen. I plan to win. I'm expecting you to make that possible."

The room had stilled. One by one the men nodded, accepting her challenge. M.L. turned her attention to

Mary. The others were talking quietly among themselves. Jason was rubbing his eyes. Frank lifted a foot to rest it on his knee. Pamela was sure she was the only one who witnessed the odd little man write something on a small card. What's he up to, she wondered, reminding herself to watch him closely.

"Gentlemen," M.L. said rising gracefully from her chair. "Till tonight. Our first official outing. Let's charm the pants off our guests."

Rising to follow, Pamela wondered when charm had become a management tactic. Charm had nothing to do with this meeting, she thought. Tonight should prove very interesting.

CHAPTER XIII

The Tudor-style room high above Manhattan's skyline was abuzz with masculine conversation. The pianist's selections of light jazz and show tunes were paced to the expectant mood. The tinkle of ice in well-filled glasses rounded out the sounds of a cocktail party in progress.

As the elevator doors opened, all conversation ceased. Centered in the illuminated carriage was a regal M.L., clad in a column of dark green velvet. The soft fabric clung to her, not an extra fold or drape to confuse the eye. At her ears and neck glowed creamy pearls, set to exhibit their size and luster, not their gold mountings.

Standing in the elevator next to M.L. Pamela watched her open her velvet wrap. Wow. She's certainly nothing like what I expected. That dress is far sexier than a lot of cleavage, Pamela remembering that when M.L. had picked her up she had been disappointed to see the plain dark gown with a relatively high cut bodice. Looking down at her own simple pants suit, Pamela felt even more out of sync than usual. Somehow even her old reliable attitude, "Fashion plates are so shallow - I'm smarter than to care about that," collapsed when confronted with the conundrum of M.L.

Watching M.L. begin to move into the room, she knew it wasn't the dress, it was M.L. that made it spectacular. The velvet fabric flirted with her toned body, like a lover's gentle touch. Starting from just above her ample bust, the soft fabric was cut to skim over her curves. And with each step the soft fabric caressed her body outlining her lean and shapely thighs. The color, rich in the candle lit room, enhanced M.L.'s auburn curls and flashing green eyes.

Following Charles and M.L. into the room, Pamela watched as M.L. moved toward her guests flashing a 300-watt smile. "Hello gentlemen. I'm delighted you could join us for my unveiling."

The room broke out in appreciative applause. The pianist picked up his pace, and conversation grew more animated as Charles began to lead M.L. around the room. Following one step behind, Pamela heard M.L. greet one man after the other with a well-researched remark. "Hi John. How's your golf game?"… "Well, Todd, last time we met you were retiring. I'm glad you haven't."

As M.L. and Charles circled the room, Pamela saw several men position themselves closer to M.L. One man moved behind as if to hear what she said. To his chagrin M.L. turned, catching him off guard. Then she greeted him in the same friendly way she had the others. Another, smaller man, had stepped directly in her path. Offering her his hand as if by taking the initiative he could gain her favor.

So far all's light and fluffy, Pamela thought. Looking ahead, she noticed a wizened man that could have been anywhere from 60 to 90. His knobby shoulders poked up through his tuxedo jacket. Claw-like hands clutched his drink. But it was his eyes that stopped her cold. They burned. Who, in the Hell? she wondered. Quickly moving closer to M.L., she was just in time to hear a surprisingly savage voice say, "So my dear. The little girl has grown into an appetizing morsel."

Pamela was shocked by his coarseness. But M.L. just laughed and replied, "Nat Fallon. You old buzzard. Are you here to greet me or eat me?"

The old man's eyes turned to stone. "Greet you of course. I'll dine on UCC later."

"You'd better check with your doctor Nat. Rich foods can kill a man your age."

With Charles nodding to the Buzzard, she saw him lead M.L. away to chat with another guest. She followed, wondering what had inspired the verbal duel? Thinking it odd that not all of the guests were cordial at such a carefully created event. Pamela made a mental note to look up Mr. Fallon and see if she could find the source for his animosity toward M.L.

The party was in full swing, the room reverberating with a sprinkling of hearty laughter following M.L.'s progress through the crowd. Having heard enough of the guests trying to suck-up to M.L., Pamela looked around for someone to talk to. In a smaller room off to the side, she spotted Frank Jackson standing next to a large hearth with a crackling fire. Walking over to join him, she saw him nod and smile at her in approval.

"I'm flattered you singled me out in this crowd of movers and shakers, Pamela. May I get you a real drink, or glass of champagne?"

"Don't tease me. But, yes I'd love a little bubbly."

As he returned with two glasses, Pamela noticed that Frank's tuxedo hugged his torso just enough to reveal his solid build. "You're a refreshing surprise Mr. Jackson," saluting him with her glass.

"And why is that Ma'am? Cause I'z black?"

"No. Because you're gorgeous."

"Why Ms. Green." Frank's sharecropper's twang had disappeared. "If I didn't know any better, I'd think you were trying to con me."

"Can't we be friends?" She held out her hand to shake his.

Frank took her small hand into a callused paw. She had to admit he did intrigue her.

"So beside my body, what interests you about me?"

Laughing, she couldn't resist playing along. "You speak my language of the underdog. So let's cut the crap. Friends!"

"Yes Ma'am. If we're cutting the crap, what do you think of our attractive leader?"

"Oh no. You first. How did you end up with this bunch?"

"I'm one of the lucky ones," he replied in a subdued tone.

"You've got my attention," she said and took a sip of champagne.

Reaching for Pamela's arm, he escorted her to a sofa near the fire. Settling back he continued his story. "When I was in high school in Harlem, I attended an assembly program. A businessman offered my sophomore class a challenge. He said he would hire any of us who maintained a B average or better. You know, work after school, full time in the summer. The kicker came when we found out at the end of the summer, that our salaries were matched in a college fund. College? Imagine my black ass in college! I didn't even think they'd talk to someone like me. That man was E.F. Haynes."

"Isn't he on the UCC Board?"

"Yes. See that guy next to Charles? The athletic banker looking type? That's E.F."

"Ah-huh! He hired you to work at UCC?"

"No. Mr. Haynes is a man with many interests. Started out in the oil fields of Texas. But, E.F. hired me for Haynes Associates, his management company."

"He looks like he was born with a silver spoon."

"Far from it. And he's never forgotten his poor beginnings. I'm only one of E.F.'s kids."

Wanting to tweak him out of his serious mood, Pamela said, "So you made your B average."

Stretching up to his full 6 foot 3 inches, Frank looked down at her. "Actually I maintained an A plus." His grin was so wide she knew he wasn't bragging, just getting even for her sarcasm.

"Class Valedictorian too, I suppose," quickly feeling shamed, because Frank just nodded and grinned at her discomfort.

"I'm sorry. I really am impressed. I don't usually meet a success story in the flesh. This E.F. sounds like a rare guy."

"Sure is. Anyway, E.F. placed me in every tough manufacturing and mining job he could find. I owe him my life. So here we are."

"So you had an easy ride to the top."

"Not quite. I worked my ass off. But you know, I'd do anything for that man."

Pamela liked his sincerity. "Frank, can I ask you a question?"

"Sure. I'm single."

Smiling, she wondered if he was about to make a pass. "No, nothing personal."

"Too bad. Shoot."

"Who's Nat Fallon?"

"The Buzzard? Why?"

"Well I may be wrong, but I think M.L. just tried to castrate him."

"She succeeded I hope."

"Almost. What gives?"

"Mr. Fallon, nee Fallonconi, isn't a very nice man. But he is a major customer who wants to control UCC."

"How can a customer control UCC?"

"If he became our largest customer for coal, he'd hold an economic club. So instead of selling him all the coal he wants, we make sure we sell it to two or three other buyers of equal size.

"But why hit on M.L.? She's new?"

"Yes. But M.L. worked for a coal mining operation that thwarted one of his takeover attempts. He's never forgiven her. If she'd been a man he would have hired her. But in Mr. Fallon's world, women don't best men in business."

"I see. So M.L. has worked with some of UCC's customers before? How about you and the rest of her staff?"

"M.L., Ed and I all worked for that same West Virginia coal mine; Jason and I met at Arthur Anderson when they hired me as a consultant for a labor study they were conducting. Charles and I worked together drafting the results of that study. The only one I've never worked with before is William Foley; he's been at UCC the longest."

"Oh?"

"Yeah. He was hired by Jack Foster five years ago."

"The previous CEO?"

"Right."

"Hi Frank. Pamela." Ed's massive shoulders blocked their view of the main room. "This a private discussion?"

"No. Join us," Pamela moving to make room for Ed on the sofa. "I understand you and Frank worked with M.L. before?"

"Sure did."

"A coal mine?"

With a boyish grin Ed nodded. "We've really come a long way, haven't we Frank? No soot in our nose or cinders in our eyes now."

"That's right Pamela, Ed and I are in tall cotton. The only real winners in this crowd "

"Why?"

"Both of us were born on the wrong side of the tracks. Yet, we're living the American Dream. I guess you could say we wouldn't have believed it possible working for anyone but for M.L."

"M.L.?"

"Yeah. She's an outsider too." Frank's comment causing Pamela to wonder anew about how the perfect lady got to be CEO.

"I understand you two are almost a team. Is that because of your areas of expertise? Or, your long friendship?"

"We're flip sides of the same coin. Frank's labor, I'm management. But we've always trained in the trenches. You could say having worked together as long as we have, we just think alike. You know of course that Frank saved my life?"

Turning to Frank, she saw him squirm, and his face began to shine. She was sure a blush hid under his espresso brown skin.

"Frank, you're full of surprises. What happened?"

She saw Frank about to object, when Ed cut in, "No you don't, Buddy. It's my story to tell."

"Why don't I go find some trouble?" Frank said getting up to leave. "Then Ed can tell all the lies he wants. See you later Pamela."

Watching as Frank walked over to talk to E.F. Haynes, she saw the two immediately launch into animated chatter, which soon began to attract a circle of men, over whom they towered. Watching them, Pamela asked Ed, "This really is a men's club, isn't it?"

"In most ways. But M.L.'s very much one of its members."

Turning her attention back to Ed, Pamela caught him studying her. His clear gray eyes suggested honesty. "Will you answer a question frankly?"

"If I can."

"Do you think M.L. can cut the mustard?"

"Yep."

"Any doubts?"

"Nope."

"But look at these guys. The customers, bankers and Board members are all seasoned executives."

"Yes."

"So?"

"M.L. is a very unusual gal. I've watched her win over cons and thugs. This crowd should be easy."

Pamela wanted to pursue her line of questions, but Ed had changed the subject. He had begun to tell the story about Frank having saved his life. "I was part of an inspection crew going into one of the mine shafts to inspect a fault that had been spotted. We had just reached two of our miners, when the wall caved in. Our emergency crew was off working on another problem, so I called M.L. on the portable radiophone. She and Frank were the only two around who knew how to launch a rescue. M.L. must have contacted the paramedics and lined up a relief crew. But Frank came in to get us, dug a passage and pulled us out. Just in time too. A second cave in started as we walked free."

"What was M.L. doing at a coal mine?"

"She was the accountant."

"A bookkeeper?"

"Officially. Unofficially she was trying to uncover a major coal theft."

"Did she?"

"Yep. Fallon's men. She could never prove it. But she discovered how the thefts occurred. And stopped them."

"Did you work together long?"

"No. She was only at the mine on assignment for E.F."

"E.F. again. Are you one of E.F.'s kids?"

"Not really."

Pamela saw his look of surprise.

"If Frank told you about E.F., he told you a lot. He must like you."

"Yeah. My sass."

While she had been sitting on the chintz sofa with Ed, Pamela had been studying the room. Ed's easy company allowed her to ask questions as one guest or another captured her curiosity. His answers, while brief were as straightforward as Ed himself.

"If that rough cut man talking to Jason is really a banker, than I have to reassess my stereotypes."

"Such as?"

"That bankers are usually connected to inherited wealth. Along with good family comes polish, right?"

"So Frank and I lack polish?"

"Touchy. OK, you're both candidates for a Calvin Klein ad. But tell me about that banker. Why isn't he classier?"

"That particular banker, Arthur Cawley, is a self made millionaire. He took a little biddy idea, patented it, and it's making millions."

"What little idea?"

"A decal for computer chips and circuit boards."

"You mean that every computer pays him a royalty?"

"Many times over."

"So, he sold the company and bought a bank?"

"No. Arthur leveraged his company into a mega-corporation and to finance future research, started a private bank."

"A private bank?"

"His bank loans money to a select group. UCC is one of his special clientele."

Not knowing where to go with this new information, Pamela was relieved to see Charles approaching.

"Pamela, Ed. I think it's going rather well. Aside from Fallon, M.L.'s sailing clear of trouble." Accepting a glass of Champagne from a passing waiter, Charles bent down, and whispered in her ear. "Pamela, do you see that man with the red cummerbund and face to match? He's a major graphite customer. If you heard any of his conversations, you'd know he's a red-necked womanizer. But when he offered to introduce M.L. to his state's senator, I knew she'd passed the gender barrier."

"You mean you set her up for a possible fall?"

"Of course. One of M.L.'s strengths is to make even the worst of our sex behave like gentlemen. If she can get them to like her in the process, then they'll do business with her. Of course they'll think they're still in control."

"You're switching the rules. Men don't like doing business with women. They don't even like talking to a female reporter."

"But all men like to talk to a pretty woman, and they'll fall all over themselves to please one."

"But . . ."

"Not now. Watch and listen. Ask M.L. about gender politics. She's the master. Anyway, when we left that crusty bastard, he was smiling."

Breaking into the conversation Ed asked, "Foley's taking his turn as M.L.'s protector?"

"Yes Ed. But he's been a reluctant escort. I don't think he likes women. I'd better relieve him before he sours the festivities."

As her eyes followed Charles, Pamela checked the crowded room. Of the more than fifty formally dressed men, she and M.L. were the only women present. So we haven't come very far have we M.L.? she thought. Seeing Jason, starting their way, she motioned for him to join them. How did this shy numbers man fit into the festivities, she wondered.

"Hi." Taking a seat across from Ed and Pamela, Jason's shoulders seemed to slump. "M.L.'s really zeroed in on the tough guys. When Fallon asked Charles about their plan for expansion, M.L.'s response turned him red. I thought the old coot would have a stroke."

"Frank told me earlier that he hates M.L. for besting him in a coal mine takeover attempt."

"That'd do it. He's a sore loser. How do you think its going Ed?"

"It may be a little early for post game analysis. But by the look of things, I think she can reach any of these characters any time she wants."

"Is tonight that important Jason?"

"Yes it is. After M.L. completes her tour of company outposts, it's business as usual. And these people will be key to implementing our long-range plans. Your book would be a strong testament of her credentials."

Shit. They are all out to impress me. Or sensor me. I'd better keep my guard up, she thought yet again.

"Do you know each of the bankers?"

"Yes. In fact, I worked with most of them when I was with the accounting firm. They may know me, but they also know I'll be carrying out M.L.'s orders. The way she's planned things, they'll be contacted one by one, as we need them. I'll go first. M.L. will come in for the close."

"The close?"

"Yes. I layout our plans. But M.L.'s going to finesse the bankers for financing. The customers for new contracts. The Board, for their support."

"And Jason will have paved the way so well, I'll be an anticlimax." M.L.'s sincerity fell softly on their ears.

Pamela watched Jason blush. They had been so engrossed in their conversation, that M.L.'s sudden appearance had been as surprising as her kindness to the nervous young man.

Looking up at M.L. Pamela said, "I understand you're a success." All the while studying the calm woman for a hint of her real thoughts.

"So far. Jason, I have been talking to E.F. He had a question about the availability of cash for our merger. Go over and see if you can calm his concerns."

Pamela saw Jason practically jump to attention, his face set with purpose.

"Does Jason always look like a terrier with a bone?"

Pamela watched M.L. laughing at her remark while she followed Jason and E.F. with her eyes. "He seems devoted to you."

M.L. turned her attention to Pamela. All the while Pamela was wondering which woman would answer her question. The relaxed female, or the curt CEO.

"That's a bonus. I demand loyalty of my staff."

Her direct stare warned Pamela, her access was limited.

"But now is the time for Cinderella to disappear and leave her minions to keep the guests happy. Can I give you a lift Pamela?"

"Thanks. If I remember our schedule, you're picking me up at 6?" She grimaced at the thought.

"Of course, if you'd rather meet me at the office later?"

"No you don't. 6 A.M. it is." Rising to follow, Pamela saw M.L. head for a side door, exiting the gathering unnoticed.

As they entered a service elevator, M.L. saw Pamela's question before it was expressed. "I'm leaving the boys to mop up."

"Aren't you curious to know if this crowd's accepted you?"

"Charles will find out all I need to know."

"How, by asking?"

"How else? He'll get their off-the-record opinions far faster than I could."

"And the others?"

"Jason is on friendly terms with most of the bankers. Frank and Ed know all of our customers. And Charles and William have a working relationship with our Board members. The entire crowd is covered."

"This is the damnedest CEO announcement I've ever heard of. First you chat them up, and then leave, knowing they'll revert to type, a men's club. M.L. I thought you wanted to be in the club?"

"Right. My men will tell me how I scored." The twinkle in M.L.'s eyes further confused Pamela. Shaking her head, she wondered what surprises tomorrow would hold.

*　　　*　　　*

The limousine had dropped Pamela off first. She had been too tired to press M.L. with more questions, during the ten-minute ride to her door. But she did notice that Ms. Perfect had retreated behind an unreadable expression.

As she climbed up the steps of her westside brownstone, Pamela wondered where M.L. lived. Did she climb stairs? Or did she ride an elevator to a cloud overlooking Central Park?

Too weary to care, she let herself into her building and climbed two more flights to her one bedroom apartment. Pamela loved her apartment. The stairs were by now, automatic. She especially liked having a street view. It reminded her of living in a small town. When not working, she would often watch her neighbors as they went about their lives. It was one of those neighborhoods without children. Mostly, young-up-and-coming professionals. An occasional elderly man or woman. And a few lovers, usually going about their daily chores blindly entwined.

But tonight Pamela had enough on her mind. Her fatigue was tension induced, usual for a first day's pressure of not knowing what to expect. It was after ten, and she needed a long hot soak in her tub. Kicking off her shoes, quickly pulling her camisole over her head, she looked over to her answering machine and saw the message light. With an exhausted sigh she tossed the rest of her clothes on a chair and turned on the machine. Her boss's voice, saying, "Call when you get in."

Punching John's home number into her phone, she grumbled, "So much for a hot tub."

He picked up on the first ring. "I'm back. What's up?"

"Just checking in. Anything interesting?"

"Everything. But I'm too tired to care."

"Take notes and keep an open mind. You're in the company of masters."

"Right. Night." Hanging up, she complained, "I'm on leave to research my book, and he has to know everything. John knows I'm sworn to secrecy for now. That's the deal. I can see everything, but can't reveal what I know until they approve my draft."

Heading for the bathroom, she felt jumpy. Her over-stimulated brain cried out for sleep. "Tomorrow. I'll deal with it tomorrow," she muttered as she slid into her hot bubble-filled tub.

CHAPTER XIV

A cross town, William Foley slammed the front door of his apartment and headed for the library. Throwing his vicuna coat on a leather chair, he poured a stiff drink of his favorite 30-year old scotch.

"Fallon. Why do I keep coming across that creep?" Picking up the phone, he called Dearling.

"Something's come up. Do you know any private investigators? Someone who can keep his mouth shut?"

Accustomed to his boss's late hours, Dearling's fatigue-fogged voice replied, "I think so. Why?"

"Call one, first thing in the morning. Have him get anything he can on an old geezer named Nat Fallon. Got that?"

"Yes. Nat Fallon. Doesn't ring any bells. Why?"

"Don't worry yourself. It's just a hunch. I thought I felt someone walking on my grave."

"You're superstitious?"

The surprised voice chilled him. All his life Foley had hidden his poor Irish heritage. Carefully living two lives. One life spent in Irish Boston as a working lawyer. The other, as a New York attorney with pseudo-American roots. Superstition had no place in the life of William Smythe Foley, corporate counsel.

"No. It's just an expression I picked up. I mean that this Fallon smells like trouble."

Hanging up Foley looked around his favorite room, unaware that his possessions were too perfect. The furniture was new, rather than inherited heirlooms with that patina of age. His clothing was ill suited to his short figure, which lacked the bearing of generations. His small, dumpy body strained the seams of his Saville Row suit, with his tiny feet too effeminate for their Gucci patent leather evening slippers.

Reviewing the cocktail reception, Foley thought about each Board member and banker he'd cornered for a private chat. He'd been careful to edit his comments, while ravenously filing away any tidbits that he might use. He knew each of UCC's Directors, having been Jack Foster's right hand. The former CEO had hired and groomed him to be his successor.

"They know I'm one of them," he said aloud. Pleased, to have felt accepted by the real power behind the corporation.

"That was before Ms. Bitch," cussing his fate to the empty room.

"She may be CEO for now. But it's my destiny." Hoisting his glass to toast his future, "To the fittest the crown. She'll be sorry. And UCC will pay for their oversight. Just wait, Ms. High-and-Mighty. You'll slip. Then it's my turn."

Removing his tie and jacket, Foley settled at his desk to concentrate on Dearling's market orders for the morning.

Unlocking his file drawer he reached for a leather folio. Opening it, he skimmed the book filled with his stock and bond holdings. A habit of many years, it always brought a smile to his normally dour face. Picking up the market's closing prices Dearling faxed over earlier that day, he entered each notation neatly by hand. While he kept his trading records on computer, this ritual was his way to touch his growing fortune.

Finished, he picked up the phone to call his older sister with the news.

"Jane? I've just finished going over our portfolio. You should be pleased. You're a rich woman."

"Willy! If you're pleased, I'm satisfied. I leave all that stuff to you."

Listening to his sister's casual acceptance of the news left him empty. He wished she cared a little more about his success. He'd created a small fortune for them. It took years of scheming. Didn't she care that their portfolio was now in the neighborhood of $2,000,000? But he knew that Jane thought his Wall Street trading was the result of luck. To Jane, it was all a paper tally. Not real in the sense that she could take any of it to the grocery store. She was so accustomed to scrimping, by now it was her way of life.

After listening to her talk on about her quiet life as a teacher in Quincy's grade school, Foley interrupted, "Jane I still have some work here. I just called to see how you were."

"I'm fine, thank you. I love you. Oh, and Willy, I'm happy your investments are going well. Good night Dear."

"Night Jane. I'll check in on Sunday as usual."

Hanging up, Foley knew Jane would never change. Even when he had handed her a $1,000 bill for her birthday several years ago, she just gave it back and told him to put it in his investment fund. She didn't need $1000. She had everything she needed. So the next year he bought her a cashmere bathrobe. The bathrobe had been a huge success. He smiled as he remembered her enjoyment of the soft, silky wool, totally unaware of its cost.

Seven years older than he, Jane had raised him while their widowed mother worked long hours in a neighborhood bakery. Drilling him in his homework. Watching out for him when he went out to play. After all he'd accomplished, Jane still tried to protect him with her love. He knew she worried about him. As if he were still the little kid running to her to patch his cuts and bruises from a fight with the neighborhood bullies. As the smallest kid in his class, he had always been in one fight or another.

With a sigh of resignation, he said "Oh Jane. You have no idea how rich you are. It won't change you. But now I want to protect you." He knew Jane loved him. And that was enough.

Swallowing the last of his drink, he finished his notes for Dearling's next day's trades. The pair were symbiotic. Not friends. Bound by a need to amass individual fortunes. Dearling wanted a fortune to gain his father's respect. William, born poor, needed a fortune to gain power.

Setting aside Dearling's written instructions, he gently stroked the leather folio as he closed it to put it away. Not trusting even his own housekeeper, although she had been with him almost thirty years, he hid the folio in a specially built drawer behind a false panel in his desk.

It was nearing midnight; the room was aglow in mock candlelight. This was Foley's favorite time of day. Listening to the popping of the old heating system, he went to refill his glass. He had nursed one glass of white wine all night. Foley never drank in public. His father had been an Irish drunk, and he vowed he'd never fall under that curse.

Stopping by his stereo, he turned on a favorite CD of *Barcarole from The Tales Of Hoffman*. Lowering the sound so it permeated the room, he returned to his desk. With pen in hand Foley began to draw up a list of targets. Weighing each entry aloud.

"Ms. Horn. Check. And double check. Fallon? That's a question mark. Cray? A definite. Haynes? Too bright to have had anything to do with giving that woman my job. BioTech's President? I don't think so. He's too old to keep running his business. He's just a matter of price."

Having revised the "Black List," his thoughts turned to Tim Lynch. If he could get Dearling to show Lynch how to get insider information, he knew the eager young broker would do the rest willingly.

Hunched over his note pad, Foley studied a list of questions he wanted Dearling to ask Lynch tomorrow. He needed information. He had to know if Answord Mining and Medical Industries were about to sign agreements with UCC. Even though he was the corporation's Counsel, M.L. hadn't included him on all of her plans. He was too visible to be able to approach anyone in those companies himself. And Dearling wasn't slick enough to bribe any of their officers. Thinking aloud, "It has to be you, boy'o. You're about to make a step off the straight and narrow."

As his list of questions for Lynch grew, so did Foley's confidence. Thanks to his sister and the nuns, he had learned that planning was the path to success. His life's blood was spent in revising those plans. Success, he thought, was just within reach.

CHAPTER XV

The alarm clock crashed to the floor as Pamela reached out to still the abrasive buzzing. With barely opened eyes, she searched the floor for the clock, her head throbbing with the jarring noise. Punching the alarm button finally silenced the offensive sound. As Pamela saw the damaged dial stuck at 5:30, her grainy eyes spotted shards of broken glass scattered next to her bedside rug.

"Serves you right. From now on it's a radio alarm for me."

Lying back on her pile of pillows with her hand on her aching forehead, she groaned as she remembered drinking too much champagne the night before.

"I must stick to white wine. Those bubbles flattened me."

Rolling out the other side of her bed, she headed for a steamy shower, hopeful of clearing her foggy head. "I've got to get it together. M.L.'s no fool. She'll spot a hangover."

By 6 AM Pamela's vision had cleared, the three aspirins restoring her head. As she stepped out the door to her building she spotted the UCC limo. I could get used to this, she thought, as she climbed into the back of the car. Settling into the wide leather seat, she gratefully accepted a cup of strong black coffee from M.L. Before she could give M.L. a thought, Pamela inhaled the rich aroma and took three fast sips.

Her appointment book had prepared her for an early morning workout. Being organized, she had thrown a new T-shirt and tights into her tote bag the night before. But she had been unprepared for M.L.'s casual appearance. Dressed in a T-shirt and well-worn jeans, her naked face was glowing with health. The casual clothes were topped off with an exquisite fox-lined suede coat, her legs encased in matching espresso-coffee suede boots. M.L. looked more like a rich man's second wife than one of the most powerful women in business.

Even more surprising was M.L. herself. All the previous day Pamela had thought of her as a machette, with the posture of a soldier on parade. But sitting next to her and listening to her chatting away as if they had been sorority sisters, was a woman Pamela would like to have had for a friend.

Echoing in the back of her head was her boss's warning, "Remember you're in the company of masters." Masters of concealment, she thought.

"Another cup? M.L. asked while reaching for a carafe plugged into a cabinet in a console of the car.

"No. This is fine. If I get too much caffeine, I'll be wired."

"I hope you're ready for a good work out? It should help wake you up."

"I'll be OK. I may start a pace or two behind, but just look around and you'll see your shadow." Shit, Pamela thought, she knows I'm hung over.

Alighting from the car in front of a modest brownstone, Pamela looked up and down the quiet tree-lined street. She knew she was in the East 50's, not so much by the corner street sign, but by the lack of commercial buildings. This was a residential block, a mix of private and converted buildings of floor-thru apartments.

Walking into the building's vestibule, Pamela asked, "How long have you been into exercise?"

"Since I turned 30. I can still remember the horror of seeing the beginnings of saddlebags and cellulite. My body was telling me to shape up, or I'd look like my mother."

"Your mother wasn't thin? With your bones, I thought thin was a family gene."

"No. Mom was matronly."

Not heavy, matronly. Now that's interesting. I must remember to follow that up, Pamela thought.

Entering the gilded cage of a small elevator, Pamela saw that there were six floors listed on the control panel. Next to each of the buttons were small tags identifying the occupant of each floor. M.L. had pushed the top button. The sign read, "Fran's Place."

"So this is a long time habit?"

"Actually it is. In my desperation to loose the fat, I found Fran. She's a treasure. I've followed her from a one-room studio to this duplex. What you see is her creation, with a lot of huffing and puffing from me."

I'll bet, Pamela thought. This woman probably doesn't even break into a sweat. It's my luck to be with an exercise freak. "I'm not very disciplined. But I must admit if Fran remade you, I'm tempted to give my body another chance. I just have to find the time."

"Interesting."

"What?"

"Time. It's all just scheduling."

"Can't be. Scheduling is a habit of mine. But, the time gets filled in by work. Anything left over has to cover eating, sleeping, and extra curricular activities."

"If a healthy body is a priority, you find the time."

Pamela wondered if that was an order.

"Follow me."

And Pamela did, from the dressing room into a pale blue carpeted studio with one mirrored wall. It was all she could do to follow M.L. and Fran through a complex routine of stretching and aerobic exercises. All the while M.L. kept up with Fran's pace. Her purple-Lycra-clad body flowing to the music as if she were auditioning for a Broadway show.

Pamela was envious of M.L.'s body. Poor thing, all she needed was a butt. Shit, she grumbled silently. I've got the butt, and no tits. Watching her own reflection in the mirrored wall, Pamela saw her straight-as-a-board chest and the square shoulders of a halfback. I doubt even Fran can help me.

After a rigorous forty minutes, Pamela found herself panting, sweating, and thirsting for a cold glass of water. But secretly pleased she had kept up. Now, collapsed on the floor, she snuck a peek at M.L., lying a hand's width away. She was absorbed in Fran's calming voice, relaxing her body one segment at a time. M.L.'s skin had a sheen from exertion. Yet her breathing wasn't ragged like her own. Thinking it might help her as well, Pamela closed her eyes and listened to Fran. To her delight and surprise her body began to unkink, leaving her with a feeling of well being. Her mind was so totally removed from her body, that M.L.'s gentle touch startled her.

"How's my shadow?"

Pamela answered with a blissful smile.

"How about a massage? I'm used to Fran's workouts. Between you and me I pretend I'm Ginger Rogers. But a massage is my treat for pushing this body so hard."

The business of undressing and wrapping up in thick buttercup yellow towels occupied Pamela's thoughts. Following M.L. to a small room nearby, she saw two massage tables. "M.L. I've never had a massage. What's it supposed to do?"

"Smooth out those knotted muscles. It's not only relaxing, I think it helps keep skin tone."

"Ouch." Her involuntary cry was the result of the masseuse having hit a bundle of knotted shoulder muscles. Having assured Brunhilda she was all right, Pamela closed her eyes and allowed the masseuse to continue to work on her neck and back muscles.

"You're not what I expected at all," Pamela said. Her eyes closed as she relaxed, beginning to enjoy the massage.

"And what did you expect?" M.L.'s voice was ebbing and flowing as another masseuse worked on her shoulders and back.

"A machette in uniform. Someone who had either slept or murdered her way to the top."

"Don't you think women have the capability to lead?"

"I guess I never thought about it. In my field, women who succeed do so on talent. It's not about leading."

"But as a feminist you must think women equal to men?"

Stopped short by M.L.'s comment, Pamela realized she did, but not in the corporate suite. "As I see it, there's equal ability, but not equal opportunity."

"I'm hoping to change that. Women now head up advertising agencies, cosmetic companies, and fashion empires. Now there's me."

It was a flat statement. She didn't seem to be bragging. Pamela wondered how she could be so accepting of the oddity of her position as the first female CEO of an industrial complex. "Aren't you frightened by being a first?"

"I don't look at it as the Holy Grail. It's a job I've trained for. Male or female. It's all the same. Each person will handle the job in their own unique way. My staff will follow my lead as long as they have faith in me."

Holy shit! She really believes that. What gives her the confidence? Pamela was also wondering if she had a life and began another tack. "Do you have many women friends?" She noticed that M.L.'s response was a tad slow.

"No. Most of my friends are men. I'm not lucky with women. Every time I think I've met a kindred soul, she stabs me in the back. Men are much easier to read. It's either a sexual attraction, or one of trust. For me, without trust, there's no personal connection."

What female doesn't have a woman friend or two, Pamela asked herself. Even she had girl friends to go to a movie or lunch with. Didn't you need another woman to dish with?

"How about your social life?"

"Is this personal curiosity, or for the record?"

"Curiosity. I can't figure out how a gorgeous, smart woman remained single. On one hand, I'm single so it makes me comfortable. On the other hand it makes me suspicious."

"Suspicious?"

"Yeah. To me all gorgeous women are mated at birth. Those that remain unattached are driven by other agendas. Work, ghosts of loves past. An empty place where emotions should be."

"I see. And what about you?" M.L. asked.

"I'm told I pick the wrong men. My friend Skip thinks I lack a sense of self-worth." How in the Hell did she get me to say that, Pamela wondered?

"Well, I fall into your pigeonhole of career driven. All my working life I've been striving for the next challenge. CEO is the icing on the cake. And as you've noticed, a work driven schedule leaves little time for nurturing a love affair."

"Unless it is a priority!" Pamela, finishing the sentence for both of them. "Do you miss having a man in your life?"

"I didn't say I didn't. I said I didn't have a social life."

"I don't get it. Do you live in a monastery?"

"What's this from a liberated sister? I could give you a long answer, but the truth is the men I might have been interested in, weren't interested in me." Rising from the table, M.L. poked Pamela, "That's way off the record."

What did I expect, Pamela thought, as she got off her table to follow.

While they were dressing Pamela watched M.L. with amusement.

"And, just what's caught your fancy now?" M.L. said to Pamela's mirrored reflection.

"For a major corporate executive you apply makeup with the skill of a fashion model. Wouldn't your stockholders be surprised."

"Scratch the cynic and I'll bet you're quite a woman." M.L. turned to look Pamela directly in the eye. "You really should do more with your appearance. You have a great body for clothes. Especially knits. If you wore colors instead of dark brown and black you'd be a knock out."

Pamela found M.L.'s appraisal disconcerting. "You're beginning to sound like Skip. I guess I never thought much about my appearance as long as I was clean and comfortable." You don't, when you know you're plain, she thought.

"I'd be happy to take you to my personal shopper at Sak's and let her show you a new You. In the right clothes you might surprise yourself."

"Right. On my salary. She'd take one look at me and bus me out to K-Mart."

Not expecting this sort of exchange, Pamela wondered if M.L. really thought her looks had possibilities. Slow down. Remember you're the interviewer. But a warm spot had developed in her skeptic's soul. M.L. was the first woman to make her feel almost pretty.

CHAPTER XVI

"Tim?"

"Yes?"

"This is Bruce Dearling. Did my check arrive in time?"

"Yes Sir. How can I help you today?"

"I noticed that BioTech dropped back to 2. I'd like to place an order for another 10,000 shares."

"Just a minute Mr. Dearling, you're accumulating a position. Are you planning to make a statement of intent?"

"No. This is to remain strictly between us."

"Then we will have to watch your future purchases. Can I interest you in another company?"

"No. Just the 10,000 of BioTech at 2. I'll send a check round later today. Park the extra funds with the others. I like your short-term selections."

"Yes Sir, Mr. Dearling. Thank you."

*　　　*　　　*

It was still early in the day and Foley had planned a full morning away from his official duties at UCC. Dearling was expected in ten minutes. Inviting him to brunch was a small gesture. One he knew Dearling valued.

His housekeeper was laying out a variety of pastries on the Library coffee table. A silver tray lay waiting for its matching coffee pot.

"Will there be anything else Mr. Foley?"

"No Violet. When Mr. Dearling arrives show him in."

"Fine Sir," she answered, closing the door silently as she left.

Violet Mason was a sparrow of a woman whose name was her most colorful possession. He counted his blessings for having saved her brother from a long stretch in jail. That was 30 years ago, and Violet had been his devoted servant ever since. As Foley's career advanced, he had rewarded Violet with increases in salary. Yet she remained a silent figure in his home. It was a Victorian relationship that suited them both.

Thinking about the evening before, he congratulated himself for having cemented his relationship with UCC's Board members. For now, he thought, wondering what they would think if they knew of his plans to unseat their new CEO.

"Mr. Dearling has arrived."

"Show him in."

Moving away from his desk, he greeted Dearling with a handshake. "We have a lot to do."

"I'm ready," Dearling said, taking a seat as Violet poured their coffee. Leaving the pot, she left as quietly as she had appeared.

He's still a skinny kid, Foley thought. Only now he's in pin stripes not chinos. An appraisal that had more to do in measuring Dearling's growing wealth than his maturity.

With his first bite of pastry swallowed, Bruce Dearling launched into his report. "Neuwirth can put together a private issue to raise up to $48 million. We can subsidize 31% or close to $15 million by leveraging our combined personal and corporate holdings. But we will have to find four or five partners for the balance."

"How about that insurance group you represent? Can they come up with $9 million?"

"Possibly. We also have the Willis Family Trust. They should be good for another $9 million. Maybe we could interest the Cutler Foundation in another $9 million. But that still leaves us $6 million short."

"This Fallon. Did your P.I. turn up anything on him?

"Yes. It seems he heads up a transportation syndicate. Nothing irregular so far. Why?"

"Do you think we could approach him for a piece of the action? He looks like he'd be a player."

"I'll send him a note and arrange a meeting. Or, do want to contact him directly?"

"For now, it's your deal. But be careful. This Fallon is still an unknown. Just let me know before you contact him."

Dearling hadn't let his love for sweets interrupt his conversation. Throughout their discussion, Foley watched as he nibbled at the edges of his pastry. It struck him that Dearling ate like he worked. In measured bites.

Suddenly hungry himself, he reached for a custard-rich Napoleon. His appetite was always stimulated by the smell of success.

"You know in six months it will be all over. Have you given any thoughts to what you'll be doing next Bruce?"

"Yes Sir. I'd like to remain at Neuwirth. If that's OK. Now that I've accumulated a small portfolio, I have plans to invest in new areas."

Small by whose standards? His father's, Foley thought. Dearling had made his first million and was planning for his second.

"Will we be able to keep Neuwirth going?"

"I think so. But I may have to sell you some of my equity. I'll need the capital."

If Foley hadn't studied him so well over the years he would have missed the avaricious grin. Only money caused his partner to reveal any of his buttoned up emotions. At the hint of gaining control over Neuwirth, he knew Dearling was fighting to contain his glee. I wonder if he really expects me to hand him complete control? He should know me better by now, Foley thought.

"How's our consolidated position on BioTech stock?"

"Good. When the buy out is completed, we'll gain in share price as well as equity. We may only have 25% of the LBO, but we'll control everything through our cumulative voting shares."

"Well done. Leave nothing to chance. We're too close." The verbal warning was unnecessary. Both had staked their futures on this shadowy fiscal manipulation, a pyramiding of funds to gain control of a burgeoning technology. Gnats about to feast at the expense of the behemoth.

Sitting back, Dearling momentarily forgotten, Foley began to compose Melissa Horn's corporate obituary. 'She meant well, but then she wasn't suited to the task.' Revenge richened the flavor of his coffee.

CHAPTER XVII

The car had left M.L. and Pamela at UCC's private entrance just before 8 AM. Arriving at her office, M.L. suggested Pamela spend some time going over background on UCC.

"Mary has gathered some information for you. Our history, product mix, and advertising. It's waiting in an office we've set aside for you while you're here."

"Will I see you later, M.L.?"

"Yes. We have a meeting here at 10. I'll see you then."

"Fine. And thanks for the workout. I haven't felt this good in years."

As Mary left to escort Pamela to her temporary home several doors down the corridor, M.L.'s thoughts returned to their workout. Pamela had surprised her by keeping up with Fran. She'd even dropped her guard about her problems with that guy she'd been seeing. What a jerk, she thought.

"How can that tough reporter let a guy treat her so shabbily?" M.L. wondered aloud.

As her thoughts returned to her day's agenda, M.L. remembered that Pamela was still watching her every move. "How could E.F. expect me to work with her looking over my shoulder? Even he doesn't do that," she grumbled.

Rubbing her neck, Melissa tried to summon up an inner calm. Deep breathing helped steady her jumpy nerves. But nagging thoughts kept interrupting her composure. Closing her eyes, hands loosely folded on her lap, she focused on her plans. But fear began to raise its familiar head. *Can I handle this? Keep our plans on track? Or is our traitor going to fuck me good? E.F. still hadn't found out anything to talk about.*

Calming her mind, she realized that this bout of self-doubt stemmed from working under Pamela's scrutiny.

Rationalizing aloud, "There's nothing new here. There's always a snake in the woodpile. I've smoked them out before, and never been bitten. Screw it." Reaching over to her in-box, she began to deal with the day's paperwork.

"Damn it! Focus." But, now, instead of thinking about the mail, she saw Hugh's handsome face, heard his sexy voice promise they'd meet again. She couldn't afford to let that happen. Not now. Being with Hugh had been a vacation. He was a rich dessert she had devoured like a starving dieter. She couldn't give up a life-long dream. Not even for Hugh. CEO was the crowning achievement of almost twenty years of single-minded ambition. Ambition to run a company. Run it as well as any man. Now, she was about to lead UCC back to strength. Restore its life-blood.

Shaking her head to clear Hugh from her mind, Melissa focused again on the pile of correspondence. Hard work was her friend. Her protection. Her wellspring of strength.

She had been working steadily. Concentrating on demands being made by suppliers and customers she had not as yet met. Looking up as Pamela entered her office, she realized it was just about 10. M.L. was glad to see her nerves were back under control, every one of her senses on alert.

As Pamela settled in a chair opposite her desk, M.L. noticed that the insecure girl she'd seen earlier at Fran's, was no longer in evidence. So her Achilles heel is her appearance, she thought, studying the strong face and wondering if it was the only one.

"What's on the agenda M.L.?"

"We're going fishing."

"Fishing?"

"Yup. For information. Information that for now is off the record. OK?"

"I'm a shadow."

Sure she is M.L. thought. With a tape recorder for a brain.

"Jason and Will have just arrived M.L. Would you like me to show them in?" Mary asked from the doorway.

"Please Mary, and join us."

"Gentlemen. Coffee?" M.L. asked, rising as the two men joined Pamela and Mary at the round conference table.

"Yes Please M.L.," Jason replied. "Don't bother, I'll get my own."

Gold star, Jason, M.L. thought as he quickly walked to the credenza and poured his coffee. She liked Jason. He was shy around the others. But after working closely together, he'd become easier with her. He was as consistent in behavior as he was in his balance sheets, she thought. Jason wouldn't betray her.

Now, as for William Foley. He's another fish. He was already seated and expecting to be served? Getting him a cup of coffee, M.L. silently remarked, the snot. Not even a thank you.

With coffee poured M.L. casually asked, "William. How close are we to finalizing our offer?"

"I've set a meeting for you tomorrow at Noon. We should be able to complete the closing formalities then."

"Where's the meeting to take place?"

"Your conference room, M.L."

"Please change that," she said, her words polite, yet her voice had hardened. "Arrange to have us meet in their CEO's office."

You pompous ass, she thought. For all your brains, you never learned the social graces of negotiation. Noticing something in his stare, M.L. wondered if it was personal? Probably just upset because I've changed his plans again, she decided.

"Right M.L. Whatever you want."

M.L. felt his barely contained contempt. But he didn't scare her. She'd been scared by professionals. Take Fallon, she thought. He's scary.

Turning her shoulder away from William Foley, M.L. gave all her attention to Jason. Her voice was all business, but softer. "Where do we stand once the agreement is signed? Can we get the loan we need within 24 hours as we promised?"

"First Security is lined up and just waiting for the formal closing. As soon as they have a copy of the agreement, they will release the $54 million."

"Any problems?"

"Not if the contract is signed this week."

She wasn't sure why she was looking at William. But she noticed him rubbing his pinkie ring. An unusually large one for such a small hand, she thought. "Is there any reason William, we can't sign tomorrow?" her voice drilled for a positive reply.

"No. Everything's set."

She was having a hard time reading William. She had watched him drag his heels on finalizing the BioTech purchase. E.F. may have underestimated you, she thought. You may have thought my job should have been yours, you greedy bastard. But if you fuck up our purchase, I'll destroy you. This meeting couldn't end fast enough. She'd call E.F. right away and alert him. She wanted William Foley tailed. She had to have something concrete before the next day's meeting at BioTech. If he was playing games, she'd need something to hang him with if necessary.

As William and Jason left, M.L. asked Mary and Pamela to stay behind. Crossing her legs and opening her notepad, M.L. looked toward the closed office door before continuing. "Mary did you get everything?"

"Yes M.L.," Mary said as she placed a tape recorder the size of a checkbook on the table and rewound it. At her touch of the play button, M.L.'s voice was clearly heard asking if anyone wanted coffee.

Noticing Pamela's grin, M.L. suspected that she was now grouped with Nixon, spies and spooks. "This isn't my usual practice. But I suspect one of my staff of treason. We're fishing for a traitor. This is top secret. OK?"

"Of course. But I didn't catch anything other than a tug of wills between you and Foley. I suspect it wasn't your first time."

"No. And probably won't be the last. Mary I've already changed my schedule. But I'd like you to call William at 4 and double check the change in venue. When you've transcribed the tape, add it to the file. Then you had better erase the cassette. That's all for now Mary. Thank you."

As Mary left, M.L. caught Pamela studying her. Here we go, she thought. Sitting taller in the straight-backed chair, she waited, fully prepared to deal with another round of pointed questions.

"Is Mrs. Hammond usually present?"

"I like to keep her by my side. That way she has all the information she needs to act as my assistant."

"Is that usual? I thought secretaries just typed, took dictation and organized things."

"Some do. I prefer a partner who understands my needs. Mary goes back to UCC's early days. As Jack Foster built this organization brick by brick, she smoothed over the mortar. I suspect she knows all the company secrets."

"But she's still your secretary?"

"For now. But I've asked Ed to create a title of Assistant to the President for her. I have plans for Mary that are better suited to her exceptional organizational skills."

"President?"

"Yes. Officially I'm President and CEO."

"Back to Mary, you seem to believe in delegation of authority?"

"Yes. But only to those trustworthy enough to follow my intentions, as well as my orders." Clever girl. I guess I'm still at odds with her concept of CEO's she thought.

"Pamela, I'd like to ask a favor."

"Ask away."

"The next two days will be important to us. Economically, as well as politically. Not only will we be tendering an offer to purchase a company. A matter that must be kept under wraps to prevent any movement in their stock. We will also be holding some sensitive meetings."

Noticing Pamela's puzzled look, she continued carefully. "By that I mean you will be present for some off-the-record negotiations. More like an airing of ideas between interested parties. While there will be nothing unusual about these meetings, they are not for the ears of the public or the press. It's private business." Well she's agreeing in concept, M.L. noticed.

"This purchase agreement. Will I know the name of the company?"

"Yes. But not until just before it's official. Since it should close prior to your submitting the first draft of your book to your publisher, you will be free to include the information."

"But M.L. Why do you want me at your other meetings if I'm expected to keep what I see and hear to myself?"

"Because I want you to experience the shadow world of business. The Men's Club. It's one few women ever get to see, let alone join. I'm hoping that once you see them in action, you'll get a better idea of what I'm up against." I wish I could read her mind. I may be making a big mistake. But she's definitely hooked. I can see the excitement percolating in her eyes.

"Yes Ma'am. I'm all yours. Thank you."

As M.L. watched Pamela getting up to leave, she saw her straight lips turn up slightly, in a little smile. Like a younger sister delighted to be entrusted with a secret.

"Then I'll see you back here at 3. If you need anything, ask Mary."

As Pamela left, M.L. let out her breath. "On track, O'le girl." With private fears pushed aside, M.L. Horn, began to attack the stack of letters Mary had left for her to sign. She was in her element, in the place she could control. The one sure facet of her complex life: Work.

CHAPTER XVIII

Dressed in the old football jersey of a long gone, but not forgotten, love, Pamela picked up the phone and punched John's unlisted office number. "Please answer. I need you." she whispered.

"Hi Boss." Thank God, she thought. "I'm sorry to call after hours, but I think I need some direction."

"Sure. Shoot."

"I'm stuck. M.L. took me to her club for a workout this morning. She was real friendly. Answered most all my questions . . . even the one about why she wasn't married. But . . . I just don't get it. Why has she opened her private life to me?"

"Let's analyze your two days. First, most of your time spent with M.L. has been with at least one of her staff. Right?"

"Yeah. Usually Charles Cray."

Secondly, did you pick her up this morning? See where she lives?"

"No."

"Were any of her girl friends present? Don't you girls usually torture yourself in pairs?"

"Not always. Anyway, I got the feeling that this Fran, the woman who runs the place, is a friend. Our class was private."

"Did you talk to this Fran?"

"Not alone . . . there wasn't any time."

"Just how personal were your questions? Did you ask about her parents, friends, boyfriends, former jobs?"

"Not exactly." She was beginning to feel like a cub reporter, not a take control professional.

"Listen Pamela. Don't rush into forming opinions of any of these people. Something will break. You still have five days before you have to submit your outline to your publisher."

"John. Are any of them on the level?"

"Probably, but they're all control freaks and will try to mold your opinions if they can. So far my research hasn't turned up anything out of the ordinary. I'll call you the moment I find anything that's not kosher. What's on your schedule for tonight?"

"Oh. There's a dinner for some New York politicos. I think the Governor and Mayor are expected."

"*Mm*. Very interesting! Pay attention to those two. See if they are friendly or get into any heated debates?"

"Why is that important?"

"Because the Governor is a Democrat and hates the Republican Mayor's lack of support. They have to work together, but don't like it. And watch M.L. See if she can get them to agree on anything. Call me as soon as you get in."

"I've been sworn to secrecy. I won't be able to tell you much."

"That's all right. Use your judgment. Just call!"

"Thanks for listening. I'll check in later." Hanging up, Pamela cussed, "Shit. She's got me so dazzled, I'm forgetting my own rules. Preparation, keep eyes open, and mouth shut. I'd better write up my questions for tomorrow. No, I'll do that later. I'm sure I'll have plenty after tonight's affair."

*　　*　　*

As the limousine pulled away from Pamela's westside apartment building, she was pleased to see that her black crepe pants suit and Lurex camisole were appropriate for the evening. Sitting across was the confidently handsome Charles, and equally composed and sophisticated M.L. Didn't she ever look ruffled? Nothing was out of place, from her hair combed into a soft bun, to another spectacular set of pearl jewelry, simple enough to have come right from the oyster's shell. Looking at the handsome pair, she thought M.L. was dressed more like a wealthy socialite, not a CEO. Her slim black evening dress was a shimmer of black sequins. But M.L. surprised her by complementing her on her own outfit.

"I love your look Pamela. Is it Ralph Lauren?"

"I'm afraid not. It's a J.C. Penny look-alike. But, thanks. I wasn't sure what to wear."

"Don't worry," Charles smooth voice was very appealing. "Men don't analyze wardrobe, just the woman inside. And, my compliments. You look sensational."

"Careful, or you'll have me blushing." Giving Charles one of her impish grins, she added, "Maybe I should dress up more often, especially if I get that kind of reaction." What was it about this guy that made her want to flirt?

As the car continued on its way, M.L. and Charles began to review the list of expected guests. Pamela detected a slight edge in M.L.'s voice, and was surprised to hear the tension. Was it apprehension? Maybe it's normal pre-event nerves. If this is so hush, I wonder if I'll hear any dirt. Something to dig around in later."

As Ben pulled up to the private entrance of UCC's club, Pamela couldn't suppress her curiosity. "Does UCC always entertain at this location?"

Charles nodded his glorious red-blonde head. "This is the most convenient place for us. And our guests seem to covet our invitations."

Gathering her satin stole around her shoulders, M.L. signaled Ben that they would be remaining in the car a few moments longer.

Pamela could feel M.L.'s eyes studying her soul.

"Tonight is one of many off-the-record occasions. By controlling the location we can offer our guests anonymity. Eliminate their fear of prying eyes and mischief makers."

There's that word again, Pamela thought. If there was one word to sum up M.L., it was control. From her clothes to her emotions. Now, it's the location of a dinner party. Does she ever let up? Pamela wanted to be the fly on the wall when she did.

"Pamela," Charles' voice, for all its honey, couldn't hide his seriousness. "It has become almost impossible to conduct exploratory discussions with people important to our future, without someone leaking information to our competitors. One way we can prevent leaks is to have private meetings. Remember that you are a privileged guest. But I'm sure your instincts will agree with our caution."

Pamela's quick mind was composing the headlines in the morning tabloids, "UCC Cuts Deal With NY's Governor. Payoff Suspected!" and nodded, acknowledging Charles concerns.

"Ready?" M.L. asked.

Pamela knew M.L. really meant was she ready to keep her place.

*   *   *

Entering the Club several steps behind M.L. and Charles, Pamela could see the room of 20 or so men dressed in evening clothes. Odd, she thought, each man stood slightly apart, not in one group. As her eye moved around the room, she recognized the State's Treasurer, the Governor, several Senators, and New York City's Mayor. No wonder they stand out. Each one is a power to be reckoned with.

After last nights spectacular entrance, Pamela expected M.L. to be greeted enthusiastically. But these men she noticed, were responding with little more than polite curiosity. As M.L. walked into the main room, their eyes appraised her body as if she were a Playmate. Pamela realized that M.L. may be a newcomer to their club, but to this group, she's only a woman.

Fascinated, Pamela watched M.L. stand her ground. Body erect, head held high as she slowly stared each man in the eye. Tonight, Charles spoke first.

"Gentlemen. It gives me great pleasure to present Melissa Horn, the new President and Chief Executive Officer of United Chemicals Corporation."

M.L. dipped her sleek head to acknowledge their polite applause, and then gave each man a dazzling smile that stopped short of her eyes. "Gentlemen, thank you for your warm welcome."

Warm shit, Pamela thought. The group looked more like lions studying their evening meal.

With Charles in tow, M.L. began to circulate. This time, with a formality that demanded each man's best manners. No golf scores tonight Pamela noticed. M.L. was pointedly commenting on each guest's efforts on behalf of the New York business community. To her reporter's mind, this was a work session. M.L. was quickly reversing Pamela's initial impression of her. Not a frail plaything, she thought, as she watched M.L. circle the group, all sails flying.

"Hi" greeted Ed, from a position to the left of her shoulder. "What do you think of New York's Boys Club?"

"Pretty stiff bunch. Usually they can't smile enough. Why's tonight different?"

"Because in this egocentric crowd, each one is a star in his own sphere. M.L. is just a mystery they have to solve."

"A mystery?"

"Will she play along with them, or is she going to make waves. Will she fight their deals with the unions? Inhibit their tax bills? I'm sure they are all hoping that she's a weak link they can exploit!"

"They might have in the beginning. I don't think they are now. But, what happens if she is stronger?"

The chuckling in her ear had to be Frank, Pamela thought. Looking up into his rugged smiling face, she relaxed and allowed him to lead her toward the bar.

"Ah Pamela, now you know the real stakes of the game. Power," Frank said as he held her elbow in one of his large paws.

Stopping at the entrance to the bar, Pamela noticed that unlike the night before, it was packed. "I've always known politicians in private, were a wet group. You've just confirmed my suspicions."

Frank offered to elbow his 6'4" frame into the crowd. "May I get you two a glass of champagne?" Ed nodded in agreement. Pamela to her own surprise, declined. "After last night, I think I'd better stick to a glass of white wine."

"The bubbles got you?"

"I should have stopped at one glass of that stuff. Any more and I'm in trouble."

As Frank moved off to get their drinks, Pamela asked Ed, "What is it these men fear?"

"That M.L.'s a loner, and not afraid to call they're bluff."

"And, this is an election year for our esteemed Governor, one U.S. Senator, and a State Senator," she noted aloud.

"That's not all," Frank said joining them with the drinks. "Jack Foster had quietly let it be known that UCC might be pulling up stakes and leaving Manhattan."

"Is that true?" Pamela's fingers were itching for a pencil.

"Ah. That depends on how these men work with M.L."

She was waiting for Frank to continue, but had to settle for his silence. This is dynamite stuff, she thought. UCC owns a half block of real estate on Park Avenue between 49th and 50th streets. And I have to keep this quiet. Tomorrow's headline could read "UCC won't take it any more. Puts corporate tower up for sale."

Thinking aloud, she said, "Frank, that could seriously hurt those up for reelection."

"Yup. I'm sorry that's all I can say for now."

Pamela meanwhile was mentally tallying the ramifications of a UCC defection. Loss of some 10,000 jobs, city and state corporate taxes, real estate taxes, not to mention the loss of all that purchasing power. That's some secret to keep. Even for me, she thought.

After some forty minutes spent sipping her one white wine and watching M.L. move easily from one politico to another, Pamela's gaze fell on an agitated Jason. He was anxiously whispering something to Charles. After a small exchange Charles patted the smaller man on the shoulder as if to gentle his concerns. Sensing something was not right, she then watched as Charles moved silently up to M.L. and gently took possession of her arm. Was it a signal? Seemingly, without a pause, M.L. brought her chat with Governor Dennison to an end. "We must talk about your idea in greater detail. Maybe we can go off to the side room after dinner?" The Governor apparently thought that was a great idea, it was the first time his smile held any warmth. It was still on his face as Pamela watched M.L. and Charles walk away.

Now curiosity had her hooked, and her eyes followed the handsome couple to an empty corner of the room. Reaching the far wall Pamela saw Charles turn his head away from the room as he began relating something to M.L. As he talked, M.L.'s forehead began to wrinkle. Not exactly frown, Pamela noticed. That would be a break in self-control, she thought. Just the same her face showed her concern.

If she was alerted before, now Pamela was worried. M.L. was staring directly at her, and signaling that she should follow her from the room. Leaving several steps behind M.L., Pamela followed her to a small unmarked door. It led to the outer area of a charming powder room. Already seated on a vanity stool, M.L. said in a cold clipped voice, "We must talk."

What was this all about Pamela wondered, as M.L. began to speak in the quietest of voices, talking not to her, but at her mirrored reflection. "I'm afraid that in my attempt to take you into my confidence, I misjudged your reputation. It seems you are well known to this crafty bunch. So well known that your presence has met with suspicion."

A danger flare was going off in Pamela's mind.

"Bringing you along tonight could jeopardize our plans. Now to correct the damage, I'm afraid you are going to have to leave."

"Even if I leave, isn't the damage done?"

"Even though you are known to play fair, you are still the Press. Tonight, however, you are certainly not welcomed by these men."

"I see. But, M.L., I don't know anything." Clenching her hands behind her back, she thought, Hell, not only is the book in danger, but so is my reputation! If I anger this group, I'll never gain access to any one of them again.

"I'm sure you know more than you think you do. However, you will honor the temporary non-disclosure agreement that Charles asked you to sign. That should suffice. This group, myself included, won't want to read anything said tonight in the next issue of *Economic World*."

Worried about losing M.L.'s trust, Pamela sheepishly said, "I'm afraid I've already mentioned tonight's gathering to John Holmes, and that the Governor Dennison and Mayor Sirocco, were expected. But I had no intention of revealing anything I overheard."

"I thought Charles had emphasized the delicacy of your position?" M.L.'s voice was quite chilly.

"Oh, he did." Pamela was deeply embarrassed by having fucked up. "I understand the necessity for my silence, for now. And, you're right to approve the final manuscript. But I didn't see any danger in mentioning my daily whereabouts to John. He's the only person other than your staff, that I've been in contact with."

M.L. turned to face Pamela. "Well nothing can be done about the past, but I must have your sworn promise not to reveal anything, anyone, or anyplace, to John Holmes, not even your mother, unless you first check with either Charles or myself. Is that clear?" without raising her voice M.L. was demanding nothing less than Pamela's immediate and total agreement.

Screw it, Pamela thought, I have no choice.

"We'll leave together and I'll ask Ed to take you down to the car. Ben will take you home. All set?" It wasn't a question.

As Pamela rose to follow M.L., she took a quick look in the mirror. Her face was red, her discomfort so visible, she hoped she'd be able to slip away quietly.

Approaching Ed, M.L. said, " Pamela has to leave. Will you please see that she gets to the car? Have Ben drive her home."

"Of course M.L." Ed looked at Pamela strangely as he led her to the elevator. All the while, Pamela was wondering what was wrong with her. She knew tonight was off-the-record. Why did she even mention it to John?

"Wake up," she muttered. "Access to M.L. and her good will are critical. Without them there is no book!"

CHAPTER XIX

Reentering the main reception area, M.L.'s gaze swept the room. Is it my imagination, or is the deal making in full swing? The Governor and Mayor had moved off to the side. She was guessing that while each man was scanning the crowd, they were really chatting about deals they hoped to close with UCC. Spotting Charles talking to the Club's Manager, she walked over to join them.

"I've removed the extra place setting, Mr. Cray."

"Thank you Lloyd. Are you ready for us?"

"Yes Mr. Cray. Would you like me to announce dinner?"

"No. We'll take care of that."

As the manager walked away, M.L. saw that Charles was relieved she was alone.

"Our guest has been left in good hands I presume?"

"Ben is driving her home. I see we're ready to feed the lions. I'll escort our esteemed Governor and Mayor to their seats," M.L. said.

"I'll take care of Stephen Lambert and Winston Armory."

Surveying the room to locate the rest of her staff, she asked, "Has everyone else been covered?"

"Yes, and Lloyd has his waiters posted inside the door to help any stragglers find their places at the table."

"Then, let's see if we can soften this bunch with more liquor and some red meat."

Time to act social, she thought, and sashayed over to her charges for the evening. She was always amused by her ability to slip into the role of a flirtatious female. A sudden thought of her mother saddened her. She would have accused her of being a Jezebel. As fleeting as it had been, she then thought of E.F. and smiled. He knew she turned on the charm to disarm her opponents. His approval always made the difference, realizing how different she had become from the girl her mother knew. Clearing her mind, she approached her guests. First she took the Governor's arm, and then directed one of her sexiest smiles toward the Mayor, capturing more than his arm.

Aside from her error of underestimating Pamela's reputation, things were going quite well, she realized, as she watched Charles locate his charges for the evening, and then signal William, Ed, Jason and Frank to find theirs. She had Charles rehearse her team earlier that day. Each had been assigned two guests to entertain and develop as useful contacts. Dinner was about to be served.

As the guests settled at the rectangular dining room table, M.L. winked at Charles. Here we go, she thought. As she waited for Charles to introduce her, she covertly studied each of their guests, wondering why she was only slightly nervous. This is my turf, that's why. I represent their future, with UCC being a major source of jobs, goods and services.

"Good Evening, Gentlemen," Charles said as he looked at each man at the table. "I couldn't be happier. Meeting, quietly like this, is an opportunity we don't share often enough. Tonight, it is my pleasure to introduce you to Melissa Horn, our Chief Executive Officer. And hopefully, your newest friend at UCC."

The applause could have been warmer she thought, as she rose from her seat at the head of the long table. "Gentleman, I'd like to offer a toast," holding a fluted glass of Champagne by its stem, and waiting for her guests full attention. "To each one of us, success. May we all profit from working together."

Was it her use of the word profit that had them smiling? "Now that we have officially met, I am looking forward to getting to know you."

She saw Charles grin as he listened to the men chuckling at her flirtatious delivery. Now that Pamela was no longer there she was pleased to see their guests begin to relax. Or was it because in the brief time they had a chance to meet her, these protectors of New York thought she'd be someone they could use?

As she stood sipping her wine, the Governor rose and turned toward her. Raising his hand for attention he said, "Friends, I'd like to add to Ms. Horn's toast. First I'd like to welcome this charming lady to our Club. I sincerely hope we can put our differing ideologies and politics aside. Here's to M.L. and UCC. May those of us here tonight, usher in a new era of good will."

If she had been given a diamond bracelet M.L. couldn't have been more surprised. Giving the Governor a toothpaste-bright smile, she acknowledged his toast and wondered what his public display was going to cost the corporation when the game of hard ball began.

"Gentlemen, why don't I save my speech for after dinner." M.L. saw that her willingness to put socializing before business was rewarded with one whistle and good-natured laughter. "So please, let us enjoy ourselves." As she sat down, the men began to chat with their neighbors, and begin to eat with a hearty abandon. Wineglasses were kept filled, and the experienced Club staff served and removed dishes without disturbing the flow of conversation.

Dining at a leisurely pace, M.L. had kept her third eye on her staff. Watching them charm each of her guests. The Governor's willingness to play along had encouraged the Mayor to open up. She was half-listening to him describe the difficulty he was having in working with the leaders of the Muslim community in Harlem. Glancing at Charles, she saw his red-gold head and handsome profile animated in conversation at his end of the table. And Ed, and Frank were equally involved with their charges. Probably trading sports stories, she thought. Jason and State Treasurer Armory were doing arithmetic on the tablecloth using their knives as invisible pens. Two of a kind, she thought. When she looked over to William she saw him engaged in serious conversation, and made note to ask Frank, sitting one seat away what he was talking about. He was such a complex and unlikable man. Maybe he never learned how to have fun, she thought.

Looking up from her creme brûlée, M.L. nodded to Charles, signaling that the serious part of their agenda was about to commence. Gracefully rising from the table, she invited Denny, a.k.a. Governor Dennison and Paul, the Mayor, to join her. "Gentlemen," she said to the rest of her guests, "Let us adjourn to the other room for an after dinner libation."

Charles watched as cummerbunds were straightened, and ties adjusted, as one by one the men began to leave the room. Standing near the door he greeted several old college chums, and was somewhat surprised to have Senator Lambert detain him with a slight tap on his shoulder.

"Spunky. I hope you're enjoying yourself," Charles said in response. They had been buddies since prep school and roommates at Yale. Spunky and Red shared a bond of family and background that separated them from most of the men in the room. They often shared secrets to help one another survive in the dog-mean world in which they worked.

"That's some Lady! You should wed that one, Red."

"Are you match making again? Last time Regina had you fixing me up with Mary Jane Hamilton. Even you wouldn't marry her. All family, and no fun. Anyway, I don't think Mother and M.L. would get along. A conflict of wills. Anyone Regina chose would have to be more docile."

"You're not going to let that stop you?"

"No. But my Boss is just that. Out of bounds."

"Maybe Regina's scared off every other female in your life. But, my guess is this one's different. Though I must admit I'd hate to bring anyone home for your mother's approval. Male or female," he said, patting Charles's back in sympathy.

Charles was uncomfortable. Spunky knew Regina and his girl friends were off limits, even for him.

"Red, this is the most animated can of worms I've been among in a long while."

"Do you have something special we need to talk about?" Charles was not fooled by his friend's relaxed charm. Spunky looked distinguishably vague at times, but Charles knew it covered a politically astute mind.

"Red, you've got a serious enemy."

Looking around the room Charles saw challenges, but no real enemies. The question in his eyes led Spunky to whisper, "Not here."

Taking his friend by the arm, Charles led him off to the now empty bar.

"I'm all ears," Charles wondering what his friend had uncovered.

"I was visiting with my brother Rob last weekend. By the way, he wanted me to thank you for sending him that stock tip. It seems he's made a killing and is now busy putting it to work. How come you never let me in on it?"

"Rob called me to see if I knew anything about graphite fibers. I told him what I knew and of a small firm in Ohio that was using them in golf clubs. He must have looked into their stock and bought some."

"That's my brother. If you can hunt, fish, or golf with it, he's interested."

"That can't be what you have on your mind Spunky."

"No. I wish it were that simple. Rob had more than stock profits on his mind. He wanted me to warn you about Fallon. He's out to scuttle your purchase of that Bio firm."

"How did you know we are about to make that acquisition?"

"I know because Fallon wanted my brother to help fund him so he could purchase it himself. You know Rob's well connected with those West Virginian money deals. Well, Fallon took him hunting. Rob shot his deer, and Fallon tried to trap Rob."

"Will Rob get into bed with that Buzzard?"

"No. He told Fallon he was pretty well covered for now, but he'd give it some real serious thought. Rob told me that whatever that man's history, he is still someone you have to take seriously."

"That bastard. I wonder if its BioTech or M.L. Fallon's after?"

"What do you mean?"

"It's an old story. M.L. and Fallon crossed talons several years' back. And she bested him."

"So Rob would be buying into a blood sport? I'll warn him."

"Thanks Spunky. I owe you for this. Thank Rob for me. And tell him to watch his back. Fallon's deadly."

Charles led his friend back to the main room where conversation was humming over brandy, coffee and cigars. M.L. was nowhere in sight. Turning back to the dining room, he saw her returning from the back hallway. Signaling her to meet him in the bar, Charles slipped out to follow.

"Yes Charles?"

"Lambert's brother was approached by Fallon to go into a deal for the purchase of BioTech."

She appreciated Charles not waiting to deliver the bad news. Her anger was on slow burn.

"How in hell did Fallon know about BioTech?" Charles demanded. "We've protected ourselves in every conceivable way. Hell, M.L., we don't even send our memos by interoffice mail."

"I think I know," she said. "I'll have E.F. check into Fallon's activities. Do you think you could check with Lambert's brother? Find out when Fallon approached him? And anything else he might know. Even suspect? I take it he doesn't like our old pal?"

"I doubt it. The Lamberts are all straight shooters. I know Rob. I'm sure he'll tell me what he knows. Maybe he can even go digging for us."

"West Virginia again, she said. Frank's old stomping grounds. Maybe he can find out what's going on in the trenches. Why don't you ask Ed whom he knows in neighboring Ohio? I suspect that's where the deal will be put together."

"Through a union?"

"Maybe. If so, it's unofficial. We'll gather our resources and meet tomorrow in my office. Oh, and Charles, let's make sure William is out of this loop. Warn the others."

"Is he a problem?"

"I don't know yet. But he's still unproven to me. So he's out for now."

"This isn't the first time you've shut him out. I don't like the guy either, but I have to admit he's one damn sharp attorney."

Not answering Charles, M.L. was now thinking about the balance of the evening. Standing just outside the comfortable room furnished in small groupings of upholstered chairs and sofas, she wondered how her guests would receive her presentation. "Has everyone settled inside?" M.L. asked.

"Yes. Shall we begin the negotiations?"

"Not yet. Let's let the Boys settle in with their brandy and cigars. I want them as relaxed as possible."

"Before you cut them down to size?"

"Would I be so rude? No, just to be able to catch them off guard."

"I see you've got an admirer in Paul Sirocco. What did you promise, M.L.? Support for his campaign for reelection?"

"Yes. But he thinks it's going to be fiscal. I'm betting I can make him practice what he's been preaching. Especially if we help some of our favorite projects along."

"You mean his job training for teens and school dropouts?"

"Among others. His heart is in the right place, but he's powerless to get anything going. He'd never last in business."

"How can you get to the Senators? They'll need backing too. We only have so much we're allowed to contribute to each campaign."

"I was thinking of your old publicity stunts. Have them cut a couple of ribbons for UCC. Smile at the cameras and make sure the photos get distributed around the State."

"Can't hurt. You really did listen and learn when you worked for me."

Acknowledging Charles' compliment with a smile, M.L. strolled into the room moving slowly toward the crackling fireplace. She saw Charles move off to the side of the room, keeping within her line of sight, but behind their seated guests. Around the perimeter of the room, she saw the rest of their team stood at the ready. M.L. knew that her quarry were all relaxed. Their jackets unbuttoned and several bow ties loosened. It was, as E.F. said, the time to separate out the bulls from the steers.

"Gentlemen. I'm delighted you could join us tonight. I've watched you all for years. Even learned a couple of things not in those text books." The laughter was deep and throaty.

"So you might say I'm eager to work with you on a one-to-one basis."

Looking around the room, she saw Senator Lambert wink at Charles. The Mayor was settling into the depth of his club chair, apparently soothed and not expecting trouble. And Denny, bless his black heart, was drawing contentedly on his large cigar. He had made his opening play, toasting to cooperation and good will. Hinting that UCC, or M.L. any way, would be welcomed to the Governor's Mansion in Albany.

"I invited you here in the hope that we will be able to work together for the benefit of New York and UCC."

Looking at her audience, M.L. saw interest but no concern. "I'm aware of your prior dealings with my predecessor, Jack Foster. And I want to offer you my continuing attention to plans you began with him. And to begin some new projects of my own."

Are you listening Governor Dennison, she wondered and was pleased to see his eyes riveted on her. Would he remember Jack Foster's threat to move UCC out of New York? As she had expected, the room began to buzz. No one talking to her, but all discussing ways they could work with UCC

"Gentlemen. I love this city. So I hope we can come to some mutually beneficial agreements." As she looked toward the Governor, she caught him nailing the Mayor with a look she knew meant trouble. Good, she thought. Denny got her implied threat, that she might still pull UCC out of their reach. A man might have cussed, ranted and threatened, accusing this group of having bled business with their ever-increasing taxes and invasive rules. But she just announced her willingness to work with this bunch. She didn't have to go into details tonight. They had all heard the rumor. Now they knew it was still possible that UCC would pull up stakes.

"Now men." Governor Dennison was the first to speak his thoughts. Standing to face the room he hooked both thumbs in the edges of his tuxedo jacket pockets, and rocked back on his heels. He was the picture of confidence. "This little lady is offering to work with us. And I'm sure we can help her out. After all we've got more than two centuries of experience sitting in this room. We can afford to share a little of that with her."

"Thank you Denny," M.L. said, struggling to hide her irritation with the Governor's chauvinism. After he sat down, M.L. once again addressed her guests.

"Gentlemen. I appreciate your good will. So why not ask me all those "what if" questions I'm sure you're just dying to get some answers to?"

Standing calmly, her eyes studying each man for his reaction, she noticed that a couple of the men groaned, then laughed and quietly counted their fingers. They'd ask questions, just to be polite, she thought. The real questions would wait until she had asked hers.

CHAPTER XX

William Foley awoke drawing his senses inward, arming himself for the next round in his daily fight with the world.

"Shit. I've overslept," he grumbled, as his turtle-like eyes registered 6 AM on his bedside clock.

"That Bitch sure looked the fool last night." His glee propelling him out of bed with a bounce. Heading for a hot shower, Foley's raptor-like mind began planning his day. He had already decided to get to the office at 10. He deserved a morning-after hour or two of leisure. He had work however, not leisurely pursuits, planned for his brief morning at home.

The glass-enclosed stall was steamed opaque. Foley, standing with his head hanging down, let the pulsing flow of hot water soothe the top of his neck and shoulders. "I love this city," he said, mimicking M.L.'s voice. "Shit. If that didn't cause UCC to lose face I don't know what would," he said, continuing a dialogue with himself. "And our good Mayor. Wasn't he something? Paulie may look like a choirboy, but rumors say that his Grandpa was a made man. He's the first generation of respectability, and has got to be laughing himself silly. No worse than our Senator Jimmy James. He's nothing more than a cardboard cutout for the upstate Democratic machine. His report on Ms. Bitch must have Albany already making plans to use her to their advantage. I couldn't have planned things better myself."

The grooming ritual complete, Foley dressed in the suit pants and shirt his housekeeper had laid out for him the night before. Leaving his tie, jacket, and shoes for later, he slipped into his silk robe and leather slippers, and headed for the Library. Violet had his black coffee and plate of scones waiting on his desk. His usual breakfast table complete with newspaper and telephone.

Rubbing his eyes he promised himself that as soon as he took over BioTech he'd get some badly needed sleep. He had been operating on five hours a night, ever since M.L. had taken his job.

Sipping his coffee he began a review of Dearling's report, reading the opening paragraph with satisfaction. It detailed their progress in the negotiations to purchase BioTech for Neuwirth Investments.

OK, he thought, now that Dearling's set our price at $200,000 above the one I submitted for UCC. He should be hearing from BioTech's attorney soon.

The rest of the report detailed funding for the purchase. Noticing that they were still short by some $6 million, he wondered if it was time to reconsider contacting his wild card. "Where is that taxi receipt," he muttered aloud. Searching his desktop of accumulated notes as diverse in size as origin, he grabbed for a two-day-old taxi receipt. Turning it over he saw the telephone number he'd scribbled on his way home from UCC's opening cocktail party. Delighted he had taken the gamble of approaching Nathan Fallon at the UCC function. Now there was one tricky player, if he'd ever spotted one. Foley wanted to get this man's attention, so he could get Fallon to invest in the BioTech syndicate. After reading Dearling's report on the man, he decided to contact Fallon himself.

Fingering the receipt, Foley couldn't help remarking, "And he started talking to me. He was sure plain about hating M.L. I wonder why?" How could he know her well enough? Even knew about Neuwirth, and said to call him if I had anything interesting. How did he make the connection? Dearling says he's OK, on the surface. Maybe, and maybe not. He knows too much.

Picking up the phone he punched in Fallon's number, at the same time noticing that it was only 6:30. Fallon said he only slept three hours a night. Told him to call any time. That's probably all I'll need when I reach 80, he thought.

"Mr. Fallon please. William Foley calling." The voice answering the phone had been young, female, and empty.

"Yeah? Got anything for me," the crass voice answered.

"Maybe. In fact I have one position open for $6 million in that deal we discussed the other night. Interested?"

"How much do I get for my $6 million? 60%?"

Shivering as if a cold hand had brushed his neck, Foley suddenly recalled an earlier conversation he had with Jason. He had been pumping Jason for names of people that played the market of mergers and acquisitions. Fallon's name came up, but Jason had dismissed him as too dangerous. Saying that Fallon would only play if he had a controlling interest in a venture. Damn if Jason wasn't right.

Collecting his wits, Foley replied, "No Sir. Your initial position would represent a little more than 12%. Actually 12 and one-half."

"Not interested." The phone connection was cut with a bang.

Slumping backward, Foley's pudgy hands were white from squeezing the arms of his chair. "Am I happy he cut me off?" He broke out in a fearful sweat as he pictured Fallon getting control of *his* business.

"Dearling will just have to find us another sucker." Closing his eyes, Foley said an unaccustomed prayer in relief, knowing he had faced the devil and escaped. What had he been thinking of? No one would control him. Not ever again. But he was still shaking from his brush with Fallon.

Picking up Dearling's report, he resumed reading. Reviewing something he controlled soon restored his nerves.

"OK," he said, his voice now steady. "With the money almost set, Dearling's next task is to convince Lawrence Henderson that Neuwirth is committed to supporting BioTech's on-going research. Now there was one strange duck, Foley thought. He couldn't find out much about the elusive scientist. Nothing that would make Foley change his plans. BioTech was just a little firm out in the sticks of Queens. Not even mentioned by the market insiders as important to the burgeoning field of medical research. Not yet, anyway, Foley thought. I'm going to put BioTech on the map.

Yeah, he thought. Dearling just had to convince the old man that he was a humanitarian. If I'm right, all Henderson cares about is continuing to spend time in that laboratory of his. Slamming the report on the desk, he almost shouted, "I want BioTech sewn up by the end of the month." Realizing just how close that was, he decided to cover his ass and tell Dearling to up the stakes another $800,000, over the initial $40 million offer. For protection. Just in case the Bitch forces me to submit a counter offer for UCC.

All these years of living in UCC's shadows, he thought, his face a mask of hate. "Fuck it," he swore. "Just 48 more hours you Cunt, and you'll wish you never heard of UCC or William Smythe Foley."

CHAPTER XXI

Has it only been six hours since we left this room, M.L. wondered, as she watched her tired staff, minus William Foley, take their seats at the table. The entire Club had been scoured. Last night's cigar butts and glasses replaced by tall floral arrangements, sweetly scenting the room.

Time for the postmortem, she thought. Last night's bunch had been the toughest crowd she'd yet dealt with. Compared to Fallon, M.L. decided the politicians were more dangerous. Fallon was merely evil. This bunch stood rooted in shifting sand. She knew only too well that their attention was divided by ego, position in the pecking order of their respective parties, their constituents, and last but not least, their degree of greed. Each one balanced his agenda differently. E.F. had given her a thumbnail sketch on the main players. Now she wanted her staff's analysis.

Lifting his steaming cup of black coffee, Charles saluted M.L. and each one at the table. "All in all I think last night was a good beginning," he said. "Now we can divide up our political friends and begin to make quiet entreaties."

"Charles" M.L. began. "I'd like to hear your postmortem. Can we work with this group? Will they accept our demands?" Secretly, she really wanted to know what the boys thought of her. Had she come across as female or bull dyke? Having no role models to fashion herself after, she had developed her own style. She thought of it as a role. One she wore like an actor, dressed for power.

"You turned their heads so far around that by the time you've made your demands, they'll give us some of what we need. Even Denny, our illustrious Governor will deal with you. If not for the good of New York, at least to look good to the State's business leaders."

Nodding, M.L. thought, so E.F. was right again. Men will do business with a woman as long as they get something they need in return.

"I'm used to union leaders M.L.," Frank said. "But I've never seen wheelers and dealers like this bunch. My street sense tells me that if you don't box them into any corners, or publicly embarrass them, they'll deal." "Frank's right, M.L." Ed jumping into the discussion. "I was talking to our Mayor. He's got so many factions screaming at him to create jobs, I'll bet that even a little help from us would go a long way. I'll draft a memo outlining his hot spots. Some parallel our own human resource needs. I figure there are at least two areas we can help him with right away."

"What are those, Ed?"

"He needs to create jobs for two groups. High school and college kids. And those on welfare."

"How about the homeless? Did he mention them?"

"No. But the way I see it, if we get people off welfare, some of the homeless will be pulled in."

"You know," Jason said. "I could use some of those college kids to help me crunch numbers. It shouldn't cost much, and the kids could earn credits toward their degrees."

M.L. watched as they each offered suggestions. Noting those jockeying for larger budgets, or more control. "Ed, why don't you write it up for me? Outline the number of interns we could hire and the length of time it would take to train them. You might see if you could attract any special talent to mainstream after graduation. And Ed, rework that budget. Give Jason someone he can work with!"

Smiling over to Jason, she knew she'd cut days off his negotiating with Ed for extra help.

"Ed, I'd love to get some whizzes, kids born with an 8th sense . . . computereze. If I'm to help Winston Armory balance his State budget, I'll need the extra hands."

"Remember our attempts to expand our recycling facilities," Frank said. "Why not encourage the city to use our facilities on a restricted basis? Charles couldn't you turn it into some neighborhood program? Use a grass roots approach to keep neighborhoods clean?"

"We sure could Frank. In fact it would also add to the Mayor's visibility. Useful with his reelection coming up."

"Fine." M.L. said. Looking at her notes she wondered what had happened to her handwriting. It used to flow like a Steuben sculpture. Now it looked like broken shards of glass. "Ed, I'll review your memo tomorrow. Jason, yours as well. Frank, why not combine Charles public affairs concept into your notes on recycling. If you're right, it could be just the carrot we need to reduce some of our City taxes."

Before continuing, M.L. waited for the men's attention, sensing it was time to bring up the problem of Fallon.

"Gentlemen. Last night Charles was given a warning concerning Nat Fallon. I'll let him fill you in."

M.L. sat back and watched as the news, about Fallon wanting to purchase BioTech was revealed. Of the entire group, only Frank and Ed had worked with her at Weston Coal. All three shared the scars of Fallon's attempted takeover. She knew they were thinking about the Buzzard's tactics. What was it Frank had said when they had been hip deep in unexplained accidents? Knowing Fallon was better than basic training. It was something you either lived through and learned from, or were mortally wounded in the process. He had his own reasons not to like Fallon. One of his goons had sent Frank to the hospital with a crushed knee.

Suddenly aware that conversation had ceased, M.L. looked at Frank. "Got it," was all he said. Nodding, she knew that he too was remembering Weston Coal.

M.L. made a note to call Frank later that morning. She didn't want him to take revenge. While they had all come a long way from the coal fields, and Frank had learned to control his temper, she knew Fallon could make a butterfly attack.

"I'll check into the official Union position on Fallon," Ed volunteered. "His status as an employer, and any public support or contributions he's made to their coffers."

"Remember Tony, Ed?" M.L. said.

"Sure do. Union Shop Steward at Weston. We were close for a while. He'd probably be able to dig around in Ohio if I asked him to. His sister had a run-in with one of the Buzzard's bodyguards. I might even pay Tony a quick visit. If I remember correctly he had a taste for Balducci's homemade sweet sausage and sun dried tomato and onion focaccia."

"Good." M.L. said, as she checked another item on her list. One left, she thought. Looking at the tired faces awaiting her next instructions. "Before we divvy up our friends for some special attention, I want you to know how much I appreciate the added hours you've put in to get these plans underway. Just as soon as this first month is over, why not take some time for yourselves."

"Great. I'll take a cruise to the Pacific," Ed said. This caused Frank to laugh. Everyone knew of Ed's fear of the sea. "And you Frank?" Charles asked, joining in the banter.

"Oh I'll rent a cottage in Mykonos."

M.L. knew Charles loved the Greek island. "How about the UCC cabin and yacht for a four day weekend instead?" she volunteered. Looking at the smiles of gratitude, she remembered why she liked these guys. They were all pros, and still they enjoyed a private life. She was jealous of their wives and comfortable homes. Even bachelor Charles, was active in social and charitable circles. Well maybe some day I'll find time for myself, she thought. But for now, UCC's my life.

"Back to business gentlemen. We had better decide who's to follow-up with each of our guests. Jason, did you get to talk with our overly burdened Mayor?"

"Yes. I believe I can help him to make headway with the holes in his budget. I don't think he knows where the serious money leaks are. Armory let slip some of his plans for the next State budget. Maybe I can work some tips into my suggestions that will counter those cuts?"

"Be careful. You don't want Armory reminded that he let that information slip. Let me see your rough draft next week. Be sure to remind his Honor, that if we aren't given special consideration with his proposed real estate and corporate tax increases, we can still pull up stakes."

"Remind?" Jason wanting to be clear on her instructions.

"Yes. No threats just yet. But I'd like you to call him today to thank him for coming. Arrange a date for lunch. After, we've had a chance to review Ed's suggestions on creating jobs."

"M.L.," Ed began. "I was talking to our Senator Lambert about his pet subject, education. I think I have a way to incorporate our ideas on special education for advanced students into his school reform platform."

"Good Ed. Why not follow-up and develop Lambert. Can you bring me a plan when I get back from next week's trip?" Looking toward Charles she saw his approval in having selected Ed to develop Lambert. She knew Charles would rather keep his friendship with Spunky in the background.

"What will you do with William?" Charles asked, giving voice to the unspoken question.

The room quieted to a vacuum stillness. Just how honest can I be? M.L. wondered. Tell them I just don't trust the man? Placing her forearms on the table, she leaned forward and said. "Of you all, William is the only one I have never worked along side of, until now. Since I have been working with him on a one-to-one basis, I didn't feel it was necessary for him to join us this morning." Her voice held a warning. For now Foley wasn't one of them.

"Anyway I have decided to have William keep company with Senator Sean Molloy. He could be useful to us in Washington, since he serves on the health care issues committee."

Taking a quick look at her notes, she continued, "Frank do you know our State Senator Roy Madison?"

"Yes. He visited our Rochester plant last year as a favor to me."

"Do you think you would have any influence with his attempts at friendlier relations with the major union chiefs?"

"We might, if we can retrain his thinking about the evils of corporate management."

"Would you tackle him? See where he's had difficulties in the past? Then see if you can identify opportunities to help him develop better relations with the key players. Let's go over your notes when I get back."

"I know Roy likes a good fishing trip. Why don't I invite him up to the corporate cabin the weekend after your return?"

"Sounds like just the macho thing for plotting against our union friends. "Lets see, that leaves you and the Governor, Charles."

"Right M.L.," Charles replied.

She saw that he was delighted that she had given him this plum. Charles and the Governor Dennison had gone to law school together. She knew he wanted the opportunity to develop him as a contact.

"I know Denny's main theme for New York is its economic revival," he said. "It's all he talked about last night. I think we can sweeten his hand for the upcoming election. Help him to develop incentives to encourage industrial investment. That of course, includes our expansion up state. I'll put together a plan and schedule a quiet dinner with Denny aboard UCC's yacht, for the weekend after next."

"Let's polish up our social skills gentlemen. Be sure our guests are made to feel appreciated."

Diving into her eggs Benedict, M.L. began listening to Frank and Ed share some of the comments made after she had left the party. She knew, because Frank had told her earlier, that she had rated comments from "That's quite a broad" to "Some piece of ass." But this morning, the conversation covered the political ambitions of their guests, each of whom had made his bid for support to one of her staff.

While savoring her coffee, M.L. looked over the rim of her cup to Charles, who caught her eye and gave her a thumbs up. The missing William Foley could be handled by Charles, she thought. Maybe he could find out what Foley had been talking to Senator Lambert about?

"Anyone going to the office?" she asked after the quick breakfast had been eaten. "You can ride with me if you like." M.L. was pleased to see them all accept the three-block ride. She liked working with them. And she remembered the old days. Working alongside Ed and Frank. She had rolled up her sleeves and was treated like one of the guys. Charles and Jason, of course, hadn't had the same blue-collar positions, but they had also treated her as a peer. Her elevation to CEO hadn't seemed to cause any jealousy in these ranks. Foley, was still an unknown. E.F. had warned her to watch the disagreeable little man. But his manner hadn't been that of a jealous employee. No, there was something else going on, she thought, making a mental note to talk to E.F. again about him.

M.L. knew she could rely on this group to back her all the way. After all, they knew she was their ticket for notice by the UCC Board.

Just before she got into the car, M.L. stopped Charles. "After Ben drops us at the office, would you swing by and pick up Pamela? Maybe you could find out if she was upset by her abrupt departure last night? You know, reassure her. We want her content, not more suspicious than usual."

"Sure thing. I like her pluck. I'll make sure she didn't take anything personally."

Entering the limousine M.L. pulled down the facing seat for Charles. As she squeezed into the remaining space on the back seat, she accidentally poked Jason in the ribs. "Even limos get crowded", she quipped. Jason's smile reflecting his good nature and moved over crowding Frank, who said, "Careful kid. You don't look big enough to need all that room." Laughing at Frank's comment, M.L. saw that Jason only took half the width of either Frank or Ed.

As the limo pulled away from the curb, M.L. picked up the car phone, and punched in Pamela's number. "Good morning, Pamela. I won't be able to pick you up this morning. Charles asked me to call and say that he would be by in about 20 minutes." Not hearing anything to indicate that Pamela was upset, she closed her short conversation. "I'll see you when you get in. Bye." Hanging up, she looked at each of her team and cautioned, "Not one word to Pamela or William. Not even a hint about anything decided or discussed this morning. For now they are both on a need to know basis!"

*   *   *

Rubbing her neck, M.L. felt drained of all energy. With the first two receptions over, and her staff developing their new best friends, she needed to time for herself.

Picking up her phone, she dialed her masseuse. "Jenny, do you have time for me? Say in half an hour, at 11?"

Sighing with relief at Jenny's being able to fit her in, M.L. cleaned the top of her desk. She would be back in two hours and do triple time to handle the rest of her work.

Grabbing her handbag and coat, she left the office telling Mary where she was going and not to contact her unless it was an emergency. She needed a break and planned to eat lunch out.

Now lying on the table, wrapped in warm towels, M.L. closed her eyes and emptied her mind. Jenny's massage had her body unkinked, and the warmth seeping into her bones from the heated oil, was relaxing the rest of her.

I need some R&R, she thought. Maybe E.F. can get Jordan Rockwell's yacht for the evening. Lifting the phone at her elbow, she dialed E.F.'s private number.

"Hi."

"Where are you Honey?"

"At Jenny's. I had the most wonderful thought. Could we dine aboard Rocky's yacht tonight? I know it's a little brisk. But we'll be inside. Just the two of us?"

"Sure thing. I know he's out at the ranch. I'll call him. Don't bother calling back. Meet me at the 23rd Street boat basin. I'll call you if there's a change in plans. Is 6 OK?"

"Yup. 6 it is. Even if I have to take work home."

CHAPTER XXII

Jumping up from behind her desk, Bridget Curry rushed to greet her boss. "Good Morning, Mr. Foley. Your messages." Standing at attention, she awaited his directions.

William Foley took the slips of pink paper from his secretary's small square hand, unaware of her anxious to please smile.

"Thank you Miss Curry. Are there any envelopes from Ms. Horn?"

"No Sir. You had a messenger delivery though. I didn't open it. It's marked confidential. I placed it on your desk."

Storming into his office, Foley slammed his door shut, and ripped open the wrapper of the sealed package. Removing an expensive envelope with an engraved return address, he saw that it was from the law firm representing BioTech. Dearling must have received it earlier that morning, he thought as his trained eye scanned the labyrinth of language, devouring the one page letter. All of a sudden the dense type blurred.

"Calm down and read the damn thing," he muttered, his eyes searching for the essence of the final sentence. 'It is, therefore, Dr. Henderson's decision not to accept your offer of purchase.'

William fell backward into his chair, shaking with rage. It can't be over, he thought. There must be a way. "I'm going to own you," he swore. "Damn the cost." His mind was a jumble looking for a pattern. Punching his intercom, he barked, "Miss Curry, get me Dearling on the phone."

Locking his short legs at the ankles, his toes just touching the floor, he began to reread the letter. Trying to focus his mind on something that made sense, Foley thought of his former boss, Jack Foster, and their conversation that had started his whole revenge-driven odyssey for power. It was one week before the CEO's sudden death. Foster had told him that he'd been thinking of retiring. That was only five months ago, he realized.

"William, I'm sorry to be the one to tell you. But the Board will not consider you as my successor."

He remembered Foster's look of resignation, and for the first time realized that even Jack had people to report to.

"I don't understand. After all you've done for the corporation, I'd think they'd trust your judgment? You're not planning to retire before the end of the year. There's still time for me to prove myself to them."

"I may be CEO, but I don't own UCC. Our Board is an unusually strong one, with three of the six Directors controlling the majority of our voting stock. I did sponsor your promotion. But is seems they've been thinking about looking outside UCC for my replacement."

How angry he'd been. He'd worked for Foster for five years of 80-hour weeks. To find out that the real power was held by the Board, had been a shock. Foster, their Chief Executive Officer, only ran UCC.

Foley wasn't going to be pushed aside, and began planning to get even. Ingratiate, interfere, and eliminate, that's how he'd do it. Now, he was so close. Without BioTech, UCC would fail. Oh they wouldn't close down. But they wouldn't continue to be a shareholder's darling. They'd end up being swallowed by a bigger fish. He wondered if after all his planning, he'd have to settle for merely ending the corporation's name.

When Foster died shortly after that conversation, Foley had enjoyed a brief period of direct access to the Board. But he had to admit he wasn't in their golden circle. They respected him. That much he knew. For two months, he'd been king. Then they hired Ms. Bitch. Oh they had been gentlemen to the core, with their spokesman, E.F. Haynes taking him to lunch and thanking him for his hard work. But in asking him to support the new CEO, Haynes was telling him that he wasn't good enough for their top job. Swearing to himself that he'd get even, he told Haynes he'd accept his offer to serve as UCC's Chief Counsel, reporting to Ms. Horn. He hadn't been asked for his loyalty. That had been assumed. He remembered thinking, only an ass assumes.

"I wonder whom she banged to get my job?" he muttered. All of his connections had failed to find out. The Board was impenetrable. His attempts at finding their individual peccadillo's all failed. It was something he still considered open business.

Bridget's buzzing snapped him back to the present.

"Mr. Dearling is on line #2."

Grabbing the phone Foley growled in a voice that wouldn't carry across the room, "Dearling, how can we reverse this decision?"

"I see. I'll get back." Slamming down the phone, he yelled "Miss Curry."

Rushing for the door, which at that instant was being opened, Foley caught an alarmed Bridget as she fell into his arms. Foley being the first to recover quickly steadied his secretary, without looking at her embarrassed face. In moderately normal tones he asked, "Miss Curry, please get me the Neuwirth file." And turning his back growled, "Immediately."

Bridget returned promptly, placing the slim file on her boss's desk and scurried away.

Foley hoped his secretary wouldn't realize the importance of the Neuwirth file. He only asked for it on the first of the month. While it contained an accounting of investments, it was one file he had never asked her to take dictation for. She had been his secretary for five years. And yet in many ways, she was a stranger. He never had her do personal errands. Not even to send a birthday card to his sister. And she only knew he had a sister because Jane had called him one day.

As Bridget closed the door, Foley booted up his personal computer. He'd had Quinn's son isolate it from the office network. Removing a small diskette from a hidden locked drawer, he inserted it, muttering as he looked at the flashing screen. "Now where do I stand with BioTech shares?" Just as he began to study the information, the phone rang. Barking at the box on his desk, "Miss Curry, I don't want to be disturbed." But the buzzing continued. Christ. Doesn't she listen, he thought, punching the intercom to get rid of the persistent buzzing?

"Sorry to interrupt you Mr. Foley. Miss Horn is on line 1."

Foley knew Bridget's accent was always more pronounced when she was under pressure. It was an Irish/Boston brogue that he was only too familiar with, having tried hard to eliminate his own. As if he could wipe away any traces of his rough childhood.

At the mention of M.L., Foley jolting upright, "I'll take it."

"Hello, M.L. What can I do for you this morning," he opened with a cat-like transition back to William S. Foley, corporate advisor.

"William, I'll want to see you later today. After our return from BioTech."

"Anything I'll need for the meeting?"

"No. Just your sage advice."

Yeah. Even she knows I've got a superior mind, he thought.

"About our meeting with Doctor. Henderson. I'd rather we kept things general. If he has any problems, let's discuss them later. Privately."

"Fine M.L. I'll see you at 11." Hanging up, Foley returned to his study of the monitor and began to chuckle. "Well, well. If M.L. wants to keep any problems between us, that's fine with me. I own more BioTech than UCC. And she can't trace it back to me."

CHAPTER XXIII

M.L. was having misgivings. She hated last minute changes in her plans. Especially when it would delay the merger with BioTech. But she hated leaks more.

Picking up her private phone, M.L. punched in Lawrence Henderson's number. The one that bypassed his very efficient secretary, Emily. This wasn't the time to announce her concerns to outsiders.

"Hello Larry. I'm afraid I have to cancel out on today's meeting. We've got some problems to iron out." She didn't hide the bitter edge in her voice. Larry and E.F. were the only people she didn't have to pretend for.

"How serious are these developments, Melissa? You sound disappointed, but not worried."

"One is only an inconvenience. The other's potentially disastrous."

"Why not start at the beginning."

As she always did with Larry, M.L. unloaded her problems in a cascade of words. "We have a leak that threatens our merger. And E.F. has saddled me with a sharp reporter who's writing a book about me. So you see we don't know who's playing games with us, and I have this reporter tied to my tail. We'll have to put off the signing. At least till I get rid of my shadow."

"That wouldn't be wise Melissa. Have you talked to E.F. about these developments?"

"Not recently. He's trying to verify his suspicions about who's been playing with our stock. And Pamela was his idea. I know you are counting on the sale so you can get your research funds. Can't it wait a little longer?"

"Not if your leak is one of your staff, as you and E.F. suspect. Changing our meeting will only put him on guard. You must keep to your schedule."

"Larry, I'm sure that we are the only ones who know you planned to sell your company to E.F. a long time ago. And, our friendship has always been private."

"One of E.F.'s better ideas. I know, let me be the fly in the ointment. Don't worry Melissa, we'll be careful."

"But Larry, Pamela can't suspect anything until the merger goes through. She's the press! I was only having her come along this morning because we were signing the papers today. After they're signed, we're safe."

"I'm aware of that little problem, and we can't tip our hand. So you must gag your staff. I'll think of something."

"Right. I'll see you at 11. Larry, thanks." Hanging up M.L. felt better. Larry would divert suspicion away from her. For all his decency, he could be a crafty devil. E.F. said he was one of the best card players he'd ever bet against.

Her next call was to alert Charles. This time her voice was back in control. "There may be a change of plans Charles. No matter what Dr. Henderson says, you're not to mention our association with BioTech in front of Pamela. Especially the merger! It's crucial that she's kept in the dark."

"What's happened?"

"I'm not sure. Dr. Henderson has indicated a change in agenda. We want to be careful not to crowd him."

"What ever you say. Do you want me to alert William?"

"No. I'd better call him myself."

She knew she could rely on Charles. It was William she worried about. What was there about him that made her skin prickle? Waiting for the phone connection, M.L. planned just how much she'd tell him."

"William. About our meeting with Dr. Henderson."

"Yes?"

"Since Pamela will be with us, I don't want you to mention our interest in BioTech."

"We're signing the merger this morning," Foley said, careful to keep his voice flat.

Unaware that she'd crossed her fingers, M.L. kept her dislike for the crafty little man from her voice. "Just follow my lead. I want Pamela kept in the dark. Do I make myself clear?"

"Are we still signing the merger papers?"

You're too sharp, she thought. "Probably not this morning. Either way, not a word in front of Pamela!"

"I hear you loud and clear."

Hanging up with Foley, M.L. thought, that was just too easy. He wasn't upset by the possible change in plans. Closing the deal and launching UCC on its new path, was his opportunity to shine. What's he up to, she wondered.

*   *   *

Now that she was on her way, Charles, William and Pamela in the car with her, M.L. felt better. She was alert and ready to follow Larry's lead. She knew Larry had handled details of the merger through a screen of lawyers. While William had negotiated the merger for UCC, he'd never met the reclusive Dr. Henderson, or seen the company. Charles hadn't been to BioTech either. Pamela was still a risk. But this time, M.L. was confident that her exposure would be limited. E.F. and Larry had kept their intended merger between themselves for two years. If word leaked now, all their planning would backfire. The ball's in your court Larry, she thought, as the small group walked into BioTech's unpretentious factory-like building.

The meeting with Dr. Henderson was being held in a molded plastic and aluminum furnished meeting room. Melissa never got over her impression that she was in a public school lunchroom.

"Miss Horn. I'm delighted to welcome you to BioTech," said the slender, white lab-coated gentle man bowing over her hand.

M.L. was amused to see Larry playing the role of corporate host. Being formal and polite, even to her. Oh

Larry, what actors we've become, she thought as she gave his hand a little squeeze.

"Dr. Henderson, may I introduce my associates? I know how you protect your time so I appreciate your seeing us today."

"I'm delighted to welcome you to my little company," he said shaking Pamela's hand first, then Charles' and William's.

"I wonder if you would like a private tour of our laboratory?" Henderson said to Pamela, before looking to the men and including them in his invitation. "Not many people are interested in our work. Miss Horn, however, thought you'd be interested in some of our projects."

M.L. saw Charles and William nod, accepting the invitation. In fact William looked almost pleased. If Larry could keep the tour controlled, it would be a good opportunity to introduce them to the field of bioengineering.

M.L. was reminded of the old sci-fi films, whenever she visited one of BioTech's laboratories. Intent young lab coated people sat hunched over long rows of tables. The rooms always filled by sounds of fingers tapping away on computer keyboards, electronic buzzing of timers and other hi-tech scientific equipment. She had convinced E.F. and Larry that bioengineering was UCC's new reality. Yes, she thought, it was time for Charles and William to be introduced to Larry's work. It offered so much hope for developing treatments to ease pain and suffering.

"Miss Horn?" Dr. Henderson's voice penetrating her thoughts.

"If you agree, I'll arrange for my assistant, Edwin, to take your associates on a tour. But, I'm afraid our meeting will have to be rescheduled. You left your office before I could reach you. We're having a small emergency with one of our projects."

"Nothing serious I hope," Melissa said, hiding a fleeting thought that maybe there really was an emergency. Looking over at Charles she saw him fingering the knot of his silk tie. But he kept his peace. William looked like a blank page. Her executive team didn't like their plans changed.

"Miss. Horn, since you have already seen our little company, I wonder if you might join me for a private lunch? Don't worry, Edwin knows more than I do about our lab. He said he'd be delighted to explain our operation."

Watching Pamela, M.L. saw that she was amused by Dr. Henderson's polite invitation. I wonder if she thinks I'm flirting with him? The thought had her smiling.

"Dr. Henderson, I'd be happy to join you for lunch. I'm sure my associates will be very pleased to have Edwin show them around, without the Boss Lady in tow. If I may have a few moments with them, I'll be ready to join you for lunch."

"I'll wait for you in the lobby," Dr. Henderson answered, and turning to the others took his time to say a personal good by to each of them.

As soon as they were alone, M.L. looked at William and ordered, "Before you leave, set up another meeting with Dr. Henderson's secretary. Make it for the week after next."

Nodding, William pulled a leather folio the size of a business card from his jacket pocket and made a notation.

"I'll trust you to keep your thoughts till later." At her curt command, M.L. noticed William frown. You don't have to like it. Just do it, she thought.

Looking over at Charles, she saw him pacing slowly around the room. "Keep Edwin to a short tour. I don't want Dr. Henderson to think we're trying to steal any company secrets." And with the word secrets, she turned to Pamela. "All off the record. Understood?"

As Edwin entered the room and introduced himself, M.L. was pleased that the ruse was working. Her little group knew what was expected of them, and was listening to Edwin explain what they would see. It was time for Charles and Will to better understand BioTech's commercial possibilities, she thought. As for Pamela, she would just tell her that they were exploring a new avenue in which UCC might be interested in a future co-venture. True, Melissa thought. If tomorrow could be called the future.

Calling after the small group as they left for their tour, M.L. said, "I'll see you all back in my office at 2."

So much for that, M.L. thought, straightening an unseen crease in her skirt. Now let's see what Larry has on his mind.

*   *   *

Seated in a Queens neighborhood Polish-style restaurant, far from prying eyes, Lawrence Henderson had just given their order to the cute 20 something waitress. Cheese pirogi with applesauce for himself. Fresh chicken salad, like his wife used to make, for Melissa.

"We haven't done this in a long time Larry," Melissa said as she eased her back against the plastic padded bench and unbuttoned her suit jacket. "But this isn't social is it?"

"I'm afraid not. I wish it were." Larry's voice sounded unusually somber.

"What's up?"

"E.F.'s right. A Neuwirth Investments has been nibbling at our stock. They're a private investment firm. But I haven't been able to find anything out about them. All the investigator I hired found out, was that their President is a Bruce Dearling."

"So, we're vulnerable. But why is Neuwirth playing your stock? To make a killing when the merger's announced?" Thinking about what she had just heard, Melissa blurted out, "That seals it. The leak, damn it, is one of my staff."

"There's more, Melissa. Neuwirth has also approached my lawyers with an offer that is suspiciously close to UCC's. That would confirm your leak."

Melissa's hand slammed down on the table so hard, that water from her glass jumped onto her plate. "It's Foley. I know it is."

"It's not Foley. He's not stupid. Bruce Dearling is representing Neuwirth. He's a nice enough sort, but no one I'd take home to Ava. He says that Neuwirth has formed a limited partnership interested in acquiring a medical research company. Their group wants to develop BioTech into a major health care entity. But when I asked for specifics he put me off."

"What exactly did you ask?"

"The market they were interested in. Was it controlled prescriptions and over-the-counter worldwide distribution?"

"Did he have any answers you liked?" Melissa felt better when she saw Larry's humor return. If he was smiling it couldn't be too serious, she thought.

"Oh yes." Larry's chuckling caused his blue eyes to twinkle. "He said I could retire in luxury."

Melissa joined in his mischievous laughter. She knew that Larry was the son of a Scandinavian immigrant who had made a pretax fortune on a patent for a process used in manufacturing aluminum.

"Have you spoken to E.F. about the Neuwirth offer?"

"Yes. In fact he suggested I play Dearling along. Then, at today's meeting, announce that you and I needed more time to make a decision."

"So we can gather our facts and confront our snake-in-the-grass with the evidence and threat of exposure."

"My Dear, are you happy?"

The sudden change of subject and concern in Larry's voice broke into her thoughts of revenge. "Don't I look happy? I've got the world. I'm CEO!" Why did his question cause her to doubt her own words?

"You've toughened. It bothers me. As if you've forgotten how to enjoy life."

"I'm just preoccupied. I'm finally flying free of E.F.'s nest, have my dream job, and I'm faced with a traitor." Why was she angry with Larry, she wondered. He only wished her well.

"Since Ava died, coming here helps me remember," he said, his voice calming Melissa's nerves. "Ava always worried you never ate enough. She loved to cook for you."

Larry smiled and began recalling happy times the four of them had shared. M.L. enjoyed reliving the memories with him. Times when she and E.F. had joined the happy couple for old-fashioned home-cooked meals on holidays and the occasional Sunday dinner.

"She treated me like family, always cooking pirogi for me. I know you loved her pirogi, but for me it was her potato pancakes. They were so light they floated above the plate."

"Instead of fattening you," Larry recalled. "She tried to fatten me up. But I fooled her. Hendersons don't have fat genes." He was pleased to see Melissa chuckling along with his memories.

"I miss her too Larry. How have you dealt with her death?" Her love for this man softened her face.

"It's been five long years. Without my research I'd be a grieving shell. Ava was everything good in my life."

"You're one of the lucky ones." The sadness of his loss made her think of her own parents. "You and Ava would have been great parents. I wished mine shared the love you two did." Seeing Larry's questioning look, Melissa wanted to explain her parents to him. "Oh, I knew I was loved, but it was as if all of Mom and Dad's love was saved for me. I could never figure out why they got married."

"People marry for many reasons. Maybe your parents needed to belong to someone. And they gave you all the love they had stored up."

"Maybe. But they were killed in a car crash my freshmen year in college. And it wasn't until a psych course in my junior year that I even tried to figure out my family's dynamics. Enough, or you'll have me crying."

"Melissa, have you ever thought about getting married?"

The question shook her. Larry never pried into her private life. Ava was the only one she ever talked to about her feelings. But she loved this man and answered, hesitantly.

"I've been so busy for so long. When I do go out, usually it's with you or E.F. I never thought I'd missed anything. Until recently, that is."

"Care to tell me about it?"

"There really isn't much to tell. I was on Largo Verde and met a very sensitive and caring man. But that was Largo Verde. You know. No yesterday. No tomorrow. So even if I wanted to find out how I really feel about him, I don't have the time. I have too much to do right now."

Taking her hand in his Larry said, "If Ava were here she'd say, make time for love. Oh how I miss her."

Seeing that her watch read 1:30, Melissa snapped back to the present, rebuttoned her jacket, and replaced her no nonsense face. "Well for now I have enough to worry about." Looking at the sad expression on Larry's face, Melissa knew he didn't want to change the subject.

Taking a deep breath she launched into their problems. "Larry did you notice a rather sloppy man standing on the curb when we got out of the cab?"

In a weary voice, Larry gave her his attention. "What else Melissa? Isn't the merger enough?"

"I hope so. Just the same, did you see him?"

"You mean the brown suit? Yes. What's this about?"

"I've seen him off and on for two weeks. If he just worked near UCC, I wouldn't worry. After all I'm driven everywhere. But the thing is he's there at odd times. And he seems preoccupied with store windows. Or the reflection he sees in them. It's scary."

"Have you seen him around the townhouse?"

"No. Not that that would mean anything if he's a pro."

"Well even if he uncovers your residence, he might not put you and E.F. together," Larry said more to himself.

"If he's a pro he will," Melissa's anger returned. Her private life was of no concern to anyone.

"The problem isn't what he uncovers, but who he's working for Sweetheart! What would happen if your relationship to E.F. were to become public?"

"The Board would demand my resignation. And E.F.'s name would be page one news. Oh Larry, I can't let that happen."

"Let's assume this guy's got your office phones bugged, and a surveillance camera following your every move. Maybe we can tip the scales by planting a little false information."

"Can we?" Melissa's optimism returned at the thought that there might be something they could do.

"You go about your business as if it's going to be a piece for television."

"You mean be even more secretive than usual." I can do that, she thought. I've mastered that little trick anyway.

"That's right. I'll talk to E.F., and then give a friend of mine a call. He used to work for the F.B.I. Now you keep to your schedule. But stay alert for any changes in our Brown Suit. I'll get back to you just as soon as I get anything useful."

Patting Larry's hand, Melissa sighed, "Let's pray he wasn't hired by an enemy trying to blackmail us."

Sipping the last of her coffee, she wished she didn't have to go back to the office. "You know Larry, being with you, even for this little lunch, has me feeling better. Can't we find time to do this again? That seems to be the only problem I haven't been able to solve. Where to buy some time."

They were standing on the curb saying their good-byes. When Larry leaned over to kiss her hand, Melissa regretted being the cause of the added worry she saw in his face. Yes, she was tense. What could he expect? But she also knew that she had to win their fight, so he and E.F. could retire.

Flagging a passing taxi, Larry gently helped her into the cab. Just as the car began to move, he warned, "Keep your wits Melissa. This traitor is probably a very lethal fellow. And it's likely he's Brown suit's employer."

CHAPTER XXIV

As Charles turned toward the checkroom to help Pamela off with her coat, M.L. looked toward the decorative stairway leading up to the famed Four Season's Restaurant.

Holding her breath, M.L. thought she recognized the lean broad-shouldered back of a man as he walked out of view. It can't be. The stride and macho assurance wasn't her Hugh.

"M.L.?" Charles said, gently touching her elbow. Snapping back into the present, she shook her head slightly to clear her vision and was careful not to look directly at either Charles or Pamela. "Why don't you two go on up? I'll be along in a minute." She breathed a sigh of relief as Charles, ever the gentleman, led Pamela away.

Once in the powder room, M.L. was relieved to be alone with her sinking stomach and tumbling thoughts. One look at her pale face confirmed her worst fears; she wasn't in control, and she didn't know what to do about it. Calm down. You want to see him again. Just slip upstairs and see if you can arrange to meet somewhere for a late night drink. What if he's not Hugh? Well, old girl, you'll never know if you don't get upstairs. Adjusting the hem of her black knit dress, M.L. headed toward her quandary. Stop it! You know it's Hugh. But will he want to see me? she worried.

M.L. couldn't remember when a short flight of stairs had been so hard to climb. Not only was she unsteady on her 3-inch heels, she could feel her body heat up and knew that meant she'd have a shiny nose and forehead.

Reaching the top of the stairs, she stopped to take a deep calming breath, adjusting her eyes to scan the room's interior, Melissa began a quick but intensive search. First she scoured the bar, famous for its Richard Lippold sculpture suspended from the ceiling above. It's dagger-like forms looked like she felt, all sharp edges. The bar was an island, off to one side of the cavernous Grill Room, mirroring her own feelings of isolation. The dark night circled three sides of the room, behind two story windows.

Suddenly, there he was, steps away. She longed to touch the lean, angular face. But this wasn't Largo Verde and they weren't alone, he hadn't even seen her. She was struck by a jealous flash when she saw Hugh was calmly chatting to a brunette with a figure that made men salivate.

Quickly turning her back on the bar she saw the reservation clerk signaling for her to go on through to the main dining room. Nodding, but unable to move, M.L. was unaware of people brushing past her. Turning slightly, hoping Hugh might be looking her way, she had to finally accept that he was preoccupied with his date.

Shutting down her emotions wasn't as easy as usual. Damn it, she thought as she headed into the dining room. It's going to be a very long evening. Anyway, with that female practically falling into Hugh's lap, what would he want with me? The idea of coming in second hit her in the stomach. She could never compete with that mantrap. Even if he saw me, what could I do about it? Pack up and follow him? I won't even get that chance by the looks of things. He can't take his eyes off her.

M.L. had settled absently-mindedly at the table, and began to half listen to Pamela chat on. As she sipped her wine she desperately tried to keep Hugh out of her thoughts. Pamela had been talking about the outstanding features of the Four Seasons Pool Room. Good. Let her talk, M.L. thought. Charles is good at chitchat. He can keep things going without my help.

"This is one great room!" Pamela was saying, looking around the enormous space. "I really like the way they've done the windows. Using fine brass chains instead of draperies. They distance us from the buildings across the street, and give the city an almost magic look. Charles, this is a prime table. I am impressed."

Charles was smiling at Pamela's enthusiasm.

"You know, these high ceilings make the tables feel farther apart." Turning to M.L. Pamela asked, "Is this a corporate favorite?"

"Yes. I don't feel I'm on display here. I can relax and enjoy my companions and the chef's excellent menu." M.L was surprised her voice sounded so calm.

"Even I like this dining room," Charles added. "It's more masculine than some of New York's other top dining spots. And, while you might not think men are concerned about their weight, I am. Their Spa Menu is among the best anywhere."

"You look content Pamela. How was your day?" If I can keep her talking, M.L. thought, maybe I won't have to.

"I'm ready for my research into the specifics of UCC, your predecessors, and of course, you. I should be ready to start my outline by Monday."

As M.L. began to reply, Pamela looked away, fascinated by something across the long rectangular pool. In an excited whisper she interrupted M.L., "There's Hugh Baron."

"Who Pamela?" Charles wanted to know.

"Only Hollywood's hottest new star. I saw his recent film 'Redemption'. He was awesome!"

"I don't see what's so special Pamela." Charles, glancing across the pool, was giving the famous man a thorough once-over. "He's handsome in a clean cut way. Looks like he'd be a normal sort of fellow."

"Oh Charles, it's not just his gorgeous face and body. He has this vulnerability that makes women crazy. There was some rumor about his hiding out just after his latest film was released. Some mystery about a breakdown, or was it exhaustion? I forget. Even if it's not true, it makes him even more interesting, don't you think M.L.?"

M.L. felt her tongue stick in her mouth. Her mind absorbing Pamela's gossip and knowing how close she had come to the truth. All she could do was nod. Dear God. Let me get through this, she prayed. Instead of continuing the conversation, she picked up her glass. To her surprise, the stem suddenly snapped, spilling red wine over her plate and napkin. A nearby waiter appeared as if by magic, and cleared the mess before she could catch her breath. M.L. was thankful that she hadn't spilled wine on her dress. Now all she could do was wait to see what Pamela would do or say next.

"Have you seen any of Hugh's films, M.L.?"

It was nice of her to ignore my blunder, M.L. thought, before answering. "No, I'm afraid not. Lately I've seen all my films on TV. There just hasn't been any time." Christ, I didn't even know he was an actor, she thought staring at her clean plate and flatware. Twisting her large sapphire ring, she avoided Pamela's eyes, hopeful that it would discourage her chatting on about Hugh.

"Ah. Our first course," announced Charles.

Bless you, M.L. thought. She needed time to absorb this new information. Quietly, she listened to Charles as he began a discussion about their dinner selections, and how pleased Pamela would be with the restaurant's cuisine.

"So this is what all those four star chefs do to keep the Ladies-who-Lunch in their size 6 clothes," Pamela said, while looking at the order of grilled vegetables being placed in front of her. "I almost came here once. But the interview had to be rescheduled for 25 minutes at the office."

"Just wait," Charles said. "I'll bet you thought eating well consisted of rack of lamb and baby vegetables. What the chef does with crab meat is a creation of sublime simplicity."

Throughout dinner M.L. tried to keep conversation going even though she had retreated completely into her protective skin. She was on automatic. It helped to restore her self-control. He hasn't spotted me, maybe he won't, she thought, slowly releasing her breath. At least now I know his name. I guess I'm safe. Safe from what she thought, remembering Larry's concern for her happiness.

As she moved her food around her plate, M.L. realized her appetite had vanished. Maybe it was Pamela's having said that she'd begin looking into her background tomorrow. That's probably all it is, she thought. Wasn't that why Pamela was here to begin with? Just as she began to refocus on what Charles and Pamela were saying, M.L. was suddenly confronted by her handsome secret.

"Melissa? It is you," Hugh said in his soft, melodic voice.

Before Hugh could say anything else, she rushed to stop him from revealing their relationship. With steely control over her nerves, she calmly said, "Hugh. What a surprise? May I introduce you to Pamela Green, she's a reporter with *Economic World*." Her impersonal words were reinforced by her hand firmly squeezing Hugh's forearm.

"And Charles Cray, Executive Vice President with United Chemicals Corporation."

Melissa was acutely aware of Pamela's melting look as Hugh shook her hand.

Standing, Charles reached across her and shook Hugh's hand in a very firm grip, while she studied them both. Hugh had a wide, open face and easy charm, where as Charles was reserved, with perfectly polished manners. As handsome and perfectly groomed as Charles always was, he couldn't compete with Hugh's sheer magnetism. Dressed in western-styled suit, Hugh was larger than life, his well-toned body revealed by the custom-cut of his clothes. She wasn't sure, but she thought that Charles was a bit stiff. Didn't he like Hugh? Could Charles be acting jealous, she wondered.

Shit. Now what do I do, she thought. Manners, as usual, won out saving her from herself. "Are you visiting?" she asked, really wanting to know if Hugh actually lived in her own town.

"Yes. I flew in on the red-eye from the coast this morning. May I introduce Judy Lewis. She's handling my TV appearances while I'm in town."

How can he introduce us when he doesn't know my last name, she thought. Holding out her hand to the 20-something woman, M.L. said, "Hello, Ms. Lewis, I'm Melissa Horn."

"How nice to meet you, Ms. Horn. You can catch Hugh on "GMA" and "Letterman" tomorrow, and on "Regis" on Friday, gushed the young beauty.

"I'm sorry I didn't hear your last name," Melissa quickly interrupting the woman's prattling. She wanted to know who this PR type was. "Are you based in New York?

"Oh yes. I work for Hugh's studio. We're making the rounds promoting his latest film. You've seen it, haven't you?" Without stopping to let M.L. reply, Judy continued. "No? Well I'll have a couple of passes for a private screening sent to your office, or if you prefer, I'll send over a cassette. You'll love it. He's wonderful. His best role yet."

"Thank you," M.L. said as politely as she could, while discretely cataloging the woman's abundant assets. Her crass manner couldn't hide her sculptured curves molded by the red Lycra dress that was short enough to display five feet of shapely legs. Then she saw that Hugh was beginning to look annoyed.

"They've put me up at the Stanhope, Melissa. Maybe we could get together for a drink while I'm here?"

That was all she needed. To have the tabloids pick up her name and hound her about being the secret girl friend of Hugh Baron, star. Wouldn't the UCC Board love that, she thought.

"Meeting you tonight, must be a sign of good luck," Hugh said. "Now I know my trip will turn out well. May I call you Melissa?"

"Please do, Hugh. Just call the UCC . . . I'm sorry, the United Chemicals switchboard and ask for me. If I'm not available my assistant, Mary, will find me," she said, thinking to herself, if you can break away from Lady Legs long enough. M.L. wasn't paying attention to Pamela or Charles as they said their good-byes. She was twisting her ring while her thoughts were following Hugh out of the dining room.

"He sure is a good looking devil," Charles, said to the silent women. Getting his attention, M.L. indicated with a look that it was time to leave. She was unaware of Charles as he signaled for their waiter, and then busied himself with the check.

M.L. was completely off balance, as the trio walked out of the Pool Room. Stopping to shake the Head Waiter's hand, she felt him slip her a small piece of paper. She dared not look at it until she was alone. The torture of waiting made her grasp it tightly. She was sure her nails had permanently impaled it on her palm.

*　　*　　*

At last. Alone, she thought, and retrieved Hugh's now damp and crumpled note from her hand. Adjusting the car's reading light, Melissa read the telephone number and immediately picked up the phone at her elbow. "Let him answer," she prayed aloud, suddenly aware of her shortness of breath.

"Lissa?" the deep voice asked.

"Yes Hugh. Where are you?"

"I'm at a friend's apartment on Central Park West. Are you alone?"

"Yes, I just dropped off Pamela and Charles."

"Can you join me?"

"Yes. Give me the address." It was hard to talk. She needed time to get used to the idea that she was going to see Hugh. "Hugh?"

"Yes?"

"Never mind. I'm on my way." I can't ask if he's alone. I'll just have to play this out, she thought. Rolling down the window between the front and back seat, she gave Hugh's address to her driver.

"He still cares," she said softly. But how much, she worried. I don't want him if he's involved. Or do I? Stop planning the next step. This isn't a merger. It's romance, she thought. The one thing I'm no good at. Falling back into the deep seat of the limousine, she felt small and scared.

*   *   *

Hugh's hand rested on the telephone receiver not wanting to be separated a moment longer from his magical Lissa. In two short weeks, Hugh Baron, nee Baronowski, had not only regained his confidence but had come to terms with his famous and very public self. And it had all been due to the generosity of this wonderful, delightful, mystery of a woman.

"Imagine finding her in New York. She doesn't belong here," he announced to the telephone. "I know. We'll do the town. I'll have Judy set up a VIP schedule, limousine and all. I'll take her shopping. No I can't do that. The crowds might scare her. Better, I'll arrange to have Tiffany's stay open a little later and have her pick out a gift." Wait a minute, his conscious cautioned. Maybe she's involved with that Charles. "No. Can't be. He's too serious. Lissa needs parties and laughter and California sunshine. She needs me. Bless her gentle heart. She has no idea how much she means to me."

*　　　*　　　*

Having let her driver go for the evening, Melissa entered the canopied entrance and rang 14C on the intercom. Hearing the buzz that released the inner door, her stomach suddenly gurgled. "Oh shit!" Opening her bag she retrieved a mint and popped it in her mouth. A quick touch-up with her compact and she closed the door to the world behind her.

"This is a long way from Largo Verde. Time to see if he's even real," her voice was a tremble and her palms were sticky.

The elevator had opened to a small hallway with three apartment doors. Just as she began to search for 14C, the door on the end of the hall opened to a sight from her dreams. Hugh in slacks and shirt opened to his slim waist, with that smile, only for her.

The arms now holding her close were his arms. His kisses, the ones she had feared she'd never again share.

"Shush Darling," Hugh said.

His kisses were wiping the questions from her lips.

"I've missed you too much," he whispered holding her gently in a warm embrace.

Closing out the world, she released herself to the moment. Snuggling as close to him as she could, all of her doubts vanished, comforted by the tenderness with which Hugh held her. "Hugh?"

"Shush. Don't talk Lissa." Wrapping an arm about her waist he led her into the apartment. "We've plenty of time. I didn't think I'd ever find you."

M.L. was so relived to know Hugh hadn't changed, she released the hidden lock on her heart. As he led her into the living room, she reached up and wrapped her arms around his neck, wanting to feel all of him. Returning his kisses with a hunger of years, Melissa melted her body to fit against his. A fleeting memory of lying in bed with him, flooded her body with a rush of energy. Not wanting to break the mood, she kept her silence, using her mouth to kiss Hugh with all of her pent-up passion.

She felt Hugh gently push her away and look at her flushed face. She knew he was looking for his Lissa. Was she still that same woman? Seeing his smile filled with tenderness caused her heart to skip. Oh God, this is so right, she thought, as she felt Hugh take her face in his hands and gently caress her cheeks. Closing her eyes she lifted her lips to his kiss, the very feel of his mouth pulling her closer to him, as if she couldn't get close enough.

"Will I ever get you out of my system," she whispered.

"I hope not."

Hugh's passion-filled voice sent a small shiver through her, as she realized, he wanted her as much as she craved him.

As with those starved for love, emotion replaced logic. And so the evening began. A touching of souls, a tempting of nerve endings. A feast of lovemaking. M.L. at first responded to Hugh's lead. Then, finding her body sensuously stretching and sliding as she rubbed against him. She was aware of his erection, first with her hands, and as her need of him grew, with her entire body.

Later, lying in Hugh's arms, she looked out of the apartment's bedroom window to see a clear sky lit by stars and a now descending moon. We haven't said more than half a dozen words, she thought.

Hugh opened his eyes slowly as she moved slightly within his embrace. He's just the same, she thought, looking into his tender gaze. He's so open to me. I can see his soul.

Not wanting to drift off to sleep and miss even one minute of Hugh's sensuous touch, she wondered how she would find the time to see him again. She knew she'd find a way. But would there be time to talk? To find out who they were outside of each other's arms? The worm nibbling her conscious, worried that Hugh wouldn't like M.L. Horn. Hadn't he been running from controlling women when she'd first met him? What made her think he'd like her anymore than he did the others? Ms. Legs certainly wouldn't control him. Not the way she fell all over him in the restaurant, she thought.

"I must have dozed off after all," she murmured as she next saw the dark sky hinting at the approaching dawn. Looking at her watch, the only item on her naked body, she was disappointed to see that it was almost six o'clock. Moving away from Hugh to caress his sleeping face with her eyes, she reluctantly leaned over to kiss him awake.

"Mm?" Hugh responded, coming to from a deep sleep. "What is it Lissa?"

"I have to go."

"How soon?" Hugh whispered in her ear as he came fully awake.

"Half-an-hour. I have to go home and get ready for work." She was leaning over his long body, resting her weight on her hands.

"When can I see you," his voice asked with an unexpected firmness.

Careful, don't seem too anxious, she thought. "I don't know. I have another dinner engagement tonight," and with a sigh of regret, turned away from his scrutiny, and lay back in his arms.

"Are you really a corporate big shot?" His question filled with doubt.

"Hugh we have to talk," closing her eyes, not wanting him to know about her responsibilities. Not yet. She needed his loving innocence.

"How about you? What's your life like? I've never met a movie star," she was careful to keep her mood light, pulling his arms more tightly across her chest.

"I don't know where to begin. I was so happy to have spotted you. I haven't thought of anything but being with you again. I never thought I'd find you in this town."

"By the way. This Judy, she's your slave if you want her!" She wanted to take the jealous words back as soon as she said them. Her embarrassment grew into anger as she looked up into Hugh's smiling face. Wasn't it bad enough she was jealous and stupid enough to let it show? "I'm sorry. You have a life. I have no right to say anything." What she really regretted was allowing a harsh tone to interrupt their remaining time together.

Chuckling even harder, Hugh shifted his position to lift her chin so she couldn't avoid looking at him. "Darling. I can have all the Judys' I want. But remember me? You're the one who captured my heart."

"Oh Hugh. What are we going to do? My life's so complicated." Snuggling closer into Hugh's warm embrace, she hoped he'd have an answer.

Whispering into her hair, he asked, "Can you take some time off, or short vacation?"

"Not for the next ten months at least," her voice was saddened at the thought.

"What?" he snapped, and bolted up in the large bed.

Hugh's surprise and confusion were only too clear. What else had she expected? Sitting up along side him, she gently explained. "I'm involved in a complex campaign just now that's important to my company. I don't get time off until we succeed."

"Lissa. What do you do at United Chemicals? Are you in advertising? Is the campaign one that your assistant could handle, for a long weekend at least? You do have an assistant?"

"Not really! It's not like that." Not wanting him to know. But why didn't she want him to know? She loved being CEO. She worked her tail off for almost fifteen years to get where she was.

"What do you do?" Hugh's voice pressed for an answer.

Gathering her strength, she replied, "I'm their CEO," and for the first time she was surprised not to find pleasure in having said it.

"Not really." It wasn't a question. It was a statement in awe.

"Yes. Don't you think I'm capable of being a corporate officer?" She was miffed that he had even questioned her. But when she thought about his reaction, she knew he was overwhelmed. He wasn't questioning her ability.

"Calm down Lissa. I don't know anything about your life and I've never heard of a woman running a giant corporation. It's just a bit much to take."

This wasn't going well at all, she thought.

Turning at her hesitant touch, Hugh looked into her face as if to find some answer.

"Regardless of our busy schedules, we have to spend some time together. I can stay in New York for a week. But I'll be starting a new film soon. It's on location in Europe. I'll be away almost ten months."

Relieved that at least he had the week in New York, she leaned back, wanting to feel the warmth and strength of him.

"Anyway, I have to get back to the Stanhope before Judy finds I'm missing. She'd have a fit not knowing where I am."

Come to think of it, she hadn't thought about his schedule, or his life. They had a lot of catching up to do. She relaxed, confident she'd be able to find some way to enjoy the time left. After all it was their love that was important. They'd make it, she knew they could.

"Darling, meet me here at 11 tonight?" his voice pleading for her answer.

"Yes. Of course I will."

The rest of the time went by in minutes. She refused to accept any reality but the present.

CHAPTER XXV

M.L. had just dropped Pamela at home. Looking at her watch, she saw that it was 10 PM, but Pamela couldn't have been more awake.

"What the Hell!" she muttered turning away from the front door to her building. I'm all a jumble, she thought, hailing a passing cab. Leaning into the driver's side window, she said, "Take me to Mickey's on third and 50th."

It was a bouncy ride with the driver hitting every pothole he saw. Figures, she thought. I'd get a driver and cab to match, both broken down wrecks. While she fought to sit upright in the back seat, the car rushed through empty late night streets. She wondered why she was rushing over to Mickey's. But was it Mickey's?

Wise up, she thought. It's really Skip. You don't even drink her conscious chided. Pay attention girl. You could do worse than Skip Moran.

Why did she have these one-sided conversations with her alter ego anyway? She always lost.

Paying the driver, Pamela got out of the cab and looked into the window of the bar. It was different.

Crowded with noisy chatter and laughter spilling out into the street. She had never been to Mickey's at night. Her hour was late afternoon. Between crowds.

Pushing open the door, Pamela didn't know where to go. Looking toward the back she saw that her booth, in fact all the booths and tables were filled with late diners. Mostly thirtyish, corporate types, all dressed in versions of T-shirt and jeans. Only unlike hers, the shirts were Polo and jeans Armani, of all things. They spent more on casual than she spent on a good winter coat. And here she stood in her best evening pants suit. I'll never get the hang of this, she thought, knowing she didn't have the knack for clothes.

"This is a pleasant surprise!" Skip said giving her a head-to-toe once-over. "Whatever's been keeping you away, has improved your wardrobe. I approve."

Turning to her left Pamela looked into Skip's very white teeth and a smile of welcome she appreciated as never before.

"I'm in need of a cup of your coffee," giving her friend a warm look that told him she was really glad to see him too.

"At this time of night? You'll be awake till dawn. How about decaff? You won't know the difference."

"OK."

"Follow me. I have a nice quiet corner at the bar where I'll be able to keep my eye on you."

The bar was 20 feet long and had a short two-foot section that bent at right angles toward the wall. Setting up a full dinner place setting, Skip next moved a barstool over and held it for Pamela to climb up on. "No one will bother you here," he said in her ear.

She could barely hear him above the noise in the room. "Skip. Do you still have that too rich, very chocolate mud pie?"

"You want dessert? What's the matter? Forget to eat again?"

"Don't be a smart ass. I was at the Four Seasons." Why was she trying to impress Skip, she wondered? "But I had fresh fruit for dessert. What I need is a lot of sugar, fat, and chocolate. And while you're at it, add a scoop of vanilla ice cream."

As he walked away to get her order Pamela's rebellious thoughts still couldn't settle. Taking a pen and pad from her evening purse, she started to outline what she knew about the complex M.L. Horn. Before she had made one note, Skip handed her a mug of strong coffee.

"Want to talk Pal?"

His sincerity helped Pamela begin to deal with her mood. Looking into his kind face, Pamela nodded. "I'm a mess. I'll be starting that book I told you about, in a couple of days. But this woman's not like anyone I've ever met. I like her. I suspect she's a manipulator, but I want to be her friend. Not that she seems the friendly type. Yet I don't see her making one wrong move. There is no perfect! So what's wrong with my senses? I should have found two or three chinks in the lady's armor by now." She gave Skip a pleading look, hoping he'd help her figure things out.

Skip lifted Pamela's hand in his, preventing her from picking up her pen. "You haven't focused on the official woman. You're mixing the public and private person. People who manage others don't share their private lives with the help. For all the human resource bull shit about friendliness in the workplace, it's still not possible to manage your friends. Have you seen her off balance? Lose it?"

"Sort of. We were in a meeting with her executive team. And she turned on the attorney. She didn't lose it, but every time she talks to this twerp, she's barking some order."

"How is she with the rest?" Skip asked.

"Like a smoothly meshed football team. Give and take. All teamwork."

"Who are these guys? Give me some names. I might have known them."

Looking up, Pamela saw Skip in a totally different way. His friendly bartender's face was drawn in tight, with concentration puckering his forehead. If she'd put his well-built body in a gray stripe suit, and cut his longish curly locks, he'd look very corporate indeed.

Skip was squirming under her close scrutiny. "What's wrong with me?"

"Not much," surprised that she was only now beginning to see the real Skip Moran after ten years of taking him for granted. "In fact, I just pictured you in corporate pin stripes, and you looked great." The look of horror on Skip's face started her laughing and he quickly joined in.

"So give me some names and quit looking at me like that. You make me feel naked."

Pamela not only gave Skip names, she gave him a thumbnail on each player on M.L.'s team. "Frank Jackson, Operations, is a black Adonis from the streets. Ed Cole, Human Resources, is every high school cheerleader's dream. Jason Simmons, Finance, is a wire haired terrier who looks at Lady Boss like a worshipful puppy."

"And the lawyer?" Skip prompted.

"Yeah, William Foley. A mystery. Boston Irish from the wrong side of the tracks is my guess. A dumpy little show off. But deadly."

"Why would you say that?"

"His eyes. Always moving. Like a ferret. And there isn't one ounce of humor in him. I don't trust people without a sense of humor. And there is something between him and M.L. If she didn't like him, why is he still there? She's the boss. What ever it is could win me the Pulitzer."

"Foley. I remember him. He's damn smart. Not many in his league. A loner. Maybe that's all it is."

"More. I'm a loner. You're a loner. Oh don't deny it. For all your buddy buddy charm, you keep to yourself. Foley's different. He gives me the creeps."

"Is that all?"

"No. Charles Cray, Corporate Affairs, a gorgeous WASP. Charming, smart, and in love with his boss."

"And what about the boss lady herself?"

"She has that 'I'm it', way about her. You know those people, they walk into a room and everyone stops what they're doing, wanting her attention?"

"Stuck up?"

"No. It's more like a presence. I'm not sure she's even aware of it. Though the lady can be quite an actress. I've watched her dazzle and beguile crusty politicians. Even I know that takes talent."

"It seems you've got the players pegged, but not your subject. You're not paying attention to how she got where she is. Look, pretend you're CEO. Then see how your credentials match up with hers. If she's as good as you think, you'll find she trained for her job. Focus on that. Where she learned all she needed to do the job."

"By the way Skip. I thought you'd like to know I'm dropping Nick." Now why did she say that? Because you chump, you always tell Skip your major decisions before you take action. And for once Pamela had to agree with her alter ego.

"Good," Skip said with a smile of approval.

CHAPTER XXVI

Tim Lynch was looking at the digital ticker tape with ever changing stock prices, primed for anything that might be attractive to his small, but growing list of clients.

"What's this? UCC just jumped from 20 to 24. I haven't read anything about them lately." Aside from Dearling, he hadn't had anyone even ask about UCC.

Dialing research, Tim asked, "You see the jump in UCC?"

"No Tim. Do you want me to check into it?"

"Definitely! Let me know ASAP." Hanging up, Tim wondered if research would uncover anything he could make money on.

Jumping at the shrill sound of his phone, Tim picked up. "Yeah? UCC's in acquisition mode? Who? Not even a clue? Thanks for nothing." Hanging up, Tim thought, well Mr. Dearling do you have UCC bugged? Just yesterday you asked for a research report on them. Let's see what you'll do with this information. Dialing the unlisted number of his strange client, Tim was not surprised to have his call picked up on the first ring.

"Yes?"

The educated voice was easily recognized. Not exactly cool, but it didn't inspire a friendly chat.

"Mr. Dearling, this is Tim Lynch. I thought you'd want to know that UCC just jumped 4 points."

"Thank you. I'll get back." Settling back into his desk chair, Dearling began twisting his pocket watch chain, mentally cursing the sudden interest by someone in UCC.

"We can't afford to keep buying their stock if it goes to 28" he said. "Then again, we might not need to. No announcement has been made about either Ms. Horn's appointment or BioTech's tests. This may just be an adjustment by one of the funds. I don't think there is any need to alert Foley yet," he decided.

Picking up his phone, Dearling called Tim back. "Tim, call me if UCC hits either 22 or 28."

Hanging up, Dearling changed his mind and decided to call his boss. As was his way, he silently practiced his opening remarks. At least he'd protect his ass.

"Mr. Foley, I don't think there's anything to worry about, but UCC's on the move. It just hit 24."

"Shit. Call me if there's any change. Immediately," Foley barked.

*   *   *

Dearling's just keeping me informed, Foley decided sitting back in his desk chair. All the same, he thought,

I'd better call Jane. Reaching for the phone, his fingers automatically found the right buttons to call his sister.

"Hello?" answered a thin and colorless woman's voice.

"Hello Jane. How are you? I haven't heard from you all week." Foley asked in concerned tones unheard by anyone but his sister Jane.

"Oh Willy, I've been up to my ears with our Church's Holiday Bazaar. But I always have time for you."

Foley was amused by the sudden brightening and enthusiasm in her voice.

"How are you doing then? Can you come home for a visit?" she asked.

"How about this weekend? I'd like to go over our family portfolio with you. I'll need you to sign some papers."

"You know what ever you decide is fine with me. But I'd love a visit," her voice slowed with hope. "I'll bake, you can lick the bowl."

Jane's soft laughter sounded good to him. Foley knew Jane hadn't had an easy life. He did owe his sister a visit; he knew his presence was important to her. Even when she had married, his sister had worried more about her little brother than her husband. He thought of her as all the family he ever had. Or was it all he accepted?

"Willy, when can I expect you? I want to get ready. I'll cook your favorite gingerbread cookies. How about corn beef hash for dinner? Are you driving up?"

"Yes. I thought that would be best. I'll see you Saturday for lunch. Bye Jane."

Hanging up, Foley was thankful his sister never got in his way. He'd been investing her money along with his for years. But then again, money didn't seem important to Jane. She always said 'after being potato poor, everything extra is gravy.'

Foley laughed when he realized that by her standards, he had made his sister Beacon Hill rich. This was the kind of money that required managing, not being left safely tucked away in a bank. And yet with all her assets, including her teacher's pension and widow's insurance, Jane still tutored high school kids in English grammar for $10 a lesson. "Pin money", she called it.

As he thought of his sister, Foley unconsciously began stroking the telephone receiver. Then prayed, "Don't go and start spending your nest egg now. I may need to borrow against the insurance fund."

Sitting straighter in his desk chair, thoughts of Jane tucked safely away, he scribbled a note reminding himself to update Neuwirth's timetable for the final move on BioTech. Lifting the phone, Foley rapidly tapped out Dearling's number.

"Dearling? Foley. This four point jump in UCC? How do we stand?"

"Mr. Foley, Neuwirth's portfolio has been moving between utilities, telecommunications, and select chemical stocks. We've tripled our capital and can buy a significant position in BioTech just as soon as you give the signal."

"Place a buy order for $250,000 worth if BioTech moves to 4."

"But BioTech closed at 3 yesterday."

"Yes. But if it jumps another point I want to catch it before it moves any more. I'm not ready to close in just now. And I don't want to make any move before Monday. I'm just protecting my position."

"OK. I'll get right on it. I haven't heard from Henderson's people yet. I'll call you when they get in touch regarding our latest offer."

Hanging up on Dearling, Foley was confident that he'd achieve his goal of taking BioTech away from UCC. "What a nice golden parachute for unappreciated me," he whispered to himself. "Not a thing M.L. can do to stop me now."

CHAPTER XXVII

n a United Chemical corporate office not far from the CEO's, sat E.F. Haynes surrounded by the mementos of his active life. Civic and charitable awards sat along side sporting trophies. Awards from organizations he had from time to time raised funds for, or made significant donations to. And silver cups and bowls for winning yacht races. It wasn't the trophies that interested E.F., though they were a reminder of being in the thick of a down wind leg to the finish. E.F. had often challenged friends on the merits of sail versus powerboats. Stinkpots to sailors. One had man aiming an engine-powered vessel. The other had man harnessing nature. Neither stink-potter nor ragman could understand the other's love for their boats.

E.F. had been on the phone with Larry Henderson for an unusual 10 minutes. But the telephone conversation between these two very old friends was coming to a close.

"It seems our snake-in-the-grass is poised for his strike. Will Gavin contact you when this kid Lynch registers Neuwirth's trade?"

"Said he would. Gavin and I go way back Larry. He runs his brokerage firm like he captains his 40-footer. Everything ship shape, no breach of the rules."

"As soon as he calls you, I'll have trading suspended pending an audit of our BioTech shareholders. Then with all shares accounted for and in our control, we should be able to confront this Bruce Dearling with your detective's findings."

"Very good Larry. I'll brief Melissa tonight. She's been handling this entire campaign brilliantly."

Suddenly his old friend's voice saddened. "E.F. I'm worried about our girl. She's loosing her sparkle. Don't you think you're pushing her too hard?"

"What are you hinting at, you old codger?"

"Happiness. The old fashioned boy-meets-girl kind."

"She's wanted this all her life," E.F.'s voice heated with emotion. "She's earned her shot at the CEO spot. Of course she's happy."

"Melissa's not a workhorse. Next time you two are curled up in that library of yours, look at her again. She's all female. Maybe you ought to treat her like one."

"I know she's given up a lot for her dreams. But damn it all, I wouldn't let her do anything that would hurt her. We couldn't be closer if we slept together."

"You're wrong. And when was the last time you slept with a woman? Or even thought about it?"

"At my age? Come on!" E.F. didn't want to continue this conversation. It was making him uncomfortable.

"Listen, I have to go. Have some calls to make," Larry's voice brought E.F. back to the present. "Just remember, I love you both."

Hanging up, E.F. began to wonder if he had pushed Melissa too hard. Then he thought about his wife Carol. After 15 years without her, she still brought tears to his eyes. How could Larry even think of his being with another woman? He knew how much he had loved her.

"Where did the years go honey," he said, accustomed to carrying on one-sided conversations with her. "You were right by my side. Living in the dusty Texas oil fields. Eating and breathing dirt. You never let me doubt our future."

Remembering their first Christmas together he saw the pine boughs tied with a red ribbon. It was the only tree they could afford. And the one homemade package for him lying next to it. Without his knowing, Carol had been saving to buy him a white dress shirt. She'd called it his going to the bank shirt. How had she done it? It had to have taken all year.

He knew she never dipped into her family trust fund, not wanting him to feel he couldn't take care of her. Yet she was so tight with a dollar even he used to complain. If they ever fought about anything it was about her penny-pinching ways. Money was meant to be spent. But he had to admit during those lean years, they never missed a meal or the rent. He had come to realize that Carol's miserly ways must have been bred into her. Even after their first well came in, she continued to hide away money from the household budget. And she went on scrimping till the day she died. He remembered finding a couple of bankbooks hidden in her vanity, with over $250,000. So silly he had thought at the time. Yet the withdrawals coincided with a party she had thrown for him, gathering together old friends, scattered by life and careers. Or, one of his birthdays. "Honey, you could make me crazy. I never understood your fear of rainy days. I loved you so much I wanted you to have everything."

But then his mind filled with pictures of the years since her death. Time increasingly filled with Melissa. She now shared his solitary life. Albeit one of luxurious comfort. Melissa never thought about money. She spent what she earned. She said that it was a score card of how well she was doing in her career.

E.F. sat back in his desk chair picturing the evening fires in the library. Melissa curled up on the sofa. Both, listening to a recording from one of his collection of jazz albums. The thought of those evenings always comforted him, but now he saw Melissa as a luscious woman, not just his housemate. Her curves amply displayed under those thin silk jumpsuits she usually wore at home. How could he have missed all those years? Regret was not something E.F. had time for. But now he wished he could relive the last ten years. Wished that he had noticed how much he wanted Melissa as a woman. Someone to love and share passion-filled hours with.

An unaccustomed rush of sexual urgency filled him. It was time to let Carol go. He was going to pursue Melissa with every breath he had. The decision made him feel alive. He needed her love and was going to get it.

Shaking his head, and he returned to his notes, E.F. was glad to see he'd checked off each point on his list that he'd covered with Larry on the phone.

*   *   *

"Gavin," E.F.'s hearty greeting was followed by a firm hand shake. He'd stopped by to take his old friend Gavin Caulder to lunch.

"E.F. You old so and so. It has been too long. Instead of going out, I thought we could have a private lunch in my dining room?"

"Always ready to share in your ill gotten gains." E.F.'s hearty laugh rang out in the wood paneled room. "I wanted to ask for your help. Staying in might be more convenient."

"Follow me. Just as soon as we've given the kitchen our order you can fill me in."

Looking around the good-sized tastefully furnished room, E.F. thought of the generations of money that had been made by Gavin's firm. The pictures on the walls were of sailing ships and early eighteenth century scenes of commerce, part of a well-known and respected collection of art. The company, Morrison, Sherman & Temple, was an investment banking house with a retail brokerage subsidiary. Gavin was in charge of their retail brokerage activities.

Over their steak luncheon, E.F. had filled Gavin in on his concerns about UCC's stock. "So I would like to call in a favor."

"And what would that be?" Gavin's New England accent more pronounced now that business was being discussed.

"Can you see if anyone in this firm is trading both UCC and BioTech stock?"

"That shouldn't be too hard, if it's our firm," Gavin answered.

"This has to be kept between us. No leaks."

"My secretary's a master of the firm's computerized files. She can set me up and I'll do the checking personally. I'll call you later. Soon enough?"

"Thanks. When this is over, how about joining me for a weekend on board the Gitana?"

"Why in earth did you name your ketch Gypsy? Golden Fleece might be better. It's always costing you money. "

"Because that's what I'm working so hard to become."

Laughter and personal stories accompanied their coffee and cigars. E.F. leaving to return to the office, was sure Gavin would find their leak.

*   *   *

The grandfather office clock reminded E.F. that Gavin would be calling shortly. The market had been closed for an hour, and Gavin's responsibilities were all timed with the market.

The ringing of the phone triggered a smile, E.F. knowing his friend's habits, could have bet he'd get back by 5.

"I spoke to one of our young Turks. It was during our conversation prompted by my review of the kid's trades, that I learned of the small brokerage account, and that of a Mr. Dearling, who are both actively trading those stocks. E.F., I kept my promise. I never let on that there was any interest in either the kid's clients or these trades. Just the normal curiosity about one of my newer employee's progress in the firm."

"Thanks. I owe you."

"If there is any business we can do together, call me."

Hanging up, E.F. made a mental note to have Melissa approach Gavin first with her plans to raise new capital.

Now, to uncover this Neuwirth's pedigree. If it's as Melissa suspects, and we have a traitor, who in Hell is it, E.F. wondered. "They'd have to be dumb to go against UCC," E.F. whispered to himself. "Didn't they know everything these days could be traced?" Leaning back in his leather chair, feet on his desk, E.F. reminded himself that UCC's executive team was hand picked for Melissa and they were far from dumb. Yet, if he was right, one was accumulating a position in both companies, while representing UCC in the merger. It couldn't be for profit, he reasoned. So if it's not profits, what else? A hostile takeover?

"Sheeit! Well I'm from Texas. I'm used to killing snakes," he all but shouted, and started building a trap. "UCC needs BioTech. Melissa has to prevail!"

CHAPTER XXVIII

nterlocking her fingers as she stretched her arms overhead, Pamela flexed her shoulders free of kinks. The conference room felt like a cage.

"Damn it. Why did I give up smoking?" she asked herself while looking through her tote bag for a cigarette. "After a whirlwind week of M.L., I was looking forward to some plain research. But I've reread all this stuff twice and still no person. She's just a statistic. Born, graduated, worked."

Getting up from the conference table covered with folders and company publications, Pamela began pacing the length of the book-lined room. Thinking of Skip's remark, look for the things that don't tote up, she began rereading the chronological data that was Melissa Lynn Horn.

"Graduated Pittsburgh High School—honor society and valedictorian. Graduated U of Virginia, then Virginia Law School. On the "Law Review" staff. First job, as assistant to president of management consulting firm. No name. "No name. What firm?" she asked aloud. "OK Skip, one for your theory," and continued reading. Spent six months as a bookkeeper for a West Virginia mining company.

"Who's the owner of Weston Coal? Again, no names. Wait, Frank worked with M.L. and Ed at Weston? They'll know who owns Weston," she said and continued reading aloud.

"Worked as account executive for Hall & Knowles, public relations. Now why does that sound familiar? Jeezus. Who hired her? How did she get this job? Was she any good? And if so, why didn't she stay more than six months?"

Pamela had already paced her way five times around the room with a pencil in her teeth, wishing it were a cigarette when she hit it. Charles Cray was from Hall & Knowles. Isn't that interesting! This smacks of a closed club. Who's pulling the strings? And if this resume is accurate, why is it only a shell?

Thinking about her own resume, she remembered including a list of her published articles, organizations she had worked for, her membership in professional associations, and she had named every important person she'd ever interviewed.

It's as if M.L. hasn't lived in the real world, Pamela thought. She's just moved from job to job. "And that's another thing that doesn't compute," she said aloud. "She is definitely the boss. She's bright. If this is her resume, she's done her time in the back office. Numbers, management, public relations." Looking up Pamela saw Charles Cray watching her from the doorway.

"What's so funny?" she asked. Afraid he'd been there far longer than she'd have liked.

"You were having this animated conversation. I was afraid to interrupt. Do you always act out your thoughts?"

"Just since I gave up smoking," she grumbled.

"How about some lunch? We could go to the dining room, or judging by that stack of files, you'd probably like to have something brought here."

"How about joining me here?" For a chat, she thought. "Just the two of us." Pamela was determined to get some answers.

Pamela watched him head for the phone. "A sandwich? Roast beef? Turkey?" he asked.

"Roast beef rare, on rye with Russian dressing and a large pot of black coffee would be perfect."

The tray was delivered in best hotel fashion too quickly for her to have asked even one pointed question. All through their hasty meal she wondered if he would ever tell her what was going on.

"I must admit I enjoy our lunches," Pamela said as casually as she could. Leaning back in her chair, her hunger sated and remnants of sandwiches and cookies stacked on the tray, she began to study her companion somewhat wistfully. "You're a handsome devil. How come some luscious young lovely hasn't snapped you up?"

"Is this an invitation? If so it's the best offer I've had in several years."

"My friend Skip says I have no taste in men. I'd marry you, just to prove him wrong."

"Mm. Not bad. I get a young, bright, lovely bride. You get a graying groom. Not an even trade. You deserve someone you're passionate about. Now, if you'd like to try out . . . ?"

His seductive smile was tempting, she thought. But she never got the good ones. Anyway he's really in love with M.L., so what's the use? Looking away she said instead, "Maybe when this is over," pointing to the pile of paper scattered over the table.

"Then I guess you had better ask me your questions. The ones that had you crazy for a cigarette," Charles sighed.

"Who is M.L. Horn?"

"Excuse me?" Charles replied, straightening up in his chair. "How do you want me to answer that?"

"Honestly! Where did she come from? I know Pittsburgh. But who hired her? What did she do, that she gets to be CEO?"

"It's all in those papers." Charles answered, picking up M.L.'s resume.

"Yeah. A management firm. Which one? Who did she work for? What businesses did she study? Why isn't any of that in these files?" her questions spilling out one on top of another.

It took Charles longer than she would have liked, to answer. Now she knew she was on the right track!

"M.L. worked for me at Hall & Knowles."

It was just as she had suspected. M.L.'s worked with all these guys before.

"I was a partner at H&K when I was hired by UCC's Board."

"Why would you leave a firm you had a piece of, for a job?" Pamela wanted to know.

"I was bored. The clients' problems all began sounding the same. So I left. By that time, I could afford to work at something I liked."

"You mean you left with all that lovely stock. And now you clip coupons." Pamela interrupted.

"Well, more like a cash buy-out. More important for your story young lady, was that I was free to look for new challenges. UCC has put the zip back into my life."

Yeah. And M.L.'s the zip, she thought. Poor guy. She was so side tracked she almost missed his next remark.

"This is a pivotal time for UCC. It was just the thing to rescue me from boredom."

"Pivotal? How? The corporation's sound. It's the leading chemical manufacturer in probably the whole fucking world."

"Success is yesterday's news. Success in a corporation this size is an everyday struggle. First, to be on top. Then, to be even bigger, before a competitor beats you out of market share."

"So. I have to listen to meaningless meeting banter, and I don't get to hear any of this?"

"Settle down, and I'll sketch the past and future of this behemoth." And he did. Pamela hanging on every word. Her eyes never leaving Charles. Her pen leaving ink tracks

She had been listening to Charles talk non-stop for almost an hour. It was a calculating insider's view of UCC. She thought of the people uprooted and moved during the years of growth, and those reassigned, retired, or laid-off in periods of economic downturns. Still in all, she was fascinated. The budget implications were greater than those of some state governments. And this was another juncture where the corporation would move heaven and hell to survive, she thought. But as fascinating as the story, Charles love for his job was just as interesting. It was if he was fighting every fight. Cheering each achievement. It's a corporation for Christ's sake, not a family business, she thought.

"Anyway, this merger M.L.'s been negotiating is vital."

"What's wrong," Pamela asked, seeing a sudden change in Charles' mood. She saw him look at her . . . no more like into her soul.

"I'm going to divulge something that has to be kept between us."

"I promise," she quickly answered, leaning closer not wanting to miss even one word.

It was with a sigh of resignation, Charles continued. "Someone is making a play for our stock, and that of the company we are planning to purchase. It could not only queer the deal, it could throw UCC into a decline."

His voice was so leaden, Pamela felt sorry for him. "So if this play against UCC succeeds, then this entire campaign is lost?"

Charles sat there looking somber, and nodded.

"We haven't been able to find out who, or what it is we're fighting. But young lady, you have just given me an idea, another avenue to explore."

"Do you have any names? Can't you trace large stock transactions these days," she asked.

"Yes. But the small investment firm doing the trading is owned by a Cayman Island corporation, a WSF, Ltd. "Well this isn't your problem, Pamela. Just remember not a word."

Nodding, Pamela was already trying to figure out who she knew in the stock market. A source she could press for some off-the-record information.

"Charles, could this be personal? Some one out to make M.L. fail?"

"Young lady, you may just have hit on something," Charles said and leaned over to give her a friendly pat on the hand.

Watching Charles closely she saw a change in expression. Was it a look of resignation? "I have a note for you Pamela. You can leave everything. It's in my office."

Bewildered, she pushed her pad into her tote and closed all the files. Following Charles out of the room she saw that he was preoccupied. His golden head bowed, shoulders slightly drooped, and hands tucked away in his pants pockets. The overhead light caught a sprinkling of silver in his red-gold hair.

What's he going to spring on me now, she wondered, her feet scrambling to catch up?

Entering Charles's spotless office a few doors down the executive corridor, Pamela followed him to his desk.

She watched as he opened a drawer and removed a small envelope. Her name had been hand written on the front.

"It's from M.L."

She ripped at the heavy paper flap, not caring if Charles was watching her or not, and read the note as if it held the key to her future. Her mind was still puzzling its contents, when the phone rang.

"Hello?" Charles said. After listening a moment he looked to Pamela and said, "I have to take this. Are you set for now?"

"Sure. I'll be done with those reports by 5. I've got to meet M.L. later.

"Good. See you tomorrow then."

Pamela was half way out the office door when she stopped. "Aren't you joining us tonight?" To her surprise Charles gave her a tight grin and shook his head no.

Pamela started down the hall thinking about the note. It said that M.L. would tell her something tonight, for her ears only. More secrets, she thought. Some were double edged, Pamela knew.

No sooner had she left than Charles began his end of the conversation. "She's got the scent, M.L. and she's not going to be satisfied with anything less than the truth."

"You had to give her the note. Oh, Dear," M.L. said, her voice lacking enthusiasm. "E.F. will be joining us tonight. I don't know what he's got planned. How much truth can we trust her with?"

After a pause to consider the consequences of Pamela meeting E.F., Charles took a breath, "Look, she's been zinging me with questions, dancing all around it. I just discussed our little problem with the activity in our stock. But, we do have her hog-tied. Her book needs our approval or she loses her deal."

"We'll see tonight. Let's go over all this at breakfast. Meet me at the Club at 7:30 tomorrow. I'll update you then."

"Fine. Be careful," he said, but knew M.L. was always careful. He hoped they could count on Pamela's sense of fair play.

CHAPTER XXIX

Pamela was on her way to another mystery location, riding in high style. "At least I'm dressed for limo travel," she murmured, thinking how unusual it was for her to be in an evening dress. The note said black tie. Somehow the usual pantsuit didn't seem appropriate, she thought. "They've had me so programmed I haven't had a chance to think."

Looking out the car's tinted window she saw that Ben was pulling up to a private townhouse, on a residential street of similar buildings. Wondering where they were, she began to look for a street sign or restaurant, something to give her a clue. CEOs live pretty well she thought, comparing her westside walk-up with the wrought iron trimmed, classic red brick building.

As the car door opened, Ben extended his hand helping her out of the deep back seat. "Is this house Ms. Horn's?"

"No Ma'am," was the quick reply as Ben steered her toward the open front door where a small neat woman stood waiting.

She looks like a housekeeper in an English country home, Pamela thought, taking in the middle-aged woman's black dress, erect back, and old fashioned hairstyle set in waves close to her head.

"Miss Green to see Ms. Horn, Martha," Ben announced. With a small tip of his cap, he whispered, "I'll be back to take you home, Miss Pamela."

Standing in the crisp early evening air facing Martha, she felt like a servant being handed over to the house police.

"Ms. Horn is expecting you, Miss," the British tinged voice confirmed her earlier impressions. Following Martha into the house, Pamela began to study her surroundings. Not your usual townhouse, she thought, struck by the richness of the entry's architectural details. The most dramatic were the Doric columns and carved moldings that defined the space, and the graceful stairway that curved up to a second floor gallery. Well if she doesn't live here, who does, she wondered?

"Please follow me, Miss Green," Martha instructed in her servant's formal voice, then turned away and headed towards a short corridor. Approaching an elaborate double door, the austere woman knocked twice, before opening one of the doors onto a softly lit room.

"Miss Green," Martha announced and indicated that Pamela should go into the room without her.

Before Pamela had taken her second step M.L. approached with a somewhat older man.

"Pamela I'd like you to meet E.F. Haynes."

So, that's the who, she thought. It was the first close look she'd had of the illustrious Mr. Haynes. This man, with a face as creased as the bark on a hickory tree fascinated her. He had the skin of an outdoorsman. Earthy humor shone in his eyes, laugh lines deeply etched at their corners. And his smile left no doubt that he was a man who enjoyed women. The aggregate picture promised adventure tinged with danger.

"Miss Green. I'm delighted to meet you. I'm a fan of yours."

It was something he might have said thousands of times, Pamela thought. But she was flattered. Maybe it was the way he kept hold of her hand. Or that little squeeze to emphasize what he had just said.

"We almost met at Monday's reception," she replied.

"I'm at a loss. I know I'd remember meeting you," he said in a soft Texas drawl.

"You were occupied with your guests." She was enjoying his flirting.

"Ah. Well, tonight I'm all yours. M.L. and I were having a glass of champagne. Will you join us?"

He's fabulous, Pamela thought. And this is some place. What does he have to do with M.L.? What's going on here? Pamela's thoughts stumbling for an answer while she automatically accepted a chilled flute from M.L. Looking again at M.L., Pamela received another shock. All week she'd been following the crisp professional, as polished as a granite carving. But this lithe creature was clad in a turquoise slip of a long dress. I'll bet that's an

Armani, she noted. Even her hair looked softer, swinging straight, and free of those funky gold tassels suspended from her ears.

"M.L. you look incredible," surprise evident in her compliment.

"Tonight is really a special occasion," M.L. replied, giving her a rare, real smile.

Even M.L.'s face seems softer, more feminine. The package was one luscious woman. Was this a glimpse of the real M.L.?

"Shall we?" E.F. said as he offered Pamela an elbow and led her to a nearby settee. "M.L. has given me a rundown of your week's activities. I wanted to meet you for myself."

Before she could reply, M.L. perched next to E.F. and raised her glass. "I'd like to propose a toast. To Pamela. To dreams. To uncharted waters."

That's a strange toast she thought, joining the handsome pair and sipping her drink. Now's the time to shut up and listen. She pinched her hand to be sure she took her own advice.

Leaning forward on the settee, knee-to-knee with Pamela, E.F. said, "It was my idea for the three of us to meet here. I don't like stuffy offices."

"This certainly isn't stuffy, Mr. Haynes!"

"Call me E.F. Everyone does."

"E.F." E.F., M.L.? Is everyone in the power set known by their initials, she wondered?

"It's somewhat formal, I'm afraid. But these rooms were designed for entertaining. On occasion they have to accommodate large groups of people."

"Social or business?"

Why is he looking amused?

"A little of one, and some of the other."

Waiting for more information, Pamela soon realized she would only learn what this man wanted her to know. She made a mental note to check into his personal life first day back at *Economic World*.

When E.F. did continue, his voice had the intimacy of having been her life long friend. "I'm interested in what you've learned this week."

"About UCC or M.L.?"

"Both. As Chairman of the Board, I'm very much interested in your point of view. Especially in how it will influence your book."

So that's what these two are up to. Trying to find out what I may write. As if her mind had suddenly cleared, she blurted out, "Did you nominate M.L. for the CEO spot?"

"I did. You see M.L.'s credentials were tailor-made for our current needs."

Is she an older man's darling, Pamela wondered, then chided herself for thinking that M.L. had been acting like the puppet.

"No, Pamela. M.L. isn't my puppet!" E.F.'s sharp tone and his accurate read, had her squirming. For all his charm, she thought, his eyes could fell a tree. But Pamela could still recall a scandal several years' back, when a single CEO was rumored to be sleeping with his attractive VP of Public Affairs. It was the corporate scandal of the time. So what was going on here? Some game, or was it the scoop of her career?

"Pamela why do you think M.L. was named CEO? You've read her resume. If you were on the selection committee what would you think of her credentials?"

Jarred by E.F.'s powerful gaze, she thought carefully about his question. He certainly got down to it. Yet nothing in his voice said she had to curb her tongue. All the same she'd be careful. She still needed her fuck you money.

"I'm fascinated by power. Always thought it was something you're born with. No offense, M.L. You've obviously done your homework, and then some. But your background . . . at least your on-the-record experience . . . I don't see it."

"How's that?"

There was something in M.L.'s voice. Was she on the defensive? Pamela wondered what she was hiding, and cautioned herself to answer carefully.

"You never stayed in any one company for more than two years. Certainly not over the real long haul."

"So?" E.F. questioned, his eyes somewhat hooded but still staring at her for an answer.

"So it just doesn't add up." Flustered by blurting out her suspicions, Pamela sat back to wait for the storm of angry denial. All she saw was an exchange of looks. Perfect for poker, Pamela noted.

"Let me tell you a little story," E.F. began, leaning back into his seat. "It might clear up some of your suspicions."

Giving Pamela the warmest smile he added, "Off the record of course!"

Smile or not, she knew this was no request. Nodding her agreement she said, "But first, since we're to be on first name basis, what does E.F. stand for?"

With a twinkle in his eyes, E.F. sighed, "Ah. Your reporter's curiosity again? My name is Emmett Frances. But every time I hear Emmett, I think of that soulful clown, Emmett Kelly. And, because I've seen enough soulful characters in this life, I try not to add to their numbers."

"I can't imagine you soulful," Pamela said. "You're too alive. Too . . ."

"Magnetic?" M.L. interjected.

"I'm really enjoying to myself. I'm surrounded by beauty and compliments. Hope I don't lose my head." His laughter was relaxing. Pamela decided to go along with the mood.

"When I graduated from college, I set off on a Jack London odyssey to find my fortune. After knocking about in the Alaskan oil fields, I took my small stash and headed home to Texas. I was very lucky and after some planning struck oil on my first try. That was easy - I fixed that though - pretty quickly, I lost everything."

"How much was everything?" Pamela couldn't help but ask.

"Let's just say my first million. No one to blame but myself - I was the one who got drunk and gambled it away. It was one of my very first lessons."

"I'd say. Don't drink and gamble."

"Not at all. I still drink and gamble," E.F.'s laugh came straight from his gut. "The lesson is, if you're good at something it probably will be easy. But don't value it any less."

"I'm afraid you lost me. Was it really easy? The first million I mean?"

"Yes. And under the right circumstances you can still turn a quick million today."

What in Hell does this have to do with M.L. she wondered, as E.F. got up to refill their glasses?

Once again settled opposite her, E.F. continued, "So, there I was, busted. Took a job as a field operations manager for North Eastern Chemicals and became friendly with a man who'd drop in on us every so often. He was their President, Tom Larsen. Tom is responsible for the man you see now."

"I don't understand?"

"Well, we were dirt poor. My mother died when I was six. Dad, just wasn't suited to raising a kid. Tom did it instead."

"I'd say a fortune helped."

"Somewhat. But that doesn't polish your insides, just hides the rough spots a little better."

Pamela could see E.F. as a tough kid. Unkempt in stained jeans and frayed denim shirt. He probably had the same rakish grin he has today, she thought.

"That was back in the 50's. In those days, it was hands-on-management. Lesson number 2. If you want something done well, do it yourself. Or, train the people you want to represent you. Anyway, Tom and I just hit it off. But that is not really the point of this tale. The point is that Tom took me in hand. He taught me the meaning of success. The emptiness of living life just to earn piles of money."

"But you did earn piles of money!" Pamela cut in.

"Yes, but my wealth has enabled me to pursue other interests."

"How?"

"That, young lady is a story for another day."

E.F. was clearly amused by the directness of her questions.

"I'd worked for Tom for ten years when I developed a new oil recovery method. I suggested that Tom register the patent.

"So Tom Larsen patented this process of yours."

"That was the strange thing. He said no. Wanted me to think of my future. I'd thought I'd work for Tom with one foot in my grave. But he told me, "E.F., you've learned all I can teach you. You register that patent and setup for yourself. I expect exclusive use of the process for five years, then I'm a customer like anybody else!"

"I was about as shocked as you look right now. To me, he was family! But he was adamant. Said I should go into business because I was good at it, and was an incredible judge of people . . . my lesson #3. Find the people who are inspired. Keep moving them up.

"I may be the skeptic of all times E.F., but no businessman is that generous."

"So young and so hard," E.F. sighed. "It's damn good business to support your people."

All goodness and charity, Pamela thought. She'd never met an executive who had a heart. "How does this relate to M.L.?" she asked instead.

"I sensed her potential the first week she worked for me. As I kept giving her greater responsibility, she grew in ability and confidence, until she got where she is today."

He puffed out the words with pride, but Pamela's mind was working overtime. "You placed her in every job?"

E.F. just nodded.

"How can you move someone around like that? Research says, you're a business man."

"I'm a business man who owns companies, has an interest in other businesses, as well as serving on the Board of UCC."

Just how extensive was E.F.'s control and influence? Just as she was about to ask, Martha entered and announced dinner was about to be served.

As Pamela stood, E.F. took her elbow and M.L.'s, leading them into dinner. This is some picture, she thought. A reporter having a cozy dinner with a titan of industry. I hope I'm not the dessert.

*   *   *

The main dining room table had been moved aside and a smaller round table placed in the center of the large square room, the table appearing to be an island of soft light. It was warmed by flickering candles reflected in the crystal and silver table settings, and multiplied by the gilt-framed mirrors encircling the room.

"I thought you'd enjoy Martha's roast prime rib," M.L. said, inviting Pamela's attention. "E.F. introduced me to her special skills with Yorkshire pudding years ago. I had always thought it was a pudding. I didn't realize it's really a sort of a scrumptious beef-flavored popover."

"How and when did you meet?" Pamela asked as E.F. had moved her chair into the table. Leaning over her shoulder E.F. said, "There's that curiosity again." It was maddening how he evaded her questions.

Throughout the delicious meal, Pamela filed away questions, not wanting to break the flow of easy conversation. E.F. and M.L. shared opinions of the coming election, the stock market, reporters and their coverage of business news. The entire meal had the ambiance of people who had gone through a lot together. It wasn't an intimate conversation so much as a conversation of intimates. Just how intimate, was what Pamela wanted to know.

As coffee was being served she finally asked again, "E.F. how did you two meet?"

"Now to the rest of my story," he replied. Clearly E.F. wasn't a man to be rushed.

"Twenty or so years ago, my wife Carol was diagnosed with an advanced case of ovarian cancer. With all of my money and powerful connections, I was helpless. I asked her what she wanted to do. And she said, to spend her last days in my company."

Pamela read true love in his sad, distant eyes, and the tenderness of his smile. E.F. was telling a story he still lived.

"We were, and had always been inseparable. But while I had my business interests, she had only me, our marriage, not even a child to share her too often solitary life. So I delegated every last business detail, and spent the happiest two years of my life, travelling with the woman I loved. To the Alps in summer, the Great Barrier Reef when New York was in deepest winter. Always returning in the spring, Carol's favorite time at home. And, as she faded toward death in my arms, I began to crave life. I needed to live."

Stopping to sip some water, E.F. looked over at M.L. and smiled. Pamela wondered if she had known his wife, because while the smile was warm, it wasn't the look of a lover. Maybe they weren't an item after all. The jury was still out on that one.

"After Carol died," E.F. obviously struggling with leaving his more enjoyable memories, "I moved out of our home and into this building. I made this place my home and my Club. A place to invite and entertain people. Lots of people. It helped to fill my days. Next I wanted a management firm to oversee my various interests. I had to free myself of the day to day details, but in order to do that, I had to find and groom an assistant.

"Let me guess. M.L.," Pamela interjected.

"Correct. Of course she was nothing like the woman you see today." E.F.'s voice and the firmness of his mouth, reminded Pamela that no matter what their relationship, M.L. was a colleague.

"M.L. came to me straight out of law school. She was beyond bright, honest and with something more - an integrity I'd missed in my busy world. The rest is history," E.F. said, and breaking into a smug grin added, "Do I need to tell you, the student eventually overshadowed her teacher."

Isn't that just perfect, Pamela thought, then asked, "But if she was your assistant how could M.L. have had the experience needed to be CEO?" Damn it! There was still something they didn't want her to know.

"Just what do you think a CEO does?" E.F.'s voice was all business.

If it was a challenge she was ready for him. "Skills of leadership, the mind of a lawyer, and abilities of a banker, and he . . . it's usually a man . . . must have vision for corporate growth. I guess that's the crux of it."

"How about morality, ethics, values?" E.F. asked.

"I'm afraid I haven't seen much of those in corporate America. I've seen too much double-dealing and back-stabbing to think they can coexist in the corporate suite."

"So when you start a story you expect to uncover evil. You don't expect competence? Experience? A track record of accomplishments? Too bad." E.F.'s face was a study of disapproval. "I wanted to hire and train an exceptional assistant. Someone to run my businesses by my standards."

"I guess it's my turn, E.F.," M.L. began. "Without knowing my side of this story Pamela, you'll reach the wrong conclusions."

Pamela sensed a reluctance in M.L. Was she getting too close, or was E.F. about to reveal more than she wanted? Pamela guessed the latter. In the short time they'd spent together, M.L. had very cleverly kept her life outside UCC, under wraps.

"I joined E.F.'s firm before I had taken my law boards. After only one month on the job, he offered me an intriguing proposition. He knew I was adrift. But, I was ambitious. I loved working for him. I wasn't sure I wanted to practice law, anyway." Looking at E.F. she said more to him, "We had long discussions about the legal profession. I had interned for three summers at a huge Washington firm and hated it. As a researcher, I got to work on criminal, civil, corporate, as well as government cases. But all I did was look for loop holes." Turning back to Pamela, she continued, "E.F. suggested my training be put to use in business, where I could build something that would benefit many people."

"But you had no business experience, what could you do?"

E.F. jumped in. "Pamela, I saw in her a generalist."

As Pamela was about to ask how, he held her gaze in his. "Patience. I'm getting to it. Yes, she's a lawyer, but M.L.'s more. Her legal training and her ability to plan effective strategies make her ideally suited for leadership. Along with her valuable knowledge of the workings of government and private sectors, she was tailor made to take UCC into the future. With special training of course."

All Pamela could do was look at E.F. She couldn't see it. What was he really telling her? He saw a pretty, bright woman and forged her into a CEO? The air in the room was getting tense. Just as she was going to break her silence, M.L. did.

"E.F.'s plan was to have me work in various positions in companies in which he had an interest. The purpose he said was to groom me for major executive opportunities beyond his company."

M.L. was warming to her story and Pamela was following her every word.

"Business tends to pigeonhole you. Doesn't let you stretch and grow. Can you imagine a woman earning her spurs, so to speak, working for one company? No corporation I've heard of would allow you to be a bookkeeper, payroll clerk, personnel benefits manager, and legal council."

Pamela heard the edge in her voice and had to agree. She could think of two spots at *Economic World* she'd love a crack at. She knew however she didn't have a chance. John wanted her to stay on her beat.

"For someone as ambitious as I was, this was an incredible opportunity. How could I refuse?"

"Weren't you scared? Worried that you couldn't cut it?"

"Of course I was scared. But I used that. Forced myself to work harder. And, before I accepted E.F.'s plan, I made him promise me two things. First he had to be brutally honest about my performance on each assignment, or I knew I wouldn't grow. Then he had to make sure no one knew of our connection. I wanted to be accepted as a regular employee. Hired for a specific assignment."

"I agreed, though it made it tougher for her."

A man places a mole inside his companies? Is this standard operating procedure? I've never heard this before, it's too scary. Pamela's hand was itching for her notepad. Questions were pushing for answers. "But how did you get here? I still don't see the big picture."

"That's my question, M.L.," E.F. said. "She's a natural! As I thought from the start. She was the most multidimensional employee I ever hired. Without question the most diplomatic - best with people. You'll find Melissa left friends and supporters at every post along the way."

"It was like solving a new puzzle each time out. I'd be hired in a junior position and given a limited task. As my various managers found that I had a consuming appetite for work, they took advantage of it. But to their credit, they taught me what I needed to know each step up the ladder. I actually found some of the most menial tasks fun."

"Weren't the regulars jealous of this new employee? You don't look like you're bush league. They'd have to be suspicious?" Now why is E.F. smiling?

"That's one of her special skills, she's a chameleon. She looks like a native, even in the hills of West Virginia."

"Look. Even I know you can't manage a payroll without a background in accounting." Pamela was having trouble hiding her skepticism.

"You're right. E.F. had me tutored for each new assuagement."

"That takes a lot of money."

"Not as much as you'd think. When your editor wants you to bone up on something what does he do?" E.F. asked.

"He has me meet with a specialist at the magazine for a briefing."

"If he wants you to learn something in depth?"

"He sends me to school, or has me meet an expert in the field."

"That's what my life has been. Playing catch up for the years a man might have spent being groomed in-house."

M.L. was certainly secure in her view of her background. E.F. just sat there as if he'd planned it all along. Maybe it was the only way she could have earned her credentials. Pamela hoped her research would turn something up.

E.F., leaning closer to Pamela, tapped her knee. "I can see by your face that you're having a hard time accepting this."

Damn the man, he had read her once again.

"You're thinking that if you write any of this, people will think I'm a doddering old fool, or M.L.'s a manipulating bitch. Neither is the case, I assure you. Check her references. Do your interviews as if this were a traditional man's career."

And forget that this is the hottest story I've ever had, Pamela worried. But that's probably the deal in order to get their approval.

"You know Pamela, if you think about it. It really was the perfect school for a woman. No corporate men's club would ever let one of us on the career path to the top. This was the only way I could've gotten here."

Am I so jaded, I suspect everyone in the executive suite? Looking at the two, she thought, maybe M.L.'s right. Women are leading cosmetic and fashion companies. Times are changing. She'd dig into this angle during her conversations with those references E.F. told her to check out.

The evening had been a surprise. She'd have a lot to think over. E.F. was right about one thing, capable or not, if their unique relationship was even hinted at, they'd be the new tabloid darlings. That would hog-tie M.L., preventing her from succeeding. If Charles was right, UCC couldn't afford any breach in confidence. Pamela was sure Charles had secrets of his own. She hoped this was the only secret she'd have to keep for now and that these two masters of manipulation hadn't been playing her for a sucker.

"E.F. I have to ask, are you two a..uh . . . a couple?"

It was Pamela's turn for surprise. E.F. looked more perplexed than shocked. His response closed one door and opened another. "We're family. Not blood relations, but family just the same."

"M.L., I know this isn't part of our deal, but don't you have any social life?" If looks could freeze, M.L.'s rigid face warned Pamela she might have gone too far.

"You have no idea what these past fifteen years were like," she said. "I've worked round the clock to be what I am. So, social life? Not on the job. As the southern boys say, 'You don't dip your pen in company ink.' Believe me I didn't have any other opportunities!"

M.L. relaxed, suddenly less defensive. "I'm not a monster. It's just that I was limited to making friends with my employers and their families. I still keep in touch with all the nieces and nephews I've accumulated along the way."

What Pamela saw was a determined young woman with no personal life. She hadn't mentioned a lost love. How can she look like that and not have had a lover? What a waste! Does she ever cry herself to sleep wishing some Prince Charming would sweep her away? Why did she even bring it up? Her job as a reporter, left her little time for romance. Could a woman have a husband and a CEO post? From Pamela's current vantage point, the answer looked like no.

"E.F. you said that there was a specific reason that the Board hired M.L.?"

"I did. It wasn't only me. Three of us have employed M.L. at our own companies. We all noticed her unusual talent for problem solving, and we've got a big one right now. If things don't shift, and fast, we'll be stuck downsizing – as they like to say these days, reengineering. None of us like it, we needed an outsider for this job. A talented leader no one knew; then we thought of M.L."

"And if she fails?" Pamela asked. "You've set her up as a sacrificial lamb."

"I can't fail. I've worked too hard. You have to help me," M.L. said. "The careers and jobs of thousands of our employees depend upon my success."

"Help you? In the book?" Pamela couldn't see how 300 or so pages would help anyone. The book hadn't even been written. It was at least a year and a half away from being published.

"I'm betting you'll find I'm real. You're too smart not to do your homework. I'm hoping you'll help us fight. By the time you're published, all of this will have been resolved and UCC will be stronger than ever."

Pamela knew they weren't telling her everything, but their story did make a weird kind of sense. With E.F.'s clout and M.L.'s abilities, maybe she could pull it off. It will certainly be a coup if they could. What a book if they can't, she thought. For some reason Pamela wanted to believe them.

"What the Hell. I'll keep your secrets for now," she said. "I can write them in later." Watching E.F. relax back into his seat, she knew he had expected her to. Shit, she thought. Then she said a silent prayer, that when the final draft was ready for print, she wouldn't be sorry.

CHAPTER XXX

"What unmitigated gall!" Melissa growled having spent the last twenty minutes storming her way around the Library. "My resume isn't real? E.F. how could you ever have thought that, that reporter would understand? She didn't spend two weeks scared shitless, while Weston fought off Fallon's men. She doesn't spend 18 hour days perfecting a budget."

Only Melissa's iron control kept her from jumping down Pamela's throat when she hadn't liked one of her questions. Now safe, with Pamela gone, she'd been watching E.F. sitting quietly drinking cognac, while she wore a hole in the library rug, walking off her anger.

"Melissa, think about your resume. If it were a man's it would read - Joined Haynes Associates as assistant to the President and worked his way up the ladder to account manager, vice president, recently promoted to Executive VP. We didn't write yours that way. We didn't want it known that you've only worked for me."

"Not powerful! Not equal to a man!" Melissa growled, only half listening to what E.F. was saying. "She doesn't think I can cut it. How in hell could I have accomplished all I have? Learned all this, if I were some fool girl the head honcho had the hots for?"

"Honey, Pamela's questions were surprisingly direct. She's not out to waylay you. I think she believes you're capable. It's your trip up the ladder she isn't sure about."

Reaching out for her hand as she passed his chair, he stopped her. "Melissa, how do you see yourself? Isn't that the real question? When Pamela asked if you had a social life I think she was looking for the other side of the CEO - the human being. I don't think she was attacking you."

Perhaps it was the softness in his voice that stopped her tirade. Thinking of her assets wasn't something Melissa often did. She knew only too well what her weaknesses were. But E.F. wanted her strengths, wanted to remind her of herself.

"I can hold my own. I'm hard working. Different. I've earned my success." Ticking each item off a mental list.

"That's it? My God Honey, don't you ever think of getting married?"

As if a piece had just fallen into place, she now knew what Larry was trying to tell her. In a far away voice, she said more to herself, "I'd like to find a man to love, the way you loved Carol." Looking into the puzzled face of her dearest friend, she saw a deep sadness. Bewildered, she reached out to gently stroke his cheek, and wondered why? They had been talking about a potential disaster. Pamela could still refuse to go along with their plan. Shaking her head she wondered where this marriage nonsense had come from, now of all times? It was then she knew she wanted Hugh. Answering Pamela, and telling her about Hugh, would have made her seem real. But at what cost?

Resuming her walk around the library, she knew she was right in not telling Pamela about Hugh. CEOs didn't date movie idols.

"Melissa, where were you the other night?"

Looking at her friend she was surprised he'd ask, E.F. had never kept tabs on her. But she saw that he was worried about something.

"When you go off with one of your friends, you always stop in the Library when you come in, to say good night. I couldn't sleep, and spent a long night reading. I missed our usual nightcap and good night kiss."

Melissa had heard the question. She just didn't know if she could talk about Hugh, even to E.F. She'd never missed saying good night to E.F. Never thought she'd be with anyone but E.F. Maybe if she didn't tell him about Hugh, he could remain a secret.

"Honey? I don't mean to pry. But don't you think you can trust me after all this time? Is there something you want to tell me?"

Looking into his wrinkled, sun-baked face, Melissa knew she'd never be able to resolve her feelings about Hugh if she didn't at least try it out on E.F. Knowing her as well as he did, maybe he could answer her question. Was she really in love?

"I met a man on Largo Verde." She sighed with relief to finally share her secret. She was so involved in her own thoughts she didn't see the flicker of alarm in E.F.'s eyes. Dropping to the floor, she sat at his feet, resting her head on his knees. Oh, if she could only stay that way forever, she thought. No Pamela. No decisions about Hugh.

"And?" E.F. asked, patting her hair, gently urging her to continue. "And he showed up in New York. Saw me at the Four Seasons with Pamela and Charles. At first I just let my emotions sweep me away. But . . . I don't know." Looking up for reassurance she saw E.F. was paying close attention. "E.F., we've never talked about my social life . . . my lack of one. But I had a very bad experience in college. It made me think I was frigid." Her eyes were pleading for understanding. "You don't know how I wondered what was wrong with me. It's kept me from having what other women have. A meaningful relationship. Hugh is the only person who's ever made me feel I was sexy. That I could enjoy sex. But is sex enough to build a relationship on?"

If she hadn't been so serious, she would have seen E.F.'s smile.

Lifting her on to her feet, he stood and gently enfolded her in his arms. "Tell me about him. Have you seen him often? Does he love you?"

Resting her head on his shoulder she whispered her hopes and fears. E.F. held her and stroked her back. He was always a good listener, she thought. After a while she moved away, and smoothed her hair. Looking rather sheepish she said, "Sorry. That was quite a mess." But she was glad she had told him her painful secrets. He hadn't laughed. Hadn't asked if Hugh was someone he'd approve of. He just held her and listened, making her feel safe.

But now she had to deal with her outburst over Pamela. Picking up the cognac E.F. had been drinking, she wondered why she'd blown a fuse. Were her emotions getting out of hand? No. She realized it was her fear that Pamela would laugh at her. She knew that if the reporter didn't believe her, no one would. Ready to face up to her fears, she said, "You're right. Pamela wasn't out to kill me. Not yet anyway. Do you think she's accepted me as CEO?"

"Yup. I'm not worried for now. I am concerned about you. Do you feel better now that you've told me about him?"

"Yes," her voice soft and self-conscious. "Telling you wasn't easy. Do you think less of me?"

"No. Of course not. I could tell you some of my own follies and failures. But that will have to wait. We have a traitor to nail, a merger to finalize. You need all of your attention focused on UCC's reorganization."

CHAPTER XXXI

Steepling his fingertips Charles Cray, was unaware of his office or the day's schedule lying on his desk. Sitting back in his chair, highly polished loafers resting on an open lower drawer, his mind was reviewing M.L.'s analysis of dinner with Pamela and E.F. M.L. felt Pamela was still a threat. From what she had told him, Charles had to agree.

It was one of increasingly frequent times he sided with her over E.F. E.F. had a keen eye for people he could trust, and those he should ignore, or get rid of. Yet, there he was once again, siding with M.L. He began to wonder if this campaign to launch UCC into the 21st century under M.L.'s leadership was eroding his loyalty to E.F.?

The ringing phone brought Charles back to the present. Since it was his private line, he was expecting it to be M.L.

"Yes?"

"Hi Charles. How about letting me buy you lunch?"

Smiling at Pamela's invitation, he absently fingered the knot of his tie. It wasn't hard to guess why she was inviting him to lunch. But that was his job. Damage Control.

"I'd love it. Where and when?" Problem or not, he enjoyed Pamela's company.

"Do you know Mickey's on Third?"

"They have the best Caesar Salad in town."

"They do? Great. How about 11:30? It should still be quiet. Ask for me."

*   *   *

Pamela was sitting at her favorite booth at Mickey's, playing with her mug of coffee. "He's got to level with me," she muttered, surprised that her nerves were on edge. She could usually relax around Charles. At least he takes me seriously, she thought. After his years as a spin-doctor, he must be expecting me to corner him for answers.

Glancing up she saw Skip come out from behind the bar and greet Charles as he walked in the front door. Skip never came out from behind the bar. At least, not for most customers. Intrigued, she saw the two men grip hands and launch into an animated conversation.

Shit, she thought. Why didn't I remember Skip still had a few friends at UCC? Muttering to herself, "Now they're laughing at some private joke." Watching Charles's red-gold head leaning toward Skip's black curls, Pamela was reminded of just how good looking both men were. Charles's long, lean frame clothed in navy pin-stripe perfection, while Skip's pure beefcake was stretching his t-shirt and well washed jeans. If this wasn't so important to me, she thought, I could think of some real interesting things to do with those bodies.

Damn it any way, she thought. I wanted to catch Charles off guard. I need some answers.

Catching his eye, Pamela waved Charles over, attracted once again by his easy smile. She saw him make some arrangement with Skip and pat him on his shoulder before walking toward her.

"Hello young lady. This is an excellent choice. I haven't seen Skip since summer."

"You two are friends?" she asked, trying not to sound jealous.

"We play the occasional game of hand ball. Have for years. Even before Skip and I worked together at UCC."

Charles removed his jacket, carefully folding it inside out and placed it on the seat next to him. Aware that Pamela was watching, he asked, "Do you mind? I feel more comfortable in shirt sleeves."

"Not at all," she answered, admiring the blue-and-white stripe shirt with contrasting white collar and cuffs.

As if knowing he still wasn't dressed for Mickey's, Charles unfastened his gold signet cuff links, slipped them into his shirt pocket and rolled his sleeves once, covering the white cuffs.

Even the hair on his arms is red-gold, she noticed. She shook her head to clear it for business.

Charles had been watching Pamela and was clearly amused. "You aren't as tough as you'd like everyone to think. In fact, I'll just bet you're a romantic."

"Sure. All my men compete for my favors with poetry and flowers."

"Skip would if you gave him a chance."

His words hit like a slap, making her hand jerk, spilling her coffee on the bare wood table. She made the thousandth wish that she had picked another restaurant. "I don't picture you in a place like this," she said, trying to regain her composure.

Laughing softly, Charles picked up one of her hands. "I like nice clothes and can afford to dine at 4-Star restaurants. But Pamela, like you, I come here to see Skip and unwind when I'm not working. Understand?"

"Sorry. Can we start again?" she asked.

Giving her hand a little squeeze, he answered, "Absolutely."

"If you come here to see Skip, how come we've never crossed paths?"

"I'm usually a late night visitor. Just before closing, when he has time to talk."

"I hate crowds too. 3 PM, is my schedule."

Signaling Skip, Charles asked, "Do you know what you want?"

At that she laughed. "I'm predictable. It's always a juicy burger with my black coffee. And you? Caesar Salad?" She was glad to see that he was enjoying himself.

"Why tamper with success? Pamela, I have a couple of hours. Would you like to join me in a beer?"

A couple of hours for me, she thought. Thank God! He's going to answer my questions. "Fine. You order. I'm not up on the lineage of beer."

Skip had simply appeared with their beer, and said their orders were on the way. In all of the years she had know him, Skip had never been anything but friendly. He always made her feel she was his special guest of the house. Did his distance have something to do with Charles, she wondered?

"Pamela, I spoke to M.L. this morning. She said she was glad you've agreed to go along with her plans. She also thought you'd have some questions."

She was aware of an intimacy in his voice. A tone that she hoped meant honesty. "She's right. I can except her desire to build a career. Wanting to be CFO. I can even understand her need for secrecy. But, I don't get E.F. His power must be enormous to have pulled all those strings for all of those years. It isn't the normal route to the executive suite."

Sitting back, his beer in hand, Pamela watched as Charles gathered his thoughts. "Remember that article you did on the banker accused of mishandling his bank's investments?" Charles said, leaning forward, forearms on the table. "You researched his education and personal background. Wrote about the man himself. His philosophy on life, charity, and the role of his bank in the community."

Pamela did remember her research. At first she was furious that someone with that responsibility would cheat his customers. They were mostly working class people in one of the poorest areas in the state.

"Which, if I remember correctly," he continued, "demonstrated so clearly that he was innocent of charges, and the Judge who tried him agreed."

"That was a major scandal. Are you trying to tell me that she's E.F.'s Eliza Doolittle?"

"Pamela, M.L. and E.F. worked with the tools available. How many women have been groomed for the corporate suite? How many bright capable females are promoted through the ranks of one organization? Not forced to jump from one proving ground to another to gain recognition?"

About to cut him off, Pamela saw him shake his head to fend off her remarks.

"I'm talking about industrial corporations, not advertising or fashion."

"That part of their story rings true," Pamela grudgingly agreed. "Maybe I need to know more about E.F. What's his role in all this? Why haven't I heard their names linked before?"

"E.F. and I have been friends since I met him at a college roommate's ranch. Some . . . ah, thirty years ago. In all that time, his name hasn't been linked to anyone. Business or personal."

"How old is he, Charles?"

"Ten years older than I am."

"How old are you?" Pamela's humor restored as she watched the gorgeous man twist in his seat. So, he was vain. Looking at him over the rim of her glass, she thought he looked a lot younger than E.F. Yet if she figured it right, he was telling her he was 55, the same age as her father.

"That's not the issue. You were asking about E.F. Let's say he's not old enough to retire."

"His kind never are. They're usually forced to. And when he retires, who takes his place? M.L.?" Something in his eyes caught her attention. "You, maybe?"

"So smart and so young," he answered.

"How could you be number two to M.L.? Aren't you more qualified for the job? You owned your own company, for Christ's sake." Watching him frown, she apologized for her language. He could really make her feel like a clod.

"My role is key to our plans. M.L., as we've tried to tell you, is the better choice to lead this transition."

Pamela saw by the firmness of his jaw and the energy in his voice, that he believed what he was saying. So she changed the subject. "So you and E.F. are old pals. Yet you look like old money, and he new, oil rich. And come to think of it, Jackson and E.F. have a history together. Are you all old buddies?" Her sarcasm broadcast her feelings about the insidiousness of a corporate men's club.

"How many of the journalist-all-stars have you known or worked with?" Charles asked. His eyes were challenging her for an answer.

"Most of those who have worked for my boss at one time or another. I guess you could say my professional world is a small one."

"Mine too. If I need a specialist I go first to someone I've worked with, or someone who's been recommended.

E.F. and I have often shared names and recommendations over the years. We run large organizations. Second best isn't good enough. What would you do? Hire a head hunter and spend months screening for someone who may or may not be as good as the men we've known?"

Pamela was upset, by hearing just how closed the top ranking employment pool was.

"Working within a small arena of professionals isn't corrupt. It's efficient, when people like E.F., M.L., and even me, pick and train only the best.

Now he's reading my thoughts, shifting in her seat, clearly uncomfortable.

"Every member of our executive team has one way or another, worked for E.F. We're hand-picked to a man as the best support for M.L."

"And her strengths are?"

"Problem solving. Strategy. One hell of a chess player. She's also an outstanding female."

"And your secret love?" Even though she'd whispered, she saw that it hurt. "Sorry. That's between you and the Boss Lady. Now's probably not the time for romance anyway."

"Thank you."

The silence following allowed both to explore their thoughts. Pamela had no wish to make an enemy out of Charles. Getting a handle on M.L. was more important anyway.

"Pamela? Can I tell you something?"

"You've been fair with me. I won't sell you out."

"Just hear me out. Don't rush to judge. Can you promise that?"

Nodding her approval, Pamela put down her hardly touched beer and picked up her coffee. She needed a sip of caffeine to keep her quiet.

"Sometimes business is a matter of perception. You develop advertising campaigns and packaging to influence the consumer. Dealing with the image of a corporation can involve some of those very same techniques. If you want to influence Wall Street you put on a dog and pony show to communicate your strength in earnings and depth of successful products. If you need to reengineer a corporation, but don't want to bring on large scale job loss along with speculation that you've lost your competitive edge, you paint a different face on it. Deflect the negative issues. Focus the eyes of your competition, Wall Street and investors, on the corporation's leadership, its build-up toward a new future."

"I'm with you so far." Pamela knew the basics. Her whole career was based on looking behind what the corporations issued as official comment. Now, she wondered what could be so sensitive?

"You don't have much time. In fact, if you're lucky, maybe one month at the most."

"Almost the lead time of a monthly news magazine," Pamela said catching Charles' eye.

"Right. Of course the daily media, even the stock market will react instantaneously. Especially, if they suspect that something's afoot. So how do you plan to realign employees, structure layoffs and close plants without word getting out?"

"You do your planning behind the scenes." She was right behind him.

"Right again. But you also create a diversion. You attract attention away from the harsh realities of reengineering and get the same media and investors talking about something else."

"M.L." Pamela whispered. She was itching to ask questions.

Holding up his hand as if to stop her runaway skepticism, Charles said, "Before you accuse me of being a chauvinist, or M.L. of not being qualified, hear me out." Getting her nod to continue, Charles took a breath before speaking.

"I didn't say fake a diversion. I said create one. M.L. isn't a fake. She knows only too well the talk she's beginning to generate. But it was her idea. Before E.F. nominated her for CEO, the Board had reviewed the reengineering plans of two other candidates. Each one a respected president of a large company. Only M.L.'s had the audacity to buy UCC the time we needed."

Charles had been talking for half an hour before their lunch arrived. Pamela was happy to take a break and put this final piece of information into place. As far as she knew, only M.L.'s team and probably the UCC Board, knew which company UCC was purchasing. And M.L.'s announcement to the press was timed for a week from Monday. Then UCC would issue a press release that would become part of the official corporate record, posted on all the wire services and available on the corporate website. After the cocktail parties earlier this week, M.L.'s position was sure to have leaked out. But Charles had never said anything about keeping the press at bay. Anything in print would be rumor, until it was officially announced, she thought. *Right now, all of my competitors are probably scrambling to get the skinny on who and what she is.*

Pamela saw that Charles had hardly touched his beer. His salad finished, he seemed preoccupied.

"Have you been fielding reporters all week," she asked, breaking the short silence.

"Yes."

"And I have to stay quiet for now. She is qualified, right?"

"She's qualified!" Charles was challenging her for a commitment.

"So far, I think she is too. And, yes I'll write the outline that way. But I want her first official interview. An exclusive!" She shot back.

"A deal! Let's celebrate with dessert."

His grin almost hid the relief she read in his face. "The chocolate mud pie with ice cream? If your diet permits," she teased.

"Two spoons? Shouldn't we ask Skip to join us?"

She knew she was blushing, but had to laugh. And, maybe Charles was right about Skip. Hadn't she been thinking along those same lines all week?

"Charles, the company UCC wants to buy?"

"Yes?"

She was sorry to see the sun leave his smile. "What was the name of the investment firm that was also bidding for the company?"

"Neuwirth Investments, a subsidiary of the Cayman Island, WSF, Ltd. What's on that sharp mind?"

"Don't the initials WSF remind you of something? A monogram maybe?"

She had all she could do from blurting out the results of her digging and her incredible find. A nugget of information that was so bizarre, she needed his reaction, or she'd bust. Pamela could see Charles puzzling over her question. It was if he was poised for the drop of a bomb. And, if her information was correct, it was nuclear.

"No, should it?"

"I see your cuff links have a crest, a family crest?" Seeing him nod, she continued. "Yet you don't initial your shirt cuff or pocket."

"William Smythe Foley," Charles spat out. His mouth, open in surprise, snapped close. "Are you sure?"

"Yes. A friend has a Cayman girl friend. She just happened to have access to the ownership of all the Island's registered firms."

"I'll be damned." Charles breath seemed to have left him. Looking at her she knew she'd given him a valuable gift.

"I owe you. M.L., E.F., we all owe you. Can you keep this a secret along with the others?"

Nodding yes. She knew the information was the their lifeline to success.

"In return, I'll tell you the name of the company UCC wants to buy. It's BioTech. But you can't breathe a word, not until the merger papers are signed. Agreed?"

"Hell yes!" So this was what being on the inside track was like, she thought. Shit, what a high!

CHAPTER XXXII

Gothic arched windows reflected a gloomy dusk, forty stories above Park Avenue. The Sky Clubrooms had the cold feeling of a tomb. The mood wasn't any less oppressive in the closed off library where M.L., E.F. and Lawrence Henderson sat lost in separate thoughts.

They were a powerful trio. M.L., a knife-slim leader dressed in a severe black suit. E.F., the image of a CEO's boardroom portrait, and Henderson the stereotype of inherited wealth.

The room held no hints of hospitality. No tray of drinks. No coffee, or little cakes.

"Melissa," E.F. said as he rose and began to slowly circle the room. "Larry and I will keep our silence. It must be cold and quick. It's the only way to kill a snake."

Nodding, Melissa looked toward Larry, waiting for his advice. Not getting any she said, "How can you just sit there?"

"Years of waiting for test results. You'll be fine. E.F. and I are just here for visual effect."

M.L. wished she were as confident in her own abilities. This was one battle that had become personal.

At that moment Raymond Costa, the Club manager, announced the arrival of William Foley. Melissa walked toward the library entrance and held the door for her nemesis. "You know everyone here, William. Why don't you join us at the table?"

Walking toward the small group seated at an antique gaming table, he selected a chair and perched in readiness.

M.L. had brought a slim file with her as she sat in the remaining chair, facing Foley. Noticing the slight flush in his face, she had to admire the calm expression clothing it. Where did she begin? She'd practiced her speech. Rehearsing for all Foley's possible reactions. Yet, here he sat poised, waiting. Giving no hint of what he was expecting.

"William Smythe Foley," she began in flint hard tones. "I should have you arrested and disbarred. Your betrayal is so foul, it's akin to murder."

The silence was filled with the electricity of her voice. Yet Foley just sat, waiting for her to play the rest of her cards.

Opening the slim file, she continued. "I trusted you with my plans. Your activities as owner of WSF, Ltd, which owns Neuwirth Investments, and the double-dealing on BioTech are not only illegal, they threaten the future of UCC. I demand your resignation, effective immediately." Still no outward reaction, she thought.

"To stay out of jail, you will sell all Neuwirth's BioTech and UCC holdings. In return, I will not have you prosecuted and disbarred. Are we clear?" Staring into his black beady eyes, she suppressed a shudder, knowing she had made a life long enemy.

"You can't prove anything," was William's calm response. Crossing his legs he sat back in his chair. "You're impotent."

The venom in Foley's voice caused Larry and E.F. to blink with alarm. Yet Foley's face remained calm. "You can't force me to sell anything not in my name. But I will resign. Effective right now," smiling with the expression of a cat toying with a mouse. "UCC needs a man in control."

They watched as Foley's all-consuming hatred was directed at M.L.

Careful, she thought. Don't rise to his baiting. "I have before me an extensive report consisting of telephone conversations with a Bruce Dearling and, your Mr. Dearling's with a Tim Lynch."

M.L. continued, purposely ignoring Foley's dagger-like stare. "I also have Dr. Henderson's account of Mr. Dearling's offer and counter offer, that include information only you could have provided."

"What?" William asked, in a surprised voice.

She saw that it was his first break in composure. Continuing to ignore him, she went on reading from the file. "I also have Mr. Dearling's sworn statement containing your plans to purchase BioTech and sabotage UCC's restructuring."

Looking up she saw the haughty William S. Foley wilt. His beady eyes boring into her. When did he lose it, she wondered. He's too smart to pull a dumb play for power against E.F.

"Mr. Haynes is here representing the Board, and Dr. Henderson is here to sign the BioTech sale to UCC." M.L. turned to Lawrence Henderson, as he nodded silently for her to continue. Henderson then turned a calm gaze on William, reinforcing his position as a silent member of this tribunal.

"Dr. Henderson, also wanted you to know that he suspected foul play. That your behavior, is beneath contempt. He won't do business with someone without ethics," she added, digging the hole a little deeper.

Shaking his head, William Foley finally spoke. "What now?" He made no attempt to appeal to E.F., and refused to look at Henderson.

M.L. knew Foley had never felt comfortable with E.F. Did he know it was E.F. who had rejected his nomination for Chairman?

"You will sign these papers agreeing to all our demands. If you ever speak of this to anyone, or if you leak any information we consider sensitive or proprietary, I will publish this file."

Foley looked at the paper in M.L.'s hand. Refusing to touch it he asked, "Where do I sign?"

To her surprise his calm had returned. She was expecting the little pop in jay to throw a tantrum. His calm told her he wasn't beaten yet.

As soon as Foley'd put pen to paper, he rose, nodded to E.F., ignored Henderson and slowly headed for the library door. Just as he reached the door her voice cut into his thoughts, stopping him in mid step.

"Don't go back to your office. Your pass is voided. The door is padlocked. Your personal effects will be sent to you."

The look he directed toward M.L. was pure evil. Suddenly it was replaced with a sly smile. "By the way," he said, as if the last thirty minutes had never happened. "Nathan Fallon sends his regards." Turning on his heel, head high, William Smythe Foley walked out the door.

Sinking back in her chair, M.L. stared at the closed door. "What in Hell can he have to do with Fallon?" she asked E.F., her voice deeply troubled. Foley's lack of verbal response, then his threat had escalated her fear.

No one spoke. Only the grandfather clock chiming the hour gave any hint of life.

"He's bluffing," E.F.'s voice broke the silence.

"He's a deviant." Larry's added, concern coloring his gentle voice.

"Fallon wouldn't deal with the likes of Foley. Fallon has to be boss. Foley'd never stand for that," E.F. concluded.

"So it's not over," she said in a trance-like voice.

"Not yet." E.F. said. "But we have our watchers in place. He can't pee without our knowing how much."

CHAPTER XXXIII

The limousine had taken E.F. and Larry to their weekly card game. Melissa walked home to change for her evening with Hugh. Each step had been accompanied by thoughts of Foley's next move.

His greeting from Fallon didn't mesh with what she knew of the Mafia capo, she thought. Fallon had once threatened her directly. As if time had frozen, she could see the Buzzard's soulless eyes when he'd said, "Think you'd be so cocky with a cut face?" She remembered her terror, his hollow cackle sending shivers up her spine. He didn't need to act on his threat, she knew his pleasure was in terrorizing her.

It wouldn't be like him to use Foley to deliver a message. Foley's call to Fallon to sell him a piece of his Neuwirth syndicate had been in the detective's report. Most of her file on Foley contained the detective's information gathered from secretaries, cleaning ladies and wire tap transcripts.

By the time she had turned onto her block, Melissa had decided that it was Foley's ego that had him believing he could use Fallon to threaten her.

Melissa remembered Freud's saying, we accuse others of the shadows in ourselves. If that's true, just what was she really accusing Foley of? Greed? Treachery? Suddenly she stopped, the blood draining from her face. It was ambition. And Freud was right. Her's had fueled her every move since college.

Melissa was horrified that there was any similarity between them. Unaware of people turning to stare as they passed, she resumed walking. Comparing her climb up the ladder to Foley's, she saw that the main difference was E.F. Because of him, she hadn't had to claw her way over people.

Could she have risen as far as Foley without E.F.? It wasn't something she'd ever considered. The unasked question that would have challenged her own opinion of her abilities.

I'm not going to let that deviate upset me. He can hate me till he's eaten up. I've won! The merger was just signed. UCC is on its new path. And, at last, my position is secure.

*　　　*　　　*

Leaning back in the taxi, Melissa wished the car would move faster through the city's dark streets. Didn't the driver know how much she needed to see Hugh? She could feel his arms around her. When she was with him she could escape reality. Hugh was her gift to herself.

Alighting from the cab, Melissa let herself into Hugh's building, pressing the buzzer to his apartment.

The buzzer's shrill sound jolted Hugh into action. Lissa's downstairs and I'm talking to this screw-up, he thought. Rushing to get off the phone with his agent, he shouted, "Fuck it! They want me in Spain next week. I'll be there. You're off the hook." Slamming down the receiver, Hugh's anger was on low boil. "I've been their box office draw for three films in two years, and the pricks are treating me like some extra. It's time to get a new agent. A bastard tough enough to get me what I want."

Rushing to the door of the apartment, Hugh sidestepped a chair and vaulted over a low table. He reached the door in time to see Lissa leaving the elevator and rush down the hall into his open arms.

Holding her close he felt his heart rushing blood through his body. Ah shit, he thought. This is what I want. Thanks to that schumck, I have only a few days to make this precious girl mine. Turning his thoughts to the curves of Lissa's body, he gently kissed her forehead, holding her close. Forgetting his problems as his hands moved over her back. He liked the feel of her head resting on his shoulder and her body molded to his.

She's so fragile, he thought. Feeling his own tension melt away, Hugh focused on Lissa, wondering what had happened. Her usual greeting was filled with fiery kisses and hands that were everywhere on him at once. But tonight she leaned into his arms. Watching her closely, he saw small beads of moisture dot the inside corners of her eyelashes. He wanted to protect her. Take her away from this hellhole of a city.

"Darling. We can't stand here," he whispered into her hair, gently guiding her into the apartment. All thoughts of his career gone. Replaced with joy in knowing she needed him. "Would you like a drink?"

"Can you make a margarita," she asked, straightening to stand on her own.

She must have had a bum day. She always drinks wine.

"We can go out if you prefer." Hugh felt her voice echo in the silence. Go out, he thought. Not on your life! Seeing her lack of interest, Hugh knew that wasn't what she really wanted. Relieved he quickly kissed the tip of her nose. His spirits restored by the joy of spending their too few remaining hours alone.

"In one of my past lives, I was a pretty good bartender," giving Lissa a smile that women swooned over. "I'm famous among the Malibu set for my margaritas." As he saw her relax, he swore he'd find out what had happened.

With one arm holding her waist, Hugh led her to the bar and lifted her up onto a stool. Walking behind the mirrored counter he began to prepare their drinks with all the flourish in his actor's bag of tricks. Watching her closely he saw her give him a look of such tenderness his heart ached.

"I feel better. You're the best tonic," she said as he poured her drink into a salt rimmed glass.

Taking a sip and closing her eyes, Hugh watched her mouth savor the tart/sweet taste. "Mm this is perfect," a dreamy look on her now relaxed face.

"Care to tell me about it?" Careful, keep it light, he thought. "Why are you so upset?"

"I don't know where to start," she said, her eyes now veiled. The dreamy mood was broken. "Let's just say I had a tough day."

"We all have those." Would she tell him her problems, he wondered? "You seem beat. Can I help?"

"I doubt it. I just fired a traitor. He hates me."

As he watched her sip her drink, Hugh wondered who and why anyone would hate her. Hatred stemmed from some deep emotion like jealousy, greed or betrayal. He'd studied enough of those parts to know that.

"When I read a script, I try to get into the soul of the guy I'm playing," he began, hoping to draw her out. "If I'm to work myself up to hating someone, I have to have been cheated or crossed. Hate's just another emotion, like jealousy."

"We're in different businesses," Melissa began, looking at her empty glass. "Emotions don't play any part in what I do."

As Hugh poured another drink, he wondered how this woman, to him the embodiment of emotion, could say that.

"What if you had something someone thought should have been theirs?"

Her question had him grinning. Almost laughing. "That's the story of my life. Before I made it, I would read for parts I'd have killed for. But they'd go to Redford or Nolte. Now it's my turn. Others get rejected."

"How do actors get through the rejection?"

"Some don't. I try to remember I'm no better than the next blond guy who is in decent shape. Save my money so when I go out of style, I won't starve."

"Why do you act? Are you driven to it? Could you live happily without the fame?"

Moving to the stool next to her, Hugh wondered if he could give it all up. He knew he could have both if she'd marry him. Without her he'd turn into a monster. Driven by ambition and a gut-deep need never to be poor again. Sweet Lissa validated everything he liked about himself.

"I struggled for years to get where I am." His jaw tightened in remembering his years of eking out the rent in jobs that required brawn, not talent. "Only a handful of us ever reach this point in films. And I've just arrived. I still have to prove to myself, that I can act. Lissa, I want it all. Academy nominations. Percentage of the gross. I want enough fame so I can pick and choose parts after my looks go. Do you understand?"

"Yes. Success keeps away the demons."

Did she really understand, he wondered? Hugh wasn't sure if he like the dejected tone or her troubled look. It wasn't his Lissa.

"Acting's not a disease. It's fun. At least, most of the time. I can pretend I'm a hero. Strong. Rich. And get paid for it."

"Oh!" Instead of laughing with him, she looked as if she'd lost her best friend.

"Oh? What's wrong sweetheart? What's knocked you for a loop?"

"The man I fired? I found out he tried to ruin me."

"How?" What had she gotten into, he wondered?

"I can't really talk about it. But this man felt he should have had my job. That I wasn't smart enough. You see, I'm only a woman." The distaste for what she was saying puckered her lovely face.

"Lissa. Why do you work? Is being CEO your life?"

"Yes. I've put years and everything I am into becoming a success. I guess you would say in my field, CEO is the equivalent of being a star. Instead of acting a part, I have power to make things happen."

Hugh was beginning to see a very different woman. She sure was passionate about that job, he noticed. Still trying to lift the dark mood he said, "Hollywood is a cutthroats paradise. Your business can't be the same," hoping she'd agree. But Lissa just sat there quietly twisting her glass by its stem.

"As an actor I have some power." Not enough, yet, he thought remembering his conversation with his agent.

"You don't understand. I make decisions that involve thousands of people and billions of dollars."

Aware that she had changed before his eyes, Hugh's laughing mood was gone. He was stunned. He didn't want to think of her life without him. But damn it all. Her sharpness scared him. This wasn't the woman he fell in love with.

"I don't know if you realize how important you've become to me." Hugh wanted to look into her eyes and plead for her to love him. To forget her job. Picking up her hand he continued before she could reply.

"You're so real. You make me feel I'm important. Me. Not the star. What I'm trying to say is I need you."

He couldn't look up. Her answer was too important. Not hearing anything, he blurted out, "Lissa, will you marry me?" Startled but relieved, he knew that was what he'd wanted all along. He wanted her by his side in Spain. Then if she had to come back to this hellhole, he'd figure something out. All he knew was he needed her.

Squeezing his hand, Melissa got off the stool. He watched her walk toward the livingroom window, her head tilted down. Looking out at the fairy lights of Central Park, twenty stories below.

Walking up behind her he placed his arms around her, his chin resting on her head. Hearing her sigh, he heard her whisper, "You're still not real to me. I don't know anything about you."

The silence was filled with his own heart beat.

"I work here," she continued, not seeming to expect an answer. "You wouldn't like my 12 and 14 hour days."

She leaned back, resting her full weight on him. Hugh felt her sadness. But holding her, he also felt her need of his strength.

"I can't even boil water," she sighed.

Chuckling, Hugh looked at their reflection in the night-darkened window. She looked so slight, in front of his broad body. The reflection not showing her curves and warmth. He was thinking how happy his houseman, Jesus, would be seeing him safely married.

"Lissa. I don't think you understand. You don't have to cook, clean or iron my shirts. All you have to do is love me."

"But darling . . ."

"Shush. I know, your job," hearing her fears, not believing they'd get in the way. Changing the subject as he cradled her in his arms, "I want you to see my new house. It sits on top of a mountain. My nearest neighbor's over a mile away. It's almost finished. You can help decorate."

"What are you doing on a mountain top? Hiding?"

"Don't joke. That's exactly what I'm doing. The public Hugh Baron is only available by appointment. I want you to share my retreat. We can ride, swim or loaf. We can raise our family, away from the noise and dirt of cities."

He felt her pull away. "I'm always on the go. My schedule is packed from 8 to 8. Next week starts one month of non-stop travel."

Hugh gently turned her around to see what she was saying. "Lissa, don't you want a home and family?" He needed her answer.

"I never thought about it. My life took a different path." Not wanting to continue, she reached up and wrapped her arms around his neck, kissing him as if her life depended upon it.

Time stood still as Hugh's need for Lissa replaced his questions. Tomorrow, he thought. I'll figure us out tomorrow. Lifting her into his arms he carried her to the bedroom. Hugh knew that after seeing him on the set,

Lissa would stop worrying about her job. Bless her heart. She had no idea how rich he was. Probably thinks the house is a log cabin. He couldn't wait for her to see the glass walls that brought nature into every room. It was being photographed for *Architectural Digest*. The interior shots were waiting for the decorator to finish. Smiling, as he thought of having her with him in Spain. They'd be in the penthouse suite of a private apartment the studio rented for his use. She'd love the royal treatment. Maybe then she'd forget that job of hers. His spirits lifted: confident that he could give her anything she wanted.

CHAPTER XXXIV

As the front door slammed close, William Foley stomped toward the bar in his den and poured four fingers of scotch. The three ice cubes he dropped into the glass melted as they hit the alcohol.

"That Bitch hasn't won yet." His fury echoed around the walls of his empty apartment. Picking up the telephone receiver, he phoned his sister. "Hi Jane. I'm going to be leaving town earlier than planned. Do you mind if I drive up tonight?"

"Of course not Willy. But that means you won't be getting here until after midnight. You know how I worry when you drive at night."

"It can't be helped. Don't wait up. I'll let myself in."

"That's all right. I'll be up. Is anything wrong, Dear? It isn't like you to start out after dark."

Just hearing her concern calmed him enough to sit. "I've been fired!"

"Who fired you?"

"The new CEO. The Bitch terminated my contract. She's threatening to ruin me. Shit Jane, she's forcing us into bankruptcy."

"Calm down. We'll have a long chat when you get here. Just like we used to."

"Yes Jane. I'll tell you about it tomorrow."

"Good. Willy if you feel tired, stop off and have a strong cup of coffee. Promise me."

"I'll be careful. See you around midnight."

Any thoughts of sleep had vanished, as Jane tried to absorb her brother's news. Pacing back and forth around her bedroom, she worried. I haven't heard Willy close to tears since his 10th birthday. When he'd been beaten up by kids who wanted his new toy plane. The plane he'd bought with money he'd made taking out old Mrs. Murphy's trash. Jane was alarmed. She loved her brother. But his anger could blind him.

"We'll figure something out. This Miss Horn must be a doozie to get you in such a snit. Oh God, protect me from my temper. One of us has to remain calm. It apparently isn't Willy."

Hanging up, William felt calmer. Jane always stood by him. With his drink in hand, he started emptying his desk drawer. All Neuwirth and Foley family files were on computer disks. A loose-leaf binder contained a duplicate record of investment transactions, tracking his activities along with copies of all brokerage receipts, and documentation of ownership. Closing and locking his financial life into his briefcase, Foley emptied his glass. Checking his desk once more for cash and car keys, he picked up his coat and headed for the garage.

Three hours later, Foley aimed his dark blue Mercedes sedan down the blackened local roads, twenty miles from Quincy, Massachusetts. The entire trip from Manhattan had been accompanied by a stream of bile-colored images of how he would take his revenge.

Clenching his jaw, his mind filled with a torrent of diabolical schemes of M.L.'s demise. First he pictured her with a noose around her neck, standing in a cemetery awaiting hanging by a group of his peers. Now, as rain spattered the windshield, it washed away a scene in which he stood over M.L. with a gun, while she cowered on her knees, pleading for her life.

Unaware of the night around him, he was suddenly blinded by the headlights of an approaching car, hugging the centerline of the two-lane road.

"Mother fucker," cursing the maniac in the advancing car. Maneuvering frantically trying to avoid it, Foley steered off his side of the road.

"Stop damn you! Why do you think I paid for disk brakes?" he yelled, as his car went into a skid. Paralyzed by fear, he felt the car's wheels lock, as they hit the rain soaked grass. His mind slowed, becoming a series of slow motion pictures that one-by-one depicted his car as it careened into a big old tree.

Foley knew he was going to die when the windshield exploded into a sunburst of light and glass. He didn't feel the glass as it sliced into his head. He felt somehow removed from his body, as he stared in fascination at the other side window, seeing flames licking at the glass. The last thing he was aware of, was the nauseating smell of gasoline. "I won't get sick," he said, passing out from shock and loss of blood.

If God kept score, then the account of William Smythe Foley, former UCC Counsel, brother of Jane Smythe Foley Ahearn, was settled.

*   *   *

The Saturday morning papers announced UCC's purchase of BioTech. Tim Lynch, having read *The New York Times* and *The Wall Street Journal* accounts began counting his profits.

"The market is sure going to love this news. Dearling's going to be very happy indeed," he gloated. Not able to reach him on the weekend, Tim made a note to call Dearling Monday and see what he wanted him to do next.

Chuckling, he started thinking about moving to a status address. "Yea. Go BioTech!" He couldn't afford stock in both UCC and BioTech. So gambling on Dearling having the inside track, he'd put his last dollar into BioTech. "Park Avenue here I come."

*   *   *

In the dining room of their home, E.F. and Melissa were discussing the same newspapers. "If I don't hear anything from Foley today, I'll phone and offer him yesterday's price for our stock," Melissa said.

"Wait until after the market closes Monday. That way we can watch to see if he dumps his holdings, and nail him. We know how much Neuwirth owns, but we haven't been able to find out how much he owns personally."

"I see what you mean. Will your broker keep you informed on what this Lynch does?"

"Yes. Gavin's been alerted. He'll call me if there's any change in the Neuwirth account. We've got him. Now that the merger is signed and you've announced our purchase of BioTech, we're protected."

"Have you given any thought to Foley's threat?"

Melissa heard the worry in E.F.'s voice. It didn't seem important to answer him. She was thinking about something more pressing.

"Damn it Melissa! Didn't Foley scare you?"

The thundering sound of his voice, followed by the rattling of glasses and dishes as E.F.'s hand slammed down on the table, made her jump. She had been thinking about Hugh. Sadly, realizing, she wouldn't survive on his mountaintop. But now E.F. was demanding her attention. Closing her mind to her problems, she looked directly at him, surprised by his flare-up.

"I don't understand? Fallon wouldn't use Foley to threaten me. He'd save that pleasure for himself."

"Wake up! It's me. I care about you. Not the G D job."

"Aren't you over reacting? Nothing's changed." She really didn't know why he was so upset. Picking up her coffee she sipped it absent-mindedly. Her emotions, hidden under defensive layers.

"Honey, where are you? Where ever it is, it isn't at work."

Looking at him, Melissa shook her head. "No it isn't. I saw Hugh last night. He wants to marry me."

"You don't look very excited about it. Hugh Baron is the biggest thing to hit the movies since Gable."

"I didn't know you knew him?"

"Don't. But I've invested in his studio. They've been budgeting on the basis of his being their cash cow."

Melissa moved her eggs from one place to another on her plate. Each little yellow pile as neat and tidy as if she measured them in place. "He wants to take care of me. Move me to a mountain top and raise kids."

Miserable, she looked to E.F. for some answers. She just wasn't sure of the questions. It wasn't as simple as yes, get married, or no, say good bye.

Getting up from the table, E.F. walked to Melissa and lifted her from her chair to hold her in his arms. "Why don't you tell me about it," he said caressing her back, trying to soothe away her pain.

Hiding her face on his shoulder, she sighed. "I told you about my lack of a social life. Hugh didn't just free me sexually. He showed me a glimpse of a life I've never expected to have. A passionate and tender relationship with a man I can trust."

"You trust me."

Melissa nodded but didn't say anything. She did wonder about the wistfulness in her dear friend's voice. E.F. wasn't sounding like his usual tough self.

"Do you want to live on his mountain?"

Moving out of the comfort of his arms, Melissa looked up and shook her head so firmly her hair briefly hid her face. As her tears began to fall, she sobbed, "I love my life. What would I do on a mountaintop? How would I work? I've reached the top. How could I give all that up?" Feeling E.F.'s arms holding her, she dropped her face onto his chest and cried. She was beyond thought. Her heart ached.

"Don't worry Honey," E.F. crooned. "I'm here. You'll find someone better."

CHAPTER XXXV

It had been raining for 24-hours and the airport runway was enveloped in an early morning fog. The limousine driving out of the predawn darkness was heading for the corporate jet's boarding stairs. As the driver walked around to open the back door he unfurled a large black umbrella. It was a dour M.L. and Charles Cray who got out of the car and climbed the stairs to the plane.

At 4 a.m. on this Monday morning, M.L. hadn't had time for her morning coffee. Hurrying up the stairway her toe caught on the top step, catapulting her into the open cabin door. Strong arms caught her before she landed on the blue carpeted entry, setting her gently back on her feet. Reaching out to steady herself, M.L. grasped hold of the steward's forearms that even her viselike grip failed to dent. Looking up at the smiling face she recognized Kevin, one of E.F.'s bodyguards.

"Why couldn't she lean on me for something other than business," Charles mumbled to himself as he saw her trip.

"Good morning, Ms. Horn, Mr. Cray, "Kevin's voice was a bright note in the pre-dawn gloom. "We'll be flying over this weather. As soon as we're above it, I'll serve you breakfast."

"Will the trip be smooth?" Charles asked the handsome younger man. "This weather looks dicey."

"It should be like glass once we reach altitude, Mr. Cray. Our ETA in Boston is a little over one hour. There'll be a car waiting for you on the field."

Looking for the phone, M.L. headed over to the recliner placed in a small area cut off from the main cabin by a panel of etched plexi-glass. Buckling into her seat, she saw Charles heading for the chair next to hers. "I'm going to have to make a call when we're clear of the tower. I'll join you later."

Nodding, Charles turned toward the front of the cabin, selecting a chair just behind the door to the flight crew. "What could be so secret she'd need privacy from me," he grumbled, buckling his maroon and green, webbed seat belt.

The cabin was one of M.L.'s favorites. It was E.F.'s newest plane and as with his others, it had been furnished for comfort. The privacy she needed was hers. Leaning back, feet elevated, she wondered what she'd say to Hugh. He was expecting to see her this evening. It would have been their last time together before he left for Spain.

I know he's not expecting me to give him an answer, she thought quietly. What do I tell him? It was a question that had haunted her and had her crying in E.F.'s arms.

After yet another sleepless night, she still couldn't be sure just what she'd say.

The green light finally signaled that she was free to use the telephone. Lifting the receiver she dialed in her personal code and Hugh's number at the Stanhope.

"Yea?" growled Hugh having been awakened from a deep sleep. Looking at her watch, M.L. saw that it was only 4:30. "Shit!" he exploded in her ear.

"Hello grouchy," she laughed. "Is this what I'm to expect if I wake you?"

"Lissa? Where are you? Are you all right?" Hugh's questions were running into one another.

Listening to the concern in his voice, she was suddenly sad. She knew what she had to tell him.

"I don't know exactly where I am, except I'm winging my way to a funeral."

"Where? Is that why you're calling at this ungodly hour?"

"Massachusetts. I'm afraid I have to break our date for tonight. This was a last minute thing. The man died Friday in an auto accident."

The silence at the other end of the phone pulled at her. Maybe she could delay actually telling Hugh she couldn't marry him. That would buy her some time to think things through more carefully.

"I leave for Spain tomorrow. I don't suppose you could fly over for the weekend?"

"Darling. I wish I could. But I won't have a free weekend for some time." No, she thought, she had to deal with him now. It was the only fair thing to do. Because she loved him, she had to let him go.

"Hugh. I've been thinking about your proposal. I, ah.."

"Don't tell me," Hugh interrupting her. "You love me but can't marry me. Well don't worry. I don't want to marry you."

His bitter voice stung her.

"You aren't my Lissa." His voice was all unleashed anger. "You've turned into a frightful stranger. The Lissa I fell in love with on Largo Verde needed me. You don't need anyone. If Lissa had to go to a funeral, she would have asked me to go with her. Needing and wanting my comfort. That Lissa would pick up and visit me on location. Want to help me finish our home. You don't want me. All you want is that job. Well, keep it. You've earned it!"

Silent tears of pain ran down her face. He was right. Lissa wasn't real. She needed Hugh, but not for any reason Hugh wanted. He needed someone to lean on him. She had long ago learned never to lean on anyone. E.F. was the only exception.

"Bye Lissa. Don't call me. I couldn't stand it."

The dead phone buzzed in her ear. Replacing the receiver, M.L. covered her face with her hands and cried out her pain.

It seemed she'd been crying for hours when the plane leveled off. It was time to rejoin Charles. Picking up a tissue, she blew her nose. Reaching into her handbag, M.L. set about opening her compact and repairing her makeup. Her heart was beyond any such fix. Staring at her reflection, Melissa adjusted her thoughts and regained her composure. Only her eyes gave her away. Well everyone will think I'm grieving for Foley, she thought, clicking her compact closed. With her emotions back in storage, she straightened her suit and walked forward to join Charles for a light breakfast.

Charles looked up at her tap on his shoulder. "Are you Okay?"

Nodding, M.L. sat in the lounge chair next to his before answering. "I've just had an unpleasant call. Do I look dreadful?"

"Nope. Come on M.L. This is me. What's wrong?"

Her hands couldn't stop fidgeting with the seat belt buckle. Her mind was someplace else. Even during the toughest meetings, she was always in control. She wished she could confide in Charles. Sadly, her mind focused instead on the business before them. Quietly, she waited for Charles to take the hint.

"What do you think of all this? Foley's death sure is convenient," Charles said, looking at her for a response.

Bless you for understanding, she thought, as she gave him a smile of gratitude. "I was wondering about his religion," she lied. "What was his family like?"

"Money. His religion was money. Our records show only a sister. He was a loner at UCC; I suspect he was the same in life."

Me, too, M.L. thought, I've been alone all my life. Now, I can't even dream of Hugh. I had to have a secret affair with a man I could never live with. The tears almost started again, as she realized Hugh was a gift, not something that could have lasted.

"I wonder if his sister is as demented as Foley?"

"He wasn't demented. Just ambitious. But his sister won't like the woman who fired her brother. You should be prepared for some bitterness."

Charles and M.L. always played "what if" scenarios before important meetings. By asking the tough questions, Charles helped her prepare for the worst.

"No I guess she won't. But was she aware of his treachery? I have to get control of that stock. Without it we're vulnerable. Do you realize just how much BioTech that bastard bought? What a hell of a way to start the week."

As they sat over breakfast of muffins and fruit, M.L. prayed things would work out. Hugh was history.

*   *   *

They stood still in a pristine New England cemetery. The bleak fall weather was unable to offer the mourners any warmth, with sunrise still an hour away. The early hour had been chosen by Foley's sister. M.L. and Charles had made every effort to attend.

Mourners. That's a laugh, M.L. thought. The only other person at the gravesite was a sharp-edged, narrow woman. She wore her hair pulled into a gray and black streaked bun caught high on her neck that cleared the collar of her charcoal gray raincoat.

Watching the angular face, tight with unshed tears, M.L. knew this woman's anguish went beyond anything she had ever experienced. Even at the sudden death of her parents.

As they lowered Foley's coffin into the dark hole, M.L. wondered if they would ever know the real story behind his death. The police had called her at midnight on Friday, having obtained her number from UCC's night operator. She had been amazed at how far E.F.'s influenced reached, when she'd arrived at the grave site, and been handed an autopsy report by a local police officer. She remembered thinking that they had to have worked through the weekend to have it ready for her. She wanted it to help her to deal with Foley's sister.

As Foley's sister bowed her head in prayer, M.L. thought of his betrayal. She couldn't pretend she had ever even liked Foley, but she would offer a prayer for his soul.

Feeling Charles' hand on her elbow, she was reminded that they were here to tidy up loose ends. M.L. had read the police report quickly. But questions remained. Could it have been a suicide? Heart attack? Was fate going to protect the bastard by his death? Maybe she could save his sister the pain of knowing the full extent of his treachery. First she'd have to meet the woman and find out what she knew. Thank God for Charles, she thought. He could charm anyone.

*　　　*　　　*

Their driver pulled up to a postcard New England cottage, amid a precise, evergreen-bordered lawn. The tranquil setting was a hopeful sight to M.L.

"Do you think Foley's sister is as serene as this house?" she asked Charles.

"Serene or controlling. There's only one way we'll find out. Ready to go in?"

As they approached the front door, M.L. moved ahead to lift the ring of the brightly polished brass doorknocker. Before she had a chance to remove her hand the door opened to reveal the lone woman they had seen at the grave.

"Miss Foley?" M.L. asked.

"It's Mrs. Ahearn. You must be Ms. Horn. Your office called earlier and said you would be attending Willy's funeral. Please come in."

The words were polite, but the grief-filled face was that of a stoic. This was probably the only person who could have loved a man like William Foley, Charles thought.

"Mrs. Ahearn, I'm Charles Cray. Ms. Horn and I worked closely with your brother."

Nodding, but not answering, Jane Foley Ahearn, turned and with head held high, led her visitors into her front parlor.

"Mrs. Ahearn," Charles began, breaking the silence in the room. It was a room without even the ticking of a clock, as if time stood still here. Charles wondered if Mrs. Ahearn ever listened to a radio or phonograph. She didn't look modern enough to own a CD player. She reminded Charles of his maiden aunt, now somewhere in her 80's.

Seeing that he had her attention, he continued, "Both Ms. Horn and I wish to express our condolences. We were shocked by your brother's sudden passing."

"Shocked but relieved." Jane's voice was filled with bitterness. "I don't know what happened. Why, you fired William. Maybe you'd like to tell me about it."

Sitting in a well-worn wooden rocking chair, Jane indicated they should sit opposite her on the sofa.

Charles prepared himself to negotiate the woman's hostility. Jane was New England winter itself. Dressed in a gray sweater set and wool skirt, she started rocking with a slow metronome-like regularity. Waiting. Watching. Saying nothing to ease the situation.

"Mrs. Ahearn," he began. "Were you aware of William's recent difficulties? Did he confide in you? Tell you about his business dealings? His investments?"

"I know William. What I want to know is what you're accusing him of. Willy told me Ms. Horn, that you fired him and threatened to ruin his good name. He didn't tell me why."

Charles didn't want M.L. to answer the grieving woman. Choosing his words he said, "I have with me a rather unpleasant document your brother signed on Friday." Handing the official papers to Jane, he softened his voice and explained, "You'll see the charges detailed, and his signature agreeing to our conditions of termination. An agreement, I might add, that said we would not ruin his good name if he went along with our demands."

"Demands?" Jane cried. "You'd better let me read your paper."

Handing the termination agreement to Jane Ahearn, Charles felt sorry for her. "I'd like you to know that this unfortunate situation isn't personal."

Withering him with a look, she said, "All Willy's fights were personal." Watching her slowly read the four-page document, he saw her eyes focus on each word. As she read, she rocked. Only the increasing tightness around her mouth and the constant rigidity of her posture conveyed her pain.

It took Jane ten minutes to read and digest the details of William's severance agreement. With a sigh of regret, she looked at M.L. "Ms. Horn, why were you named CEO? Not my brother?" Her voice had lost some of its anger. Under her controlled tone was a barely concealed plea to understand.

"Mrs. Ahearn, I want you to know that William was one of the brightest attorneys I've ever worked with. He had the respect of our Board. Especially our former CEO Jack Foster. You might know that Mr. Foster had recommended William for the position when he retired."

She knew, Charles thought, watching Jane's expression soften as M.L. praised her brother.

"What happened?" Jane whispered.

It was his turn to answer. "The Board had a particularly delicate plan for the next CEO to carry out. William wasn't the right person to execute that plan. But the Board recognized his strengths and asked him to support Ms.

Horn. He was very important to UCC's success. If you could tell us what your brother said, maybe we could help you understand what happened?" Charles wanted her to understand. He didn't want to trash Foley to this woman who now had only memories of him. But they needed her help. She seemed intelligent. If she knew the facts, then maybe they'd get it.

M.L. had been sitting quietly. "Mrs. Ahearn, I'm not aware of anything I've done to inspire your brother's hatred. Are you?"

"Yes. You took his job."

"I was hired. I didn't take his job. It was never his."

"In his mind, it was. My brother was very ambitious. His stock portfolio was his way of earning the fortune he felt would protect him from poverty. But your job meant the Board's approval of his abilities as a leader. It would have given him power and professional stature. You took that away from him."

She's protecting the bastard, Charles thought.

"Mrs. Ahearn," M.L.'s voice was strong with conviction, "What your brother did, his vendetta against me, could have ruined the company. The corporation had no choice but to terminate him."

"He wouldn't do something like that. William wouldn't hurt your company. He wanted to hurt you."

"You don't understand. His activities were criminal. We had no choice but to fire him."

Charles had been watching the two women. One loyal to her family, the other her company. Maybe he could help. "Mrs. Ahearn. William was double-dealing. He represented UCC in the negotiations to purchase a company that would have given U.C.C new life. He was also negotiating to purchase that company for himself. Surely you understand that this conflict of interest was wrong."

Looking at her visitors Jane suddenly rose and walked from the room.

M.L. and Charles looked to one another in surprise. Afraid to say a word, they waited for the proud woman to return.

It didn't take her long. Mrs. Ahearn walked into the room and over to Charles, handing him a battered briefcase. "I can't go through Willy's papers yet. It's too painful."

Nodding in understanding, Charles lifted the accordion bottom, brown leather case on to the old sea chest that served as a coffee table, and opened the latch. If it had been locked, it had been broken in the crash. Reaching in he carefully withdrew an envelope holding several computer disks and a two-inch thick leather loose-leaf notebook. Opening the file, he saw that it contained a carefully documented record of Neuwirth transactions and the various accounts into which Foley had placed considerable shares of BioTech and UCC stock.

Charles let out a soft whistle in surprise. M.L.'s termination and stipulation document had the outline of Foley's activities. But here was the play-by-play of his treachery. Looking up at Foley's sister, he saw that she had finally accepted his guilt. The proof, plain even to her, that Willy had crossed some invisible line.

"Willy always kept immaculate records. What are those papers? I'd like to know." There was resignation, more than curiosity in her voice.

Charles quickly scanned the binder before turning the book around for her to see. "This document show's the formation of a syndicate. You see William's listed as primary shareholder. The firm forming the syndicate is Neuwirth Investments. This document show's that WSF, Ltd. of the Cayman Islands owns Neuwirth Investments. It also shows that William was the sole owner of WSF. In fact, Mrs. Ahearn, William was Neuwirth Investments." He stopped, not wanting to explore the actual stock purchases in BioTech or UCC.

"I see," Jane said. She was a tall woman who seemed to grow taller as she tried to shore up her grief, as if she were girding herself to face William's betrayal.

"Mrs. Ahearn, according to this file, you are the beneficiary of William's illegal trading. In addition, you are the sole surviving beneficiary of the Foley family portfolio. I'm not exactly sure of the current market value, but I'd say you are one very rich woman."

"I'm not in need of ill gotten gains, Mr. Cray. Willy wanted money."

"Mrs. Ahearn?" M.L. asked when the older woman had neither moved or spoken for some minutes.

Coming to as if from a trance, Jane sat in her chair and began rocking. The room filled with unspoken thoughts.

"What can we do for you?" M.L. asked. "This was between your brother and the company, not you."

Looking at M.L., Jane nodded in thanks. "I'll sell you back the stock at a fair price. In return, I want you to destroy that paper and restore my brother's good name."

That was all they wanted. It was even in the stipulation agreement. Is that where his sister had gotten that idea? Charles wondered.

"I'm not sure how you go about setting a fair price," Jane continued. "But I don't want what wasn't supposed to be Willy's in the first place. Who else knows you fired Willy?"

"Our Board, and the president of BioTech," M.L. answered quietly.

"Is there a way to keep anyone else from knowing about this?"

Charles, looking over to M.L., raised an eyebrow as if to get permission. He saw she understood and nodded for him to answer.

"I think there is a way to protect your brother. Since you are his heir, why don't you agree to dissolve Neuwirth Investments and sell the stock to UCC? We will handle the details, and work with your attorney to make sure your rights are protected. Then I can issue an official obituary concerning the untimely death of UCC's valued Counsel. All William's company benefits will be protected, and no one has to be the wiser."

That was cheap at any price he thought and hoped Mrs. Ahearn would agree.

"You have my promise," M.L. began. "I will see that not one word of this matter escapes our control. William will have a quiet and dignified departure from the company."

Jane sat with eyes closed in prayer. Her chair stilled. "Ms. Horn, Mr. Cray, I loved my brother. He wasn't a bad man. He just worried about being a failure. Our father deserted him before he could be shown how to be a man. I fear Willy always thought it was because he wasn't a good son. He's with God now. Thank you for allowing him to keep his reputation here on earth."

Closing her front door on her departing visitors, Jane clasped her arms to her chest to stop her trembling. Alone finally, with her tears and emptiness. "How I miss you Willy," she whispered. "Even the death of my husband didn't leave me as empty as this." As she cried for Willy, she added this new pain to a lifetime of woes. Her drunken father, over-worked mother, two miscarriages that left her marriage as barren as winter trees. Seeking comfort in habit, she headed for the kitchen to brew herself a cup of tea.

CHAPTER XXXVI

Dragging herself into the library of their home, Melissa fell into the deep club chair, kicked off her shoes, and dropped her briefcase at her feet.

"Was the funeral that bad?" E.F. asked from the matching chair across the room. He had been waiting for her to return from Quincy. Sitting with his legs stretched out in front of him, he slowly sipped a drink.

"Not really. Got everything we needed. Foley's sister will work with us."

"Then why are you in the dumps? You've had tougher problems."

"After-the-war letdown, I suppose." She knew that wasn't the reason. Why had she lied? Because, it was easier than facing the truth.

E.F. had gotten up to pour her a drink and walked over to her chair. "Here. This will chase away those blues," he said, handing her a bourbon on the rocks. "Why not come sit by me? We can talk."

Getting up and heading across the room on lead-like feet, Melissa plopped down on the sofa.

"Honey, what is it?" E.F. asked, sitting down next to her.

"You know me too well," her voice as flat as a rain-filled sky. "Hugh's dumped me."

"Dumped you? Isn't there a little more to it?"

She hurt so badly, the words stuck in her throat. "What would you call it when he has a fit about not being invited to Foley's funeral? Then tells me not to call him. Ever."

"I can't believe from what you've told me about him, that's what really happened. Try again."

Looking over to her dearest friend, she couldn't stop her tears. "He said I wasn't the woman he met on Largo Verde. His Lissa. That's what he calls me. His Lissa would need him. Want him by her side. I didn't need anyone." Hiding her head on his shoulder, Melissa's tears stopped only long enough for her to blow her nose. Putting her head back, she felt E.F. tighten his arm around her and realized how safe she felt with him, sheltered and protected.

"Honey, maybe he's right. Maybe he wasn't the one for you. Hugh apparently didn't understand who you are."

"What's the matter with me anyway?" her anger beginning to flare. "I was going to tell Hugh that I couldn't marry him. Why am I upset because he's come to the same conclusion?" she asked.

Leaning closer to E.F. she let her thoughts drift. Her emotions were raw and her body felt as if she'd been beaten up from the inside out. Not aware of what she was doing, Melissa snuggled against her caring friend, her body now intimately overlapping his. As E.F. began to stroke her hair, his hand moved to lift her face. Looking at him, she saw into his deep love for her, and a newly exposed sexual yearning. Drawn to him, she reached up and gave him a tender, hesitant kiss. One kiss led to another, her passion building slowly, as E.F. returned her kisses with increasing fervor.

She was surprised when E.F. lifted her off the sofa and led her to the nearby elevator. But she followed not caring where he was going. Closing the door on the small wood paneled enclosure, she watched as he pushed the button for his private rooms. In all of her years living under E.F.'s roof, she had only been to this part of the mansion once. Thinking back to the time when she had spent 24-hours nursing him back to health, during a rare attack of the flu.

Leading Melissa down the hall, E.F. opened the door to his bedroom and looked at her, waiting for her response. His expression was asking her what she wanted to do. Melissa knew this was the turning point in their long relationship. Maybe she shouldn't cross that unspoken threshold. But this sudden rush of emotion for E.F. was racing her blood. She wanted him. She wanted . . . what was it she wanted? Love? Desire? Safety? She had always loved E.F. Her mind was also telling her he wasn't like Hugh. Then thinking how much she and E.F. already shared, knew this was something she had to do. Needed to do. Throwing both arms around his neck she devoured him with her kisses, and feeling the strength of his response reach into her heart, Melissa knew this moment had been a long time in coming, not only for her, but for him.

Clinging to him, Melissa let E.F. guide her toward the mahogany four poster bed that took up the entire corner of the large room. Stopping by the bed she hesitantly reached out to touch the rich satin fabric of the bed cover, tracing the quilting pattern with her fingertips, and wondered how it would feel against her bare skin.

Feeling E.F. slowly unbutton her suit jacket, she turned to face him and stood still wondering what he was thinking while he focused on his task. As he draped her jacket on the upholstered bench behind him, she saw that his eyes had never left hers. Studying his expressive features, she saw a naked need, the lust and love clearly visible on his ruggedly handsome face. Feeling hot and desirable, she closed her eyes, melting in his embracing arms as he held her tightly to him. As his first kisses on her ear began to rob her of her thoughts, she felt E.F. begin working his way down her neck, his tongue tracing little circles, each one starting a new wave of chills radiating out over her body.

Melissa's new found sexual passion fueled her responses. Her hands pulled at his tie, unknotting the densely woven silk and ripping it from under his collar. Tearing open the buttons on his shirt, she reached under the soft cotton fabric as sheer as a nightgown, and let her hands gently roam over the smooth skin of his back. A fleeting thought of Hugh's hard muscles floated just at the edge of her mind. E.F.'s back was hot and smooth, with a covering layer of soft fat. It wasn't a fair comparison she thought, E.F. was a man, not a fantasy. A man she could love for a lifetime.

In a surprisingly expert move, E.F. had her skirt, pantyhose and panties off without her even knowing how he'd done it. Lifting her in his arms, he placed her on the bed, resting her head on the satin covered pillows, looking at her as if she were a rich dessert. Removing all but his briefs, he then lay down next to her.

Melissa had been watching closely as he finished undressing her. It was as if she were an observer sitting somewhere above the bed. His sure movements quickly removed her blouse and bra, then gazing at her naked body, he lovingly and gently caressed her breasts. One part of her body shivered at his sensitive touch, while the other, her mind, was empty of all sensation.

Self conscious at his enthusiastic admiration of her body, she reached up and pulled him close, kissing his face and mouth, any part of him in reach. Closing her eyes, she began to grasp and knead his body with her hands. Her mind was now occupied with E.F.'s body, exploring it as if it held a secret to her happiness. As she reached his growing erection, Melissa's passion cooled. Jerking her hand away she fought her thoughts, frantically trying to recapture her mood. Something was clearly very wrong.

"E.F.," she whispered.

Moving away, he looked down at her, his face lit with love. His mouth plump from ardent kisses. She had never seen him as a sexual being, but this earthy man was very sexy, a thought that only confused Melissa even more. If she found him sexy, why was she about to stop they're lovemaking?

"I'm . . . not sure." She was suddenly frightened. It was wrong to have let things go this far. Feeling guilty for arousing his passion, she wondered how she could stop now? It just wasn't fair. Her own emotions were raging within her. But her thoughts were rapidly reclaiming her body.

E.F. didn't say anything, so she didn't know what he'd do. Then he began to caress her cheek. Opening her eyes, she watched him work through his thoughts. What would he say? What would he do? Was their relationship forever compromised? Suddenly she was more afraid of his response, than of giving in to his sexual needs. Her own passion had turned to fear, guilt killing her sexual needs.

As if he knew what she'd been thinking, E.F. lay back down next to her, and stared at the ceiling. His breathing was ragged. His face flushed. "Honey? Are you sure?" His voice echoed with his pain.

"Yes. I'm so, so sorry." Tears were choking her words. "I don't understand what happened. One minute I was crying on your shoulder, and the next I was hungry for you." Not wanting to hurt him even more, she kept trying to explain. "It's not you. It's me."

"No Honey. That's not it."

The sadness in his voice let her know that he understood, knew what she was going through. Turning away from her, he sat up and picking up his shirt, began to dress. "I've only recently realized that I love you very much. Honey, I love you too much to push myself on you. Maybe in time, we can try again."

Melissa saw his pain in the bend of his head and sag of his shoulders, knowing she'd hurt him deeply.

"Oh no. I didn't know. E.F . . . .?" He didn't answer, just sat with his back to her and shook his head. Silently she swore she'd do everything she could to make it up to him. If it wasn't too late. She had to, what ever it took.

CHAPTER XXXVII

November 2, 1998

It was almost 1:30, M.L. and Charles had been working their way through lunch at the Four Season's Grill Room, since Noon.

"Here's next year's plan for the Board," M.L. said, tossing the twenty-page report to Charles sitting across from her. Just as the report left her hand, a corner of the heavy folder hit her wineglass, sending it flying to the floor. At first she just sat staring at the spreading red stain on the carpet at her feet, then burst into a torrent of tears.

Handing her his handkerchief, Charles watched helplessly as she held the white folded square over her eyes, and continued to cry silently.

"M.L.?" Charles whispered. People at neighboring tables were beginning to stare, making him flush with embarrassment. She was clearly not herself. Charles suspected it had nothing to do with the spilled wine. Reaching for her hand and squeezing it as hard as he dared, he raised his voice slightly, "You're attracting attention."

M.L. hadn't seemed to hear him. Charles knew if she had, she'd be shocked, at the scene she was making.

Glancing up to the approaching waiter, Charles signaled for him to clean up the mess. Through it all, the waiter politely concentrated on his task, picking up the broken glass and cleaning up the spilled wine, then leaving as quietly as he had arrived.

Charles had been watching M.L. as she sat there, unaware of the waiter, or of the increasing attention of neighboring diners, tears streaming down her face. She had the same devastated expression he'd seen on the plane to Foley's funeral. Only this time, he saw her break down and didn't know why.

They'd been having a very productive discussion about the success of the past months and plans for the coming year. Then, this outburst. He was at a loss. M.L. was unlike any woman he'd ever met, with a steel control over her emotions. She just didn't do things like this. Certainly not in public!

"Melissa?" He never called her by her first name. It wasn't that she had told him not to, it just didn't fit during office hours. M.L. was more appropriate, it fitted her position. To his dismay, he had few occasions to use her name, rarely having been with her outside business.

"What's wrong? What can I do?"

She just sat there and cried. Her eye makeup had left streaks on her face, her nose red from the punishment it was taking from his now wet handkerchief.

The waiter had left them several minutes before, when M.L. looked up at Charles and strangled a cry, "Get me out of here."

"Melissa?" he spoke hesitantly, not wanting to upset her even more.

"For Christ's sake. Get the damned car. Get me out of here. Just get me out of here," she hissed.

Signaling for the check, Charles quickly signed it, adding a healthy tip, while he waited for M.L. to fix her makeup. As she put on her sunglasses, he helped her up from her chair, taking firm hold of her arm to keep her from stumbling.

"Ready," he asked. Getting a nod, he guided her past the concerned headwaiter and down the restaurant stairs to the waiting limousine. Helping her into the car, Charles followed, settling into the deep seat next to her.

"Drive through the Park, Ben." Looking over to see if she had even heard his directions, he watched as she blew her nose and continued to cry.

"Damn it Melissa. Tell me how I can help you?" The desperation in his voice seemed to have reached her. As she looked up at him, she shook her head then turned away to stare out the car window. Within seconds of the last of her tears, she found her voice. "Ben, stop the car. I'm getting out."

"Melissa, we're at 59th Street and Madison Avenue. You're in no condition to be walking the streets of Manhattan," Charles' voice reflecting his growing panic.

"I'll return this tomorrow," she said focusing on wet crumpled mess that was his handkerchief, then at him. Lifting her hand as if to ward him off, she opened the door and got out of the car.

Charles was so distressed he was tempted to call E.F. For all of the years they worked together, he knew E.F. expected him to watch out for her.

"Mr. Cray," the driver asked, "Where to?"

"Follow her. I want to be sure she's safe."

As the limousine pulled away from the curb, it slowly followed M.L. as she rushed up Madison Avenue. At 60th Street, she turned toward Fifth Avenue and in the following car, now stopped at 60th street and Fifth Avenue for a red light, Charles watched helplessly as she crossed the broad tree-lined avenue against the light, and ran into Central Park. They couldn't keep following her now. He'd have to let her go, a thought that was so painful, he flinched.

"What now, Mr. Cray."

"Back to the office Ben. I'll try to raise her on her cell phone."

*　　　*　　　*

Rushing blindly past the curious on lookers, Melissa dashed past parked horse drawn carriages and into the sanctity of Central Park. Taking her first full breath since her outburst started, Melissa began to feel the calming influence of the over hanging trees. A sudden breeze brushed her hot face, cooling it and restoring a sense of control. The Pond lay in the foreground, and the calm scene drew her forward. Heading down the paved path toward the water's edge, she sat on a vacant bench overlooking the miniature lake, and tried to make sense of her roiling emotions. There were few visitors wandering nearby, the park empty of noontime regulars and too cool for children and their nannies.

Maybe I should just jump in, she thought, as she stared at the water. I'd just swim to the opposite shore, was her following thought. She took comfort in knowing that even if someone were to see her red eyes and nose, New Yorkers were all absorbed in their own lives, so much so, that they wouldn't even stop to see if she was all right.

"Am I cracking up?" she asked in a whisper. Leaning back on the bench she tried to make sense of her unaccustomed tears.

"I'm a fuck'n success. What's my problem? How could I lose it like that?"

Thinking back to the previous six months, she realized that there had been other warning signals. Amid her triumphs were numerous hollow victories. "Hollow? Is that what my job has become? I'm one of the most powerful women in the country, and here I sit dissolved in tears?"

Then she pictured herself lying next to E.F., and not making love to him. She could still feel her pain, of giving in to temptation, at the expense of the only person in her life she loved. E.F. had never referred to that afternoon again. He pretended it had never happened. But alone in her bed, she spent many a sleepless night regretting the whole, ugly scene. If they had made love, would she now be happy? It was a question that still eluded an answer.

Then she thought of her behavior at work, thinking back to a meeting a couple of months before, when she yelled at Jason for not having some figures ready on time. Jason, who would do anything for her.

"Thank God I held it together as long as Pamela was around. She was on my tail with a magnifying glass," her voice echoing with relief.

Getting up to follow the path just above the lake, she heard the buzz of her cell phone. "Damn it. Can't I have some time to myself?" she cried, the sound of the phone setting her teeth on edge. Reaching into her oversized handbag, she pulled out the annoyance, knowing it was probably an emergency. Without a second thought, she pulled back her arm and hurled the small instrument out into the middle of the pond. "There. I'm free." With a smug expression, she watched the sinking phone create a series of circles rippling the pond's surface.

Stretching her arms out to embrace the air, Melissa took in the beauty of her surroundings. Even though the trees were almost bare, they were alive. Stepping gingerly at first, she headed toward the path above the pond, deciding to follow it wherever it led. As she approached The Wollman Rink, she thought of having loved to ice skate as a child. Why had she never skated here, in one of the prettiest spots in New York? Reaching the promenade above the rink, she looked out over the expert skaters carving their dance patterns into the ice. Looking up, she took in the drama of the Central Park South skyline in the distance. To her left was the green copper mansard roof of The Plaza Hotel, and if she looked to her right she saw the large red letters on a rooftop, spelling out the name of the Essex House. The buildings of varying architectural styles seemed to appear magically over the tops of late fall colored trees surrounding the rink. It was a spot often celebrated by artists and photographers, and never failed to give her a sense of joy.

Strolling up the hill, Melissa walked past the Checkers House, and headed toward the famous Carousel. Stopping just in front of the red brick enclosure, she could see the brightly painted horses with fanciful personalities that seemed to have jumped off the pages of a children's fairy tale.

They look perfect, she thought, poised for flight, awaiting their riders. Studying the colorful animals mounted on golden poles, she thought of their constantly circling rides, never able to run free. Melissa realized she too had a prescribed path in life, and wondered if she had become a wooden character?

As Melissa stood studying the colorful horses, listening to the cheerful sounds of the pipe organ, she saw a young girl dressed in torn blue jeans and equally bedraggled sweaters, staring at her. She couldn't be more than ten, Melissa thought, intrigued to see that she was by her self.

"Lady? Are you Okay?" the sweet voice asked.

"Yes."

"Are you sure?" the little girl said with a frown of disbelief on her dirty face.

"I will be. I was just sad. I'll be all right. I just need to be by myself for a while."

"Me too. By myself," the girl echoed. Looking once more to see if Melissa was all right, the girl ran away.

"And who said New Yorkers weren't friendly?" Melissa said, smiling at the way the little girl had reached her heart. "I may be a mess, but I'm all right. At least I will be when I figure things out," she decided. It was the first hopeful thought she'd had in months.

Feeling lighter, almost content, Melissa continued her walk taking a path that ran in front of a baseball field, and headed toward Central Park West.

"I need a drink. That's what I need," she said spotting the rooftop and outdoor lights of The Tavern On The Green up ahead. Picking up her pace, Melissa strolled up the path, reaching the road just in front of the famous restaurant, where she was assaulted by a speeding rush of humanity on racing bikes and inline skates, dressed in costumes of the cult of youth.

"Shit. Where have I been to have missed this?" she exclaimed with the wonder of a visitor to a new country. She had always been fascinated by the underground and off beat cult-like clusters of younger New Yorkers. They were the ones that created the street fashions sold in Soho, and introduced nose rings and body piercing to Madison

Avenue. Inline skaters had their own customs and fashions. The cyclists usually dressed in body-hugging Lycra. Both groups of street-wise athletes wore protective headgear and assorted pads. The speed and the youth of the crowd, all in their late 20's, created a vitality that for some reason she found threatening. Was she that old? When had that happened, she wondered. Staring at the grace and stunts of the youngsters, Melissa asked silently, is this a sign for me to lighten up and begin to live my own life?

Braving a break in the energetic crowd, Melissa dashed across the roadway, weaving between acrobatic skaters, and into the main entrance of the restaurant.

"Ms. Horn," the reservation clerk called as she approached the desk. "It's been a long time. How may I help you today? Lunch? A quiet table outside?"

"Yes. A quiet table outside, Gordon. It's a gorgeous day."

Following Gordon outside, Melissa felt as if she were playing hooky. No one knew where she was. Without her phone, she couldn't be reached. Heaven, she thought. Sheer Heaven.

Giving the waiter her order of a dry martini, straight up, she tried to remember when she had last been alone, alone during the middle of a business day. Years, she realized. Settling back on the wood chair, and looking at the paper lanterns surrounding her table, she relaxed happy to be the only one sitting out doors.

"Miss? Are you from New York?" a deep masculine voice asked.

Seeing a pair of feet wearing highly polished black loafers in front of her, she was intrigued by the lack of socks. Looking up, she saw a man of approximately her age, dressed in ironed jeans, black turtleneck sweater, and a well-worn Burberry trench coat.

"Yes?"

"I was wondering if that was Sheep's Meadow, across the road? I'm a writer and like to keep assorted facts tucked away in the back of my head. Just in case I ever need them."

His smile was warm. He even looked like the photo of a writer on the jacket of a best seller, she thought. Feeling like a flirt, she gave him one of her warmest smiles. "Yes. It is. The location for those concerts in the park you may have heard about. Where are you from?"

"Wyoming. Just here to visit with my publisher. My name is Wade Jefferson."

Holding out his hand, Melissa took it and felt calluses of an outdoor man. He may be an author, she thought, but he was all male.

"Would you care to join me? I'm playing hooky," he asked.

She was enjoying herself and laughing with this handsome stranger felt right. "I'd be delighted to. Hooky? Do you teach?" The glint in his eyes told her that he was joking.

"Sometimes."

Laughing and thinking that she would just enjoy this stranger's company for awhile, Melissa decided to put herself and her problems on hold. Is it really this easy, she wondered?

CHAPTER XXXVIII

Approaching the townhouse, Melissa took out her key, not wanting to waken Martha. The night sky was filled with stars, the crisp air strangely invigorating. She was feeling light hearted, like singing. She began to hum, *Isn't it a lovely day*. Flirting with Wade was just what she had needed. Since he was leaving town in the morning, she didn't even have to think about seeing him again. "It really doesn't matter if the skies are gray." she sang.

Just as she was about to turn the key in the door, Martha pulled it open. Melissa was shocked at the woman's appearance. Usually crisp and formal, Martha's face was that of a ghost, drawn and pale, and her uniform wrinkled.

"Oh Miss Horn. We've been trying to reach you for hours," she cried. "It's Mr. Haynes. He's been taken to New York Hospital."

Standing there, Melissa felt her heart drop to her wobbly feet and had to reach for the doorframe. "What happened?" she barely whispered. "When? Is anyone with him?"

As she heard the story from Martha, her mind was yelling . . . and you were out flirting with a stranger. How could you? Her guilt bringing on tears. Hearing the end of the story, she turned and ran to the curb, where she shouted down a passing cab.

It was a silent ten-minute ride. Melissa's anxiety about E.F. was intensified with her fear of losing him. As if her mind had just shut down, she sat there, eyes vacant, arms hugging her chest.

When the car pulled up to the emergency entrance of the hospital, Charles was there to help her out of the car. Looking up into his face she saw a deep sadness, worry etched on his brow.

"We've been trying to find you all day. What happened to your phone? It isn't working. We checked."

There was no reproof in his face, just worry.

"I dropped it," she lied. "Tell me. How is he?"

"Here you are," said a disheveled Lawrence Henderson, running to greet her at curbside. "We were having lunch and E.F. said he didn't feel well. He was nauseous. Then, he just slumped over. He's in ICU, the doctors are still watching him."

Charles heard the words tumbling out as if in their rush to tell the bad news, he could hurry it away. Watching M.L. he saw her walk over and put her arms around the distraught man. It was a private moment he'd never witnessed before. He knew Larry and E.F. were very old and close friends. Watching M.L. and Larry leaning on one another for comfort, Charles knew that she was part of that family. Strange, all these years, but I was never as close to M.L. as I thought, Charles realized.

They led her into an empty waiting room, where a man's voice called to them, "Dr. Henderson?"

"Yes Doctor," Larry answered, holding tightly to Melissa's hand. They waited for the young man, who couldn't have been more than thirty, to approach. Dressed in green scrubs, he looked like a harried intern from a movie.

"Is Mr. Haynes all right?" Melissa asked.

"He's stable. We've been watching him and have to run some more tests. The early results are in, but it will be morning before we know exactly what we're dealing with. Has he had heart trouble before?"

Charles watched, as M.L. shook her head no. How did she know, he wondered. Then he saw her look to Larry for confirmation. Larry also shook his head no.

"Well you got him here in time. We'll take good care of him. Could someone help me finish up Mr. Haynes medical history? His doctor is with him now and we'll compare notes. But there are still a couple of questions I need some answers to."

"I'll go Melissa," Larry said. "Doctor, I'll give you what ever I can."

"Are you the immediate family?" the doctor asked.

Melissa nodded yes. Charles didn't say anything. He just kept watching to see that she was okay.

"If you want to see him for a few minutes it should be all right. But just small talk. He's had a rough time of it."

"Thank you Doctor," Charles said, taking M.L.'s arm and heading into the intensive care unit.

A nurse showed them to E.F.'s bed behind a wall of curtains. The noise of the unit was somewhat muffled by the draped enclosure. As Charles stood at the foot of the bed, he watched M.L. walk to E.F.'s bedside. Reaching a shaking hand to touch his, she then closed her eyes as if in prayer.

Looking at his friend, Charles saw the perpetually tanned face now looked like aged parchment. His eyes lay closed, as if in sleep. It scared him to see how tired and helpless his friend looked. Suddenly one of the monitors began to beep a little faster and E.F. opened his eyes to look directly at him. With a weak smile, E.F. nodded and closed his eyes once again.

Charles knew that E.F. was relieved he was there, knowing he would see to everything.

"Charles," M.L. said, in a voice he barely recognized for its frailty. "Would you leave us alone for a few minutes?"

Looking at E.F. and seeing that the monitor's rhythm had returned to a steady beep, he quietly left the area. He didn't go far. *Just in case she needs me,* he thought.

As Melissa gave E.F.'s hand a gentle squeeze he opened his eyes again. This time he didn't smile. "I'll be fine Honey. Don't worry. Charles will see I get the best attention money can buy."

"E.F., let me do it," she pleaded. "Let me take care of you. Charles can take over at the office."

"No Honey. I can't let you do that." A sudden pain caused him to moan. The monitor jumped and a nurse came running, pushing the curtains aside and shouting orders. Signaling Charles, who had been close on her heels, to go, she began checking the monitor.

When M.L. didn't move, Charles gently put his arm around her waist and pulled her with him. Seeing her face wet with tears, he led her out to the waiting area, thinking how desolate it looked this late at night.

"We have to let the doctors take care of him. We'll only be in their way."

M.L. nodded but had retreated to some inner world. Charles didn't like the way she looked. What was this between E.F. and M.L.? It was as if her husband or father was lying in that bed, not a friend and business mentor, he thought.

As Charles settled on the sofa next to her, Larry returned with coffee. "The doctor thinks he had a mild heart attack and said to be prepared for a long siege. That the original episode could be followed by another."

"I think it just was, Larry," Charles said, his eyes never leaving M.L.

"Melissa?" Larry said. "I've brought you some coffee."

Melissa nodded and took the cup. She didn't sip it.

"Larry, I'm worried about her."

Larry handed Charles another cup, and shaking his head sat on a chair near Melissa. "Melissa?" Not getting a response, Larry sat back and waited. She placed the cup on the table in front of her and sat like a limp rag doll, staring into space. Then she began to shiver.

Charles saw her rubbing her arms to keep them warm, and quickly placed his jacket over her shoulders. Looking at her closely, he saw that she didn't even know he was there.

For two hours, all three sat waiting for word about E.F.'s condition.

The silence was hard on Charles. "E.F.'s really very healthy." he said. "Even if he's had a heart attack, there's no reason to think the worst. He'll pull through."

"That's right Melissa," Larry said. "Didn't that nutritionist he hired several years back put him on a low-fat, no salt diet? He's been watching his health for years now. E.F.'s a bull."

Worried when she didn't respond, Larry leaned forward to hold her hand. Maybe it was his touch, but Melissa's eyes began to focus on him.

Charles was relived to see some signs of life after hours of her trance like silence.

"Larry, can I go to him?" she pleaded.

"Not yet. We're waiting for the doctor."

Just then a young woman called from the open doorway, "Dr. Henderson? I'm nurse Scott. Mr. Haynes is being moved to a private room. Once he's been settled, you can go on up for a brief visit."

"Can you tell me his condition?" Larry asked.

"For the moment, he's resting comfortably. In the long-term, they won't know the extent of any damage until they've completed their tests."

"Thank you."

"Mr. Haynes will be in room 435 in this building. Just follow the signs."

"Larry, find out if I can stay with him tonight? Just until I know he's going to be all right?" Melissa was frantic, clutching his arm to make sure he heard her.

"E.F. wouldn't like that. He'd want you to get your rest and come back tomorrow."

"He's right M.L. There's nothing you can do," Charles said.

"No! I have to be sure he's not going to die."

She had just spoken their fears. E.F. might die. Their friend, the gutsy man who could do anything from breaking a horse to building a fortune, might die. Charles knew M.L. would sit a silent bedside vigil to keep death away. Tonight, tomorrow, for as long as it took.

*   *   *

She had been sitting at E.F.'s bedside all night. Except for two short trips for coffee and to the bathroom, Melissa had been praying so hard, she'd lost track of time. A sudden sound made her jump. Looking at E.F. she saw that he was reaching for something on the table by his bed. With a hand to her heart, she was relieved to see the sound was only a cup that had fallen to the floor. Quickly filling another cup from a carafe of water, she handed it to him.

"Welcome back. Are you in any pain? Do you want me to call a nurse?" His color is a little better, she thought. But when did he get so old?

"No. Just tired. I'll survive."

His voice has aged too, she thought. "Larry and Charles said they'd come by later this morning."

"What are you doing here Honey? It's five in the morning."

"Praying."

E.F. nodded and closing his eyes drifted back to sleep.

Getting up she began to walk slowly around the cramped, darkened room, talking to herself. "You've always been there for me. What would I do without you? You must get well."

Then she remembered the day E.F. told her he was going to have her nominated and named CEO. At the time she thought how normal it had all seemed. Of course she was excited, somewhat terrified perhaps, but she also knew she had long been ready for the responsibility. The time since had been the most exciting in her life.

Stopping to smooth a lock of E.F.'s hair, she began to cry. "I owe everything to you," she whispered. "These past months have been a dream. I never expected to reach this far. You were always there to listen to my plans. Hear my problems and support my solutions."

Yet, dropping back into the bedside chair, it suddenly dawned on Melissa that through it all, the judgments and actions had been hers. Sitting a little taller, she remembered first showing him her plan to restructure UCC. He had read it quickly. All twenty pages. Then he'd said "I couldn't have done better myself." - was this just his nurturing kindness . . . or might the words have been the truth? Had she grown into E.F.'s confidence at last?

Such odd memories for a bedside vigil - but somehow that moment had presented a turning point for her, for both of them. The student had caught up to her mentor - she could run with the front of the pack, and she knew it now.

Tears flowed down her cheeks, a sob caught in her throat. She loved E.F. with all her heart. Looking at him lying on the white sheets, she couldn't recognize the drawn, tired figure as the brilliant, virile man with whom she had shared her entire adult life. This man should be retired, and live a quiet life of golf and early cocktails. Not directing worldwide enterprises, worrying about the insane machinations of overwrought corporate executives pushing harder and faster because bigger was better, and richer was safer. He certainly didn't need to keep protecting her from the Foleys of the world.

With a bone-deep ache, she realized that she wanted him safe and healthy, able to sit back and enjoy the products of his fruitful life, able to appreciate her growing up. To be proud of her accomplishments.

"Dear God," she prayed. Folding her hands she pleaded, "Please make him well. Give him the strength to accept what I must do. I can't hide behind him any longer."

*   *   *

The soft chiming of the apartment doorbell startled Charles from a morose review of the news release he had written late last night. It was short and to the point. *UCC's Director, E.F. Haynes had suffered a sudden heart attack and was being treated at New York Hospital. An update on his condition would be issued as soon as the doctors had compiled their findings.*

Dragging himself to the door, he opened it to find a listless M.L., coat unbuttoned, hair a mess, oblivious to anything but her pain. Reaching up, he put his arm around her shoulders and gently pulled her inside. He was shocked to see the depth of despair mirrored in her eyes. Guiding her to his small kitchen, Charles sat her in a chair, and poured a glass of brandy from the bottle he had used to get him through the long night.

"I had nowhere to go," M.L.'s grief filled voice whispered. "Charles, help me."

Here was the woman he had loved silently for so long, finally needing him. Leaning down, and lifting her to her feet, he held her in his arms, and felt her body tremble as she shed new tears. "Cry. Don't worry. I'm here."

"What am I to do?" she wailed.

For once Charles was afraid for this strong woman, as he watched her give way to her emotions. "Talk to me. Tell me what's wrong."

"Oh Charles," she sobbed. "For all my adult life, E.F.'s been my rock. My strength. My life."

Charles didn't like what he was thinking. He couldn't help but ask. "Are you two lovers?" To Charles great relief, he felt her nod her denial.

"It's more, we're family. I've never even thought of life without E.F.," she cried.

"Here drink this," Charles said handing her the brandy. "Is that all you're afraid of?"

"No. I just realized that I have to move out. Begin a life on my own. How can I even think about myself with E.F. on the edge of death?"

He didn't want to hear this. This was a woman he didn't know. Someone weak. Shaking her shoulders to jar her back to some sense of herself, Charles knew he was witnessing the death of the M.L. he thought he knew.

"I just talked to his doctor. E.F.'s going to make a full recovery. He's lucky. But it will take some time for him to regain his strength."

Was she listening, he wondered? Lifting her face to get her attention, he shouted, "He's out of danger. He'll be alright."

Ah, that's better he thought as she finally seemed to recognize the hope in his words.

"Really okay?"

"Definitely!"

"Then I have to move quickly. Get him home and safely cared for. When he's well, I can move out. Not before he's well."

To Charles, her plans sounded more like a mantra. Something she did automatically. While she seemed back in control, somehow she didn't sound quite real. Then he saw her look to him for understanding.

"M.L., why? Why now?"

"Because I have to find out who I am."

"You know very well who you are. You're Melissa Lynn Horn and CEO of UCC."

Suddenly he saw the loneliness, the emptiness of her life. What had her life been? He'd never questioned it. She was the golden girl. Had everything and his love, and he now knew, the love of E.F. and Larry.

As if she had read his thoughts, she asked, "And? What else? What does this officer do outside the office? Who are her friends? Where is her husband, her family? Doesn't she deserve to be a person and CEO?"

Then it struck Charles, that unlike himself, she had given up her whole life for her career. He'd never questioned his not having married. It was a choice he made because he wanted her. No woman had even come close. But, now he saw that she hadn't even had a choice.

CHAPTER XXXIX

March 5,1999

Seated in her new fire engine red Jeep Cherokee, Melissa waited in the parking lot of the Port Washington station for Pamela's train. She hadn't seen the plucky reporter in six months, and was curious to know what she'd been up to.

On a Tuesday at 10: 30 in the morning, there weren't many passengers on the train from Manhattan. Now as she looked toward the platform stairs, she watched the arriving passengers as they headed toward parked cars, or waiting family and friends.

Well there she was at the top of the stairs, her storm coat flying open, with newly falling snowflakes gathering on her straight brown hair. I am glad I invited her out for a visit, Melissa realized. Its time to come clean.

Observing Pamela as she approached the car, Melissa noticed how much she had changed. She walked with a more womanly stride, instead of her former headlong rush to get to where ever she was going. I knew there was a woman under that tomboy. Could that knit dress be a

Calvin? I've changed as well, she thought, taking stock of her shearling jacket, black turtleneck, jeans and cowboy boots. Reaching up to wave, she smiled as Pamela began tossing questions into the open car window.

"Where have you been? I've been calling you for weeks. I heard a rumor that you resigned. You couldn't have! Could you?" she cried.

As Pamela's hands punctuated each question, Melissa saw clear disapproval and disbelief written on her face. "No hello? How are you? You look great?" she asked from the driver's seat, laughing at the sight of Pamela's reddening face.

"I've been away. Now that I'm back, I thought you might like to come out to suburbia and talk about . . . things," smiling to coax the anxious reporter into calming down and putting her questions on hold.

"I give up," Pamela said, laughing as she stepped up onto the high seat. "I can't help it. M.L., in a jeep? I'd have expected a limo, or a Mercedes station wagon."

Melissa smiled, and engaged the clutch of the 4x4, pulling smoothly out of the parking lot. Glancing over to Pamela she was glad to see the normally intense woman had begun to relax.

"You even look different. No makeup?" Pamela asked, studying Melissa as she tried to keep her eyes on the road.

"I wish," Melissa sighed.

Turning in her seat to get a better look at her, Pamela exclaimed, "Your hair . . . it's not perfect, and your nails aren't lacquered red. There is something very different going on here," she said as she continued giving Melissa a careful once over. "What's up?"

"I'm not working. I'm dressed for comfort."

"Any way, it's great to see you M.L. Now, seriously, this rumor has me crazy. I've become your number one fan. And I'm in the final edit of the book."

"If I did give it all up? Would you think any the less of me?" Carefully keeping her eyes on the road, Melissa got only a quick look as the pretty face composed itself into a scowl.

"It wouldn't be the M.L. I know," Pamela barked back.

"To answer one of your questions, I did resign."

Almost jumping from her seat, Pamela shouted, "Why?" Staring back out the window, she grumbled, "Shit, is this off the record, as usual?"

"No, this time I'm giving you a scoop. For your exclusive interview and to help you put a new finish on your book. Details later." Delighted with her surprise, Melissa watched Pamela slowly close her mouth.

"It's not fair to drop a bombshell like that and expect me to sit quietly. As a favor to you, I'll wait until we get to wherever it is we're going. If nothing else, following you has taught me patience."

"I missed you too." Reaching out to pat the back of Pamela's hand, she added, "You remind me of what normal was."

"Me normal?" Pamela said to herself.

Melissa wondered what Pamela's reaction would be as she turned into the gated drive and headed down a tree-lined street, dotted with large homes hidden behind screens of foliage. Pulling up into the driveway of a Tudor style house of mansion sized proportions, she headed for the covered side entrance connecting the garage and the house.

"Wow! When did you move out here?" Pamela's voice filled with awe.

"Last month."

"Before, or after you resigned?"

She's still got it. That incredible ability to fill in the gaps, Melissa thought. "After." Looking at Pamela's nodding head, she realized that it must look as if she had gone off the deep end giving up a mega-career for suburbia.

"Come on. I'll give you the grand tour," Melissa invited, as she hung her coat on a peg in the back entrance entry hall, and saw Pamela do the same with hers. She was proud of the house, and Pamela was her first guest, other than a few local, newly made friends.

As she led Pamela through the main floor and entertaining areas, Melissa was surprised to see the talkative reporter was speechless.

"You don't like it?" Melissa asked, hoping that Pamela's silence wasn't disapproval. For some reason it was important that the younger woman appreciate just how much this house meant to her.

"Are you kidding? It's just too much for a hobo like me. I'm westside Manhattan. This is Fitzgerald's East Egg. The house is fabulous, and for all its size, homey, not a stiff show place."

"I've rented it furnished, for the year."

"Why so short a lease? Aren't you going to stay retired?"

There she goes again, another leap toward the truth, Melissa thought. Smiling at how close she had come, she decided not to take Pamela upstairs, instead she headed for the glassed-enclosed garden room and lunch. Pamela had come all this way for answers and wouldn't be happy until she heard the entire story. Melissa realized she was looking forward to opening up and sharing her climb to power with the energetic woman. After all she too had worked hard to earn her byline and reputation as an outstanding journalist.

As they entered the slate-floored room, covered with a series of needlepoint floral scatter rugs, Melissa saw Pamela stop and stare at the view outside the wall of windows.

"Awesome. What a setting! Every bush and tree look like they were painted in place by an artist. Do you spend much time here?"

"Yes. Each window in the house overlooks park-like views filled with trees and flowers. Nature did her best for you today, Pamela. She dusted the gardens with a snow coat of magic. How about a beer?"

"Beer? No champagne?"

Laughing at Pamela's teasing reference to her high-style entertaining as CEO, Melissa replied, "I prefer domestic, but I also have a couple of imported brews, if you'd rather."

"Domestic is great."

Seeing Pamela's approving nod as she looked around the room and its furnishings, Melissa said, "The bamboo and cane pieces remind me of a place I like to visit."

"Where is that?"

"It's a retreat. An island I go to when I need down time. Come on, let's eat, and you can ask all those questions."

Walking toward a buffet set up on the long wrought iron and glass table, Melissa saw a smile of pure joy on Pamela's face, and it caused her to break out in a hearty chuckle. "I really do enjoy you. I'd like us to become friends. Shake on it?" She was rewarded by Pamela's enthusiastically grasping her outstretched hand.

As Pamela began to fill her plate with cold roast chicken and assorted vegetable salads, Melissa was reminded of their previous meals together. The CEO and the clever reporter, always fencing around one another, searching for the person behind their jobs. Well today she'll finally meet the real me, Melissa thought, praying she'd like the woman she found. She had E.F. check and learned that Pamela was working on the final draft of the authorized biography of Melissa Lynn Horn. She wanted to have her incorporate some new information.

Playing with the silverware, Pamela was clearly uncomfortable about something. "What did you mean by my being normal?" she asked quietly.

Melissa saw that for all her brashness, Pamela was unaware that she was a loner too, and didn't fit the mold of a single career woman. "I just think you and I are a lot alike. If you think of normal as being married with a couple of kids, I guess I'm a misfit too."

"Are you going to tell me what this is all about? You talking about kids is what's not normal."

Melissa just sat and nodded in agreement.

"You know M.L., all the time we spent together you accepted me for me, and showed me how to expand my horizons."

Pamela's sincerity was touching. "Since we aren't working and now we're friends, why not call me Melissa?"

"But . . ."

"I know, I promised you a scoop."

"You'll really tell me all?"

"Yes. Don't look so surprised." Watching the younger woman take an absentminded bite of her lunch, Melissa wanted to know more about her life. To see if she had found balance between work and having a personal life. "How about you? What have you been up to? I haven't seen your byline lately. What's happened to that ambitious reporter I feared?"

"More like mistrusted, than feared," Pamela shot back.

"Not exactly. We didn't know if you'd like us."

"I tried not to. Ask Charles. But I couldn't seem to make it stick. Not only were you more competent than many men I know, you had style, and even a sense of fair play."

Waiting for Pamela to continue, Melissa thought about the inherent struggle the tough reporter must have had in writing about a corporation she was conditioned not to trust.

"Did your resignation have anything to do with E.F.'s heart attack?"

Typical, she thought. Smack on target. Melissa nodded. "E.F.'s back to normal, thank God. But, yes. His heart attack scared me. It forced me to face some unpleasant things about myself."

"Such as?"

"That I had been hiding behind him. Afraid to take control of my own life."

"You are the most in control person I've ever met," Pamela corrected.

"I guess you would think that. You only knew the CEO. That job is all about control." That Pamela had thought control was something bad, worried her. "My career was my life. But I had no control of me, the person, or of any part of my private life."

"You were the success story of the century," Pamela all but shouted, waving her fork like a sword.

"As CEO, I accomplished my goals. The merger with BioTech is a rousing success. Our shareholders are happy with an increase in dividends, as well as a stock split." Melissa took a small bite of chicken, and thought sadly that she should have been rejoicing. She was proud of her achievements, she just wasn't proud of this woman's vision of who she was as a person.

"So? Now it should be easy. You can have your minions run things, while you look for new ways UCC can make even more money."

"How are you and Nick?" Melissa had purposely changed the subject to see if Pamela was really more like her than not.

"What?"

"There was a Nick in your life. What happened? If it's not too personal, that is."

"Too personal? Hell, I've asked you worse. Did I tell you about my friend Skip?"

"Remember, I know Skip."

"Right. Well, he finally got it through my thick head that Nick wasn't worth the trouble. All I got was an occasional evening of sex. And even that wasn't so great. Skip got me thinking about how I'm always attracted to cads. So Nick's history."

"And Skip? Charles thinks the world of him. He'd be in Jason's position by now if he hadn't left UCC."

"I forgot, Skip and Charles are buds."

"That men's club," Melissa couldn't keep the sarcasm out of her voice.

"I was hoping you would change all that," Pamela said wistfully. "But, yes, I'm crazy about Skip. We're working on it," a small grin broke out on her normally serious face. Then it disappeared as she shrieked, "Hey, what's gotten into you? You never had time for gossip."

"I haven't had time to be . . . just me. The me that my career overtook."

"What do Skip or Nick have to do with your decision to quit?"

"It got me to thinking about my . . . brief . . . ah . . ."

"Fling?" Pamela cut in.

"Yes." She was having difficulty continuing. Maybe she shouldn't, Melissa thought.

"What happened?"

Seeing genuine interest, Melissa thought that maybe sharing her loss would help. Pamela had long since proved trustworthy. Playing with the untouched food on her plate she answered, "It was me. He needed more. I realize now, that it was one of the prices of my success. But, he made me see that my life had become empty. Of course I did resign. So maybe the lesson was worth the heartache."

"He, wasn't by any chance The Hugh Baron?"

There was no evading it. Studying Pamela for her reaction, she answered in a whisper, "Yes."

"Jesus. Is he as sensitive as those roles he plays?" Pamela asked, elbows on the table, leaning across her plate to catch Melissa's answer.

Letting her full fork drop to her plate, Melissa said more to herself, "Yes."

"But the job came first?"

Nodding, M.L. couldn't keep the melancholy from showing.

"And he wanted you home with his kids?"

"How did you know?" Genuinely surprised at how quickly Pamela had put the painful story together.

"I didn't. But if you couldn't have landed a guy like Hugh Baron, no one could. I always thought the beautiful women could get any man they wanted."

Beautiful? Apparently that was how Pamela saw her. Accepting the compliment, she thought this conversation was proving very interesting. "Dream on. I've the same problems you have. Finding a good man and knowing how to keep him."

"Melissa?"

Had she been wandering? "Yes? Sorry, I was just thinking about something."

"I was saying, rumors are, you asked to be let out of your contract. Did you? Or, did they force you out?"

Melissa remembered drafting her own press announcement. "It was me, Pamela. My choice, not theirs," her firm voice confirming her words.

"Didn't they even try to keep you?"

Melissa was pleased by Pamela's indignation. Flattered, that she wanted to defend her right to the job. "They asked me to take some time to reconsider. They wouldn't accept my resignation until I had."

"They? Or E.F.?"

"Both, actually. The Board first. E.F. worked on me privately."

"I don't understand. You were our great hope. You broke the damned glass ceiling. You made our fantasies, reality."

"You can still hope and dream. It's always easier after the first. But I'd had it. I wanted my life back."

"You loved that job. I watched you. You were that job."

Melissa sat studying Pamela's determined face. She was right of course. Being CEO had been her life's ambition. She'd earned it, and she was good. Very good, judging by the recent corporate earnings.

"For Christ's sake! You were in the million dollar club," Pamela's anguish clearly visible.

"It was never about the money. Money doesn't hug back! It's just . . . somehow being CEO was no longer enough."

Watching Pamela try to accept this bit of information, Melissa decided to try explaining it on a personal level. "I had cemented over a large portion of my life. If I hadn't chosen the path I did, maybe I could have explored those other areas of my life. And, maybe in doing so, I could have put my personal fears to rest."

"Fears? Like phobias?"

Looking at the tough reporter, M.L. wondered what she feared? Failure? Embarrassment? If they had anything in common, maybe she'd understand. "Inadequacy. That I couldn't cut it. The one goal I'd worked for all of my adult life."

"But you did!" Pamela said quietly. "You did it. Not E.F. Not the Board. You."

"And I was protected the whole time. Bless E.F.'s heart. I still wonder if I'd even have gotten there without his support, much less done it as well."

"Are you telling me after all this time, you were his puppet?" the horror of that thought echoing in Pamela's voice. She was thinking of the rewriting she'd have to do, and the final copy was due in two weeks.

"Certainly not!" How can she get me so riled up, Melissa wondered. Taking a calming breath she leaned forward, moving closer to Pamela. "Look at William Foley. Good or bad, he created his own destiny. I always knew if I got into trouble, E.F. would be there to bail me out."

"Did he? Bail you out?"

"In a way. How many people get specialized tutors on every area of corporate control?"

"Look, Melissa, from what I know, you did it. E.F. didn't come up with that plan and then lead UCC's reorganization. You did! To me, that's significant. And, I told you, John Holmes has had me tutored from time to time. Most anyone who's on top of their job continues to learn new things. Your lessons were just . . . more private."

Watching a frown begin to form on Pamela's brow, Melissa confided, "I felt like a hamster on one of those exercise wheels. I wanted . . . , no I had to get out. Out of that job, out of New York. In your words, I needed my space."

That must have hit home, she thought watching Pamela fidgeting with the silverware again.

"You live with E.F."

"I lived in an apartment in his building. How did you find out?" The conversation was now in whispers, like those used when sharing secrets. Yet no one was around. Melissa made sure that they would be alone by giving her housekeeper the day off.

"When you disappeared, I looked for you. I couldn't find your address, so on a hunch, I asked a friend who works in the city's building permits office to look up E.F.'s building and tell me if he found anything interesting."

"Very clever of you. And?"

"It seems he had a separate apartment built some years ago on the top floor. The rest was just a good guess. Is he the reason you resigned?"

Why hadn't she expected that to come up? Pamela was always surprising her with her questions in which she had some truth nailed cold. Now that the secret was out, how was she going to deal with it? Needing time, she sipped at her coffee, and studied Pamela's face for a hint at what she thought about her living arrangements with E.F.

"E.F. wasn't the entire reason for my resigning. However, our symbiotic lifestyle did play a part in showing me that I had no life of my own. Hell, I don't even own a frying pan. I've never furnished a home. All I do is read, study and work."

Calming down, she looked at Pamela, pleading for understanding. "I had to distance myself from M.L., the cool executive. For a little while, anyway."

"Will I ever see her again? The cool executive?"

"Probably. But, not at private lunches, like this. You see, after taking a month off I withdrew my resignation."

Leaning back in her chair, she saw that her news had the impact of having told Pamela she'd won a million-dollar lottery. Her grin said it all, that Pamela knew being CEO was just too good a job for her to give up.

Having trouble sitting still, Pamela asked, "So where have you been?"

"Getting a life."

"Come on, give. All of it."

"I moved here, to Sands Point. Bought a Jeep and signed up for membership in the Yacht Club. I begin sailing lessons in the spring," smiling at the surprise on Pamela's face.

"You moved to Sands Point, to live the life of the idle rich?"

"I go back to work next month, so I'm not idle." Seeing her shock, or was it disbelief, Melissa wondered why her living out here sounded strange? "I told you, I'm renting this house. I barely own a couch remember?" Then smiling because she knew Pamela expected her to be surrounded in luxury, she added, "Of course the house comes with a pool and if you look over there, a water view," she teased, her voice filled with sunshine.

Horrified, Pamela all but shouted, "If you don't cook, or garden, what are you doing in suburbia?"

What fun, Melissa thought enjoying this sharing of her new life with Pamela. "Reading, swimming, working out at a nearby health club, shopping. I'm finding out what I want to do with my life . . . outside of my job."

"I want to know why CEO wasn't enough? What made you have to resign? I can't see you sitting around a pool drinking wine and playing bridge with the neighbors."

The questions suddenly sobered her, forcing Melissa to remember her decision to tell E.F. she wanted to quit.

Taking a breath she said, "It suddenly dawned on me, even CEO is just a job. The one I wanted maybe, but . . . it was something you leave at night, to go home from. I didn't have a home to go to - or anyone besides co-workers to be with."

Sitting straighter in her chair, she knew she'd made the right decision. "I asked myself, why shouldn't I have both?" Looking around the room she saw the new miniature geranium bush she'd bought for the room. Getting up she picked up her knife and went to cut a bloom for Pamela. Smelling the blossom she handed it to her. "Here. Why not stop and smell the flowers too?" Studying Pamela for her reaction, she added, "I'm going to buy this house."

"You have it all, don't you?" Pamela said with some envy.

"That's a fantasy. Maybe if I have a life, I can find the rest."

"Any prospects?"

Shaking her head, Melissa looked Pamela directly in the eye. "Not yet."

"And, Hugh?"

Maybe it was the hope in Pamela's voice, but Melissa knew she had done it again, hit a nerve. Slouching down in her chair, she stretched out her legs in front of her, crossing her feet at the ankles. "E.F., Hugh, even Charles . . . and don't tell me you weren't tempted to pair us up, because he told me you might . . . they will always be in my heart."

"It's not fair. You have them all in love with you."

"E.F. is my family, friend, mentor and soul mate. I'll always love him, Pamela. Hugh was my first love, and my coming of age as a woman. But, even I realize how different our needs are. He has to have a woman willing to be his satellite. I need a man to understand that I love my work.

"And Charles? He'd jump at a chance to marry you."

"I hope Charles will be a life-long friend."

"Here you are, handing me a plum. An insider's look at power, and the woman who broke the mold. How come? You are the most secretive person, male or female, I've ever met."

"I'd like you to finish your book by showing women the costs of single-mindedly chasing a career. The danger of losing your humanity in your rush to success."

"The feminists won't like that."

"You've kept on my tail ever since we met. In many not so discreet ways, you led me to believe I owed my Sisters something because I had made it to the Corporate Suite. If you really believe that, you have to show them the costs."

Pamela took out her note pad and jotted something down.

"This is more than a mere corporate celebrity book about the first female CEO. This is my pay back Pamela, to all women on the way up. It's the bottomline, about the costs and penalties of a corporate success. That a dazzling salary and glamorous perks come with a high price . . . a balanced life."

"You want an unvarnished piece? How about Hugh? Can I mention him?"

It was her turn to squirm. "I would prefer your not mentioning Hugh by name. He isn't the issue here anyway. It could be any successful man. Don't you agree?"

Pamela began to write on her pad. "You know he has to be included," she countered. "What about E.F.?"

"You do come up with the hard questions. Why not interview him?"

"Wouldn't he want to muzzle me?"

"It's my guess he won't. Why not talk to him and see?"

"And you want creative control of these changes?"

Looking at Pamela, she made a hard decision. "No. Write the truth. All I ask is not to smear anyone. They don't deserve that."

"Are you sure, Melissa? You don't have to do this. I won't tell all your secrets. I think E.F. and Charles are right, that the truth would handicap you in the Men's Club."

Smiling, as if she had more secrets she wasn't going to tell, Melissa threw out a challenge. "You're a pro. Let's see how you do." She was betting that Pamela's skill and knowledge would keep what ever she wrote from being tabloid style sensationalism. "I'm looking forward to reading your final draft," Melissa said.

"Have a new title in mind?" Pamela asked, while mentally revising her outline.

"How about, CEO?"

The two women regarded each other for what seemed like an eternity. Finally, Pamela, a wicked smile on her face, picked up her beer, and asked, "Madame CEO?"

"Yes?" Melissa inquired grinning.

"You'd better start thinking about a long national book tour."

"Why?"

"Because this is the stuff movies are made of, and your story could be a blockbuster! To CEO!", Pamela toasted.

Melissa tipped her glass to Pamela. "To CEO."